MAX SEVENTEEN

KATE JOHNSON

ISBN: 1537554468
ISBN-13: 978-1537554464

ACKNOWLEDGMENTS

Thanks must go to:
Everyone who cheered me on while I was writing the Mad Space Book and pushed me to get it out there. You guys are awesome. Specifically:
The RNA Conference Naughty Kitchen Focus Group: Janet Gover, Immi Howson, Alison May, Lisa Hill & Ruth Long, who always reassure me that I can tell good stories when I'm pretty sure I can't. Also Jane Lovering for the phrase 'milking the wine goat' which has no relevance here but makes me giggle like an idiot.
Jan Jones for making me get up off my arse and get this published in the first place.
Kiera Bruce for unfailing encouragement every time I posted something bonkers from this book on Twitter.
Rhoda Baxter for proof-reading and scientific advice. I still don't know if photosynthesis packs would work, but they sound plausible, right?
And last but most, Ruth Long (again) for volunteering to edit the book and making me believe it might actually be worth it.
I really, literally, couldn't have done this without you guys. Thank you.

CHAPTER ONE

Max was running.

The day was hot and bright, because days were always hot and bright on this crappy planet at the arse-end of the universe. Cheaply terraformed, barely able to support the dreg ends of life, farted at by the sun on a regular basis. Nobody lived here if they didn't have to.

At this moment, Max was sincerely considering how much 'have to' there was about living on Zeta Secunda, a planet so shitty it didn't even have a proper name. There was a spaceport a few clicks away, but spaceports required ID and security, and Max was fresh out of both. Well. Fresh out might be a stretch. Probably that last ID had ended up in the same place as that last decent pair of boots: inside those fecking sand-beasts. Ten feet long, and that was just the jaw. Max had been lucky to get out alive.

For a given value of luck, anyway. That bunch of culchies were still mad at Max for something. Hard to figure out what. Might've been the card sharping. Might've been the fake money. Might've been that fella left with his pants hanging out the window.

Either way, Max was running.

Sand fountained up ahead, and a whine whistled past. Grand, so they'd found their guns. At least here in the badlands they were the cheap old kind with bullets, which required aiming and accuracy, neither of which this lot seemed to have. Quite probably they were hungover. Possibly also still drunk. Not that Max could judge, brain still throbbing with last night's poteen.

Max was running on empty.

"I see you, kid!"

Max ignored that, and leapt over some low rocks to the sand below. Ahead, there was nothing but more rocks and more sand. So much more sand.

"Ain't nowhere to hide!"

Yeah, *obvs*. Sand, rocks, more sand. Max was dark with dirt and sun and vaguely sand coloured, but not nearly enough. There was nowhere to go, no shelter, no respite. Sooner or later they'd catch up.

Another smash. Another whine. Closer this time.

Max stumbled, foot rolling on a stone, knee thudding into the sand. Hell of a day to have fallen out the window with no clothes on.

The sun was fierce punishing. The desultory government advisories for Zeta Secunda included not going outside without solar protection. They meant proper pharma grade sunscreen. They didn't mention the fucking sand. Max didn't even have a shirt.

"Run, punk, run!" Those yahoos were getting closer. Some terrible little land buggies, or maybe horses. They used both around here, and it wasn't as if the wind was giving away any clues. No bugger was rich enough for a heavy-air vehicle. The HAVs and the HAV-nots, Max thought hysterically, stumbling on.

Smash, whine. Closer together. Sound and sand hitting at the same time.

Shit, not this time, don't let me die like this! I've got

no fucking pants on!

The ground shook with the vehicles, pounded with the hooves of the horses. Closer, closer. Max kept on running. The sand gave way, shelving and sliding. Burned like the lava it once had been, grinding and grating, raw against raw skin. Max slid, the sand like waves made out of grit, desperate not to scream.

Sand fountained, the herald of impeding doom, and Max scrambled to bleeding feet, limping on over unforgiving dunes. The shadows closed in.

Max kept on running.

The engines of the Dauntless hummed smoothly, at a frequency that seemed perfectly calculated to grate on Riley's nerves.

Just four more years, then you can quit this fascist popsicle stand.

Fantasies of ripping out that Service chip they'd implanted and hurling it at the captain made up quite a lot of Riley's downtime.

"Sir?"

The captain gave no indication she'd heard.

"Sir, it's about Pherick. Pherick Green, the coolant engineer? It's just, he's been gone three standard weeks now, and—"

The captain tapped something on her tablet and didn't look up. "Green is on personal leave."

"Yes, sir, I know. But we're not allowed personal leave longer than—"

"The Service is capable of making exceptions," said the captain coolly.

Really? thought Riley. In whose favour? Eleven bloody years I've been committed to the Service, and when was the last time I got any leave?

The dark thought occurred that on Sigma Prime, you could commit murder and still get out of jail in less than eleven years.

"I understand you are friends," said the captain, and there was something in the way she said it that made Riley uneasy.

"We work together."

"I see. And Ensign…" she tapped her tablet, "Yakira is not an acceptable substitute?"

"Ensign Yakira is doing a fine job."

"Then what is the problem?"

The problem? Riley wanted to say. The problem is that Pherick just disappeared one day, barely a few hours after telling me he'd uncovered something really disturbing but he couldn't tell me what. The problem is that his brother Jameson went AWOL on an away mission three months ago and he's not even supposed to be part of away missions. The problem is I think something very strange is going on here and I'm kind of scared that if I start asking questions about it, I'll be the next one to disappear.

Out loud, Riley said, "I just wondered when Pherick would be back, sir. I owe him a drink."

"I'm sure you'll be buying it soon. Was there anything else?"

You'll be watching every single thing I do on this ship from now on, won't you? thought Riley, but said, "No, sir. Thank you, sir."

The cool, neutral corridors of the ship closed in like a jail as Riley strode away, plotting escape.

Max was waiting.

"Prisoner 131-10-17," said the computer, her voice oddly judgemental for an artificial intelligence. "Please step forward into the the isolation chamber."

Max was already moving forward as the computer went on, "Failure to comply will result in punishment."

"I'm moving, I'm fucking moving," Max muttered,

stepping onto the printed footsteps and trying not to notice how sticky they were.

"Your trial is about to begin. If you have been—you have chosen not to be represented by a lawyer," the computer said, glitching the way it always did when confronted with something unexpected. Unexpected to it, anyway. Max had heard it too many times to count. "Please step forward alone into the courtroom."

The plastic walls closed in, and the tube rose up. Max was alone in a small chamber, visible from all sides. The courtroom was half empty, just the judge and requisite number of law enforcers. Nobody cared about a case like this.

"The charges against you are of public disorder, public indecency, whoring without licence, petty theft, and illegal gambling," said the judge dispassionately. She looked bored as hell. Out here in a backwater town on a third-rate planet, there were never any exciting cases. Zeta Secunda didn't even have Service protection. "How do you plead?"

Max was guilty as hell and knew it. "Not guilty."

The judge sighed and flicked on a vid screen. On it was footage from that hole of a bar, with Max using a hidden mirror to cheat at cards.

"Oh come on! Why aren't they being persecuted too?"

The judge said nothing, and flicked to another section of footage. This was Max lamping the disgruntled gambler over the head with a poteen bottle.

"Well all right, but they came after me, you know. I was just defending myself."

The next clip was Max landing painfully on the ground outside the bar, dusting off the sand and running away.

"You left without paying," the judge said.

"The money was in my room."

"And you were naked."

"They were threatening to kill me! I didn't have time for clothes."

The judge considered this. "And the whoring? There is no licence registered to you."

"Did I take money for it? It's just sex," Max said, hands spread, "and last time I checked, that ain't illegal."

"This is not your first time in the dock. According to the evidence it seems you are in fact guilty of these charges."

Max made a face. "All right, so I am. Look, I really don't want to end up back in the slammer. Can't I pay a fine?"

"You have no money. It was returned to the men you swindled." The judge regarded Max, who gave her a winning smile. Kind of. Max wasn't very good at winning smiles.

"You really want to stay out of jail?"

"Yes! What can I do?" Max looked over the judge's severe uniform and added saucily, "I can be a very good sport."

The judge narrowed her eyes, and Max winced. *Probably not the best move against an accusation of whoring.* "What can you do? You can stop committing crimes. Until then," she pressed a button and the cuffs on Max's wrists rose of their own accord to lock into a dock at the front of the plastic box, "someone else can be responsible for you. You are sentenced to one year of servitude—"

"What? Servitude?" Max gabbled, panicked.

"—during which time you will wear this marker." The restraints fell away, to be replaced with a single cuff on Max's right wrist. A slave cuff. Oh shit, oh shit!

"No no, I didn't mean it, jail is fine, really!" The judge programmed something on her keypad, and a spike drove itself into Max's wrist.

"The cuff has sampled your DNA and will physically bind you to your new master."

Max had seen these things before. They could be linked to horrible little tablets which the slave's owner could use to issue any command they damn well wished, and the slave would be forced to comply.

"Please, your honour, not slavery. Please!"

"After a period of one year you may attempt to buy your freedom. Until that time, you will be legally considered the property of whoever buys you."

"Please—"

"The auction is tomorrow. Try not to do anything that will bring you back into my court," said the judge, and the siren sounded to signal that sentence had been passed.

Max was in trouble.

Riley avoided the slave market. Most systems had banned it some years ago, but out here, on a planet still in the process of colonisation, the legal attitude to slavery was kind of murky. The Zeta system wasn't even in a position to have signed the Service's charter; the Dauntless was more or less here to check on their progress.

The presence of a slave trade would not, in Riley's opinion, do much to aid Zeta's application. Protestors and picketers from more sophisticated systems harangued the buyers and sellers, but this didn't seem to be slowing trade at all.

They stood in rows, roughly divided into groups based on training and ability. There was a special section away from the rest for the whores. They called out, male and female, as Riley passed, from under an awning that did little to shelter them from the pitiless sun and the ugly birds cirling, predatory, overhead.

"Hey sexy! You wanna buy me? I give you a real

good time. I know a lot of tricks!"

Riley ignored them. The rest of the Dauntless's crew, on the other hand, paused to flirt and fondle them, making false promises their salaries couldn't fulfil. Riley ignored them too and mooched on.

"Go on, soldier! Like it rough, do you?"

"The Service does not approve of slavery," Riley intoned dutifully and the slaver snorted, because what the Service approved of and what the Service did behind closed doors were two totally different things.

Buying a slave would be enough to get you dismissed. Yeah, but Riley didn't want to be dismissed. Riley wanted to leave. The Service would never let a trained engineer out of their sight for long. They'd have to believe—

Something glinted in the distance. A small merchant ship, the kind that switched its licence and registration every time it flew into heavy air. The kind that had lots of hidden corners and crew who didn't ask too many questions. The kind a person could disappear on.

I wish...

Past the slave market, there were heavy air crews touting for business. Riley casually wandered in their direction. Not that heavy air was the way to go, but even the Service couldn't stop a body looking at some land-bound vehicles.

"Can I help you, officer?" asked a slim, dark-skinned man. His HAV was old, rusty and battered, but Riley recognised it as a Vector, an ex-Service vehicle.

"First thing I ever took apart and put back together was a Vector." The metal beast looked smooth to the touch, the air above it hazing in the punishing heat. *Don't fondle another man's vehicle.* "Some days I wish life was that simple again."

The man grinned, reading Riley's face. "Surely the Service has everything an engineer could wish for, mon ami?"

"Yes indeed. In fact they're with me every step of the way," said Riley sourly, and this time the man laughed.

"Ah, but you wouldn't like a freelancer's life, I'm sure. We could fly away at any minute, somewhere unknown and unplanned." He let that hang there, then added casually, "Besides, after Service ships, who'd want to fly on an old Scimitar?"

That got Riley's attention, as it had probably been supposed to. "You fly a Scimitar?"

"Best there is. She ain't pretty, but she's a thing of beauty."

Riley nodded. Oh, but the Scimitar was a lovely piece of kit. One of the first commercially available designs, hardly changed since its introduction. There was nothing fancy about it, no holos and no luxury, but to any engineer worth the title, there was no finer vehicle.

"You want to see her?"

Riley hesitated. On the one hand, yes, this was the perfect answer, but on the other hand…well, other arm, really, the arm that held the Service's eminently trackable chip…it was impossible.

"I'm not sure the Service would approve." Riley made a gesture that may or may not have drawn attention to the chip's location.

The skinny man's eyes gleamed. "Oh, I'm sure they don't need to know."

Max was waiting.

"How many you got?" asked the man in the land train cap. Max's heart sank. The land trains were big, lumbering beasts, slow but irrevocable. They tracked ore across the planet to the central depot where it got shipped off-world. They were so low-tech they still ran on furnaces.

This wasn't what Max had meant by 'special skills'.

"I'm a tech—"

"No need for tech," said the man from the land-train. "We need labour." He looked them over speculatively, and Max tried to look small and weedy.

The trader rolled his shoulders tiredly. They'd been out here all day in the burning hot sun, and most of the slaves with actual special skills had been bought. Some were trained in beauty work, some had med skills. Some could cook or spoke varied languages.

But nobody wanted a tech. Especially one with a prison cuff on.

"To be honest, mate, you'd be doing me a favour taking this lot off my hands," said the trader. "One less night to feed and house them."

Max snorted. Last night's accommodation had been heavy on the concrete and gruel, and light on mattresses and food that actually tasted of anything.

"If they ain't sold by close of business, they're back in the general market. Or the whores."

That got Max's attention. "I could do general labour…"

The trader gave a slow smile. "Funny how they all say that. All right then, take the lot, for…say…five thousand."

"Five?" yelped the land train man. "For this scrappy lot? That's daylight bloody robbery. Two."

Max tuned out. On balance, knowing the exact monetary value of your own life wasn't all that comforting.

The other slaves stood around, disinterested. Max had talked to a few of them, learned the basics of their backgrounds. Two were convicts, serving out longer sentences than Max. Their previous owner had died, which meant that the blood bond on the cuff was void. However, the court service had tracked them down pretty easily via the cuff, the moment the bond was broken, and was selling them on already.

The message was clear: you don't get to run away from an indenture. They'll find you wherever you are.

Three of the remaining slaves had been born into it, and these were the three who stood quiet and resigned. On this piece of shit planet, a person could spend their whole life in chains and never know the bittersweet taste of freedom. They'd die slaves, just like their parents, and their children, over and over with no release and no hope of it.

Unlike Max, they didn't complain. Unlike Max, this would never be over for them.

The last one was a man who'd sold himself into indenture to pay off his debts. Max knew these sorts of debts. They were the kind that doubled overnight with interest. Theoretically, he could one day be freed, but they all knew the poor bastard would be a slave for the rest of his life.

"Done," said the trader eventually, and spat in his hand. The man from the land train thumbprinted the payment scanner, and was handed the control tabs of the slaves he'd just bought. To Max's surprise, they were tiny things, no bigger than that thumbprint, and each hung on a thong the owner could sling about his neck.

Before he did that, he was handed a needle by the trader, and used it to prick his thumb. Then he pressed the bloodied digit to the first of the tabs.

The indentured man flinched. Next was one of the convicts. Then Max, who yelped as the cuff gave a sharp shock.

"Now, I can do that any time I want to," said the man from the land train. "Any infraction, any lollygagging, any insubordination, you get a shock. Any attempts at escape or attack on me or my staff, you get a shock. And for your information, should I die of accident or injury, you still ain't free. Soon as this bond is broken the courts will know about it, and send increasingly strong shocks until you're handed in or imprinted on a new master. Got it? Right then, my chavvies, off we go."

Max was out of luck.

The captain and owner of the Scimitar had named it Eurydice. Riley had a good enough education to understand the reference: the wife so beloved her husband had ventured into the underworld to retrieve her.

"Does that make you Orpheus?

"Yeah," said the captain. He was a hawk-like man, sharp-featured and slim-hipped. Riley was to learn he didn't say much and never gave anything away. "Justine?"

Justine was tall and aristocratic, with full lips and heavy-lidded eyes. She looked Riley over, then said, "Give me your arm."

She shoved back Riley's sleeve to reveal the bloody patch of skin where the Service's tracker had been for eleven years. The skinny man, who'd introduced himself as Émile, had beckoned one of the scruffy kids who infested port towns like this, and offered him twenty bits if he took Riley's tracker. The kid agreed, apparently aware of the fact that this would require his arm being cut open so Riley's tracker could be shoved in before it registered the lack of warm flesh.

"Wait, that's no good," Riley said. "It's traceable. They'll find you, realise you clearly aren't me—" they all looked between Riley and the kid and nodded, "—and start checking camera footage. They'll see where I've gone and come after the Eurydice."

"Then we'll all be in the shit," Émile had agreed. "Well, I'm afraid, then—"

"No, hang on a sec. Shit." Riley had been raised not to swear and never to refer to scatological terms, but these people were pirates. Better start fitting in. "That's the answer. There are septic tanks round the back of the slave market, right? Near the brothels?"

The kid nodded. "They have to close all the windows. Me mam don't like it."

"How often are they emptied?"

"Most weeks, more often if the land train is in town. They run on shit," the kid explained helpfully.

Riley smiled. "Then I think you know where to dispose of this chip, kid."

Émile flipped the chip straight from Riley's arm into the boy's, before it could register the lack of warm flesh, and then the kid ran off, taking the only method of tracing Riley with him.

Justine inspected the cut, then flicked her gaze at Émile. "You're a fucking butcher, Émile."

Émile shrugged, unrepentant. "Worked, didn't it? We've got ourselves a Service-class engineer now."

Justine narrowed her eyes at Riley. "How do I know you aren't a spy?"

Riley shrugged. "I guess you don't. Just like I don't know you aren't a honey-trap."

Émile snorted with laughter at that. "Got you there, ma soeur."

"Honey-trap?" barked a bearded feller carrying crates into the ship's hold. "Justine? When was the last time anything got between those lovely legs?"

"Fuck off, Murtaugh." Justine's hand rested on the ex-Service revolver at her hip. It appeared to have been modified, which could either mean someone on the ship was a great tech or that Justine would explode next time she used her own weapon.

Murtaugh just grinned and carried on.

"Where you from?"

"Sigma Prime. North continent."

"Ooh, a Primer!" cried Murtaugh. "La-di-da."

"You left the Service, what, five minutes ago," Justine said, "and you're already looking for a new job?"

"It's because I left the Service five minutes ago that I'm looking for a new job," Riley said. "My face gets seen around here, I'm dead."

Justine folded her arms and regarded Riley the way people regarded livestock.

This was clearly the person Riley had to convince. "Look, maybe we'll all hate each other. Either way, I need to get off this planet. Let me come with you to your next stop and if it's not working out I'll get off there."

Justine said nothing, but checked the data displayed at her wrist. Whatever she saw there seemed to be acceptable, because she glanced at Orpheus. He gave her the barest nod.

"All right then. A couple of weeks as a trial period. You can start by fixing the hydraulics on this door. Opens with the screech of a thousand dying souls."

"Ever the poet," murmured Captain Orpheus, loping past like a jackal.

"Whatever the captain says goes," Justine said firmly. "You take your orders from him, and when we're on a job you knuckle down with the rest of us, understand?"

"I'm Service," Riley said bitterly, "I know how to follow orders."

"Good. What you do with your own personal life is your concern, but we stick strictly to consensuality on this ship, you follow?"

"Consensuality?" said Riley, and couldn't help glancing back in the direction of the slave market, hidden now by the bulk of the spaceport. "No slaves then?"

Justine, Murtaugh and Émile all seemed to freeze for a moment. Nobody at all looked in the captain's direction.

"Captain doesn't hold with it," Justine said shortly,

and that seemed to be an end to the matter.

Riley nodded, relieved. The Service was bad enough, but those poor bastards out there had no hope of freedom.

"One question: what kind of jobs do you do?"

There was a different kind of pause as the rest of the crew thought about this. Then, "Whatever pays," said Orpheus.

Riley looked up at the rusted, peeling hull of the Eurydice, a ship designed for medium-haul transport, a ship that could out-manoeuvre huge Service troop ships and out-shoot wealthy pleasure-cruisers. A ship with lots of hiding places and a crew who knew how to get rid of Service chips...

Murtaugh lifted his bearded chin and gave Riley an appraising look. Justine raised one eyebrow. Orpheus might have been made of stone for all the clues he was giving.

"Sounds good," said Riley, and with that left the Service behind.

Max was in hell.

The land trains were big, slow and ugly. So were most of the slaves working on them. Max's job was to shovel fuel into the engines, which burned fiery hot and stank like sewers. Mostly because what they were fed with was sewage.

The overseer who'd bought them that day in the market turned out to be called Herrick, and he was a humourless jobsworth who rather liked the power of inflicting shocks on the slaves for minor infractions. For Max, this included everything from 'being cheeky' to trying to make the furnace more efficient.

"But it'll need far less fuel and we won't have to stoke it so often!"

"I'm not having you tampering with the Zeta

Secunda Ore And Mining Company's land train,"
Herrick replied. Herrick was very proud of working for
the Zeta Secunda Ore And Mining Company. Nobody
could figure out why.

The slaves were given the meagrest of foods and
strictly rationed water allowances. Since the furnace
room was punishingly hot, they saved most of their
water for drinking, and as a result most of them stank
like hell. After a few weeks, it was more or less
impossible to tell what anyone's original skin colour
might have been under all the dirt and soot.

"We can fly in the fucking sky but we can't find a
more efficient method of powering a land train," Max
muttered, shovelling more shit into the furnace. They
were all instructed to add to the fuel supply, by means of
a bench with a hole in it over the sewage compartment.

They worked in shifts, sleeping at the back of the
engine compartment where it was marginally cooler and
fresher. All day and all night, the compartment shook
with the rhythmic thud of the engine and the scrape of
the shovels.

Every few days they'd stop to take on fuel and
supplies, and those were the best days because they all
got out into the fresh air and sunlight while they loaded
and unloaded the cargo. The Zeta Secunda Ore And
Mining Company's land trains carried their own cargo,
and whatever other heavy goods the planet needed to
transport long distances.

Day and night began to blur. Days of the week had no
meaning. Through an agony of aching muscles and
burning thirst, Max eventually lost track of time and
stopped even caring about it.

Max became no one.

"Right," said Émile. "This is the layout of every land
train Zeta Secunda owns. The scammel at the front,

comprising the engine hauling it all and a forward compartment for Company staff, followed by fuel storage. They're connected by a walkway. Avoid the fuel storage. It ain't pretty."

"Ugh, these are the ones that run on shit, aren't they?" said Murtaugh.

"Very efficient and self-renewing source, mon ami," said Émile. He seemed to be the ship's de facto number three, making plans and doing research and, incidentally, cooking better food than Riley had ever had in the Service.

His sister Justine acted as medic when necessary and co-pilot when not. Although no one had said as much, it was reasonably clear the only person she ever took orders from was Orpheus himself. Riley had never seen her use the pistol at her hip, but was in absolutely no doubt she'd be lethal with it. She had that look about her, like the Service's trained kill squads.

The captain stood at the head of the mess table on which the plans were displayed. Whipcord thin, silent as a cat, face unreadable. Riley hadn't seen a single emotion pass those features in…oh, it must have been three months now, working on standard calendars.

"Yeah, but tell me we ain't gonna be running Eurydice on piss?"

"If that happens," said Riley, whose job it was to maintain the fuel cells, "I'm definitely looking for a new job."

"Behind the fuel tank is the first of seven cargo compartments. Storage varies per route. Some of them hold mostly ore, some the refined product, some are for private cargo. All have guards posted at each end, and the private cargo has an extra guard inside. That's a potential twenty-one guards, although we're unlikely to have to deal with more than fifteen or sixteen."

Riley frowned at that.

"What about slaves?" asked Petal, the tiny slip of a girl who piloted the ship and had a terrifying way with a knife.

"Company keeps its use of slaves on the down-low. Now we all know they buy 'em up like nobody's business, but the official line is they don't 'endorse' slavery."

Petal snorted. Murtaugh rolled his eyes. Orpheus said in his gravelly voice, "Find out. We don't kill slaves."

Justine said, "There'll be a bounty for returning them. You should do it, Primer. You have an honest face."

"I have an AWOL face," Riley reminded her, as the others laughed.

"No Service here though, Primer."

"They might have no jurisdiction here but trust me, the Service keeps an eye on this place. Unless you're trying to get rid of me, I suggest Petal."

Petal blinked her big brown eyes and gave a sweet smile. It fooled no one.

"We're not getting rid of you," Murtaugh told Riley. "You fixed the aft head and now we can all breathe!"

"It was your own damn fault the thing overflowed in the first place," said Hide. He and Murtaugh appeared to be the muscle and general dogsbodies around the place. Murtaugh was the more jocular of the two, and Hide was simply enormous, but Riley had watched them sparring when there was nothing else to do, and wouldn't bet against either of them in a fight.

"Attempting a more efficient fuel system?" Petal asked innocently.

"Blame Émile, those curries—"

"No one's blaming anyone," said Justine loudly, like a teacher settling down a class. "Émile, anything else we need to know?"

Émile scanned his datapad. "Aside from the guards and slaves there should be some crew, mostly in the compartment forward of the engine. It's upwind," he added with a half smile. "Drivers working in shifts; probably four. The cargo manager and assistant. Couple of engineers. The slave overseer and assistant. Which reminds me, Primer…"

Émile dug in his bag and tossed Riley a couple of wide strips of leather. Riley, who'd idly noticed that the captain, Justine, Murtaugh and Hide wore these on their wrists, looked up enquiringly.

"Does this mean I'm in your gang now?"

Murtaugh guffawed.

"They're for the slavers. They try to slap a cuff on you, the leather will stop the probes getting through."

Riley didn't know much about slave cuffs, and didn't want to. "Really?"

They all nodded, no trace of mocking.

"It's organic," Émile said. "Fools the sensors."

"It was organic," said Riley doubtfully, picking up the vambraces. They were perhaps three or four inches deep, fastened by means of straps wound around and around, and had probably once been a uniform brown before salt and sweat wore lighter areas and…well, it had probably been blood making those darker stains.

Clearly, these had given someone else good service. Probably Riley's predecessor, about whom there was a conspicuous silence. Judging by the blood staining this leather, the poor sod had died on the job. Or maybe this was the blood of the Eurydice's enemies. Or…

Slowly, Riley said, "They're looking for DNA?"

Orpheus grunted. "Very good."

This was high praise from Orpheus. Even Justine looked impressed. "The probes imprint with DNA and transmit it to the owner's tab. There's a lot of mixed blood on there, Primer," she said.

"Lovely," said Riley, beginning to fasten one on.

"Stick a piece of steak in there before we go out,

they'll be even more effective," said Émile, and Riley had no idea if he was joking or not.

"That's pretty high tech for a train that runs on piss," said Hide.

"Lot of money in slavery," Petal told him. He was about seven times her size. "Like the captain always says: follow the money."

Riley doubted the captain had ever said that. It seemed far too long a sentence.

"Then why ain't we stealing slaves?" said Murtaugh.

"Bad business," said Justine, without looking at Orpheus.

Riley adjusted the first cuff and reached for the second. "I don't suppose there's any other kind of armour?"

"We're not the Service," said Justine crisply. "Émile, where's the payroll kept?"

"Right. Well, there's a specific person on the train whose job it is to look after the money. Every bit in, every bit out. Miners don't trust credit payments, so it's all in gold. Personally signs it all in and out with a thumbprint. Now, since the rest of the train is cargo or sewage, we'll be concentrating our attack on the forward compartment of the scammel. Primer, you'll be—"

Riley raised a hand. "I'll be asking why the scammel?"

Justine sighed. Her brother, more patient, repeated, "Because the rest of the train is cargo or sewage. They're not going to keep the safe there, are they?" They all laughed at that. Apart from Orpheus, whose gaze Riley suddenly felt very keenly.

"I would," said Riley.

"What, in a tank of piss?" Murtaugh spluttered. The laughter turned to sounds of disgust. But Émile looked thoughtful.

"It's the last place anyone would rob…"

"Including me!" said Petal.

"Whereas the scammel is actually pretty vulnerable," Riley went on. Émile, Justine and the captain were all paying attention now. "Easy to ram, for instance, especially with something airborne."

Émile shook his head and pointed to the plans. "It has a pilot and anti-climbers. Cattle rams."

"Those are for smaller objects," said Riley. "How fast do these things go? Two of them hitting head-on would cause a hell of a crash."

"They'd jackknife. Overturn," Émile said.

"You're not suggesting we get another convoy to ram it with?" Justine said.

Orpheus watched them like a sphinx.

"Well, if we did we'd just nick the payroll of that one," said Riley. "Plus we'd never be able to get it going far and fast enough to be effective before we were noticed. The Company would rather blow up the whole train than let pirates take its money."

"True enough," said Murtaugh. "So who's going shit-diving, then? My money's on you, Primer."

"You already fixed the head after all," Hide said.

The two of them laughed, but no one else did. Everyone was watching Riley.

"Immovable object, unstoppable force," murmured Émile, pushing his fist into his palm.

"Some of them transport pyrite ore," Justine said, and snatched the datapad off her protesting brother. "That'd go up like fireworks. Where were the schedules?"

"An explosion of shit would definitely halt the clean-up operation," Petal said.

"You'd need to make sure they were actually going to hit each other," Émile said. "They're not like real trains with fixed rails."

"Would we even need to be on the first train?" Petal said. "We could just make it look like they were going to crash…"

"Depends on whether you want everyone on it dying in an explosion of sewage," said Riley.

"We were probably going to kill the guards anyway," said Hide. Murtaugh looked as if he was still catching up.

"I could think of worse fates for Company men," said Orpheus softly. If he'd had a tail it would have been twitching.

"And the slaves?" said Riley, meeting his gaze for probably the first time.

Orpheus said nothing for a moment. Neither did anyone else.

"Can you reprogram the navigation?" said the captain eventually, eyes still on Riley, who was beginning to sweat.

"I don't know the system. But probably." Riley was a mech, not a tech, but there was a considerable degree of crossover. And after the Service's security protocols, how hard could the Zeta Secunda Ore And Mining Company be to hack?

"Émile, look it up." Orpheus suddenly seemed to come to a decision. "I need schedules of two likely trains. Justine, you'll take the Vector and get the slaves off the first train, then the second. Learn the terrain. Dump them somewhere with water. Petal, Murtaugh, you need uniforms, you'll be guards on the second train. Move through the compartments until you find that bastard with the safe but don't kill him till I give you the word. Hide, you're with me doing the same on the first train. Émile, you're on the ship at the weapons array. I need you locked onto the first train with a grenade in case the Company doesn't blow it up. Primer."

Riley waited, tense as a bowstring.

But instead the captain turned to Émile. "Can the nav be changed remotely?"

Émile's eyes scanned the data rapidly. "Think so. Have to hack in, but…think so."

"Be sure. Primer, you need to change the nav and scramble communications on the second train. You're with Justine. Everyone study the plans and prep."

With that, everyone scattered, leaving Riley locked into Orpheus's gaze and wondering if this was how it felt to be a mouse watched by a cat.

"You'd better be right, Primer," he said.

Max slept a broken sleep.

Then woken by a shock from the slave cuff, as usual, and handed a small flask of water. The compartment was already as hot and vile as hell. Then again, it could be midday already. The vents along the side of the compartment, too small to get a person out of, showed a sliver of blinding daylight. But on a planet where the solar cycle was 74 hours and they weren't far off the equator, blinding daylight didn't do much to indicate the time of day.

The other slaves were already singing, a call-and-response chant that had been going on since Max fell asleep. One or two slaves sung out the call, and the rest of them responded with a chorus that was mostly whoas and ahhs.

"…been working on the railroad, from Alpha to Psi…"

"Whoa-oh-ohh-a oh-a oh awhoa-ah whoa-oh!"

"One day I'll make Omega, and that day I'll die..."

"Whoa-oh-ohh-a oh-a oh awhoa-ah whoa-oh!"

Today, Max was sent to the fuel compartment with a yoke. This job was equally as backbreaking as shovelling shit into the furnace, but at least allowed some fresh air. The downside was that it also involved the risk of carrying a yoke with two fully-laden buckets across a narrow walkway consisting of perforated metal and an unconvincing handrail. Below it, the land train's massive wheels churned on and on, sending sand and dead insects flying up into the face of anyone who dared to look down.

"If you fall," said one of the other slaves to Max on the first day, shouting over the roar of the engine and the noise, "you're mincemeat. Even if you went clear of the wheels—" they both paused to look down at the huge tyres, wide enough to flatten a tall man, "—the desert'd probably kill you. Or the gyps."

The gyps were the huge, hook-beaked scavenging birds that plagued the storage tank, feeding on sewage and the giant roaches infesting it. Occasionally one would swoop down for a peck at a slave crossing the walkway.

"Cheerful thought."

This shift consisted of endless trips along the walkway, feet moving in time to the rhythmic chant, shovelling the buckets full, then shuffling back and trying not to look down, followed by dumping the contents of the buckets in the larger hopper near the furnace, then starting again. Over and over.

"Some day they'll liberate me and then I can sleep…"

"Whoa-oh-ohh-a oh-a oh awhoa-ah whoa-oh!"

"I'll take my compadres and the rest you can keep!"

"Whoa-oh-ohh-a oh-a oh awhoa-ah whoa-oh!"

Max's eyes burned with sweat and dust, hands already a mess of blisters and calluses from the buckets and shovels. There were bottles of disinfectant around the sleeping quarters, which was really the Company's only nod to hygiene. They cleaned the shit out of their burns and blisters and away from their mouths and that was about it.

The sun burned through the scrap of blanket protecting Max's scalp. They were all peeling in the heat.

Back inside, a new leader had taken up the call of the chant, and Max's cracked lips formed the response without making much sound. The air was too dry for singing.

"One day they're gonna pay us, and I'm straight for the door…"

"Whoa-oh-ohh-a oh-a oh awhoa-ah whoa-oh!"

"I can buy me feather pillows, and I'll still spend some more…"

"Whoa-oh-ohh-a oh-a oh awhoa-ah whoa-oh!"

"There's a shiny silver dollar that'll buy me a whore…"

Max trudged out again without hearing what else the singer was going to buy.

"Just a few more hours," whispered the slave passing on the return journey, and Max cracked a smile.

"You stop telling yourself that, after a while."

Herrick the overseer sat by the door, fat and complacent with that rope of tabs round his sweaty neck. Early on, Max had wondered why nobody tried pushing him over the railing of the walkway, but he never went near the thing without sending a pre-emptive shock through the cuffs of any of the slaves nearby. It had happened to Max while carrying two full buckets of fuel, which had predictably gone everywhere and needed to be cleaned up. Nobody volunteered to help.

Herrick had curled his lip as if it was Max's fault.

"You are for hurting, kid!" he'd roared.

Max hated everybody.

Riley had plotted the route meticulously and gone through it several times with Émile. A small course correction here and there would have the northbound juggernaut rolling on towards the southbound, and none the wiser. Murtaugh and Petal had hung around the assembly yards, discreetly slapping control devices on the inside of the engine's wheel-arches. Riley had tested them with tiny corrections, the kind the driver would just assumed were the normal variations of the massive vehicle moving at speed over rough terrain.

They'd worked.

Jamming comms was easy. The wrong kind of signal sent at the right time would cause static which, again, they'd think nothing of until it was too late.

That morning, they'd left the Eurydice docked in a spaceport, Émile going about an ordinary refuel and resupply, and flown off in the Vector towards the northbound train's path across the desert. Riley and Justine sat up front where they were visible, dressed in civilian clothes. In the covered compartment at the back were Petal, Murtaugh and Hide, and the captain, each dressed in the guard uniforms Petal had winnowed out of the assembly yards.

Justine pulled the HAV alongside the land train as it lumbered inexorably on. There was a guard monotonously pacing the back rail of the last compartment, a moving target on a moving vehicle. He raised a hand to the Vector and Justine waved cheerfully back.

Then Petal stood up in the hovering HAV as Riley flipped open the roof, narrowed her eyes, selected a knife and threw it in the blink of an eye. The guard slumped forward, but Petal was already moving, using Riley's seat and shoulder as a springboard to leap forward and catch the guard as he fell. She tossed him in the back of the vehicle and leapt over the rail onto the train's final compartment.

Murtaugh stripped the guard of his ID and followed, making the Vector dip and sway and Justine curse.

"He's more your size," Riley just about heard Petal say, and Murtaugh nodded and disappeared into the compartment.

A taut minute or so later, Murtaugh tossed a second body off the back of the train, this one narrowly avoiding hitting Riley in the face. Hide and Orpheus grabbed it and shoved it into the covered compartment.

Murtaugh saluted them with—oh, sweet Jesus! He was holding a severed hand. Riley recoiled, and Justine smirked as she pulled the vehicle away.

"You think that's gross, Primer, this might not be the job for you," she said scornfully.

Riley glared at her and glanced back at the hand, trying to ascertain its purpose. Thieves in old legends used the hand of a dead man as a warning system. But this crew was too practical for that. *Maybe it's a trophy?*

Then realisation dawned. "The compartments are fingerprint-locked?"

"Émile thought they might be. We weren't sure." Justine flicked a look at him as she sped away from the convoy. "It's not like he was going to be using it."

"Jesus," muttered Riley. Swearing came easier these days.

Justine smiled, her pointed canines showing. She swung the Vector round in a wide arc to approach the front of the juggernaut from a different direction. Behind her, the two men were methodically stripping the dead guards of their clothing.

None of them said much as they flew away towards the southbound train. In total contrast to the bickering, joking, family squabble of the crew on board the Eurydice, right now they were all totally focused on the job. Even Murtaugh had stopped making salacious jokes once he got on board the Vector.

Something tapped Riley on the shoulder: the severed hand of the first guard. Hide was grinning as he waved it. "For the other train. I'll get you one for this."

"Cheers," Riley muttered, taking it and chucking it

with distaste on the floor. Justine quirked an eyebrow but said nothing.

They reached the back of the southbound train, the train they were going to bomb, and Hide put a neat bullet between the eyes of the rear guard. Even quicker than the first time, he and Orpheus dispatched the other guard and disappeared into the train, leaving Riley with another severed hand.

"Don't mix them up," was all Justine said.

When they reached the front of the train, barrelling on at a rate of knots, Justine swung around and piloted up alongside the fuel storage area.

"Endless night!" Riley gagged. "The smell!" It was like a living thing, invading the sinuses, eye-wateringly strong. Above the storage tank, gyps flapped and squawked.

"Best be fast then," Justine said, and Riley stretched up to press the severed thumb against the panel by the door.

Nothing happened.

"Told you not to mix them up!"

"I didn't!" Riley tried again, grabbed for the second hand and tried that just in case.

"Try the other fingers," Justine urged, the Vector dipping as she tried to get it closer, and Riley did, each in turn, several times. Nothing.

"Maybe he didn't have access!" Justine shouted above the wind.

"Maybe we should have kept that ID," Riley shouted back.

Justine said nothing, but reached down and handed Riley her Service pistol. The one that had been modified and might backfire and kill the shooter.

"Fortune favours the brave," Riley muttered, and aimed, wincing.

The lock exploded, the door flying open with the

force of the wind. It bashed Justine's arm before it clattered off into the background.

"You okay?" Riley began, because something moving at that velocity could have taken her head off, but Justine brushed at her arm as if shooing away an insect, and turned her attention to the train. Either she'd got damn lucky or she had an incredible tolerance for pain.

Riley was beginning to think that the latter might be an advantage on this crew.

The sudden rush of air from the departing door had knocked the inhabitants of the compartment off their feet, more than one of them getting covered in their stinking fuel. It also toppled the woman sitting on a stool by the door, and before any of them could save her she'd fallen out of the train to the burning desert below.

Riley twisted back to see her body rolling over and over, flopping like a rag doll.

"Come on!" Justine yelled, but the slaves seemed frozen. "This train is going to crash!"

Riley stood up, reaching out to the nearest slave. "You'll die if you stay. Come on!" The man hesitated, and Riley lost patience and yanked him forward. He stumbled and fell against the floor, bringing his stink with him. Riley reached for another, and this one, eyes wide, accepted the offer. Before long the other slaves followed suit, some of them leaping into the HAV, which started to buck wildly. One misjudged and fell, screaming, into the gap between vehicles. The gyps swept down in a screeching cloud.

Riley didn't look this time.

The Vector was meant as a swift ground transport, a more manoeuvrable type of van, and not intended to carry so many people. By the time they'd filled the HAV, the engine was starting to sound laboured, the vehicle dipping wildly. The whole place stank.

"We've got to go!" Justine shouted.

"There might be more—"

"We can't cope!" She nodded frantically at the display, which was beeping with red lights.

"Please!" yelled a skinny kid from the train, arm stretched out.

"I'm sorry," Justine muttered, too quiet for anyone but Riley to hear, and peeled the Vector unsteadily away.

Riley didn't want to look back but did. Slaves were still leaping from the compartment, falling and rolling on the burning sands. Already, the birds were circling.

"It's better than being in that shithole," said the one nearest Riley, watching the bodies fall.

Nobody said much as they flew away from the speeding train. They'd agreed on a location to hold the slaves, set up the day before with food, water and supplies, and Justine took the Vector there as fast as possible when it was so heavily laden. The plan, as far as Riley knew, was to come back and pick them up again later, then lead them to the nearest town and lie in a wide-eyed fashion about finding these poor refugees from the train crash. Oh, and would there be a bounty?

They were leaping to the ground before Justine had even got the landing gear on the sand.

"We'll never get the smell of shit out," she muttered as they watched the slaves fall on the supplies.

Riley swung down to pick up the canister of fuel they'd stored, and said to the nearest slave, "There's a river down there to wash in. It's fast though, and we don't know what's in—"

"Fresh water!" whooped the slave, and raced off in the river's direction, hollering to the others, who quickly followed.

"Quickly now, while they're distracted," Justine said, and Riley hopped back into the stinking vehicle. They flew off with the roof down, trying to get some fresh air. Riley made a mental note to scoop up some water to slosh over the HAV when they returned with the second set of slaves.

"How're we doing for time?" Justine asked.

"Right on schedule." If the southbound train hadn't been blown up by the right time and place, Émile had orders to fire on it. Orpheus and Hide had plans to steal a small HAV, a new Hades model that was listed in the cargo manifest of their train; and if that went wrong, Hide explained, they'd drop and roll as soon as the train was slow enough, and then run like buggery.

As for which of them actually captured the payroll, it came down to who found it first.

Everyone was betting on Orpheus.

They flew back to the northbound train, and this time Riley didn't need to use either the thumbprints or Justine's pistol. The door to the furnace compartment was hanging wide open.

It was full of burnt sewage and burnt bodies.

For a second they both stared, then Justine peeled rapidly away from the train. "The fuck happened?"

There was no way to contact the others, not with the signal scramblers in place, but Riley tried anyway. Nothing.

"Self-sabotage? Slave revolt? Trying to override my nav changes? Maybe they heard about the first train…"

"They shouldn't know about the first train yet! Didn't you scramble their comms?"

"Yes! But what if they found the scramblers? Or boosted the signal? I don't know what they've got up there!"

Justine swore creatively and at length, and then glared at the desert for a few moments while Riley frantically tried to think of a plan.

They couldn't comm anybody on either train, which must mean the scramblers were in place. So why had the slaves gone? And where? How did they know something was wrong?

"They must have discovered Petal and Murtaugh," said Justine, at the same time the thought occurred to Riley. "Shit!"

She swung back to the juggernaut, still speeding on northward, and started shouting orders. "I'll go fore, you go aft. I'll land on the engine roof. There are footholds to go back along the tank roof. Got it? Shoot anybody you see. We might have to crash this train by ourselves."

This was an even bigger risk than what they'd planned: risk of destroying or losing the payroll, and risk of, well, dying.

"It might already be on its way," Riley said, pointing. There was a sandstone cliff off to the north of the juggernaut. It was supposed to be on the west. "Someone's altered course. Or the driver is dead."

"Make the crew your top priority," Justine said, focusing straight on the train ahead. "Get them off that vehicle. There'll be other trains."

And other plans less stupid than mine, Riley thought, watching the sand and wind scour the fuel tank. The metal of the roof had a heat-haze over it, and as the HAV landed, Riley reached back for the med kit and some pre-emptive bandaging. Burned palms would do nobody any good.

Justine passed over a pistol, nodded, and was gone.

Climbing along the top of the train as it rattled on over the desert didn't look easy, and proved to be even harder. The wind whipped blinding sand into Riley's eyes, even round the sunshades. Through slats in the compartment roof, the smell of fermenting excrement was vomit-inducing. Gyps darted close, screeching at the prospect of fresh meat. Riley crawled on hands and knees, reaching the end and climbing with some relief down to the walkway to the next compartment.

The door was unlocked. Great start. Riley darted in,

leading with the pistol. A bullet whined past.

"Petal?"

"Fuck you!" screamed an unfamiliar voice. Riley aimed at it and shot. Jesus, this pistol was as lethal as the other one! It made mincemeat of the guard hiding at the far end of the compartment.

Riley glanced around on the way through. Storage compartments, nothing with any kind of locking system on it. The second compartment was the same, except that the guard there was already dead. The third was never going to be so easy.

This one still had a locked door. Riley considered the odds, then swore, holstered the pistol, and began climbing up the side of the container. There was a hole halfway along the roof, blast-marks aimed outwards. So this was where they'd fought.

There were two compartments rattling along behind this one. Riley glanced back at the couplings, bright in the sunshine, then down through the hole into the darkness.

"Petal? Murtaugh?"

A shot answered back, blasting too close for comfort. Then more, from inside the compartment, pinging off the internal walls. So at least one of them was in there. And so, maybe, was the safe.

"What the hell," said Riley, and dropped down through the blast hole.

Max was screaming.

Nobody could hear, because they were all dead. And even if they hadn't been, the sand and wind blasting along the walkway were enough to drown out all sound.

The bodies of the slaves were specks in the distance now. Herrick had started throwing them out of the compartment, one by one, for no reason Max could discern. Peering in through the entrance to the engine compartment gave a view of a spitting, foam-flecked man frantically jabbing at tabs whilst around him the slaves screamed and clutched at their cuffs.

"Was it you?" the overseer yelled. "Are they your friends?"

"No sir!" cried the unfortunate slave in front of him, and was simply shoved backwards out of the door.

"Was it you got your friends killing our guards? Was it you?"

One boy dropped to the floor, writhing in agony. Blood seeped from his nose as Herrick yelled and ranted. Had he gone insane? For one thing, nobody was fuelling the furnace. Sudden fluctuations in fuel were very bad for it, leading to unpredictable speed jumps or hikes.

Max's cuff suddenly burst into shockingly painful life as the train jolted, and the shovel was the only thing blocking a fatal fall to the racing ground. Blood ran.

Somewhere in the distance, an explosion boomed. The slaves screamed and sobbed. "We're all going to die!"

Hell with this, Max thought. *You can die if you want. I ain't planning on it.*

Herrick had his back turned. Crawling forward, grabbing the shovel, Max raised it.

The shovel swung, hitting the overseer in the back of the skull. A heavy man, he fell forward, blood oozing from his skull. Before he could even raise his hand, Max swung again, and again, smashing the shovel down on the man's ruined head until blood flecked them both.

Suddenly disgusted, Max dropped the shovel, and then as the other slaves stared, appalled, turned the grotesque man over and started rooting through the mess of tabs around his neck.

"You killed him!" gasped a small voice.

"We're all going to die now!"

"We've got a day at least," Max snapped, wondering

like hell how to find the right tab.

"The cuffs will kill us!"

"Then you're dead already," Max snarled, and then felt the pulse of the right tab. Snatched it free, cradled it close. Looked up at the shocked slaves.

"Well, get yours—"

The seldom-used door next to the engine slammed open, rocking on its hinges. "Mr Herrick, the driver says —oh my God!"

With that, the young man stumbled, as the engine hit a rock or something and rocked violently. Max watched in horror as he fell against the sewage hopper and, with grim inevitability, it tipped forward.

The young man screamed as the excrement flowed over him, then swept him into the furnace. Max leapt back out of the compartment, grabbing onto the walkway as the explosion rocked the engine and the land train's wheels swooped sickeningly close.

Max was hanging on for dear life.

A shot rang out, knocking Riley back against the nearest storage container. "Don't shoot! It's me!"

"Primer?" called Murtaugh as Riley scrambled for cover.

"Yes!" Riley yelled, then swore as an unfamiliar face popped out behind a large box.

Riley shot at it instinctively, and then there was silence for a moment.

"Primer?"

"I'm okay," gasped Riley, which was something of a lie given the blood dripping down over those protective hand bindings. That shot had gone in somewhere around the upper arm. The pain was beginning to spread.

"Did you get him?"

"Yes." Riley slumped back against the wall.

"He was the last one in here," Murtaugh said. "There

were some forward—"

"Gone. As far front as the furnace. What the hell happened?"

Murtaugh appeared over the crates and extended a hand to pull Riley upright. The compartment swayed.

"We made it fine this far, and then one of them caught sight of us and started shooting. We put him down, but his mate started calling for help, and all hell broke loose. There was some kind of jolt up ahead. We don't know what. That bastard," he peered down at the man Riley had just killed, "got Petal in the leg."

"Is she okay?"

"Minor graze," said Petal, limping forward. The leg of her trousers was wet with blood. "The safe is in the last-but-one compartment. We had to kill four guys in there. And I saw it first," she added, elbowing Murtaugh, who sighed and shoved the sweat out of his eyes.

"Is Justine coming alongside?" That had been the plan, to get them off the same way they'd got on. But now...

Riley shrugged helplessly. "I don't even know. We landed on the roof. There's something wrong, the train is going too fast and in the wrong direction." *It's probably going to hit those cliffs. And we're going to jackknife round into them.* "We have to get off."

They stared at him. "But—"

"Justine—"

"Knows what she's doing." *I hope.*

"We can't jump. Not at this speed. It'll kill us," Petal said.

"There was nothing in those compartments we could use? A HAV or even a land-buggy?" Riley asked, despite knowing there was nothing so big on the manifest. If only they'd been on the other bloody train!

They shook their heads. "Ore in the final one and small items in the next." Clearly none of the crates in here held anything big enough to be a vehicle either.

Riley glanced at the front of the container, and wondered what Justine was doing in the forward compartment. If she was still alive or not. If she could avert the crash that would kill them all.

"Then we head for the Vector on the roof," said Petal, working her leg and wincing.

"No time," said Riley, "especially not with two of us wounded."

Their eyes met. It's us or Justine.

"We could uncouple from the compartment in front," Riley said finally. "We'll roll to a stop and the train will crash without us."

"But…Justine—"

"Or we stay linked up, and we all die. In about… three minutes."

There was a terrible silence.

"Fuck this," said Petal, "I want to live." Murtaugh nodded, and wrestled open the door at the front. Hot sand blasted in as he took aim and fired at the walkway. It clattered away, but the coupling beneath it stayed firm. Eyes rolling, Riley stepped forward.

"It needs physically uncoupling." Which would be fun with half an arm out of action.

"You're the engineer," Murtaugh said, and Riley sighed.

"Yeah. Lucky me. All right…hold onto my legs."

Riley inched forward over the hot metal of the coupling, glad for those protective bindings. The steel was sizzling in the sunshine, the hitch of the coupling almost within reach.

"Got it?" Murtaugh rumbled.

"Nearly!" Riley felt the metal jink and then give, and looked up into the eyes of a slave clinging to the back of the compartment they were about to send flying off into the face of a cliff.

"Please!"

The slave reached out, and so did Riley, and their hands met as the carriages pulled free and they were suddenly yanked backwards. Riley grabbed onto the slave, who was filthy with blood and dirt and God knew what else, and let Murtaugh drag them both back into the compartment.

They lay together on the floor, panting, watching the forward half of the train rush away towards the cliff. *I'm sorry, Justine.*

Riley sat up, feeling like shit, and avoided the eyes of the others. The final three carriages were rumbling slower and slower, although the deceleration seemed to take forever.

"Who the fuck are you?" the slave croaked, and Riley turned to help the poor wretch to its feet.

Their hands clasped, and a jolt went right through Riley. The slave gave a stifled scream and fell back to the ground, lying in a crumpled heap.

There was a bloodied slave tab in Riley's equally bloodied hand.

CHAPTER TWO

Orpheus was pleased, at least as much as Orpheus ever seemed pleased about anything. He'd acquired the sleek new Hades HAV as well as the safe from the second land train, the one Riley and Justine had been on. Justine, who for all Riley's worrying, had dispatched the inhabitants of the forward compartment all by herself, climbed back up to the Vector, and was just about to fly back alongside to collect the others when Riley uncoupled the carriages.

The captain flew them back to the Eurydice in his shiny new toy, which Riley and Petal did their best not to bleed all over, while Murtaugh and Hide went to pick up the rescued slaves in the Vector and take them to the nearest town. As they left, Justine was already issuing orders about how many slaves each of them took to each official post at a time, to waylay suspicion.

Émile greeted them with a yelp of delight at the Hades, and eyes wide with surprise at the slave Riley was carrying.

"You decided to keep one?"

"Didn't have much choice," Riley said shortly.

Petal had explained how the shock they'd both felt had been the slave tab imprinting on Riley. "So you're now the legal owner. Captain'll be happy."

Orpheus had given Riley a stonefaced look when he heard the news, and Riley was too tired to try to work out what it was supposed to mean.

Justine led them to the ship's small sickbay, where she assigned the unconscious slave a bed and treated Petal and Riley's injuries. Petal hopped off to her quarters, cheerful on painkillers, and Riley sat on the other bed, staring at the slave. A skinny, shaven-headed boy, face obscured by blood and the permanent stench of sewage.

"You can wash your own property, you know," Justine said, checking with gloved hands for any serious injuries.

"He's not my property. You can't own a person."

"Law says different," said Orpheus's low voice from the doorway, making Riley jump. The man was like a bloody cat. "That's a convict cuff. You own the indenture until the sentence has been fulfilled. Or one of you dies."

"It was a mistake," Riley said. The captain just grunted.

"Can't we take it off? I'm sure I can deprogram it, and—"

"No!" Justine and Orpheus said it at the same time, the most raised Riley had ever heard the captain's voice.

"Tamper with a convict cuff, try to remove it, and the convict dies. The probes already go direct into the vein, and at the first attempt to remove it they…" Justine made wiggling motions with her fingers.

"They wrap around the vein and rip it out," Orpheus said, his eyes like chips of ice. "Death occurs in minutes."

Riley felt wretched enough about all the slaves who'd

died today without adding another to the total.

"You need to wear the tab, too. It needs regular skin contact from the owner or it'll assume the slave has stolen it."

"Marvellous."

"Can't feel anything broken," Justine said, and picked up a scanner. "No swelling or signs of internal injury. Malnourished, for sure, and dehydrated, but nothing that can't be fixed. Help me get these filthy rags off him."

Justine cut through the top half of what had probably once been prison scrubs, and with some distaste Riley started tugging the trousers over the slave's bare, encrusted feet.

And then Orpheus started laughing. Riley was too astonished at the sound to do anything but stare at him. Then Justine joined in, tired and slightly hysterical, and Riley realised they were both laughing at the slave.

Who, without her trousers on, was revealed to be most definitely female.

Riley stared down at the incontrovertible proof that his slave was a girl. "Oh fuck," he said.

Max was dreaming.

They were dreams of fire and blood, of running and climbing up, over, around, under. Of screaming metal and howling wind. Of heat and the scour of sand, of the smell of shit and burning flesh.

Of someone reaching out, offering help that swiftly turned into pain.

"You decided to keep one?"

Out of the frying pan, into the fire!

"...deprogram it. Wrap around the vein and rip it out."

Like fuck you will.

There were hands, grabbing and squeezing,

undressing, baring. Someone swore.

Max lashed out.

Riley leaned against the wall, watching the girl sleep. It wasn't a restful process. She shifted, kicked, jolted half awake and moaned as if she was in pain. Justine had assured him this was more or less normal for someone sleeping off a heavy tranquilliser, not to mention the effects of her maltreatment.

What hadn't been normal was her sudden violent attack on the three of them, apparently utterly unconscious.

They'd ended up putting her in the brig, which was really just a storage locker with bars across half of it, and a few security cameras. Justine had started getting pissy about the slave throwing tantrums in her sleep and destroying half her sickbay, and there were no other rooms. Riley sure as hell wasn't letting the hellcat share his.

So she lay on a mattress from the sickbay, wearing one of Riley's shirts ("You're a big bastard, it'll be a fucking ballgown on her") and some of his blankets. There were little cuts on her face, on her buzzcut scalp, and burns on her hands. She was skinny like a whip and just as strong. Riley was, as Justine had said, a big bastard, and it had taken all his strength to hold her down as she'd thrashed and sworn, semi-lucid.

Riley gingerly touched his nose, which she'd broken with her knee.

How the hell did you take responsibility for someone like this?

The door cycled open, which was the only way Riley would have known the captain had entered. Maybe he had special boots that muffled sound or something. It was uncanny.

Orpheus stood in silence for a long moment, arms

folded, then just as Riley was about to speak, said, "I know her."

That got Riley's attention. "What? How? Who is she?"

Orpheus said neutrally, "A whore."

Riley stared at the lean, bruised, shaven-headed spitfire curled up in his shirt, and said, "I'm sorry, what?"

Orpheus almost smiled. "You do know what a whore is?"

"Yes, I know. But she doesn't..."

He trailed off as they both looked at how much she didn't.

"I've known career soldiers who'd look like fluffy little kittens compared to her," Riley said flatly.

"She had more hair then," Orpheus volunteered. "And she smiled."

Riley couldn't imagine that, either.

"Scar on the inner thigh," Orpheus said.

Riley had noticed that. Justine had insisted he be the one to bathe his property, probably because she didn't want to risk her own life and limbs doing it. The girl was covered in small scars, from bullets and lasers and knives and what might even have been a whip. "Where?"

"There was a whorehouse. Omega system. One of the moons."

"Sixtus Quattro," Riley said automatically, starcharts flashing up in his head. There weren't many inhabitable moons in Omega. "Or Septimus Sei. Otto is just a Service base."

"And the Service don't have whorehouses, Primer?"

"Not for pirates," Riley replied, and got what Orpheus probably counted as a smile.

"I had a room there. She made a play for me. A very definite play. Thought it was my lucky day."

Riley tried to imagine a world where being targeted by a whirling dervish like this girl would be considered lucky, and failed. The thought of going to bed with her frankly filled him with terror.

"Of course, I realised later, it wasn't me she wanted, so much as my room. The only one where you could escape out of the window and be over the roofs without being seen."

"She stole from you?"

"From her employers. The windows were alarmed, but she got past them somehow. Took half their money." Orpheus almost sounded admiring.

They both watched the sleeping girl, who dealt a hell of a gut punch to some invisible adversary.

"But when you say whorehouse..." Riley began off-handedly.

Orpheus cut his eyes at Riley, a slice of pity therein.

"I mean, you're saying she was one of the...that she was definitely a...?"

"Whore. Yes."

She fought violently against her blankets.

"Well," said Riley. "Fuck."

"Indeed," purred the captain.

Riley narrowed his eyes, and hesitated. "Uh, when you say she...was a whore but she...only wanted your room, I mean...did you...?"

The Sphinx smiled. "You're a very lucky man, Primer," he said, and slunk away.

"Wait," said Riley, spoiling the captain's exit. Orpheus paused in the doorway. "Did she give you a name?"

Orpheus stared at the sleeping girl for a long moment. "Max," he said eventually. "She said her name was Max."

Max woke to the thrum of an engine.

It wasn't the hellish blast and thud of the land train, it was the purr of a well-tuned spacecraft. She was on a ship. No recollection of the how and why.

No...wait. The train had blown up, or crashed or something. Everyone was dead. She'd survived the blast by dint of being out on the walkway, although it had half collapsed and nearly thrown her under the land train's massive wheels. Clinging on for dear life, determined that this was not going to be the end of her, Max had clung and climbed, hand over hand, to the fuel tank. No going forward, unless she wanted to risk the furnace and another bloody explosion.

There was a HAV resting uneasily on top of the engine compartment. An old one, clunky and ugly but built like a rock, and apparently undamaged by the blast below it. So. Whoever had landed it was probably behind Herrick's suspicion of treachery and his subsequent psychotic episode.

Max considered trying to steal it, but there was still a fire raging inside the engine compartment and the metal handholds leading up to the roof were molten with heat.

Back, then, away from the fire. If this thing was going to crash then Max would prefer to be at the non-impact end.

Inch by excruciating inch, she made it to the top of the fuel tank, and then over it. Down to the walkway. The door to the next compartment was open. Did that mean that the attackers were in there? And what was that going to mean for Max? *My enemy's enemy is...probably still going to shoot me in the head.*

Still, where the hell else was there to go?

Max took a deep breath—which, given the proximity of the fuel tank, was a stupid thing to do—and started across.

After the blinding sun, the inside of the compartment was impenetrably dark. Aware that her silhouette was an obvious target, Max quickly dipped to one side and pressed back against the wall, waiting. Nobody fired. As her eyes adjusted she saw a body slumped on the floor. A train guard. Shot with something that left a huge blast where his head used to be.

So my enemy's enemy has modified bloody weapons. Well, that's just grand.

She crept through that compartment, and the next, and had just got to the back door of it when there was a clatter, and the walkway ripped away, nearly flattening Max before it wheeled off into the desert.

Someone lunged out of the third compartment.

A man, big and bloody, crawled out along the coupling as if to undo it. If he did, Max was dead. Even if she leapt across the gap she'd probably be dead.

She flung out a desperate hand. "Please!"

And he grabbed her, and the next thing Max remembered was pain, crippling pain, shooting through the cuff and up her arm.

Only nightmares followed.

In restless, tangled dreams, there were people speaking. Talking about her slave cuff and Septimus Sei. Endless night, that had been a long time ago. She'd escaped Septimus Sei a dozen years ago. Maybe more. Hard to keep track with all the different planets and their weird-ass calendars.

She risked opening her eyes.

Oh great. I'm back in a fucking cell.

She had a mattress and blankets, however, and she was clean, and someone had bandaged her wounds. The small cuts had been closed with skinglue and the burns had silver dressings on them. She wore an oversized shirt and not much else. Her head felt woozy, as if with the aftermath of tranquillisers.

All this was being catalogued in the back of Max's brain, whilst she processed the really big piece of information on the other side of the cell bars.

He sat with his back to the wall, arms resting on his knees. And given the size of the bugger, she'd give even odds the shirt she was wearing was one of his. He was tanned, so he'd probably spent a lot of time dirtside recently, and his hair had a short, military look about it. She'd have said he was Service in disguise if it wasn't for the leather wristbands, an old trick the Service never had to worry about.

He wore her slave tab around his neck.

"Morning," he said, and glanced at the micro he had tangled up in the straps of his right wristband. *A southpaw.* "Just."

"Forgive me for sleeping in," Max snarled, lip curling. "Some bugger drugged me."

"You were trying to kill us all," he said mildly.

"Probably had reason."

He shrugged. His sleeves had been rolled up, displaying muscular forearms and a bandage around one bulging bicep.

She motioned to her nose, and his fingers moved up to his own. It looked sore, cut across the bridge. He winced when he touched it.

"Did I do that?"

He nodded.

"Good."

His eyebrows went up at that. They were fair, like the stubble on his scalp. Bastard probably had long lines of blue-eyed blonds on both sides, stretching back to Earth like some unbroken bloody daisy chain of racial purity.

"Good? I did save your life, you know."

"Thanks. Thanks for that," Max said with as much sarcasm as she could. "And I suppose you took on my indenture purely out of the goodness of your heart too?"

His fingers touched the tab hanging around his neck. There were a couple of other tchotchkes there too, a religious symbol or something and a couple of colourful beads.

"It was an accident."

Max snorted.

"I reached out my hand to help you," he said, eyes wide and blue and guileless. "I didn't know you were holding your slave tab! How did you get it, anyway?"

Max rolled her shoulders, which didn't ache as much as usual. They must've given her a general painkiller.

"I bashed the overseer's skull in with a shitty shovel," she said, and kept her eyes on his to catch his reaction.

To her surprise, he laughed. "You did? Jesus. You do know that the longer you're away from the owner of your tab, the worse the shocks will get?"

Max shrugged. Her plan had been to cross that bridge when she came to it.

"You just don't give a shit, do you?" he said, getting to his feet. He was a big guy, and seemed to know it as he looked down at her. Undeterred, Max scrambled to her own feet, probably flashing him a glimpse of what she wasn't wearing under his shirt.

The fact that he averted his eyes told her all she needed to know. *Well well. Do we have a gentleman here?*

Max wasn't short by anybody's measure, but her new owner towered above her. Broad-shouldered with it, too. He could probably crush her skull like a melon if he chose to.

He crossed his big arms over his big chest, and looked down at her with those innocent blue eyes. Eyes which suddenly seemed a whole lot more calculating.

Then he said something that managed to surprise the hell out of her.

"Can I call you Max?"

That had done it! The shaven-headed woman stepped

back in surprise.

"How do you—" She glanced down at the crook of her arm, where Justine had discovered an implant. A tracking device, put into anyone who'd ended up on the wrong side of the system. It identified her by a number, but there had been no name attached.

He let her sweat for a minute or two, then relented. "My captain has met you."

She shrugged, wary as a cat. "I've known a lot of captains."

"You might remember this one. You used him to abscond from a brothel with half the owner's money."

Her lips quirked nostalgically. "Oh yeah. Skinny feller. Didn't say much."

Riley hesitated. "Were you…was that your line of work?"

She looked amused. "Line of work? Yeah, if you want to put it that way. My 'line of work' was fucking strangers for money." She dipped her head and looked up at him from under her lashes, the spitting hellcat suddenly transformed into a purring sex-kitten. "And I enjoyed it. I was a good whore. Men asked for me by name."

Riley's mouth was suddenly dry. He coughed, and she smiled.

"Is that what you want me for?" Max asked. She toyed with the gaping neckline of the shirt. "To fuck?"

"No," he said, a little harder than he'd intended. *Great. Now I'm insulting her.* "I mean…no. I wouldn't take advantage like that."

He wanted to reassure her that she'd be safe on this ship, in his protection. That nobody would lay a finger on her. That he'd castrate any man who tried. But she just gave him a once-over and said, "Not even if I wanted you to?"

Endless night! "You've just met me," Riley

spluttered. "You know nothing about me!"

She shrugged. "Never knew nothing about my clients, neither."

"I could beat you black and blue. I could be full of the worst perversions you've ever heard of."

"Again, like some of my clients." She looked him over again, and smiled, showing her canines. "You ain't full of perversions. Sweet as vanilla, you are."

That shouldn't have been as annoying as it was. "I do have your tab," he said, holding it up and poising his finger over it. "I could shock you until your heart stopped."

Max just yawned and sat back down again. "Then you'd have a dead slave," she said.

Riley let the tab drop and grasped the cell bars, looking down at her. She really wasn't afraid of him.

He'd always been a big guy, unfashionably tall and broad, so fond of engines he'd spent most of his youth carting around huge, heavy bits of metal to fix whatever he could scrounge up. He wasn't given to violence, but then she didn't know that. If she remembered anything of her rescue she might remember him covered in blood and swearing. It was not, therefore, unreasonable to expect her to be at least a little cautious around her new owner.

Was she completely mad? Or did she know something he didn't?

"Look," he began again, "all this is accidental, but there doesn't seem to be—"

"Oh, you just happened to prick your finger, did you? How'd you get blood on the tab?"

He gestured to the bandage on his arm, which ached as the anaesthetic wore off. "I got shot."

Max raised a single brow. "Probably shouldn't've been robbing a train then, should you?"

She was just trying to provoke him. Riley tried to

ignore that, and continued, "There's nothing we can do about it now. You've got less than a year to go on your indenture. I can either sell you on or you can stay here on the ship and work for a living."

"Living?" she scoffed.

"Share in the prize, just like the rest of us get. If you pull your weight. Can you do anything useful? Apart from sex," he added before she turned those sex-kitten eyes on him again.

"What could be more useful?" she purred. Then she tilted her head and regarded him, apparently serious this time. "I'm a tech," she said. "That any good to you?"

If it was true, it was bloody good to him. "What kind of tech?"

"Whatever I can get my hands on."

"Training?"

She gave a mocking shrug. "Self-taught." When that failed to impress, she added, "How'd you think I got out of that brothel with half their money?"

Ah. "You're a hacker?"

"If you want to call it that."

People spoke of hackers in derogatory terms, but that was because they didn't understand their worth. Riley had some ability with electronics, but his heart was in mechanics and his hacking skills were not exemplary. If Max really was a hacker, and she really was any good, she'd be very useful to the Eurydice.

Riley folded his arms.

"How are you with engines?"

"I could learn."

There was the rub. "Are you willing to learn? Because I've got to tell you, Max, you really haven't done a lot to endear yourself to me so far." His nose throbbed as a reminder. "I could pretty easily boot you off the next time we make landfall and sell you on to the highest bidder. Crew'd like that. They're mercenary bastards. And you are basically another mouth to feed."

He watched that sink in. Yes, it was cruel. Yes, he was quite unlikely to do it, knowing as he did what her fate was likely to be. But on the other hand she was being a really big pain in his arse and as the most untried member of the crew, the last thing he needed was to shove a truculent slave under their noses.

Especially when Orpheus had made it clear how little he held with slavery.

"When are you next making landfall?"

"Day or two." They still had Murtaugh and Hide to pick up, along with whatever bounty they'd managed to glean from returning the slaves.

The irony of this profit was not lost on Riley.

Max uncurled her legs from under his shirt. As she did, he saw the curved scar on her inner thigh, before the fabric fell and covered it when she stood.

"Look," she said. "Thing is, you basically seem too good to be true. There's got to be a catch somewhere."

"I'll let you know when I find it."

Max chewed her lip. It was dry, bitten, blistered. Her hands reached for the bars above his, and Riley stepped back, because he wasn't a fool. She slid her fingers over the warmth his had left, and met his eye.

"All right. Give me some clothes and some food, for God's sake give me some water, and I'll behave. I'll prove my worth to your crew. By the time we go dirtside you won't want to sell me on anywhere."

Riley looked her over, the spitting hellcat and purring sex-kitten who'd suddenly transformed into a puppy looking for a home. *Like hell it'll be this easy.*

"I'll talk to the captain," he said. "No promises."

As he left, she said, "There never are."

CHAPTER THREE

The crew were sitting around in the mess room, looking suspiciously casual. Émile was reading a magazine upside down.

"Turns out she's a lost princess from old Earth," he said, and while most of them snorted at that or rolled their eyes, Émile said, "Really?"

"No, not really, you fathead. She's an indentured slave. Petty crimes. The sort you lot are good at."

Neither he nor Émile had been able to make much of the chip embedded in Max's arm—he suspected she herself was the cause of that—but the cuff had told them what her crimes and sentence were.

"I told her—" Riley hesitated, and glanced at Orpheus, "—that if she pulled her weight on the crew we'd let her stay. She says she's a tech. Until we next make landfall?" he added to the captain, who gave no visible reaction. "I could sell her on. But she'll just end up back on a train like before, or something worse."

Émile looked like he was about to say something, but Justine elbowed him and he stayed silent.

"Does that sound acceptable?"

The crew glanced at each other, and nobody seemed to object. Eventually all eyes turned on Orpheus.

"She's your responsibility," he rasped.

"Sure. Of course."

"She fucks up, it's you going out the airlock."

"A charming thought. I'll take care of her. Émile, is there any food going? Water?"

Émile glanced at something in the oven. "Give it ten minutes."

"Bring her up here," his sister said. "We should get to know our new crewmate."

Riley couldn't help his gaze drifting towards the back of the ship, and the airlock.

"Fair enough," he said, more jovially than he felt. "I'll fetch her. Uh. Does anyone have any spare clothes?"

Her new owner came back an indeterminate amount of time later. Max, who knew she was being watched, lay down on her pallet and feigned sleep. She'd almost managed it for real when the door hissed open, and she sat up in time for the big bastard to open the cell door and throw some clothes at her.

"The cook donated some items," he said. "He'll be wanting them back."

Max picked up a soft sweater and a pair of trousers. Probably both would adapt to fit. She was tall, and had never been much for curves, so they'd probably be okay. No shoes, however.

"I'll have cold feet," she remarked, pulling off the shirt that was more like a dress.

To her amusement, her new owner spun around and stared at the wall. "Ship's floors are warm," he said, sputtering only slightly.

Max grinned and stretched, enjoying the pull in her muscles. "Can't help but notice I'm all nice and clean now," she said, not picking up the clothes. "Did someone wash me?"

His ears turned red. He nodded.

"You must tell me so I can thank them."

"It's fine."

"Was it you?"

He nodded jerkily.

"Thank you. Sir."

His fingers flexed, but he said nothing. Interesting.

"So is that Service discipline," Max asked conversationally, "or will it be Primer modesty?"

"What?" He spun back, then comically slammed his eyes shut and wheeled away again at the sight of her nakedness.

Max laughed softly and picked up the trousers. "The way you hold yourself," she said. "Service, am I right? Either that or you were born on a Prime planet. I know how terrified you all are of natural human functions," she mocked gently.

"I—it's none of your business," he said. "Are you dressed yet?"

"Yes," said Max, and he glanced back to see the lie of it. She casually pulled on the sweater and bent to pick up the shirt. "Yours?"

He took it, cheeks pink. It was kind of adorable.

"Thank you. Sir."

"Don't do that. My name is Riley."

"Sir Riley."

He rolled his eyes. "Remember what I said about selling you on?"

An empty threat. If he wanted to punished her he'd use that hellish little tab.

"You want me to call you Riley?" He nodded. "Riley it is. Lead on then, sir."

Max trailed after him out of the brig and through the

hold. "Don't touch anything," he said, and she saluted him whilst running her grubby eyeballs over everything.

He took a deep breath before leading her up the steps and into the mess room, where four pairs of curious eyes turned on them. "Everyone, this is Max."

"I'm his slave," she added cheerfully, and Riley glared at her.

"Don't start, all right? Sit down, don't make trouble. Émile, that food ready yet?"

Émile nodded, his gaze assessing. He poured a big glass of water for Max and slid it across, and by the time he turned back with her food the water was all gone.

"God I needed that," she gasped. "I'm so dehydrated I haven't peed in three days."

"Thanks for sharing," Riley said. "Eat."

He didn't know what the food was, but it looked like some kind of stew. Émile placed it down and reached for the cutlery stored in a pot in the middle of the table, but Max was already ahead of him and tipping up the bowl to slurp noisily from it.

When that wasn't fast enough, she shovelled it into her mouth with her unbandaged fingers, the rehydrated proteins and freeze-dried vegetables and the thick sauce. It ran down her hands, over the burn dressings, all over the table. Her face was smeared with it.

They all stared at her, even Riley, until he felt Orpheus's gaze on him. Their eyes met, and Riley was the first to look away.

Nobody spoke until Max had finished that bowl, whereupon Orpheus took it away, and her eyes followed it mournfully, lighting up again as he silently refilled it and put it back in front of her.

"Really?" she said, like a kid at Christmas. "I fucking love this crew."

"Just use a spoon this time," Orpheus reminded her, holding one out, and she wiped her hands on her trousers and took it from him. Émile winced, and Riley wasn't sure if it was at the abuse of his food or his clothes.

She shoved more food into her mouth, and only then seemed to realise she was being watched. "What?" she said. "Never seen anyone hungry before?"

Justine cleared her throat. They all stirred into action, setting out bowls and glasses and organising themselves around the table. Max continued eating, gulping down hot stew as if she'd never see another meal again.

"Slow down," Riley said. "You'll give yourself indigestion."

"You slow down," she responded around a mouthful of food. "I am literally starving. I'd love indigestion. It sounds awesome."

Someone laughed at that, but when Riley looked up all he saw were blank faces.

They served themselves. Riley sat beside Max, fascinated at the speed with which she could make food disappear.

"Bread?" he offered, and she moaned like a woman in pleasure before grabbing the roll and tearing into it with sharp little teeth.

Petal cleared her throat. "Any word from Murtaugh and Hide?"

"They've turned in half the slaves. Said the authorities were starting to get suspicious so they might sell on the rest privately."

"Can they do that?"

"It's just a blood transfer," Justine said, and cut her eyes at Riley. "Primer here can tell you all about that."

Riley gave her a tight smile and tried not to feel the weight of the tab hanging around his neck.

"They'll contact us in a day or two. Not sure where they are now. They were moving on quite fast."

"Prob'ly east or west," Max said through her food. "Trains run north to south around there and I s'pose they'll want to keep away from that. Did you make 'em crash on purpose?"

A slight pause. Then Justine said, "Yes."

"Nice. Good haul?"

Another pause. "Not bad."

"Cool. Any more of that stew thing going begging?"

Émile ladled out some more for her. "It's nice to be appreciated," he said.

"Mate, you give me food this good every day and I promise you I'll get down under the table and give you a blowjob while you're doing it."

Riley nearly choked. Émile actually did, and while Justine was thumping his back, she said drily to Max, "You're not his type."

"Really?" Max looked vaguely surprised, and then the penny dropped. "Oh. Gotcha." She pointed her spoon at Orpheus, who was watching the entertainment with what passed for amusement on his face, and said, "You. I'm your type, right? I think I fucked you once."

Riley, spoon halfway to his mouth, paused in horror. The rest of the table went very quiet.

"Yeah," Orpheus said eventually. "And we had sex, too."

Max snorted with laughter and crammed more bread into her mouth.

"They thought I was your accomplice. I had to kill some people to get out."

He delivered this with a total lack of emotion, as if killing people was like filling in a form: a necessary part of life.

"Sorry," said Max unrepentantly. "Needed cash, didn't I? I'd've shared it with you, but…well, I wouldn't actually."

"Any of it left?" Orpheus enquired idly. The breadknife in his hand started to look somewhat threatening to Riley.

"Do I look like someone with five grand in her back pocket? You'd be amazed how soon I ran through it. Still, it got me off that stinking moon, so I s'pose it was worth it."

"Wouldn't you have earned more by staying there?"

That earned him a look of contempt. Her audacity was breathtaking.

"No." She shovelled more stew into her mouth. "I got food and bed and clothes, and one of them I had to share and the second I never got to keep on for long. It wasn't what you might call an investment opportunity."

"And on that note," Riley said desperately, "Max was telling me she has some tech skills."

Max gave him a scornful look. The rest of them didn't seem impressed at such a lame segue either.

"What kind of tech skills?" Émile asked.

"What d'you need?"

Riley wasn't sure, but he thought he saw the glimmer of a smile on the captain's face.

They're keeping me, thought Max as her new owner took her back to her cell. "We actually don't have any other rooms," he said, somewhat apologetically. "Um. But I won't lock the door, so. I know it's not exactly… cosy," he added, looking around as if surprised to find a lack of soft furnishings. "Do you want an extra blanket or something?"

"No, it's grand," said Max, because there was no point pushing her luck. "It's better'n anything I had on that fecking train. There's even a dunny."

"A…?"

Bless his innocent little socks. Max pointed to the rather basic toilet and sink combo in the corner. "A dunny? A crapper. A john."

"The head," he corrected, "since we're on a ship." He fiddled with the cell door for a moment, testing that it wouldn't stay locked when he shut it. "All right then. I'll wake you up tomorrow, yes? The nav files need defragging, and I could use a hand retuning the aft thrusters."

Max nodded absently and ran her hand over the cell bars. "Sure you don't want to stay?" she said, glancing back at him. He was big and muscular, not bad looking really, and he might take more kindly to her if she pleased him well enough. And Max knew she would.

"Somehow I don't think you're offering me a game of cards."

She looked up at him with heat in her eyes.

Riley just sighed. "You don't have to sleep with anyone you don't want to," he said.

"What if I want to?"

He spread his hands. "Then fuck the whole crew if you're that way inclined. But this," he pointed between the two of them, "is not happening. So stop propositioning me, all right?"

"All right," Max agreed, somewhat stung. "Sorry I offended your maidenly virtue."

He rolled his eyes. "Good night, Max."

"Night, sir."

The door cycled shut behind him, and Max wondered what she was supposed to do now. Rest, probably, after all that trauma, but she'd been unconscious most of the day—might even have been longer, she'd never thought to ask—and sleep didn't hold much appeal.

The ship's engine pulsed quietly, purring like the well-maintained machine it was. Riley appeared to be a decent mechanic, then. She wondered if he'd actually find any use for her tech skills.

She amused herself with the control panel to the outer door, programming it to chime when someone tried to open it from the outside. That was about all the tech available to her, apart from the cell door and there was no fun to be had there. Out in the hold there were probably piles of things that needed fixing, or which could be improved, but she wasn't sure it was a good idea to go out there and just start fiddling. Not until she'd figured out the surveillance cameras anyway.

Speaking of which…

The camera was located in a panel above the door to the hold. It was hard to reach, and she knew she'd be watched while she tried to disable it. Probably a job best left to another day then, accessed from the ship's systems instead of the source.

With nothing else to do, she lay down to sleep, and had almost managed it when the door chimed.

Needs an intercom, she thought as she got up to open it. A job for tomorrow, if she could find the parts.

The captain stood there, frowning at the control panel on the other side of the door. "So that's what you were doing," he said.

So you were watching me. Thought so. She folded her arms and regarded him. "Well ain't I just the popular one? I do hope you brought a card to give the butler."

His gaze was assessing, his eyes narrowed, his face giving nothing away. He hadn't changed much since she'd seen him on Septimus Sei. A bit more weathered, maybe. Longer hair. Might be a new piercing in his ear. She hadn't made any effort to recall the details.

He watched her watching him, then rasped, "As you remember me?"

Max shrugged. "I wouldn't recall you at all, but you have the distinction of being the last man who paid to fuck me. Well. In money, at any rate."

She stepped back to let him in, and went back to sit on her mattress since there was nowhere else to park her arse. He strolled after her, leaning in the entrance to the cell and looking down at her with narrow cat's eyes.

Yes, that was what he resembled. Not a soft,

pampered pet but one of the rangy creatures you sometimes saw in alleys, crouched over a kill with an attitude that said they'd murder you if you interrupted.

Like Riley and the others on the crew, he had various tchotchkes around his neck and on his wrists, and even woven into a narrow braid or two in his long hair. His clothing was dark, his jaw unshaven, his weapons belt slung with knives and holsters for guns. There might even be a sword strap on there.

This man was dangerous, and she didn't think killing gave him many sleepless nights. But he'd shown a silent understanding to her at the dinner table. She wondered what was in his background to have formed him into this man.

She could ask, but she was reasonably sure he'd never tell her.

Since he didn't seem inclined to speak, she said, "What fine weather we're having."

"We're in space."

"Sun still shines, don't it? Tell you what, it's a relief to be off that godforsaken lump of rock. Nothing but sweat and sand down there."

"Still plenty of sweat on this ship," the captain said. "If you're prepared to work hard, which you should be if you want to stay."

Max stretched out on her mattress. "I haven't decided that yet."

"It's your decision to make, is it?"

She snorted at that. "I want off this ship, all I've got to do is stick my hand down Primer's pants. He'll scream in terror and have me back on the surface before you can say 'virgin'."

That almost earned a smile from the captain. "Petal thinks he's saving himself for marriage."

"Which one's Petal?" At dinner there had been a tall, queenly woman, beautiful and composed, and one who was tiny and doll-like, with big eyes and an air of innocence Max didn't believe in for a second.

The captain put his hand out low to indicate a short person, and added, "Looks like butter wouldn't melt."

"Would it?"

"She's on my crew," he said, as if that was an answer.

Max raised herself up on her elbows and looked him over. "What are you, then? Pirates? Bandits? Bunch of opportunistic culchies?"

He shrugged. "Yes."

"Awesome. What's the ship called?"

"Eurydice."

She repeated the word, turning the unfamiliar syllables over in her mouth. "What's your name, then?"

"Orpheus."

"Fancy."

"Any more questions?" he enquired.

Max tilted her head and smiled. "Did you come here to fuck me?"

If she'd expected him to laugh or splutter she'd have been disappointed. He couldn't be more different from Riley.

"Depends. Will I have to kill my engineer?"

Max frowned. "I don't follow."

Orpheus's hand, slender and scarred about the knuckles, slid to the knife at his belt. "If he tries to defend your honour. A man challenges me to a fight, that's a dead man."

She didn't doubt it. "He said I could fuck the whole crew if I wanted to."

For a second his fingers lingered lovingly on the hilt of the knife, then they slipped to the belt's buckle and began undoing it. "You'd be unsuccessful with Émile. I don't think Justine swings your way either."

She noticed he didn't mention Petal. Interesting. Max hadn't had a bit of soft for ages.

She watched him remove his weapons belt and begin to pull his shirt off. "So that's a yes to the fucking?"

He paused and looked down at her lolling on the mattress. "Do you want to?"

In answer, Max sat up and pulled off her borrowed sweater. Beneath it she was naked. "What the hell else is there to do?"

CHAPTER FOUR

She had fast fingers.

Riley glanced up from under the aft thruster's huge magnetic rings, to watch Max spinning a lightpen in her fingers. Over and over it spun, and she wasn't even looking at it. The silver bandages on her burns flashed and twinkled in the light.

"Pass me a 9 spanner?"

She went right for the correct case and handed him the wrench without stopping the spinning. Riley took it, yanked the final bolt into place, tested its give. The problem with this kind of thruster was that the magnets surrounding it were susceptible to corrosion. He's known they needed maintenance, but hadn't realised it had got this bad. He'd had to replace a whole section.

"Whoever had this job before me wants shooting," he muttered, peering up at the rest.

"What?"

He looked up at her from his position on his back on the gridded metal catwalk. "The previous engineer. Ship was in a hell of a state. Émile had been keeping it going but engines aren't his forte. He couldn't even hear this one was keening."

"Keening?"

Riley pushed out from under the thruster and sat up, swiping sweat from his forehead with the back of his arm. "Can't you hear it, a different note from the engine when something's wrong?"

Max shrugged. "I can tell when it's running right. Can't say I noticed anything sounding wrong with this one."

"Oh, the primary engine is fine. Sweet as a nut since I replaced the source tube last month. This one is mostly for VTOL. Heavy-air work."

Max nodded slowly. "Do you ever use it out here in the black?"

"We could, but it's not usually necessary. Hence why we can bring it in like this for in-air maintenance." He flipped the access panel shut and sealed it securely in place, pushing against the thruster until it fell into its cradle. He bolted everything back into place and began the sequence that pushed the thruster back into space through a double airlock. The lights cycled through red towards green as it fitted into place, the small viewscreen giving him a visual of the engine out there in the black.

Finally he pulled off one heat-resistant glove and ran his finger round the edge of the micro he wore at his wrist. "Comm Petal."

The screen replied that it was comming metal. Riley rolled his eyes at Max. "No, I said comm Petal. Jesus."

"Comm metal Jesus."

Riley swore at his micro. Max laughed. She had, he wasn't particularly surprised to discover, a filthy laugh.

"I can probably fix that for you if you want. The cheap ones are always a bit shit."

Riley, who'd acquired the micro following the robbery of a cargo ship, could only agree. He tapped in his request instead of speaking it, and the micro beeped before Petal appeared, backed by the screens and switches of the cockpit. "Petal. Give the aft thruster a burst, will you?"

"One sec. It's facing the wrong way."

"Start her out low," he added, as the thruster began to pivot to face backwards.

Riley moved back, automatically pressing his arm in front of Max to get her to move too.

She looked amused. "Don't trust your own engineering?"

"No harm being cautious," he replied calmly.

"Never seen the point, meself."

No, she probably hadn't. He reached out to stop that damn pen spinning in her hand. "Let me listen."

The visual overlay on the viewscreen lit up with a red light, and with a whirr and a roar the thruster came to life. Small blue lights lit up along the viewscreen, indicating the amount of power used. Ten percent, and she was running nicely.

"Bring her up to forty," he said, and a man less in tune with his ship wouldn't have even noticed the difference in speed. Petal had one hell of a delicate touch on the controls. "All right, seventy."

Max's feet shuffled on the floor as the ship accelerated. Justine had finally consented to lend her some boots to keep the catwalk grid from shredding her feet.

"You want to take her up to full speed?" Petal asked. Her attention was on the nav array in front of her, not on Riley's face on the micro strapped to her wrist.

"No, she's running fine. We'll test her out when we next make landfall. Cheers, Petal."

She nodded, and tapped out.

Riley stretched his arms up and out, working the knots from his muscles. His arm throbbed, reminding him it had only been a day since the train guard shot him, and he grimaced. He hadn't really slept well last night, half expecting an alarm to go off because Max had decided to stage a hostile takeover of the ship or murder them all in their sleep.

Instead, nobody appeared to have heard a peep out of her until Riley went down and woke her up in the morning. She'd rigged a sort of doorbell from the door controls, which was interesting. He wondered if she'd tampered with the security camera, but she didn't appear to have gone anywhere near it.

Riley knew he should turn the damn thing off and give her some privacy, but he really wasn't quite sure he trusted her just yet. He'd made a pact with himself to not watch the footage, though.

"All right," he said on a sigh, rubbing the back of his neck. "Lunch, then we'll have a look at the nav files." He reached for the laser pen she was still clutching, and was surprised when she just gave it up.

"Lunch?" she said, in the tones of one who hadn't been told there were three meals in one day.

"Yeah. Whatever Émile's made. Lucky for us he's a better cook than mechanic."

She snorted at that, and helped him pack up his tools, getting them all in the right place without having to ask. A good sign. They were a mismatch of old and new tools, heavy old spanners and brand new laser cutters that had probably been half-inched from some other ship.

Riley felt a momentary pang at the thought of the state-of-the-art tools he'd used in the Service, and then he told himself that only a bad workman blames his tools, and he could do perfectly well with whatever came to hand.

He stowed the tools in their correct hatches, then led Max forward to the galley.

"Something," she said, "smells bloody amazing."

"Almost as good as the maintenance chute," Riley said, and she gave him an odd look. "What?"

"You are such a mech-head," she said. "Most people think fresh bread smells better than ionised xenon."

"They don't know what they're missing," he told her, rounding the corner to Émile's expression of sudden horror.

"What?" he said again.

"Chér, you're filthy! Don't you get that engine grease on my table."

Riley raised his hands peaceably. "I was just going to wash. What smells good?"

"Made some fresh bread. And there's ham and pickles."

Max's stomach gave a loud rumble.

"What kind of ham?" Riley asked, taking a wipe from the dispenser and cleansing the dirt off his hands and forearms. He held one out to Max, who wasn't nearly as dirty, not having had her head stuck under an engine all morning.

"Cheaper not to ask," Émile said. "Named meat is expensive."

Max snorted. Émile put two large plates of food down, and she stared at them like a dog who's been told not to move.

"Go on," Riley sighed, and she attacked the food, still on her feet. Half a loaf had disappeared before she got round to sitting down.

"And you can wash those clothes of mine," Émile told her, looking over the sweater and trousers with distaste.

"Anything," she moaned through a mouthful of ham. "Just keep feeding me."

Riley quirked his brows at Émile, but said nothing as he helped himself to more bread. "The third magnet on the aft thruster had a big corroded patch," he said, gesturing with his hands. "Had to replace the whole section. No wonder it wasn't running right."

"I've been doing the best I can," Émile began.

"No, you've done a great job," Riley said, which was true only to the extent that Émile had done a great job for someone with little aptitude or training. "Who was the mech before me?"

"Her name was Fatima," said Justine, entering the mess room from the other door. "She grew up fixing machinery on her daddy's farm. Unfortunately that didn't translate well to light-air work."

"Nice girl though," Émile said. "Lovely singing voice."

"Always important in a mechanic," said Riley, who couldn't sing a note.

"What happened to her?" said Max, spraying crumbs everywhere.

"Got on the wrong side of Madam Savidge," Justine said. "Something about an unpaid bar bill."

"Dare I ask who Madam Savidge is?"

"A filthy rotten blackhearted schemer," Émile said, putting some more ham on the plate Max had nearly cleared, "who just happens to run the best brothel in London."

Riley searched their faces for clues. "London?" He knew of about twenty. "London Sigma, New London, Real London, New New London? Help me out. Earth London?"

Justine glanced at her brother, who just gave a half smile. "You'll see," was all she said.

"You lot are helpful," Max said.

After lunch he took her to the cockpit, where Petal was leaning back with her feet on the console, reading a magazine on her tablet. Through the clear screen, Riley could see it was an article about the new Excalibur class of racing ships.

She looked them over and said, "Nav files?"

"It's next on my list," said Riley, who had catalogued so many things that needed fixing on the ship he'd never finish them all in his lifetime.

Petal swung to her feet and yawned. "Buzz if you need me," she said, and wandered off.

"We are on autopilot, right?" Riley said, and she just waved her hand as she left.

"She's not an idiot," growled Orpheus, who Riley hadn't even noticed lurking in the shadows forward of the nav console. He very much hoped the captain hadn't seen him jump in surprise.

Max just rolled her eyes and flung herself down into Petal's vacated chair. Riley pulled over the comm seat to watch her.

Her fingers moved so fast across the console he hadn't a hope of keeping up. She opened up the directory containing the nav files on the screen in front of her, flicked through a few files, then frowned and turned slightly to the secondary screen on the right. With one hand on each, she continued searching separate directories.

As a child, Riley had been sent to piano lessons, most of which he'd spent trying to figure out how the instrument worked. When he'd finally been forced in front of the keyboard, he'd found it difficult to co-ordinate left hand and right, especially since his more agile left hand kept wanting to play the melody.

The way Max's fingers flew across two separate screens made him think of the finest concert pianists he'd ever seen.

A shadow fell across him, and he looked up to see Orpheus watching her work. Hard to tell, but Riley fancied he might be impressed.

Max was muttering to herself as she worked.

"Storage is fine, the file dump is...yeesh. But there's plenty of room, it shouldn't be..."

"There's plenty of room to operate," said Riley, leaning forward to read the second screen, where she was checking out the data storage. "But the files are in a terrible tangle."

"Every time you access one it's shoved back somewhere random," Max said, peering at the first screen. "Makes no sense. Who files stuff like this?"

"I know, it's like a library where all the books that have been read are put back in the wrong place," said Riley, "which is why it needs defragmenting. I've already done it once—"

"You'll be doing it every day," Max said, "if you don't redesign it."

"I don't have that kind of skill," Riley said, glancing at Orpheus.

"Well then," Max flashed her teeth at him, "ain't it a good job you know someone who does?"

Orpheus grunted, and she glanced up at him. "It'll take me a few days," said Max.

"We'll need the files in that time," Riley began.

"No, I'll duplicate and work on that. Got a spare tablet? Lemme transfer," she murmured, fingers flying. "You can use the system as it is until I'm ready and I'll transfer it over. Yeah?"

Riley hesitated. Someone with Max's skills could fill the new system with bugs he'd never be able to untangle. He traded a look with Orpheus, who had evidently been thinking the same thing, because he said, "Single glitch with this and you're out the airlock."

Max's fingers didn't hesitate as she grinned up at him. "Don't you trust me, Cap?"

"I don't trust anyone," he grunted. "Primer, defrag the system while she's working on the new one."

Riley saluted, which seemed to annoy him, and

scooted back over to the comm to use the screens there. Orpheus sidled away, but Riley didn't miss his gaze flicking to the camera in the corner. He'd be watching, although God only knew where from.

Riley started the defrag process, which was slow and boring, then glanced over at Max, who was totally absorbed in her work.

"You don't have to go to this extreme," he told her.

She didn't look up. "Can't leave it like this. Bugs me."

He watched her fingers fly. "What does?"

"Something badly designed. Inefficient. Unmaintained. It's like…why would you do that, when it could be better?"

He felt himself smile. "Why should you put up with 'good enough' when it could be improved?"

"Yeah." At his tone, she looked over. The way she looked at him made him feel he was being re-evaluated. "You too, huh?"

He nodded, and for a tiny moment there was some appreciation between the two of them.

"Takes more skill with tech though," said Max, looking back down at her screens.

"Like hell. I'd like to see you fit a helicon double-layer thruster single-handedly."

Max smiled without looking up from her datapad. "In my sleep, mate."

"In your dreams, maybe. The plasma vessel weighs more than you do."

"Well I'm currently half-starved, aren't I? Lemme get back up to fighting weight and we'll see. And I get to keep my hands clean."

Riley grinned and opened his mouth, but right then his micro pinged and he tapped it to answer. Émile's face peered up at him anxiously. "There's that problem with the garbage disposal again…"

Max snorted out a laugh. Riley ignored her. "Can it wait?"

"Um. Not really. Slight overflow issue."

"I keep telling you, shred the metal first."

"Oh. Well the shredder's kind of in need of some work too…"

Riley sighed and swung to his feet. "All right, I'm on my way. Max, you're with me."

"But—"

"The file system can wait."

"No, just—"

Riley dangled her slave tab in front of her, and she stormed to her feet, glaring.

"Time to get your hands dirty, princess," he said.

"Oh, fuck you."

He followed her out, grinning.

The new file system was still unfinished by the time they made landfall, but Riley and Petal had both inspected it and seemed reasonably pleased. Riley asked endless questions, most of which Max didn't know the answers to. She supposed if she'd been taught electronics formally she might know how to talk about it formally, but she'd always operated on sheer instinct and that was much harder to describe.

Petal occupied herself with piloting the ship and fashioning elaborate braids in her ebony hair. Émile cooked, gossiped, and introduced Max to the world of Omicron soap operas. Riley despised them, which made Max all the keener to watch them.

Justine strode around like an Amazon queen, tall and beautiful and so bloody sure of herself Max wanted to smack her. When she checked the dressings on Max's burns, her tone was that of a mother with a naughty child who just couldn't keep things clean.

And then there was Orpheus, who Riley called the

Sphinx. Max didn't know what that was, but she looked it up and found it was some kind of creature with the body of a lion and head of a man. Max knew perfectly well that Orpheus had the body of a man, but she agreed with the second description she found of a sphinx, which was someone inscrutable and mysterious. Three nights she'd spent with him now, and she'd be hard-pressed to find any words to describe his character at all. Max could usually get the measure of a man she'd got naked with, but Orpheus never revealed anything of his nature to her.

Riley didn't know she was sleeping with the captain, of course. He'd let her disable the camera in her room out of courtesy, and unless he went digging for data, he'd never know that after he went to bed, Orpheus would glide down to the hold and spend an hour or so getting sweaty with her. He always left shortly after, and never made any reference to it at any other time.

Strange man.

After a few days orbiting Zeta Secunda, Justine took the shuttle riding Eurydice's back and departed for the surface. When she came back it was with two large men and a bulging wallet.

"...and I says, well that's the wee favour I was looking for, lassie!" guffawed one of them, a bearded fellow with a glint in his eye.

"She take you up on it?" Justine asked, taking one side of a large crate and helping him carry it into the hold.

"Course not," rumbled the second man, a giant who'd make Riley look delicate. "Got eyes in her head, hadn't she?"

Someone else with eyes in his head was Riley, who leaned against the bulkhead with an ease she didn't quite believe in. Max sat a few feet away on the metal steps to the engine bay, working on the code for her new filing system. The newcomers didn't seem to have noticed her.

"All right Primer? Survive your first train job?" called the bearded one.

"Looks like it," Riley called back. His arms were folded across his chest, sleeves rolled up as ever to show the bandage on his upper arm. After a few days with him, however, Max had realised that he wasn't just being vain and showing off his muscles. He spent so much time poking about in filthy machinery that there was no point rolling his sleeves down.

Even now there was a streak of engine oil across his forehead.

"I want a go in that new HAV," said the big guy.

"You'll be lucky. Captain isn't keen on sharing his prize," said Justine. "And speaking of prizes…"

Her gaze lingered on Riley, and both men turned to him excitedly.

"Really? What'd you get?"

He sighed. "She's not a prize," he said. "She's a human being."

"She?" The bearded one looked delighted, although his face fell a little when he followed Riley's head-jerk in Max's direction. He leaned in close and whispered loudly, "Are you sure she's a she, Primer?"

Riley's ears went red. Max snorted. "You wanna find out?" she said, setting down the datapad and making to take off her sweater.

"Nobody's getting undressed, Max," Riley said loudly, and added to the bearded guy, "Tact, Murtaugh, for fuck's sake."

"I'm sure she'd be bonny enough with some hair," he said, looking her over uncertainly.

"A gentleman indeed," Justine said. "Hands off, you two. She belongs to Riley."

"For the hundredth time," Riley began, and Max waved her cuffed wrist at them, cutting him off.

"I'm only 'technically' his," she said, making speech-marks with her fingers. "And you can talk directly to me, you know. I ain't gonna bite. Least, not 'til I know you better."

Murtaugh frowned for a second, then he grinned. "I like her," he said to Riley.

"A relief to us all," murmured Justine. "Murtaugh, come on, get these crates unloaded. Émile wants to know if you've brought him any fresh supplies."

"Load of bloody vegetables," rumbled the other guy, who she assumed must be Hide. To Max, he nodded and said, "Miss."

"Call me Max," she said.

"Miss Max." He lumbered off.

She found herself smiling. They could be fun, those two.

Riley unfolded himself from the wall. "They give you any trouble, you tell me," he said.

She looked him over. He was a big guy, but for all his strength she doubted him in a fight against either of the other two. They were clearly the muscle aboard the Eurydice, and she didn't expect they'd fight fair. Especially not against someone like Riley who probably thought punching below the belt was out of order and would never hit a girl.

"I can look after myself," she said, picking up the datapad.

"Sure, which is why you ended up with a convict cuff. You got that programming finished yet?"

She frowned. Maybe he did hit below the belt, only he did it verbally. How like a Primer. "Almost," she said. "Why? Gonna kick me off this boat once I'm done?"

He gave her a weary smile, and said, "Well, that depends on how well it works."

It turned out that Max's new file system did work.

She demonstrated it later that evening at the dinner table, on her datapad, and Petal abandoned her food to play with it.

"Uses less processing power for one thing," Max said, "so it's more efficient, therefore faster and less likely to interfere with the ship's other systems. I can have a look at them as well if you want?"

"One step at a time," Riley said. "We'll implement this one first."

"What's our next destination?" asked Justine.

Orpheus looked around at them all for a moment, and then said, "London."

Murtaugh and Hide cheered. Even Petal looked up from the new nav system and grinned. Justine nodded, and said, "Good, we need to bank this profit. Émile, can you get on to the Prideaux brothers and see what the situation is?"

Émile nodded and had his tablet in his hand before he'd even set down his coffee.

Riley glanced at Max, who was the only other person at the table who seemed utterly nonplussed.

"All right, I give," he said. "What's London?"

Orpheus gave him a long, inscrutable look. "You'll see," was all he'd say.

CHAPTER FIVE

Riley hadn't been in bed long when his micro buzzed with a text from Petal.

"You want to see London, come up to the bridge."

He got up, pulled on his clothes and headed towards the bridge. Then he stopped, and made for the hold instead. Max would probably want to see this too. Since Orpheus had dropped the news last night, they'd been trying to figure out which of the many Londons was within easy travelling distance. None seemed to be, and Riley wasn't sure they had the provisions for a longer journey.

He tapped the control panel for Max's quarters, and the light flashed, letting him know she'd heard the chime.

It took her longer than usual to answer the door, and when she did, she was wearing a shirt and nothing else. The room behind her was dark.

"Sorry to wake you," he said, his words slowing as he realised she didn't look particularly sleepy. "But Petal said we're approaching this London. Do you want to come up to the bridge and see?"

KATE JOHNSON

There was a pause, during which Riley tried to work out what wasn't right. She looked slightly flushed, and wasn't meeting his eyes.

"Are you all right? Are you feeling okay?"

"Fine and dandy," she said, looking up with a bright grin. "Just let me get dressed and I'll be right up. You go. I'll follow."

"I'll wait out here."

She hesitated again. "No really, go. I'll catch up."

Riley's eyes narrowed. "Max, what's going on?"

She glanced back over her shoulder, and then a voice rasped, "You might as well tell him."

Riley's stomach plummeted a couple of fathoms. "Captain?" he said, and his voice came out lower than he intended.

Orpheus emerged from the gloom, fastening his trousers. He wore nothing else. And Riley belatedly realised what was wrong with the shirt Max was wearing: it was the captain's.

"You," he choked, as Orpheus gave him a calm once-over. "You're—"

"It's not what it looks like," Max said hurriedly.

"What it looks like? Jesus Christ!" His hands had already formed into fists and he was snarling at Orpheus. "I'll fucking kill you. I said—"

"You'll try," Orpheus said, still calm. "Pity. You're quite a good engineer."

Riley's fist swung back, but before it could connect with Orpheus, Max had flung up her arm to deflect it. She used the momentum to push his hand away and and then grasped it away from his body.

"Riley, calm down, and listen to me. He's not forcing me, or raping me, or whatever else you're getting your knickers in a twist about. I'm just sleeping with him, that's all."

His chest heaved. Max's eyes looked up at his, steady

as he'd ever seen them.

Behind her, something glinted in Orpheus's hand. Where the hell he'd been hiding that knife Riley didn't want to know.

"And you," she said over her shoulder, "whatever you're planning, stop it. Nobody's fighting anybody. Calm down. It's all perfectly consensual, all right?"

Riley stared down at her uncomprehendingly. He'd told her she didn't have to sleep with anyone. He'd rescued her from that fate. From men doing what they wanted with her. He'd given her purpose and value among the crew.

"You don't have to be a whore any more," he said, and she looked at him like he was the biggest fool who ever lived.

"You'll never get it, Primer," she said, and released his arm. He realised he'd had his right hand free the whole time, but once she'd grabbed him he'd never thought of using it.

So is that Service discipline, or will it be Primer modesty?

They were both sneering at him.

Riley squared his shoulders and looked down at them both with contempt. Max, whose face was flushed and whose legs were bare because she'd been fucking the captain, and Orpheus, with his tattooed chest and concealed knife and his braids tousled because he'd been fucking Max.

"You're right," he said, "I won't."

"Well, that went well," Max said, as Riley's furious footsteps echoed away. He hadn't even bothered to shut the door.

"It's none of his business," Orpheus said. He was watching her, his eyes doing to her body what his hands had a few minutes earlier.

"Kind of is, though," she sighed, and pulled off his shirt to hand back to him. Orpheus took it and watched her get dressed. "I mean, the minute we make landfall he's probably going to sell me on."

"Why?"

She threw up her hands. "'Cos he doesn't want to own a whore. I dunno. He prefers the world sterile and sexless. I'm safer when I'm a bloody tech."

"He's a Primer," said Orpheus, as if that explained it. It probably did.

"Let me guess, they only have sex for reproductive purposes? Or are they all grown in test tubes? Why does he get to impose his bloody morality on everyone else?"

"He's a Primer," Orpheus repeated. He ran his finger round the edge of the micro on his wrist and commed Petal. "How far out are we?"

"Couple of hours 'til we hit orbit, then it depends on destination. I can clean that up if you've a specific target in mind."

"Nassau. I need to see the Prideaux brothers."

While Petal changed her course settings, Orpheus pulled his shirt on and sat down to put on his boots. He didn't seem remotely concerned about Petal seeing him with his shirt off, or catching a glimpse of the metal bars that would identify Max's cabin.

Eventually, she said, "Okay, three hours fifteen to Nassau. I'll ping the Prideauxs." There was the sound of the cockpit hatch cycling open. "Hey Primer. You wanted to see London?"

Orpheus grunted and ended the call. He stood up and said to Max, "You want to see London?"

"Might as well see what the fuss is about," she said, and followed him from the room. She and Riley had been trying to work out which of the Londons it might be, but none of them were remotely in this area of space. She'd been quite impressed by his knowledge of starcharts, and—

Well, anyway. That was all for nothing now.

"Is there a slave market in London?" she asked gloomily as she trudged through the hold after the captain.

"There's not much you can't buy and sell there," he replied.

"Right. So this is probably goodbye, then."

Orpheus glanced back at her. "You're leaving?"

"You really think he's going to want to keep me after this?"

"After you fucked someone of your own free will?" Orpheus paused, and looked her over. "He's not that good an engineer," he muttered.

"You'd kick him off the crew? For me?"

"Can't keep you without him," he reminded her.

She followed him through the mess room, where Murtaugh and Hide were organising and reloading their various weapons. Due to the terms of the indenture, she had to have a master or the courts would come and find her. And until they did, the cuff would continue sending stronger and stronger shocks until eventually they killed her.

She ran her fingers over the cool metal of the cuff. It hadn't seemed to occur to Riley to use the evil little tab at all. His wrath had all been directed at Orpheus.

"You could take my indenture," she said hopefully to him.

"I don't own people," he replied tonelessly, and cycled open the door to the cockpit.

Petal was at the nav, Justine the comm, and Riley stood forward of them, down in the observation area. He was staring out at...

"...there's nothing there," he said, at the same time Max thought it. Ahead of them was a field of stars and not much else. Except a blank patch where there were no stars at all.

"A hole in the world," Justine murmured. "Look closer."

"I am. There's nothing there. No…stars." He turned, frowning, and faltered only slightly when he saw Orpheus and Max there in the doorway. "Is it a black hole?"

"Depends on your definition," said Petal. She was smiling slightly. Max watched with interest as Orpheus wandered closer, put his hand on her shoulder and leaned forward to look at her screens. It was an intimacy Petal didn't seem to mind at all—and, Max noted with detachment, neither did she.

"Any word?"

"Not yet. If you're not sure of our welcome I'll put us into orbit for a few hours. There's no hurry."

Orpheus grunted and straightened up.

"Orbit? Orbiting what?" said Riley, staring back into the black nothingness. It seemed to be getting bigger.

"Is it an asteroid?" said Max, moving past the control desks and into the observation area, where Riley pointedly moved away and didn't look at her. She rolled her eyes at his back.

"We're three hours out. If it's an asteroid it's a fucking big one," said Justine.

"Then what is it?"

"A deep black pit," said Petal, sounding as if she was enjoying herself.

"A hole in the world," added Justine.

"Full of vermin," rasped Orpheus.

"Yes, but what does any of that mean?" Riley said, exasperated, and Max held up her hand.

"Wait, did you say Nassau?" She turned back, and Petal was grinning at her. "You called it London and Nassau, and…we're three days out of the Zeta system, heading towards…what, Epsilon?"

"You saw it in the nav files," Justine said.

"It's not in the nav files," Max said, hopping back up to peer at Petal's screens. "It doesn't appear on any starcharts because it's not supposed to exist. It's a rogue planet, isn't it?"

Petal nodded, and showed her the sensor screen. It tracked their course towards a mass about the size of the moon Max had been raised on.

"A rogue planet?" Riley said, curiosity evidently getting the better of his anger with Max.

"Don't tell me you don't know what they are?" Justine said.

"Of course I know, but...I didn't know any that were habitable. If it's not attached to a star system then it can't have any light or heat. How can life survive in that?"

"The heat comes from the planet's core," Petal said. "It has a little light from stars and...currently I think Epsilon might be lending it a little, but it's mostly artificial."

"Is there any native life?"

"In the sea," Justine said. "Take my advice, Primer, and don't go skinny-dipping."

Max was still trying to make sense of the data on Petal's screen. She'd heard rumours of this place but assumed that was all they were, just rumours. The infamous pirate planet, abandoned by civilised people and outside the laws of any solar system, where dark deeds were done and the worst scum of the universe made their homes.

"I just didn't think this place was real," she said, staring at the blackness and still not really believing it.

"You'll see," Orpheus said, and that was all anyone would tell them for the next three hours.

The rogue planet, which the crew still referred to as London, had its own atmosphere which appeared to be breathable. They loaded the saleable goods onto the shuttle, and the Eurydice burned down through the mesosphere and approached the surface in total darkness.

Max, strapped into her seat in the cockpit opposite a silently furious Riley, strained to see out of the window.

"So far it ain't impressive," she said, and then they broke through a layer of cloud and multicoloured jewels began winking up at them.

The surface of the planet was in almost total darkness, but here and there were flickers of light, illuminating strange shapes rising up towards them. Max tried to make out the data on the nav screen over Petal's shoulder. A small dot had been labelled Nassau, and there were others called Providence and Clew Bay.

"It's all water," murmured Riley, staring out of the window, and when Max focused, she could see giant waves just rolling around the planet's surface. She'd never seen that much water all in one place.

"But where's the land?"

"There isn't any," said Justine. "Not any more."

"But…"

"You'll see," she said again. Max was starting to get sick of that answer.

The ship descended towards the clusters of lights, which bobbed and swayed gently in the swell of the waves. They didn't look stable enough for landing, but she'd underestimated the scale of them.

They reared up, towers of boats and buildings and platforms all tethered together into a kind of floating city. As the ship zoomed in, Max could see other vehicles swooping around in the air, and even some floating on the water. A HAV slid by, so close it nearly brushed them, and landed on top of what Max realised was a giant ship with buildings on it.

"They were pleasure-cruisers," Émile said, watching her take it in. "The place was full of them, just sailing endlessly round and round the world. Big as cities. Rich bastards from all over the systems would pay obscene amounts to take vacations here."

"But why? It's dark and cold…"

"Think about it, chérie. Which system are we in?"

"We're not," said Riley. "So the laws of each system don't apply here." He gazed at the bright signs on a nearby building, advertising girls and boys to suit every predilection. "You could do anything you wanted."

"Ah. That kind of vacation," Max said.

"That was a while ago, of course. Long before living memory. Rumour has it an asteroid hit, caused a tsunami that rocked around and destroyed half the world. Suddenly less desirable as a holiday destination."

"But people still come here," said Riley.

"Vermin," said Justine plainly. "The scum of the universe. No laws here, no authorities, no rules. No one to answer to but the scum that's floated to the top. The Prideaux brothers run Nassau, more or less."

"For now," growled Orpheus.

"Don't look so scared, Primer. Just 'cos there aren't laws doesn't mean the place is dangerous. No more than any other planet."

"People here make their own justice," said Petal quietly. She guided the ship towards a landing deck in the middle of the ocean and opened a comm channel. "This is the Eurydice. Cleared for landing?"

"Cleared," replied a voice. "Good to see you, Petal."

"Good to be seen," she replied, bringing the ship down nearly into a landing bay. The engine wasn't even off by the time Orpheus was out of his seat. He led them to the shuttle, and Justine piloted it over the dark water to the cluster of lights and huddle of buildings nearby. There was, Max realised, just nowhere to park a light-air vehicle of any size next to the collection of buildings.

Justine parked the shuttle in a bay at the top of a tall

building, and they rode the elevator down to the ground.

"I'm meeting the Prideauxs," Orpheus said, and jerked his head at Murtaugh and Hide. "You're with me. The rest of you, do what you want."

With that, he was gone into the dark night.

"He doesn't hang about, does he?" Max murmured. She looked at the others. "What's there to do for fun around here?"

Émile grinned at her. "Whatever your little heart desires, chérie. Are you staying at Renata's?" he asked his sister, who nodded, shouldered her bag, and strode off.

"See you there later," said Petal, and skipped away from the building's entrance.

That left Max with Riley and Émile, who took pity on them both.

"Renata's is half a dozen blocks that way," he said, pointing. "Called the Brazen Head. Tell her you're with us and she'll give you a room. Oh, and avoid the Cauldron if you can."

Riley nodded and turned away, then stopped, sighed, and turned back. He handed Max a roll of money and said, "You should buy some clothes. Don't go mad."

Surprised, she took the money and stared up at him. "You're keeping me?"

He shrugged resignedly. "Who you sleep with is none of my business, is it?" Under his breath he added, "Even if he is a psychopath."

Then he was gone, and Max was seized by a gleeful Émile. "Let's go shopping!"

The city of Nassau was unlike anything Riley had ever seen. Made of ships and platforms piled on top of each other and tethered together with bridges of varying sturdiness, there was a constant slight creak to it as the waves rolled by.

The blocks Émile had mentioned were somewhat theoretical, as in fact were the streets. They were lined with a variety of lanterns and were full of people, and Riley was somewhat surprised to see they all looked pretty normal and didn't appear to be trying to kill each other. Quite a lot of them looked him over somewhat speculatively, most of them somewhat brazen women, some of them ratty youths eyeing the bag he carried. Riley ignored them, until he felt a tug on his arm and slammed his hand down to grab a struggling, skinny kid who'd been about to cut away the micro on his wrist.

He lifted the kid off his—or possibly her—feet, and looked into defiant brown eyes. This was probably Max a dozen years ago, he thought, and put the kid back down. "You want to be walking away right now," he said, and the kid nodded hurriedly and ran away.

Riley glanced around, at a bunch of people who were suddenly completely ignoring him. He felt absolutely no shame at flexing his muscles as he shouldered his way through them. Sometimes being a big bastard had its advantages.

He crossed half a dozen bridges over the black water, zigzagging in the vague direction Émile had indicated, past buildings made out of sailing ships and space ships and one that seemed to have been fashioned from the bones of a huge animal. HAVs whirred overhead, docking in the upper levels of the buildings, almost too high to see. The shop signs were written in half a dozen alphabets, but most of them had large graphic representations of what they sold. Very graphic. There was more porn on this street than Riley had seen in the rest of his life.

Primer modesty.

He passed brothels, bars, shops selling every kind of stolen and illegal materials, until he came to a building of sorts with 'tHe BraZen hEad' painted on the peeling door. Above it hung a wooden head with bronze paint flaking off it.

In the absence of a buzzer, he knocked, and someone leaned out of an upper window and yelled, "Yeah?"

"I'm with the Eurydice," he said, peering up into the gloom.

"Really?" The owner of the voice sounded sceptical.

"Émile told me to come here for a room," Riley added, trying to make out the speaker above.

"Ah, well, if Émile said," came the answer, and the door opened with a click and a buzz. Riley entered, somewhat hesitantly, to an entryway containing a cargo lift and not much else.

"Fortune favours the brave," he muttered, and shut himself in. There was only one choice of destination, so he pressed the button and the cage clattered upwards, through a shaft lined with cables and pipes. It didn't look encouraging.

But at the top, light suddenly flooded in, and Riley opened the cage to a softly-lit courtyard lined with tiles and crumbling murals. A long bar ran along one wall, stacked with bottles of what seemed to be every liquor known to man. Steps led up to a gallery running around the whole courtyard, and another one above that, girls in bright dresses leaning over them. One of them wolf-whistled at him.

The woman who sashayed over to him wore a low-cut dress and a lot of fake hair. She looked him over, lingeringly. "You're with the Eurydice?"

"I'm the new engineer," said Riley, taking in more details. The bright coloured lanterns hanging from the galleries, the men lounging at tables drinking, the girls laughing at their jokes. Improbably, a vine twined itself around the stair banister.

"Ah yes. Poor Fatima. That woman Savidge is a menace. You want a room, baby?"

Riley tore his attention back to her. "Is the rest of the crew staying here?" he asked doubtfully.

"Sure." She gave him another once-over, and smiled. "Murtaugh and Hide always want a girl when they come here. Orpheus suits himself. Émile brings his own entertainment. You don't have to take a girl if you don't want to, baby."

"Good to know," Riley said slowly. So, Renata was a madam and this was a brothel, even if it sold itself as a tavern. He didn't suppose there was much call for respectable hotels in Nassau.

"Or is it boys you like?" Renata asked.

"Not especially," Riley said vaguely, and snapped his attention back to her. "All right, sure. A room, please. No girl."

"Suit yourself," said Renata, and clicked her fingers for attention.

One of the girls wandered over, gave Riley an appreciative look, and said, "Follow me."

She led him up the stairs and round to a door that proved to have a fairly reasonable-looking room inside it. Riley figured this must have been part of one of the old cruise liners, its grandeur somewhat faded now. The light in the corner was flickering.

"A hundred bits the night," said the girl, and Riley reached for his cash. No point trying to pay on credit these days. The Service would track him down in no time. "Or fifty, if it's just the room."

He gave her a sideways look and paid her the fifty. She pouted.

"Is there a market around here?" he asked, going over to the flickering light and prodding it.

"What're you selling?"

"Buying. Parts for the ship." It was always worth checking the exterior of the ship when they made landfall, and making repairs that were unfeasible out in space. His body was telling him it was the middle of the night, but he was too restless to sleep. Seeing Max with Orpheus had...unsettled him.

"Ah, you probably want Metal Joe. I'll show you if you like."

Riley pulled his gloves from his bag and twisted the filament on the light. The flicker stopped.

"Impressive," said the girl. "What else can you do with those hands?"

Riley ignored that. "Where will I find Metal Joe?"

She sighed, and started giving him directions. Riley thanked her, took the room key, then set off into the endless night to look for supplies. He found a warehouse of partially stripped ships and spent a happy few hours poking around. Metal Joe proved to be a big guy with a prosthetic arm he seemed to be constantly improving. Even as he chatted to Riley he was fiddling with the pneumatics.

Gathering parts for the ship and doing some basic maintenance was almost the distraction he needed. Almost. Max's long bare legs kept flashing up behind his eyes, and her wary dark eyes as she said, "You're keeping me?"

Well, what else was he going to do? Sell her on because she'd had sex with the captain? That wouldn't make any sense. He'd meant it when he told her she could sleep with whoever she wanted. At least, he thought he had.

"It's none of your damn business," he told himself as he locked the shuttle and made his way back to the Brazen Head. He took himself up to the courtyard, threw his bag in his room, and ignored the come-ons from the girls lounging decoratively about the place. Someone was playing a fiddle, but it couldn't quite mask the loud cries and groans coming from the room next to Riley's.

He made his way back down to the bar, where Émile

was sitting with a bottle of rice wine. "Care to join me?"

Riley shrugged and took a seat. Émile wore a new hat, perched at a jaunty angle, and had a few more rings on his fingers than before.

"Been shopping?"

"Oh yes. Your girl enjoyed herself."

"She's really not my girl," Riley sighed.

Émile gave him a speculative glance. "She could be, you know."

"No."

"I know she's got a mouth on her, but the captain doesn't seem to mind."

"Well, the captain can have her." Had everyone else known about this?

"Not your type?" Émile went on. "I mean, I know you don't play for my team, but I suppose maybe you might prefer…girlier girls."

"Why is everyone so obsessed with my sex life?" Riley snapped.

Émile shrugged and poured him more wine. "Because you don't seem to have one, chér. I mean, even an ugly old freak like me can find someone to warm his bed in a place like this. It's good for what ails you."

"Yeah, well, what's ailing me right now is that everyone else is poking their noses in where they don't belong." Riley drained his glass and poured more. "Where is she, anyway?"

Émile jerked his head in the direction of the gallery.

"Is she okay? I kind of yelled at her earlier."

"She's fine. Once she realised you weren't going to sell her."

Riley opened his mouth, closed it, then sighed and said, "She'll be okay with him, right? The captain. He won't…hurt her?"

"Shouldn't think so. He's got better uses for violence." Émile smiled. "And I think she can take care of herself."

"Yes, which is how she ended up with a bloody slave cuff in the first place."

Riley fingered the slave tab hanging round his neck. The reason they were worn like that, Max explained, was that they needed regular contact from the owner or they'd start shocking the slave. The list of things that cuff would shock her for seemed endless.

"You could have used that, you know," Émile said, watching him. "To punish her."

Riley let the tab drop back against his chest. "I don't want to punish her." *Liar.* "I'm not going to. She can sleep with whoever she likes."

Émile glanced up, and his expression changed slightly. "You might need to put that in writing," he murmured.

Riley followed his gaze, and saw Max exiting one of the rooms upstairs. She turned back to say something to whoever was in the room behind her, and Riley knew he should have turned away at that point, because he didn't really want to see Orpheus half naked again.

But it wasn't Orpheus who followed Max out. It was Murtaugh, and then Hide came after him.

Riley stared.

Murtaugh was buttoning his shirt, and Max was barefoot. Hide's hair was wet, as if from a shower. It was pretty obvious they hadn't been sitting around having a nice chat all evening.

He watched them come down the stairs, Max laughing as Murtaugh caught her round the waist and gave her a big kiss.

"You have got to be fucking kidding me," Riley said, and poured more wine.

CHAPTER SIX

Max faltered slightly as she saw Riley sitting there in the courtyard, gazing up at her with a look she couldn't quite identify. Was he jealous? Disgusted?

No, she realised as she straightened away from Murtaugh. He was disappointed.

Well, screw him. She raised her chin defiantly and sauntered over to the table, picking up the bottle of rice wine there and taking a swig.

"Thirsty?" smirked Murtaugh.

"You boys," she said, wiping her mouth with the back of her hand and grinning. "I'm fucking starving, too."

Hide waved to the woman with red hair who'd greeted them so enthusiastically. "Renata! This girl's worked up an appetite."

"I know, baby, I could hear." Renata placed down some fresh glasses and handed them a tablet with the menu on it, and Max smiled her thanks and flopped down in a chair.

"What looks good?" asked Murtaugh, leaning over her shoulder. That felt mildly strange, intimate almost, which was absurd given the things they'd been doing for the last hour or so. Funny how putting clothes on made all the difference. "Oh hey, deep fried mosasaur."

"The fuck's a mosasaur?" Max asked, but never got a reply.

"Azad, my man!" cried Hide, raising his hand for a stranger to slap and punch in an elaborate handshake. Murtaugh did the same.

"What's occurring?"

"Bit o' this, bit o'that," said Azad. He had a thick silver bar stuck through the septum of his nose and looked Max over dismissively. "Got a new stinger ray last week. Nicked it off these Omicron bastards."

Both Murtaugh and Hide's faces lit up, even more excited than when Max had idly suggested a threesome.

"Give us a go, laddie!"

The three of them wandered off, both food and sex apparently forgotten at the prospect of a new weapon. Max watched them go fondly. Nice lads. Uncomplicated. Refreshing after the captain's intensity and Riley's prudishness.

She ordered a couple of things from the tablet menu, including the mysterious deep fried mosasaur, and Émile passed her a glass of rice wine. Actually it was surprisingly good, not the rot she'd expected. Max wasn't exactly a fine wine connoisseur, but she'd nicked a few nice things over the years and could definitely tell the good stuff apart from the bad.

As she put the glass down, she caught Riley's eye. He raised his eyebrows at her, his expression like a schoolteacher who'd found his pupils smoking behind the garages again. She held his gaze, raising a brow of her own, and he was the first to look away.

"Both of them?" he asked quietly, refilling his own glass.

She shrugged. "Sure, why not?"

"Why not?" he repeated, incredulous.

"Chér, leave it," Émile said, touching his arm, and was totally ignored.

"I just don't see how you can—"

"Oh, you want me to draw you a diagram?"

"I can see the fucking *how*," Riley snapped, "I just can't fathom the fucking *why*."

She felt her lip twist into a sneer. "Then there's no hope for you, Primer."

"Christ, the pair of you," Émile muttered.

"Lover's spat?" enquired Petal, plopping into an empty chair, and her arrival at least made Riley shut up. Beside her, Orpheus dragged another chair closer. The way he looked at Max made her suspect he knew exactly what she'd been doing with Murtaugh and Hide.

"Chérie, your hair!" cried Émile, and Max glanced at Petal, then looked back a second time, appreciatively. Petal had exchanged her shiny dark braids for a mermaid's mane of blue, green and violet, shimmering in the lantern light. She'd also had a new stud put in her lip and scraps of lace festooning her hairstyle.

"I needed to cheer myself up," she said, picking up the wine bottle and finding it nearly empty. She signalled for another and laid her head mournfully on Orpheus's shoulder. "Shahzad's retired."

"She's very upset," Orpheus said gravely, putting his arm around her.

"Okay, I'll bite," said Riley drained the last of the bottle into his glass. Max was surprised. Three refills since she'd sat down. She wondered how well he could hold his drink. Probably it was all thimblefuls of ratafia where he came from. "Who's Shahzad?"

"My favourite girl," said Petal dramatically. "She was *so* beautiful. Hair like spun gold. Lips like pillows. And oh my god, the things she could do with them."

"I don't need to hear this," said Émile, laughing.

"And now she's given up to go and have babies with

a bloody *man*," Petal wailed. "It's not fair. I loved her."

Orpheus took out a small silver case and started rolling a cigarette. "Can I bum one of them?" Max asked, and he shrugged and handed it over. Something else for Primer to disapprove of.

The wine arrived, and with it a couple of bowls of food. Max stubbed out the cigarette, stuck it behind her ear, and fell on the food ravenously. She was still none the wiser on what mosasaur was even after she'd tried it, but it tasted good and she was too hungry to care.

"Just to be clear," said Riley to Petal, "this Shahzad was a whore, right?"

Orpheus cut him a look Riley didn't seem to notice.

"You got a problem with that?" Max said.

He threw up his hands. "No," he said. "Course not. Why would I?"

She rolled her eyes and carried on eating.

"There must be others, chérie," Émile consoled. "At other houses. Madam Savidge always had the best, it's true—"

"I'm not going anywhere near that butcher," Petal shuddered. "Not after what she did to 'Tima."

"Fatima knew what she was getting herself into," Émile said. "What about the Golden Butterfly? Some beautiful girls there."

"Like you'd know," Max said, running her finger round the bottom of one bowl and licking it.

"I can appreciate a pretty girl, aesthetically," Émile protested.

"Ask Renata," said Orpheus, his arm still around Petal, who was curled up against him like a child. Interesting. Max might have said they looked like siblings, but for the fact they looked nothing at all alike. Petal with her china doll prettiness and Orpheus with his hawk-like sharpness could never have swum in the same gene pool.

"I could," Petal said dejectedly. "But her girls don't specialise. They just don't know what to do with another set of breasts, not to mention—"

Riley spluttered out half the drink he'd just swallowed, cutting Petal off.

"You're scaring Primer," said Émile, passing Riley a napkin. He got a glare for his troubles, as Riley refilled his glass. "You want to slow down a bit there, chér."

"I really don't," Riley replied. To Orpheus, he said, "How long are we here for?"

"Couple days. Need to talk to Azrael."

Both Émile and Petal, her romantic woes apparently forgotten, sucked in a sharp breath.

"Are you sure?" said Petal, looking up at the captain.

"What about?" asked Émile.

"Can't say," said Orpheus.

Riley groaned. "Can't or won't?"

"Don't you trust us?" said Max.

"Don't take it personal," Petal said. "He doesn't trust anyone."

Except you, Max thought, but kept that to herself.

"Besides, chérie, we hardly know you."

Riley snorted at his glass of rice wine. "Orpheus knows her pretty well. Murtaugh and Hide, too."

A slight pause. Max didn't think Orpheus would care, but then again it was hard to tell. For all she knew he was going to storm off and kill the other two.

But all he said was, "Wash before you come to me."

She grinned and fired off a salute with one hand, using the other to polish off the last of her fried mystery meat.

"Seriously?" Riley said, his words starting to slur a little now. "You don't even care?"

Orpheus gave an infinitesimal shrug. "She goes her own way," he said.

Riley slumped back in his chair, which creaked a

little under his weight, and sloshed more wine into his mouth. "Unbelievable."

"Where's Justine?" Orpheus asked Émile, who gestured upstairs.

"Asleep. Which sounds like a fine idea to me." He stood up, nodded to them all, and set off up the stairs. Some of the girls greeted him as he went past, but none of them tried anything with him.

Max pushed her bowls away and said to Petal, "You going to ask Renata about her girls?"

Petal shrugged half-heartedly. "Probably not. Most of them are busy anyway."

Max looked at her curled up against Orpheus, petite and pretty with her mermaid hair and scraps of lace. She could feel Riley's gaze on her.

"I'm not," she said.

That got everyone's attention.

"You're not what?" said Petal slowly, straightening up.

"I'm not busy. And I have a room. And I don't charge."

Riley's jaw actually fell open.

"And I do know what to do with another pair of breasts," Max added.

Petal gave her a speculative look. Then she glanced at Orpheus, and the look that went between them wasn't quite asking permission, but more…recommendation.

Then Petal stood up, climbed onto Max's lap, and kissed her. She was so small, tiny after Hide especially, and she hardly weighed a thing. Her lips were soft but surprisingly demanding.

Max gave back as good as she got.

"That is hot," whooped someone, as Petal climbed off her lap and drew Max with her up the stairs.

"I don't fucking believe this," said Riley, and the last she saw of him as she led Petal to her room was the rest of the rice wine going in his direction.

Riley didn't entirely notice Orpheus slinking off. By this point he wasn't noticing much, except the shadows moving behind the shutters of Max's room. He knew he should look away, think about something else, but he couldn't.

Émile wasn't attracted to women and Justine probably bit the head off anyone she had sex with, which really left only himself as the only member of the Eurydice's crew Max hadn't taken to her bed. No, he might as well use her word: fucked. Not that he wanted to fuck her, but...hell, if the ship had a crew of a hundred would she go with all of them in one night, too?

He picked up the bottle, but it was empty. Huh. Turning in his chair, he waved it at one of Renata's girls. "Can I get some more?"

She swayed over in his direction. "Some more what, darling?"

"Wine. Rice wine. Please."

She took the bottle from him and drawled, "Sure that's wise?"

"Do I look," Riley said, "like someone who gives a fuck what's wise?"

She made a gesture to somebody else that seemed to be an order for more wine, then hitched her hip on the table close to him, and leaned down so her cleavage was level with his face.

"You're a big one," she said.

"Yeah, I get that a lot."

She giggled flirtily. "I bet you do. And that crew, honey," she rested her fingertips against his chest and trailed them downwards, "they're a fine crew and they'll all have your back, but there's not much to interest you on it, am I right?"

"There's a damn fine engine," Riley said.

"Mmm, and I guess that's how you work out your frustrations, isn't it? On an engine."

Riley blinked up at her. "Why does everyone want me to have sex?"

She gave him a look. "You do know what kind of place this is, right darling?"

He blew out a sigh and reached for his glass. Still empty. But right then the girl who was practically sitting in his lap magically produced a bottle and held it to his lips. Then she missed and poured it all over his neck and chest.

"Oops," she said, and leaned forward to lick it up. It was pleasant, her tongue rasping against his neck, and Riley let her for a moment—but even blind drunk, he was who he was.

"No. Stop it. Get off."

She sat back, looking hurt. "You don't want me?" she pouted, all expert make-up and artificially tousled hair. The lamplight flickered across the generous expanse of her cleavage.

Above and behind her, Max's door opened, and Petal wandered out. She wore her shirt and weapons belt, but nothing more that he could see. She turned back to Max at the door, rising up on her tiptoes to kiss the much taller woman. Her shirt rode up, giving everyone below a view of her backside. Men roared in appreciation.

Petal turned, one hand on the hilt of a knife at her belt, the other raising a single finger. The roars turned to laughter, Petal wandered off down the gallery, and Max shut the door without even looking for Riley.

"Oh so that's it," said the girl leaning against Riley's table, and he realised she'd watched him watching the two women. "Which one is it?"

"Neither," he muttered.

"Now honey. You can't fool me. It's my job to know what men want."

Riley took the bottle from her and drank from it. The rice wine was starting to taste sour. "Do you like it?" he asked.

"Rice wine? Sure—"

"No, your job."

She tilted her head and sat back on the chair next to him. "Sure, honey. I know I'd like it with you," she added, and reached out her hand again. Riley pushed it away.

"Would you still do it?" he asked, looking up at Max's door. "Even if you didn't have to?"

"You ask weird questions, mister."

"Would you?"

She shrugged, apparently never having contemplated the question before. "Dunno. Never thought about it. If a rich man came and whisked me away, d'you mean?"

Riley scrubbed his hand over his face, which was starting to hurt. There had been a lot of wine. "S'there always got to be a man?"

Her expression was uncomprehending.

"Ne'er mind," Riley said, and lurched to his feet.

"Whoa," she laughed, steadying him. "Careful there, big guy. You need a hand getting up the stairs?"

"I'm fine," Riley said, with a drunk's grip on the rest of the rice wine. "Night."

"It's nearly morning, honey," she called after him as he made his way through the maze of tables and chairs to the stairs, only stumbling once or twice.

How can you tell? he thought, but didn't say it, concentrating instead on making it up the stairs and along the gallery to the right room. It was the right room, right? Yes, the one with the green door and the empty brass plaque on it. He knocked.

Max had just finished washing when the knock came. Ugh, if that was Murtaugh or Hide again they could piss off. Or Orpheus, but then she didn't think he'd visit twice in one night, and it had, technically, only been earlier in the night that he'd come to her quarters on the ship. Right now, all she wanted was to go to sleep.

She wrapped a towel around herself and picked up the small pistol Émile had, without much enthusiasm, helped her pick out earlier. Then she opened the door, and her eyes went wide.

"Riley?"

He gripped the doorframe with one hand and a bottle of rice wine with the other.

"This is my room," she said doubtfully, looking him over. "Yours is—"

He lost his balance at that point and stumbled into the room. Max caught him and righted him, leaning him against the wall. He closed his eyes and swayed in place for a moment, but stayed upright.

"Whoa. You are toasted. How much have you had?"

"Not enough," Riley muttered, opening his eyes. "I still don't...understand."

"Understand what?" said Max, pulling on some underwear. Riley looked away, and she didn't even bother to point out that he'd already seen her naked.

"Why you...you know. With so many people."

"Why I 'have sex'," she said, making quote marks with her fingers. "You're old enough to say it. And I do it because I like it. Simple as that."

"Really?"

"Yes, really! Jesus, what went so wrong with your experience of sex that you don't understand other people enjoying it?"

Riley slid down the wall to sit on the floor, his shirt riding up as he did and affording her a glimpse of some spectacular musculature. *Such a waste.*

"Comfy?" she asked, stepping into some shorts and a shirt.

104

"I was dizzy. Air gets thin. When you're tall."

"Right, that's the issue here." She watched him drink some more, oblivious to her sarcasm. "Can I have some of that?"

He held out the bottle, and she sat down on the floor opposite him, her back against the bed. Took a sip, then said, "Why are you here, Riley?"

He rested his head back against the wall and said, "Honestly, I've no fucking idea." He seemed to relish the swear word.

"Did you come to fuck me?"

He shook his head.

"Good, because I'm fucking knackered."

"'m not surprised."

"Oh yeah? Speaking from experience, are you?"

Wait, maybe he was! Maybe this painfully correct man had been whored out as a youth, or even younger, and that was why he was so hung up about sex. Maybe his experiences of being touched were so bad he couldn't bear the thought any more.

No. Of course that wasn't it. He was just being a Primer.

"What, three men and a woman in one night? No. Can't say I've done that. Max...don't you ever just wanna say...no?"

Her fingers tightened on the bottle, and she took a drink before handing it back. "Course I do," she said. "And if they don't listen, I beat the shit out of them. Wouldn't you?"

He drank from the bottle before answering. "Never had to," he said.

"No. I suppose when you're half as tall again as everyone else, you don't get too many people picking fights with you."

"I'm hardly two metres," he protested, head beginning to droop, "according to the Service."

"The Service," Max said, getting to her feet in front of him. "Now that's a conversation I'm going to enjoy having with you. Come on now, time for bed."

Riley looked up muzzily at the door, but she ignored him and put her feet over the top of his. Taking his hands, bottle and all, she hauled him to his feet and he fell against her.

"Christ, you're a big bastard," she gasped, turning and dropping him back onto the bed. Her thumb stoppered the bottle before it could spill everywhere, and she gently removed it from his hand.

"This is your room," he mumbled, as she tugged off his boots and swung his legs onto the bed.

"Yep. So if Orpheus knocks in the night, you can entertain him. He's actually a surprisingly gentle lover," she said, just to see his face.

"Tried men," Riley mumbled. "Didn't like it."

For the second time that night her eyebrows shot up towards her hairline.

"Did you try women?" she asked, and he nodded sleepily. "Did you like that?"

"Mph," he grunted, and she supposed that was all she was going to get out of him.

Riley woke to a pounding head, dry mouth, and pulsing sense of regret. The last time he'd felt this bad he'd ended up on a Service ship leaving Sigma Prime for good.

Peeling open his eyelids to what seemed like a star going supernova but was only, in fact, a lantern on the ceiling, he looked around. Well, at least he'd made it back to his bed. The micro on his wrist hold him it was midmorning, which didn't make sense for a moment, until he realised they weren't on ship's time any more.

Someone knocked at the door, and he sat up, groaning, only to see someone else get up and open it.

Frowning, head throbbing, he watched Max open the door just enough to see out.

"You seen Primer?" Justine's voice said.

Oh, shit.

"Nope. Just woke up. Not in his room?"

"Wasn't answering. Thought I'd check, see if he finally took his chastity belt off."

"Doubt it," Max said. "He was on the sauce last night. Probably still asleep."

"Probably. I'll comm him."

Max nodded and shut the door. She leaned back against it, looking over at Riley, and put her finger to her lips as Justine's shadow passed by the shutters.

Before he could work out what was going on, his micro pinged. He answered, and there was Justine frowning at him.

"There you are. Are you in your room?"

"Where else would I be?" Riley croaked. "Guess I overslept."

"Late night for us all. Captain wants you to go visit Azrael with him later."

"Me? Why?"

"I dunno. You can ask him. See you downstairs at noon."

With that she was gone, and Riley looked over at Max, trying to work out if he'd got away with that. It looked like he had.

"You can thank me later," she said, straightening up. She was dressed in clothes he hadn't seen before, trousers and boots and a weapons belt over her shirt.

Riley reached with a slightly shaking hand for the water glass by the bed. Max's bed. This was Max's room. What the hell was he doing in Max's room?

He drank some water to steady himself, aware of her watching him the whole time. "Tell me we didn't," he said, guilt churning his hangover into nausea.

Max smiled in that sex kitten way she had, and said, "Well, we almost did. But you wouldn't take yes for an anwer."

He flopped back onto the bed with a groan, realising as he did that he was still fully dressed. He pressed one arm over his face to block out the light.

"And I slept in your room," she added, before he could ask. "You took up my whole bed."

"Sorry," he mumbled through his arm.

"I mean, do you have to get them made special or something?"

He moved his arm enough to squint up at her. She didn't look upset with him. In fact she looked reasonably cheerful.

"Cheer up, Primer. No one knows you spent the night in here but me, and I can keep quiet when I need to."

"Why do I get the feeling this is going to cost me?" Riley muttered. He sat up again, and Max gave him what she probably assumed to be an innocent look.

"It'll only cost you one thing," she said. "A name."

Bewildered, he said, "What name?"

"Whoever it was who fucked you over."

Sudden nausea assaulted him, and it had nothing to do with last night's rice wine. The nausea of panic, of disgust, of self-hatred.

"Why do you want to know that?" he managed.

Max shrugged one shoulder.

Riley calmed himself, drank more water, then glared up at her and said, "You don't ever say this name again, d'you hear? I never want to be reminded of it."

"Sure thing."

Riley took a breath. "Elandra," he said, the syllables bile in his mouth. "Her name was Elandra. Happy now?"

"Ecstatic," Max said cheerfully, and peered out the door. "Coast's clear," she said, as if he hadn't just dragged himself through the worst memories of his life.

"You can go back to your room now."

Riley did, but not before he'd swiped the rice wine from the floor, and glowered at her on his way out.

The Brazen Head had hot showers with unlimited water, a luxury after the rationing aboard ship, and Riley stood under his for an unfeasible amount of time, trying to steam away last night's alcohol. Last night's clothes reeked of rice wine, so he put on the only spares he had and ventured out to buy more. Working on the ship's engines frequently had him coated in grease and sweat, and while Riley might be a pirate now, he still had some standards.

In the markets of Nassau, it seemed everything in the world was for sale, whether you wanted to sell or not. Three people tried to trade Riley for his micro, and at least two more tried to steal it. One saw the tab around his neck and offered cash money for his slave, without even asking for a single detail.

He stowed his new gear back on the shuttle, and made it back to the Brazen Head in time to meet Orpheus in the courtyard.

"Do you want me to bring anything?" he asked.

"No. We're just going to talk."

"About what?"

"Business." Orpheus set off towards the stairs, the opposite direction from the one Riley had expected.

"But...if we're talking business shouldn't I know a bit of background?" He didn't even know what was in most of those crates.

"No. Just keep your mouth shut and follow my lead."

Riley silently followed him along the gallery and through a series of doors. Looked like he was there as muscle, then. An intimidating presence. Why he hadn't brought Hide, Riley had no idea. The guy was much bigger than he was, and much more experienced in a fight.

Orpheus led him through an absolute warren of rooms and corridors. Every now and then they'd emerge into the open air, into a courtyard or across a roof, occasionally taking one of the high, narrow bridges across the winding streets.

Far below them, dark things moved in the water.

Eventually they reached a space that looked as if it had once been a warehouse, or maybe a parking garage. It was crumbling, the electrics fizzing, and there was a hole in the floor below which water could be heard.

Riley turned to Orpheus. "So this is where we're meeting—" he began, and then Orpheus shot him in the chest and the world went dark.

CHAPTER SEVEN

She should have been more suspicious when Justine asked her to go to the piercing place with her.

"Not a big fan of piercings," Max said. "Too easy to get ripped out in a fight. See?" She pointed to the notch in her ear. "Bloody hurt, that did. Same reason I don't have my hair long any more."

Justine, whose hair was a luxuriant wave of shiny perfection, simply shrugged. "Well, I'm going. Maybe you can get a tattoo."

"I dunno. Too easy for people to ID you by tattoos."

Justine looked Max over slowly, taking in her big boots and her skintight trousers and the sleeveless t-shirt Émile had said gave her 'man shoulders'. She ended at the buzzcut gracing Max's head, and then she said, "Trust me, you're easy enough to ID as you are."

Max wrinkled her nose at that, but she followed Justine anyway. Mostly out of boredom. The others had either wandered off or not been seen that morning, and Renata's girls were starting to give her dirty looks for stealing their custom.

"So where's this place then?" Max asked as she

traipsed after Justine.

"In the Cauldron."

"Sounds fun."

Justine rested her hand on the gun at her hip, and said nothing. Max noted the way she constantly watched their surroundings, checking for lines of sight and escape routes. She wouldn't be someone to get into a fight with.

"So what's the deal with Petal and the captain?"

"What d'you mean?"

"I mean how she's all cosy with him. Last night she was all cuddled up with him."

"They're friends."

Max snorted. "I don't think he's the type to have friends."

Justine shrugged. "Know him that well, do you?"

Max couldn't help grinning. "Better than you do, mate."

Justine merely rolled her eyes. "You think because you've fucked him, that means you know him?"

Max wasn't sure it was possible to get to know a man like Orpheus all that well, no matter how intimate she'd been with him. But annoying Justine was fun.

"You should try it," she said, as they stepped out onto a bridge over the black water. "He's a bit intense, but he knows what he's doing."

"How do you know I haven't?" Justine said, not looking back at her.

Max laughed at that. "Because I *know*, love, all right? Neither has Petal, obviously, but she does love him."

"They've known each other a long time."

"Longer than you?"

"Yes."

"How long have you known him?"

Justine led her into a dark building, then out across a roof terrace. A man guarding the exit with a large cutlass nodded to her as they went by.

"You're not very curious, are you?"

"Just making conversation. Murtaugh's been on the crew three years, Hide four. They said you were already on board when they joined."

"And so I was."

It was like getting blood from a stone. "How come you and Émile talk differently?"

"We grew up speaking a different language," Justine said, as if Max was being particularly thick.

"No, I mean, you talk different to him."

"Different from," Justine murmured. "I had elocution lessons. Guess they stuck."

"How come he didn't?"

"Father said it was a waste of time," said Justine dispassionately.

"Oh, that's nice. Are you older or younger than him?"

"We're twins. Didn't Émile tell you?"

Max was amazed. They didn't really look alike enough to be siblings, let alone twins. "Get out. Really?"

"Why would I make it up?" Justine pushed open a door and glanced inside. Then she gestured for Max to go first. She did, and had just noticed Riley hanging upside down from the ceiling when something hit the back of her neck and the world went dark.

Max came to as they were hauling her up by her feet. Murtaugh and Hide, the bastards, looping the chain around her ankles to a hook hanging from the ceiling. Max struggled like a fish on a line as they swung her out over a great big hole in the floor. Her arms, tied behind her back, hung at a shoulder-wrenching angle.

"What're you doing?" she yelled. "Riley, what the fuck?"

He swung beside her, too far to reach even if her hands hadn't been tied. He looked dopey, as if he still hadn't come round from whatever he'd been shot with.

There were two darts sticking out of his chest.

"Wake up, you bastard. Murtaugh, what the fuck is going on?"

"Sorry kid," said the man she'd been having sex with the night before.

"He's just following orders," rasped Orpheus, and she twisted to see him standing there with a bottle in one hand and his gun in the other.

"What orders? What are you doing?"

Below them, something moved in the dark water.

"Start on her," said Justine, moving up next to the captain. She had a whip.

Max's level of panic continued to rise.

"He's so chivalrous he'll talk to stop her getting hurt," Justine added, and Orpheus nodded.

"What?" Max looked wildly at Riley, who was staring muzzily about. He didn't look like he was about to talk to anyone. "What are you going to do?"

"This," said Orpheus, taking a swig from the bottle and nodding to Justine.

She heard the crack of the whip before she felt it, snapping across her stomach where her shirt had slid down. Then the pain spread, a fiery line of heat on her skin. Max yelled and swore, jerking about on the end of her chain.

"What do you want?"

"Your name," Orpheus said calmly.

"Max! You know my name! It's Max, Max Seventeen!"

"Seventeen?"

"131-10-17," Max said, desperately. "They used to write the 10 like an X, so…"

"Who did?"

"The orphanage! They never gave me a proper name, I had to make it up! Why does it matter?"

The whip cracked out again and Max howled. This at

least seemed to have the effect of waking up Riley, who focussed blearily on her and said, "Max? What's going on?"

"They're insane, that's what! She's fucking whipping me!"

Blood trickled down Max's stomach, between her breasts, down to her chin. It ran down her face, into her eyes, and dropped off her scalp into the darkness below.

Something big moved down there.

"What the hell?" Riley said. He thrashed around on his chains, but even if he'd got free the only way would have been down into the dark water. "What do you want?"

"Your name," Orpheus said, taking another swig as if he was at a bloody dinner party.

"You know his bloody name," Max snarled, but Riley was silent. He curled up at the waist, trying to see his feet, but they were shackled and bound just like Max's.

Orpheus nodded, and Justine snapped the whip at Riley. It hit across his back and side, ripping open his shirt and sending blood soaking through the fabric. He flinched and grunted, but he didn't scream.

And then he said reproachfully, "That was a new shirt."

Max laughed. She couldn't help it.

"You think this is funny?" Justine snarled.

"Your face is funny," Max croaked, and was rewarded with another lash. She screamed.

"Name," said Orpheus again.

"It's Thrynn," Riley said. "Riley David Thrynn."

"Your ship?"

"Eurydice."

Justine whipped him again.

"Your ship?"

"Eurydice," Riley repeated.

This time Justine hit Max. Four lashes and she felt

like she was on fire.

"He's fucking telling you!" she yelled.

"Your ship," Orpheus said again, soft as a cat.

There was a longer silence, then Riley said, "Patrol J75, Vanguard. Destroyer F32, Valiant. Patrol J26, Dauntless. Scimitar C2984B, Eurydice."

He looked up at Orpheus with contempt.

"Your rank?"

"Engineer First Class. Serial number 592-246-094."

"Home planet?"

Riley said nothing. The whip cracked again across Max's back.

"Name, rank and posting are all you're fucking getting," Riley said.

The whip hit Max again.

"I'm sorry," Riley said to her, as her blood dripped down over her scalp and fell into the dark water. Max made the mistake of looking down. Something in the gloom had very big teeth.

"You're attracting sealife," Riley said to Orpheus, as if hanging upside down and being whipped didn't bother him at all.

"Mosasaurs," Justine said. "Answer the question."

Riley started to laugh. "I've already told you. Why do you care?"

"I've got the whip," she replied. "Home planet."

"He's from Sigma fucking Prime," Max gasped. "And I'm from Omega Septimus Sei. Stop fucking whipping me!"

"When we have the information we need."

"Which is?"

Orpheus took another swig before responding. "Your interest in my ship."

Riley somehow managed to shrug. "I needed to get off that planet."

"Why?"

"Because I'd just gone AWOL. Short memory, Orpheus?"

This time the whip cracked across Riley's chest, and Max yelped in sudden horror because she could no longer see her slave tab hanging round his neck.

"Where's my tab? Don't let the monsters have it!" she yelped, more panicked than ever.

In response, Orpheus raised his hand. Dangling from it was Max's tab, and the other bits and pieces Riley wore round his neck. "Maybe I'll keep you," he rasped.

While relief overwhelmed Max, Riley thrashed as if in panic, until something else glinted amongst the tangle of threads. The small silver symbol he wore around his neck, apparently. The sight of it seemed to calm him.

Then Justine whipped his chest again, the lash ripping the first gash wider open, and he swore and spat.

"Again," said Orpheus, who'd watched this all with a look of disinterest. "Why are you on my ship?"

"Because I left the Service," Riley said wearily. Now his blood was dripping down into the water, his shirt soaked with it.

"You sure about that?"

"Yes. Émile ripped out my Service chip."

"Why?"

"So they couldn't find me," Riley said, as if the captain was an idiot.

"Why?"

"Why, Orpheus, always with the why? What are you, a toddler?"

Justine flicked the whip again and Riley tried to dodge it, but it caught him across the back of his shoulders. He snarled at the pain of it.

"I left because I didn't want to be part of it any more."

"Why?"

"Because they're a corrupt bunch of arseholes who

pressed me into service in the first place," Riley yelled, so loud Max flinched back. "But at least they never whipped me!"

For a long moment the only sound was his creaking chains as he swung there. Then he tilted his head at Max and gave her a half smile. "Last time I got really drunk," he said. "Woke up on a Service transport." He huffed out a laugh. "This time I get really drunk, I wake up as mosasaur bait."

"Still, probably better than the Service," said Max.

Riley laughed tiredly and looked down into the water, squinting to see. "Saw the bones of one of these in the market," he said. "Jaw bigger than I am."

"Oh, so they'll eat us whole," Max said, somewhat delirious.

"Two sets of teeth, though. So you don't escape."

"Shut the fuck up," Justine said, and the whip cracked out again. This time it hit Max across the chest, the end of it snaking across her jaw. She yelped and writhed, especially when the whip snapped out again, but this time it was aimed at Riley.

"You're getting nowhere," Petal said, and through the blood in her eyes Max watched her upside-down form saunter into view. She fingered one of the knives at her belt. "You want me to try?"

Riley started laughing.

"What's so funny?" Petal said. "I could castrate you from here, Primer."

"And then you'd have to come over and fetch your knife back," Riley said, "and all that blood would have a ten metre lizard jumping out of the water. You'd be so dead."

"We all would be," said Max, who was becoming increasingly certain this was the way the day was going to go. "Fuck it, I was going to die old, in bed with five young men."

"Then start talking," said Orpheus. "About the land train."

"You know everything I know!"

Orpheus cut his eyes at Petal, and something whistled towards Max. For a moment she thought it had missed, and then the pain blossomed in her calf and she twisted and craned to see a knife sticking out.

"That's the thanks I fucking get for last night?"

"Last night doesn't matter," Petal said quietly. There was already another knife in her hand.

"How do you know Riley?" Orpheus asked, those narrow eyes fixed on her.

"For God's sake," Riley muttered.

"You know this," Max said. "He rescued me from the last carriage."

"You didn't know him before the train job?"

"No!"

"What were you doing on the train?"

Max waved her shackled wrists at them, managing to stick her finger up at them as she did. "Slave! Indenture! You've read my record!"

"You can read mine too," Riley put in. "I expect I'm on an AWOL Wanted list somewhere."

The whip lashed out at him again. "Wasn't talking to you," Justine snarled.

"Thought I'd," he panted, "save you the effort."

"How did you escape your previous owner?"

"I bashed his brains in with my shovel," Max said, rotating gently as a result of her struggles. "He was killing slaves because he thought they were working for you."

"There's irony," Riley said, and she couldn't tell if his gasp was laughter or the pain getting to him.

"Then you climbed back all by yourself just to where the safe was being held? What a coincidence," Justine said.

"I didn't bloody know, did I? I was just trying to escape the fire! Look, if you hadn't robbed that train I'd still be on it."

"Don't you wish you were?" Riley said.

"There're moments," she replied, and made the mistake of looking down, just as a huge eye stared up unblinkingly from the depths below. It was several metres below, but still the size of a dinner plate.

Max screamed.

"Or maybe not," Riley said, and that got their attention back on him.

"Now Primer," rasped Orpheus. "We come to you. How did you know," he took a swig from his bottle, "which wagon the safe was in?"

"I didn't. Remember? I guessed it wouldn't be at the front. It was pot luck."

"You left me to die," growled Justine.

"So did Petal and Murtaugh," said Riley, and there was a pause.

"Sorry," said Petal.

"Didn't really think you were the dying type," Murtaugh added.

"And none of us did die, and you got the safe, and all the other goodies, so what is your problem?"

Orpheus gestured with his head, and Murtaugh and Hide dragged over a crate into their view. To Max it looked like any one of the other crates she'd loaded and unloaded with the other slaves. It had a Service marking on it, but then a lot of them did.

"My problem," said Orpheus, "is this."

And he opened the crate with a hiss of dry ice. Max was facing away and couldn't see until she swung back round, but she heard Riley's shocked intake of breath and horrified, "Endless night."

"What is it?" she asked, craning to see, but upside down all she could make out were lots of small chambers, filled with misshapen…things.

"Samples," Justine said. "Cells. Embryos."

Max blinked, but none of the shapes made sense to her. And then one did, and she gagged as she recognised the shape of it.

"And they're human," said Orpheus. "Now," he levelled his pistol at Riley, "Engineer First Class Thrynn, tell me what the fuck the Service is doing with those?"

CHAPTER EIGHT

Riley was trying very hard to think clearly what the best answer would be to avoid more pain, but half a dozen lashes and the threat of being eaten alive by a creature with two rows of teeth weren't exactly conducive to rational thought.

He looked at Max, swinging upside down beside him with blood dripping down her body, over her head and down into the water, and while he hadn't seen whatever it was that had made her scream, he had a pretty good idea she wasn't the type to be terrified of nothing.

Then he looked back at Orpheus and that crate of… things. And he knew there was nothing he could say that would make any difference.

"I'm an engineer," he said tiredly. "I fixed engines and food processors and bloody nav chairs. There's…I dunno, a couple of hundred million people in the Service. You think they tell us all every one of their plans?"

Justine raised her whip again, but Orpheus held up his hand to stop her. He drank from his bottle again, then sauntered closer.

"What's your real rank?" he said, soft as anything.

Riley looked at Max, wanting to apologise for what came next. She shook the blood from her eyes and fixed her gaze on Orpheus, mad with fear and fury.

"I was an Engineer First Class," Riley said raggedly. "I started as a cadet, then a third class engineer, then second, and then—you'll never guess—first class. I don't know anything about any embryos. Maybe the Service is running a fucking fertility programme," he added, voice breaking on a laugh, "I don't know."

Orpheus looked down at him, then shifted the aim of his gun to Max.

"Don't you fucking dare," she began.

"I can't tell you anything else—"

"Can't or won't?" Orpheus snarled.

"Can't, I don't know anything else! Max, I'm sorry. This psychopath—"

Right then said psychopath nearly lost his footing as the floor bucked and trembled.

"The fuck?" someone said, and Riley started laughing. He couldn't help it.

"I told you," he said, and Justine and Petal started backing away from the hole in the ground. Murtaugh yelped, "It's the monster!" and he and Hide ran for the exit.

"Cowards!" Justine yelled after them, but she was backing away too, looking panicked.

"Oh Max," Riley said, "we're going to get eaten by a dinosaur."

Her eyes were huge. "But I don't want to!"

Riley laughed so hard tears were streaming from his eyes. "Don't think we've got much choice," he hiccuped, as the floor shook again.

Then, to his eternal astonishment, Orpheus grabbed a long pole with a hook in the end, and reached out to grab Max's shackled wrists. He hauled her away from the edge of the hole, and when she was over the shaking ground, he aimed at the chain holding her and shot it.

Then as it fell, he grabbed the crate Justine was hurriedly closing, and they hustled it out of the warehouse.

Max lay crumpled and bloody on the floor, but as it shook again and Petal ran after the others, she looked up. She writhed uncomfortably, but managed to wriggle her legs through her arms so her hands were in front of her.

"Little help?" said Riley, still swinging there, and Max looked around. But not, as he'd hoped, for the pole. She looked for the pile of things Orpheus had taken from around Riley's neck, grabbed them and shoved them over her own head.

"Max?"

She got shakily to her knees, and tried to make it to her feet, but between the shackles and the knife in her leg she couldn't manage it, especially when the ground shook again.

Riley, hanging helplessly above a bloodthirsty mosasaur bigger than the building they were in, began to seriously panic.

"Max? Just unhook me, would you?"

She knelt there looking up at him, once more in charge of her own slave tab. If he was swallowed by that creature, she'd be free again, at least until the courts found her. But a person could get a long way in a day, especially a person as resilient as Max.

From beneath him something roared, a scream muffled by the water. It reached directly into the prehistoric bit of Riley's brain and flipped a switch marked Panic Like Fucking Hell.

"Max, please. Please."

With one arm, she swiped her own blood from her face, and then she grabbed the pole—and used it to lever herself to her feet and begin limping away, chains clinking.

"Max! No! Please don't—"

Max shuffled around the hole, and reached out with the pole.

"Shut up and let me concentrate," she said, and Riley did as he was told.

Below him, the dark water churned, and teeth taller than Riley snapped in frustration.

The hook scratched down his back before Max got a grip on the manacles, and at first he thought she'd done it on purpose. Or that she lacked the strength to reel him in. But, limping backwards, she dragged him back over the edge, the chain creaking as it clanked through the hook on the ceiling.

When he felt the concrete under him, Riley could have kissed it. Instead he found himself grappling with Max, who was trying to get the gun holstered at his hip.

"What're you doing?"

"Can't break the fucking chain with my bare hands," she grunted, as the floor bucked again and water sloshed out of the hole in the floor.

They both watched it, horrified, then Riley said, "Well, bloody hurry then!"

She shot the chain out from between his feet, then hers, and he'd just started to run when his feet were knocked out from under him and the chain still attached to one side of his shackles began dragging him backwards at terrifying speed. Right down into the mosasaur's double-fanged mouth.

It's not supposed to end like this, Riley thought futilely.

"Run," he screamed at Max. "Just run!"

But she stood her ground and fired at the chain the monster held, and the pressure stopped, and Riley scrabbled to his feet and shoved her ahead of him.

She was limping, dragging her leg, and he thought

they'd never be clear of the place before the creature below broke through. But the crash, when it came, was from above, as something shattered the ceiling and they both dived for the exit. As the floor beneath them began to crumble, Riley shoved Max through the door and glanced back just time time to see a HAV swoop down on the monster surging up.

Its jaw really was bigger than he was.

Then adrenaline kicked in and he ran with Max, half holding her up, shoving her across the adjoining roof and to the nearest exit and across a bridge and not stopping until the floor had stopped trembling and she literally couldn't walk any more.

She collapsed against the wall and held her hands up for mercy.

"Just a minute," she wheezed, and Riley leaned beside her, glad for the respite. He looked down at her leg, which was red above and below the knife sticking out of it. Like him, her shirt was ripped open in half a dozen places and hanging off her shoulder where the whip had cut through it. Her face and neck were streaked with blood and sweat, her wrists shackled in front of her, both ankles dragging chains.

"Do I look as bad as you do?" she gasped, and Riley couldn't even summon the breath to laugh.

"I'd say he looks worse," said a voice.

"No, he can stand," said a second.

Two men stood watching them. They were neatly dressed, not in Primer fashions but as respectable businessmen. They were both smoking cigars, and stood outside a set of double doors which looked better maintained than anything else Riley had seen in this place.

He swiped the sweat and blood from his eyes and looked around. They were in a small courtyard, with plants and painted walls and tiles that were mostly uncracked.

"Sorry," he said. "We—there was a mosasaur or… something, and—"

"Oh, we know."

"Who d'you think sent the harpoon?"

"So that's what it was," Riley muttered. He straightened, and gave them his best diplomatic smile, which probably would have gone better if he hadn't been caked in his own blood.

"We can't allow dinosaurs to destroy our London," said the man on the left.

"I suppose Orpheus got out?" said the man on the right. They weren't identical, but both were so bland that if they'd swapped places he wouldn't have been able to tell.

"Fucking bastard," Max said. She looked dreadful as she heaved herself upright against the wall. She still held Riley's pistol in her manacled hands.

"Yes, that describes him quite well," said the man on the left.

"Look, I'm sorry to intrude," Riley said, "but we'll be right on our way if you'll just show us the exit?"

"The market is that way," said one, pointing down a flight of stairs.

"The Cauldron is that way," said the other, pointing at the alley they'd just run down.

"But I suppose you know that," the first one added.

"Cauldron," Riley muttered, closing his eyes for a beat. Wasn't that what they made stews in? *For the feeding of mosasaurs*, he thought hysterically.

"Rough district."

"Full of criminals."

"And the rest of the place is so charming. Come on, Max. We need a blacksmith."

"Oh," said one of the men, "we'd be happy to oblige."

Beside him, Max froze, and Riley was glad that her instincts were telling her the same thing his were. Namely, that an obligation to these two wouldn't be one to be worked off lightly.

"Very kind," he said, "but we've trespassed enough on your time."

He ducked his head under Max's chained arms so she was half draped over his shoulder, and they shuffled down the stairs with two pairs of eyes burning holes in their backs.

Riley made it all the way to Metal Joe's before he stopped feeling them.

Max didn't remember much of the journey back to Renata's after they left that courtyard with the two weird men. She'd expected the pair to follow them, and later was reasonably sure they'd sent someone on exactly that task, but she was finding it hard to concentrate on getting one foot in front of the other, so her attention hadn't really been on it.

Riley took her to some workshop where their chains were cut off, and then he half carried her to her room at the Brazen Head. Someone yelled at them halfway up the stairs, and plenty of the girls shied back from their grisly appearance, but they made it without a pair of sinister men materialising or anyone else trying to attack them.

Riley got her to her room and she collapsed on the bed, rolling with her last bit of energy onto her left side, which hurt marginally less than the rest of her.

He stood there, chest heaving, blood everywhere, blue eyes burning at her, and instead of complaining or collapsing or coming onto her, he said, "You all right?"

Max started to laugh, and once she'd started she couldn't quite manage to finish.

"Take that as a no, then," he said, and with a sigh

dragged a stool over and reached for her. Weirdly, the thing she noticed was the extremely dirty bandage still wrapped around his arm from getting shot on that damn land train.

"I'm all right," she said, shoving herself back upright again. Christ, everything hurt.

"No you're not, neither of us are," Riley said, gently tilting her chin to look at the cut on her jaw.

"Been worse."

"Yeah." He gave her a bit of a smile, and then widened it to a grin. "Hey Max," he said, reaching behind her ear, "you've still got that fucking dart in your neck."

He pulled it out with a sharp sting, and she stared at it, so small and innocent-looking.

"Where's yours?"

He looked down at the ruin of his shirt and shrugged. "Guess they got whipped out."

With that he stood, wincing, and rolled his shoulders. That made his face go white.

"Okay. I'm going to see if I can scrounge up a med kit. 'Cos I'm bloody well not asking Justine for help. I'll do you if you do me?"

Max was too tired to make an innuendo out of that. She just nodded, and wondered if she had the energy to stand under the shower and get some of this blood off.

It turned out she did, although the hot water on her lacerated skin made her sob with pain. She was making a mess of Renata's towels when someone knocked at the door.

"Yeah?"

"Can I come in?" rasped a voice that wasn't Riley's at all, and Max dropped her towel and grabbed a gun instead. She had it aimed at Orpheus's head the second it appeared.

His gaze travelled lazily over her nakedness and the

damage his orders had inflicted.

"I saw you come in," he began, and Max was already shaking her head.

"No. You. Fuck off. Three seconds or I'll blow your fucking brains out and feed you to the monsters."

He raised his hands, although she didn't expect that meant he was any less lethal.

"One."

"Max…"

"Two," she snarled, advancing, and he stood his ground.

"What're you doing?" said Riley from behind Orpheus. He took in the situation, looked exasperated, and said, "Jesus, man, what's wrong with you? Get the fuck out, or I'll kill you myself."

A long second passed, and just as Max was about to say 'three', Orpheus silently backed away. Riley glared at him until he was gone, then slammed the door behind him and exchanged a look with Max.

"You're not going to shoot me, are you?" he asked, and she lowered the gun, and moved forward to lock the door. Riley held a med kit up in one hand, and a bottle in the other.

"What's that?"

He sniffed, and made a face. "Possibly rum."

"Sounds good." Max took the bottle and drank straight from it, letting the stuff burn down her throat and warm her belly. She felt Riley's eyes on her when he thought she wasn't looking, then when she met his eye, he looked away.

"Want me to put some clothes on?" she said, taking pity on him. The poor guy hadn't even had the chance to wash the blood off yet.

He turned away and washed his hands while she found a pair of shorts and eased them past the knife wound in her leg. The knife itself she'd added to her own weapons belt, with the intention of throwing it back at Petal if she ever got the chance.

"Let me see that," Riley said, motioning for her sit down. She took the bed; there wasn't really anywhere else.

Riley managed not to perve as he sat down and lifted her foot in his big hand. He peered at the puncture wound, probably an inch or so deep, and made a face.

"You should've left the knife in 'til I got back," he said.

"Bit hard to take a shower that way. Couldn't get undressed. And those trousers are new, you know."

His eyes glimmered with warmth as he glanced up. From the med kit he took an ampoule, uncapped the needle, and said, "Brace yourself," as he stuck it in next to the wound, then got her to hold a pad over it. By the time he'd got the skinglue ready, the pain had almost disappeared.

Max flexed the muscle in her calf, which didn't hurt but made it bleed more. Riley just rolled his eyes and mopped it up.

He worked intently, cleaning, sealing and dressing the wound, and then he glanced up and almost immediately away again. Max grinned.

"They're just breasts," she said. "Tell me you've seen 'em before?"

"Yes, I've seen them before," Riley said. "I just haven't applied medical treatment to them."

"Well then ain't you just the lucky one. A free grope, as it were."

The look he gave her said he didn't find that amusing.

There were three cuts on her front, two crossing her belly and creating a red X that made Max slightly queasy. Riley focused on that first, treating it as methodically as he had the wound on her leg, and then managed the trick of moving up to the lash cutting across her chest without focussing on her breasts.

"You really are a gentleman," she teased.

"A dying breed," Riley agreed so drily she wasn't sure if he was joking or not.

"Nearly literally, today," she said, and hesitated. "D'you think he'd have gone through with it?"

"Well, he practically did," Riley said, not looking up. "He only cut you down."

The look on his face when he'd thought she was going to leave him. Max couldn't laugh at that. Well, she probably could.

"Yeah, check me out being all merciful. Course I'd have left you," she added breezily, "but I can't stand unfinished business."

"And what would that be?" Riley said. "Hold that."

She pressed together the two edges of skin that ran diagonally from her breastbone to the outer curve of her breast. The lash had missed her nipple by an inch or two, for which she was profoundly grateful. The alternative didn't bear thinking about.

"Well, you've got your hands all over my tits," she said. "Turnabout's fair play."

He hesitated only minutely in applying the skinglue, his ears going a bit red, and then he said, "You'll get your chance."

Max's eyebrows shot up. "Primer, you surprise me."

Riley finished with the skinglue, applied a dressing, and sat back on his haunches. He reached for the shirt which was still partly tucked into his belt, and with visible pain, pulled it off.

Max winced when she saw the state of his chest. Justine had hit him twice in almost the same place, and it had opened a large, bloody gash there. The edges of it were crusted with dried blood, and more was seeping out.

"Jesus," she whispered.

And then, because she was Max, she let her gaze take in all the beautiful muscles he'd just displayed to her.

Riley shrugged. "Yours looked worse, I'm sure," he said, and picked up a wipe to clean his own blood off his hands. "She hit you more than me."

"You were counting?"

"Seven, to my six. Plus the knife."

"Yeah, and what did I ever do to them?"

"What did either of us do?" Riley said.

"He reckons you know something about some embryos," Max said.

"Well, I don't."

"Were they even alive?"

"How the fuck should I know? They were on ice, so…yeah, probably, cryogenics or something."

"You've started swearing more," Max observed. Nearly getting eaten by a dinosaur seemed to have had quite the effect on him.

"Can you fucking blame me?" He reached for the ampoules again. "Just the one on your face and then I'll start on your back."

It was weird, having him peer so intently at her face as he fixed the cut there. Max didn't think she'd ever had someone that close and not kiss them. She thought about that for a moment, let her gaze wander to his surprisingly full lips and the dark gold stubble surrounding them. What would it be like to feel his body move closer to hers, his hands caressing, his big arms going around her? To feel the stubble on his scalp under her fingers and let him return the favour, to run her hands over those amazing muscles and have him—

"Max?"

She blinked, and he was frowning at her. "You okay? You kind of drifted off there."

She swallowed, mouth suddenly dry. "Yeah, sure.

Tired, you know?"

He grunted, and gestured for her to turn around.

As he began working on the cuts on her back, Max wrapped her arms around herself, feeling the cool clean bandages he'd applied. For such a big buy, with big hands, he had a very delicate touch. She supposed that was engineering for you. Big muscles for the big stuff, and gentle fingers for the fragile stuff.

Funny how she'd never thought of herself as fragile before.

"This isn't your first time, is it?" Riley asked quietly from behind her, and she realised she'd been drifting again.

"Whu'?"

"There are old scars here," he said, and those big fingers gently traced the lines of them across her back.

"Oh," she said, glad he couldn't see her face. "Uh. Yeah. Bunch o'culchies caught me outside their cattle ranch. Accused me of rustling. Man, I didn't even know what that was. I thought they meant, like, rustling petticoats. You know."

"You don't have to draw me a picture."

"No. Right. Well, if the lad I'd been, er, rustling with, hadn't come out and seen me and explained...well I only had the two lashes and they weren't that hard. Just a horsewhip." And all he'd done afterwards, that rustling lad, was laugh at the misunderstanding.

Max had punched him in the mouth and stalked off to the sound of laughter.

"Still left scars though," Riley murmured. "Hang on a sec, I need your hands. Here," he placed one to his liking, "and here." He adjusted her fingers, again a curiously intimate gesture, and she felt the gentle burn of the skinglue as he ran it along the cut. Pressed into a fresh wound, it stung like anything, which was why she'd been glad the med kit contained those little numbing syringes.

By the time he was done with her back Max could hardly keep her eyes open. But he'd done her such a favour and she didn't want to let him down, not now, so she pulled on a clean shirt and said, "Go take a shower. I ain't got any clean towels, you'll have to use your own." Not that she was so picky herself, but he had all those Primer values, and besides, there was no sense contaminating his fresh wounds.

Primer values? said a small voice inside her. He's filthy with blood and sweat and he's never once complained as he fixed you up.

He peered at her, chewed his lip thoughtfully, and said, "You want to sleep, I'll get someone else—"

"Who, Justine?"

"No. Maybe Renata, or one of the girls. They're keeping out of…whatever happened today, apparently."

He took a swig of rum and got to his feet, stretching and then looking immediately as if he regretted it. The wound on his chest let out a trickle of blood.

"Go," said Max, "wash."

She kept herself awake while he was gone, thinking up all the things she was going to do to Orpheus when she got the chance. Assuming they stayed on the Eurydice. After today Riley might decide to stay off the ship, and she couldn't blame him. Once more, an uncertain future.

She knew Riley was approaching her room again from the chorus of wolf-whistles that had accompanied him when he first left it, shirtless in the lamplight. As he knocked and came back in again, she sat and appreciated how very nicely put together he was. Well, he had been, 'til Justine started dissecting him.

Then she forced herself to concentrate on the task at hand.

"Start with my back," he said after a moment.

"You're dead on your feet, and I can finish the ones at the front by myself."

"Don't be ridiculous," Max began, but the last word was drowned by a yawn. Riley just gave her a tired smile and sat down on his stool.

Max had dressed wounds before, but they'd usually been her own and she'd rarely had access to proper instruments. This kit was basic, but well-stocked, and everything was actually clean. More than once, she'd had to do it the archaic way, with a curved needle and thread, tying off the knots and pulling out the thread a week later.

She barely managed all three of the cuts on his back. Her fingers got clumsy on the last one, the one that had gone across his shoulders and the top of one arm, but he didn't complain. He just reached round, took her hand and said, "Enough. Enough, now."

"No, I can still…" Max began, yawning again.

Riley stood, turned, and looked down at where she knelt on the bed. "Get some sleep," he said. The cut on his chest still looked awful.

"But you're…"

"Capable of doing this by myself, more than you are at this point," he said gently. He looked around, found the slave tab and other gubbins she'd draped over the bedpost, and looped them over his arm. "Thanks for saving these," he added, looking at them.

"Looks like you're stuck with me," Max said, falling back on the bed and watching him collect up the rest of his stuff.

"Could be worse," he smiled. "Now. You're armed? Good. Don't open the door to anyone else. I don't trust them. Don't go out until I come to get you, all right? If you need me, then…uh…bang on the wall, or something."

Max smiled. "Riley, what kind of place is this?"

His ears went a little red.

Max got to her feet and limped to the picture hanging on the wall between their rooms. It was a crude depiction of a nude, and even Max knew it was worthless. But behind it was a hole in the wall, giving a nice view of Riley's bed.

He blinked, and then his cheeks went a bit pink, too. He was adorable.

"People pay for that," Max said as she replaced the picture.

"They'll pay for anything," he muttered. He sighed, and rubbed at his face. "All right, then. Yell if you need me."

Then, to her utter astonishment, he leaned forward and kissed her forehead. "Night, Max."

"Night," she mumbled back, and fell into a sleep full of monsters, blood, and big naked men coming to save her.

It was technically morning when Riley hauled his carcass out of bed, dressed it, and dragged it next door to Max's room. There was no answer when he knocked, or called her name. He was about to go back to his room and see if there was a spyhole into hers when he heard a cackle of laughter from the courtyard below.

In the slightly brighter gloom that passed for daylight in this hellhole, he could see Max down there at a table, arm-wrestling a bloke Riley might have thought twice about taking on. She was winning.

He jogged down the stairs, hand on the gun at his hip, too tired for trouble. He couldn't see any of the Eurydice crew down there, but he wouldn't put it past any of them to lurk in the shadows.

Max slammed her opponent's arm down on the table and thrust her other fist triumphantly into the air.

"Cheat!" cried the big guy. He had tattoos all over his

scalp. Everyone else jeered, including Max.

"How the fuck could I've cheated?" she said. "Come on, pay up."

He grumbled, but chucked some coins in her direction. Max grinned and scooped them into her pocket, then looked up at Riley, who stood with his arms folded, shaking his head.

"So do you go out looking for trouble, or does it just...find you?" he said.

She shrugged. "Little from column A, little from column B," she said. "C'mon, I'm making money hand over fist here. Literally."

He had to concede she had a point. "How much?"

"Fifty bits so far. Sexism is alive and well here, y'know? None of 'em reckon they can get beat by a girl."

Riley looked her over, all buzzcut and bandages, and shook his head again. If these guys thought her gender made her weak, they were fucking idiots.

"Go on then," he said, taking the seat opposite her. "Loser buys breakfast."

She chewed her lip. "Your arm. I didn't put that skinglue on so it could get torn open again."

He grinned at her. "It won't. Because that's on my right arm and we," he put his left arm on the table, "are doing this my way."

"What? That's not fair!" Max said, as the men around her cheered.

"Didn't say it had to be fair."

She glowered a moment, then lifted her chin and took his left hand in hers. "Onetwothreego!"

Christ, she was strong. Not that he should have doubted it after last night. Her hand gripped his tight and pushed, hard, towards the table. Riley narrowed his eyes and pushed back.

"Ten bits on the girl," said someone.

"That's a girl?" said someone else.

A man who'd evidently just arrived jeered, "Ten bits on the girl? Don't be fucking stupid. Seen the size of his arms?"

Riley tried not to smile. He'd always been a big guy, and the last three months on the Eurydice had really put the shine on the muscles he'd developed in the Service. He hadn't arm wrestled in years, though, and Max was taking it seriously, her brow furrowed and her teeth gritted.

Riley pushed back harder, and she resisted him, a vein popping out on her forearm. She had the build for this, tall with shoulders that could probably hoist a pig, and he'd never seen a woman with arms like—

Suddenly, she winked, and her arm crashed against the table as the crowd roared.

"Told you, don't bet on a girl!" crowed the newcomer.

Especially one who cheats, Riley thought, giving her a severe look. Max made a show of shaking the pain out of her hand and raising her palms in defeat. He wasn't taken in for a second.

"What do you want for breakfast?" she asked, as someone handed her a tablet.

"An explanation," Riley said, low enough that the dispersing crowd couldn't hear.

"Ah, c'mon, Primer, slave can't beat her master. It'd make you look bad."

"And you care about that because…?"

"If I'm gonna be stuck with you then I don't want people thinking you're a wussy," she said.

"Hmm." He sat back and watched her tap out her order. "How'd you sleep?"

"Not bad, so long as I didn't," she stretched over the table to hand him the tablet, and winced, "move too much." She rubbed gingerly at her back. "Jesus."

"Yeah," said Riley, who'd slept in short bursts in between accidentally moving.

"Fuck. Thought skinglue was supposed to knit skin together?"

"Not instantly," Riley said, and gestured her to come closer. Sighing, she did, and he could see the dark fabric of her shirt wet with blood. "Max...I did tell you to rest."

"Who died and made you God?" she muttered, but she let him lift her shirt and look at the cut across her back that had split open.

"Takes a few days to knit it back together," he said, "even if it's not deep. Come on, I'll re-do it."

"And miss my breakfast?" Max said. "G'wan, you get the stuff and I'll order yours. What d'you want?"

Marvelling at her insouciance, Riley picked out a few things, including fried mosasaur for the bloody sake of it, and loped back up the stairs for the med kit. Halfway there, he made the mistake of glancing at a hand raised in greeting, and found himself meeting Émile's gaze.

He looked away, but the contact had been made, and the other man ran after him to his bedroom door.

"Chér," he panted, "I've been looking for you."

"Well, I haven't gone anywhere," Riley said, unlocking his door and keeping his hand on his gun as he strode in and grabbed the med kit. Trying to catalogue what was left in it, he shouldered past Émile and locked the door again.

"Chér please. Max wouldn't talk to me. She's been making money from the boys downstairs," Émile said as Riley headed for the stairs.

"Yep. For some reason people keep underestimating her."

"And you," Émile said. "Riley, please. I didn't know they were planning that."

"I don't care," said Riley, who didn't believe it,

either. Sure, he didn't think he'd seen Émile in the warehouse, but being upside down, half tranquillised, in the dark and repeatedly whipped, his perception hadn't been at its best.

"I mean, he said Azrael, but I thought that meant…" Émile trailed off, wincing.

"What? Who is Azrael?" Had Azrael ordered what happened last night?

"He's…it's code," Émile said. "For something we don't trust. Chér, I thought they were going to, you know, haze you. Frighten you a bit."

"Émile, I've been hazed. Cleaning decks with a toothbrush. Having your skivvies stolen. Scorpions in the bed. That's hazing. Not whipping and stabbing."

"Scorpions sound dangerous," Émile said hopefully.

"They weren't lethal." When Riley had found the creature arching its tail over his pillow, he'd scooped it up with a bucket and chucked it into the barracks next door, to much cheering. "You know what is lethal? A mosasaur."

He reached Max, who was sitting with her boots on the table, scowling at Émile.

"Did they haze you when you joined the crew?" Riley asked, taking a seat and motioning Max to stand. As he folded back her shirt to show the bloodstained bandage on her back, Émile's voice faltered.

"Well, chér, they…uh…"

"What? Whipped you? Stabbed you? Strung you up above an ocean full of prehistoric monsters?"

"He was testing your loyalty," Émile tried.

"Yeah, well, he tested it too far." Riley peeled back the bandage and heard Émile's shocked intake of breath at the ragged, oozing wound on Max's back.

"He can go fuck himself," Max added over her shoulder.

Riley considered whether to add anything to that,

then decided it was pretty succinct as it was.

"He thought you could be a Service spy," Émile said.

"Well, he can go on wondering," Riley said, wiping away the blood from Max's back. "So can the rest of you. Piss off."

"You're leaving the crew?" Émile said.

Riley paused. He looked up at Max, who glanced back down at him with a look that said it was his call.

"Yeah, looks like we are. I'll get my stuff later."

"Chér—" Émile's hand touched Riley's shoulder. He looked at it, then deliberately pushed it away.

"I'll bring your stuff here," Émile said. He sounded upset.

"Take it to Metal Joe's. We're leaving when we've had breakfast."

Émile nodded, and withdrew. Riley refused to believe he was as unhappy as he sounded. This was the guy who'd levered the Service chip out of Riley's arm with a knife, after all. Even if he hadn't been party to yesterday's events, he sure as hell wasn't an innocent.

"We really quitting?" Max said.

"Think it's for the best, don't you? I mean, you can stay if you want. I'll give Orpheus your tab—"

"Fuck no." He smiled at that and got back to work fixing the cut on her back. "Jesus, I can't believe I screwed him."

"I told you he was a psychopath."

"Yeah, but that can be kind of hot."

Riley replayed that last sentence in his head. "Max, don't take this the wrong way, but you are really fucked up."

"Tell me about it," she said.

CHAPTER NINE

Max was mildly surprised to find that Émile had, in fact, taken their things to Metal Joe's. Well, really they were Riley's things, since she didn't actually own anything but what she'd bought in Nassau market, but he didn't seem annoyed at any omissions.

"Honour amongst thieves?" she said, and he just grunted.

Metal Joe's workshop was full of stripped down bits of machinery and tech, and once he'd established that Max knew what she was about, he let her wander around and investigate. She found a wrist micro that had lost its waterproof coating and gone rusty, and waved it at Joe.

"Mind if I have a fiddle with this?"

He shrugged. "If you want. I was just going to use it for parts."

"If I fix it, can I keep it?"

He gave her look. "You ain't gonna fix it, kid. I couldn't."

Max gave him a tight smile and said nothing. *Ain't this just my day for being patronised?*

"We need somewhere to stay," Riley was saying to

145

Joe. "Just temporarily. Unless you know any crews looking for an engineer and a tech?"

Joe scratched his head with his prosthesis. "Not offhand, no. What's wrong with the Brazen Head?"

"Got tired of the company."

"Really? Some good girls there. Tell you what though, the best ones are at Savidge's."

"I've heard enough to be wary of Madam Savidge."

"Oh, she's not one to be crossed, but her girls…"

Max smiled to herself as she carefully removed the rusted components of the micro. She wondered if there existed such a woman as could tempt a saint like Riley. This Elandra he'd told her about, she must've been an absolute goddess.

"How about somewhere—and I'm just throwing this suggestion out there—somewhere that isn't a brothel?"

Metal Joe looked confused. "But where else would have beds?"

Riley rolled his eyes at Max, who snorted. "He's got you there, Primer."

"Just somewhere we're not going to get robbed blind or stabbed in our sleep," Riley said. "Basic cleanliness would be a plus, too, but I realise that might be pushing it."

"You are picky, ain'tcha?" Joe said.

They wound up at a place that didn't seem to have a name, just a sign outside depicting a three-eyed raven. It was darker and less convivial than the Brazen Head, but it was also cheaper and no one there seemed to be pals with Orpheus and his crew. In fact, the mention of his name set one man to spitting.

"Fucking cunt. That cruiser wreck was mine and he knew it. Just because that damn ship of his was faster…"

Riley flicked a glance at Max, who had bummed another smoke and was enjoying the story of how Orpheus had screwed over a rival captain and gone on to make a fortune from scrap. The man was smart, even if he was a bastard.

"Speaking of," Riley said to her, low-voiced, "I'm going to start running out of money soon. We need to find work. Not that kind of work," he added quickly as Max opened her mouth. How did he know? "I can probably do a bit for Metal Joe, but keep your ears open if anyone's looking for a crew."

She nodded, and said, "Why not that kind of work?"

Riley sighed and scrubbed a hand over the golden stubble at his jaw. "You don't find it...demeaning, to screw people for money?"

"And piracy isn't screwing people for money?"

"Don't twist my words."

She shrugged. How could he ever understand? "Do you know why men take whores?"

Riley raised his palms. "Saves the bother of trying to get a woman to like them?"

"No. Well, yes, but...it's because it gives them power. In any other relationship, the one who gets to say no is the one with the power, yes? But when a man is paying for your time, he's in charge. You can't say no."

"Yeah," Riley said, "that's what I don't like about it. It's like...paid rape."

"Not if you choose your lovers," Max said, taking a drag of her cigarette. "Half the time they don't even realise they've been chosen. They still think they're in charge."

He sat back in his chair. "Like that time you chose Orpheus because he happened to be staying in the right room."

Max grinned despite herself. "Worked out for me, didn't it?"

Riley took a sip of his drink and eyed her over the top of it. "Can I ask you something?"

She gestured that he could. Didn't mean she had to

answer.

"Why did you go on sleeping with him? Did you... like him?"

"I wasn't falling in love if that's what you're worried about. I slept with him because...he was there. And I was horny, and I knew he was good."

"That's it?"

"Why else would you do it? I mean, not you, Primer, 'cos I don't think you do it at all..."

He ignored that. "And the others?"

"Seemed like a good idea at the time. Plus it really seemed to piss you off."

Riley saluted her with his drink. "I'm glad I amuse."

She looked around at the half-dressed women and leering men. None of them really appealed that much. On the other hand, there was Riley, right next to her, big and wholesome and just begging to be corrupted.

"Are you really saying I can't fuck any of them?"

He sighed.

"'Cos I get lonely, you know. A girl might go mad if she's not allowed some satisfaction."

"Max..."

"It's cruel of you to keep me for yourself when you won't even have me. Unless," she put her hand on his hard thigh, "you've changed your mind?"

Riley looked down at her hand, then up at her face. He leaned in, and for a moment she really thought it was going to happen. Then he said, "Max," all gentle-like. "I'm fifty percent skinglue right now and so are you. Are you seriously telling me you're in the mood for sex?"

He had a point, but she was damned if she was going to miss this opportunity.

"I am if you are," she breathed.

He sat back and took another swig. "Looks like a quiet night for both of us then," he said, and bloody winked at her.

Max stuck her finger up at him. "Bastard."

Riley gave Max free rein to do what she wanted the next day, while he fixed up things for Metal Joe in return for pay. It was decent, rewarding work, but he couldn't do it forever. Not least because the perpetual darkness of this rogue planet was beginning to unnerve him. Sure, it was black out in space, but then it was meant to be. If he had to have his feet on the ground he wanted some damn sunshine.

To cap it all off, it was raining.

Max, who'd fixed the broken micro and was now proudly wearing it on her wrist, sauntered in mid-afternoon with a package of greasy food in one hand and roll of money in the other.

Riley looked up from the engine he was about to install in an old Vector, and gave her a look. "Do I want to know?"

"Probably not." She shoved the money in her pocket. "I did keep my knickers on, if you're bothered."

Riley looked back down at the engine. "I wasn't aware you owned any."

She wrinkled her nose at him and took a bite of whatever disgusting foodstuff that bag contained. "I've been asking around," she said, talking through her food in a manner that would have given Riley's mother palpitations. "About crews. I did hear one or two were looking for a mech, but…"

"But?" Riley tested the tension on the pulley holding the engine, and adjusted it.

"Well," she made a so-so motion with her free hand. "There's one, the Siri, under Captain Chaudhri. I tracked him down to Madam Savidge's. By the way, they're right about those girls. Christ, they're phenomenal."

"How nice for them," Riley said, checking the Vector was in position to receive the engine.

"I mean, there was one in the courtyard, she was doing the most amazing thing with her—" She clocked his expression. "Right. Yeah. Chaudhri. He was there enjoying himself, and he was being watched over by these two guys. Massive fuckers, they were. Make you look like a little girl. And they had slave cuffs on."

"He keeps slaves?"

"Looks like it. And yeah, I'm aware of the irony." She took another bite. "So I asked if they liked working for him and they were all, like, blank. And Chaudhri saw me talking to them and shocked them. Like, really painful." She rubbed her own wrist in sympathy. "So I got the fuck out of there, obviously. Then I got talking to this other guy, he's the QM on Konstantin's freighter, forget the name of it, and he said Chaudhri's famous for nicking other people's slaves. Kills 'em for their tabs. Half his crew's indentured."

"Remind me to steer clear of him," said Riley, who had no particular wish to die at the hands of one sadistic pirate so soon after he'd escaped another.

"Yeah, that's what I thought. Konstantin sounds all right, by the way, but he's a family crew, the mech is his brother and he's training up a nephew, so no help there." She chewed, thinking. "Then there's Captain Mai and the Akimi. Great pay from what I hear, but it's danger money cos she hunts mosasaurs."

"No mosasaurs," Riley said, suppressing a shudder.

"S'what I thought. Actually, interesting biological sidebar, apparently they aren't mosasaurs, really, because they died out on earth millions of years ago, but no one knows what they really are so that's what they call them."

"Don't suppose you get too many xenobiologists around here," Riley said, assessing the engine bay one last time before picking up his gloves. "Can you help me guide this in? The exhaust, here, needs to align with that pipe there, and I can't see from over here."

She nodded and put down her half-finished food, wiping her hands on her shorts. They were, he noticed, very short indeed, or maybe it was just that she had very long legs.

Concentrate, Riley.

"Right, just tell me when it's in the right position," he said, and began hauling on the rope to lift the engine. It was bloody heavy, and his abused back and shoulders protested.

"Sure," Max said. She watched him drag the engine up above the Vector, then shuddered and said, "Can't look at ceiling hoists the same way any more."

Riley just grunted at that.

"Anyway," she rattled on. "I went to a few more bars and played a few games of poker—d'you play?" she asked hopefully.

Riley shook his head. The Service had disapproved of gambling, and besides, he suspected he had too honest a face for poker.

"Never mind. So I'm playing with this crew from the Imperator. Nice bunch of lads. Quite a few of them ex-Service, like you. Can tell from their bearing. I asked them why they left—whoa, to the left a bit there…"

Riley adjusted the rope in his gloved hands.

"Yep, that's it. And they said, these lads, they'd never wanted to be in the Service in the first place. Couple of them press-ganged, like you were. Apparently the Service gave itself the right to press anyone with the right skills or training, which is charming."

Riley, who already knew this, concentrated on paying out the rope and dropping the engine into place.

"But he said, this guy Elvis, he said one of the reasons he'd left was cos he kept getting asked to do stuff he didn't consider, you know, all that proper. And he wouldn't say what, but I wondered if it was to do with that crate Orpheus found. Like if they're shipping something illegal or summat. Hold on, it's nearly there. Just…"

She reached out to steady the engine and turn it slightly as it went in. "Oh yeah baby, put it in," Max mumbled, apparently without realising he could hear.

Then it slid down and to the rear of the engine bay, a beautiful elegant motion that always impressed Riley. There was a click as it locked into place, and he let go of the rope with relief.

He moved round to the back of the engine bay and slid underneath to check the fitting. Perfect.

"Hand me the spanner, will you? The number seven."

It appeared in his line of vision and he took it, bolting the engine in place.

"Is that why you left?" Max asked.

"The Service? Told you," Riley said. "Never wanted to be there in the first place."

"Why didn't you leave sooner?"

Because they almost broke me. They had me believing I owed them my loyalty. "Lack of opportunity," he said. "First few months was a training camp on one of the Omega moons. No way off that. Then a patrol ship out in deep space. Hardly made landfall for years. They don't let you out of their sight until they're sure they have you. And they make damn sure you know what happens to deserters."

"What does happen?"

Riley concentrated on the last bolt. "Well, they kill you, if you're lucky."

"And if you're not?"

He pushed back out from under the engine and wiped the sweat from his face. "Well, you die either way, it just depends on how." He'd done it, too. If the order came to fire, you just fired. A tracker chip running at less than 40% and that was it, shot down by a ship the poor sod likely never even saw.

"Elvis said he had to shoot deserters."

Riley's fists tightened. "Yep. They have a knack for knowing who's... dissatisfied," he said.

People disappear all the time. Doesn't mean they've deserted. Doesn't mean they're dead. What are they hiding, Thrynn?

Max read his face. "D'you want to go talk to them? They might make good allies."

"And they might be Service spies."

"For God's sake, don't tell Orpheus about them."

Riley wiped his hands on a rag and climbed into the Vector's cab to start her up.

None of this sounded particularly promising. He was leery of talking to the Imperator crew, just in case they actually were Service spies. Not that he expected they'd send anyone out to look for a patrol ship engineer, after all—but the world was full of bad luck. Maybe he could ask Max to go back and talk to them.

He glanced at her, perched on a rusted plasma vessel finishing her chunk of fried whatever. Her long bare legs swung, the bandage on her calf standing out white against her bronze skin. She was licking her fingers, eyes closed in bliss, and just for a moment he let himself imagine that he'd put that look on her face.

Then he shook himself, and started the HAV engine. Bad enough he owned a slave, but perving over her was out of the question.

The engine sounded well enough, but Riley knew he could tune her up. The better shape she was in, the more she'd sell for, and the more money he'd make. Then maybe he could buy passage off this godforsaken rock and he and Max could find work elsewhere. Maybe one of the spaceports. No, maybe not. They were always crawling with Service.

He switched off the engine and climbed down.

"Max?"

She looked up, a smear of grease on her cheek.

"What do you want to do? I mean, long-term."

She tilted her head, as if she didn't quite understand the question.

"We're kind of stuck with each other for the foreseeable, but what do you actually want to do? Stay here, get on a ship, settle on another planet?"

Max looked genuinely puzzled, as if he'd suddenly started speaking a different language, and he realised it was probably the first time anyone had given her a choice about her future.

"I dunno," she said eventually. "Look, basically if you ain't beating me or starving me, I'm quite happy to do whatever you want."

Riley's heart broke a little at that. "That's it? Not being beaten and starved is your idea of a happy future?"

She shrugged. "Better than the alternative, ain't it?"

The inn at the sign of the three-eyed raven livened up a bit in the evening, which Max enjoyed and Riley disapproved of. Well, mostly he ignored it. Scenes of brawling and debauchery seemed to completely pass him by.

What had that woman Elandra done to him?

He leaned back in his seat, looking her over, and Max suddenly felt self-conscious. She hadn't tried to be pretty for years—had pushed hard in the opposite direction, in fact. Pretty was trouble. But the way Riley was looking at her kind of made her wish she had more hair and fewer scars.

"What?" she said.

"Nothing. How's that cut on your back?"

She reached down to rub at it. "Fine. Well, I mean, not fine, but…"

He nodded. "Might scar a bit."

"Hardly my first," she scoffed.

"No." He took a swig of his drink, chewed his lip, and glanced around at the general debauchery. "You can join in if you want," he said. "Don't have to sit here talking to me all night."

"What's this, Primer? You're allowing me to have sex?"

"I never said you couldn't. I said it'd probably be a bad idea with all that skinglue, and I didn't want you whoring yourself out, but if you want to shag around then be my guest. I can't stop you."

Max tried to read his face, but for someone so honest-looking he could be a bit impenetrable sometimes. "I don't get you," she said. "I can screw whoever I like so long as I'm not getting paid for it? Thought you said we needed money."

Riley sighed and glanced over at a topless girl rubbing her considerable endowments all over an enthusiastic man with a broken nose.

"I mean, you sell your skills, right? Why can't I sell mine?"

"Reprogramming tech, you mean?" Riley said, looking away from the whore. He didn't seem to be impressed. To be honest, neither was Max. The girl was being far too obvious.

"You make mock, but I am seriously good in bed," said Max. It was true. She'd been trained by the best.

"I'm sure you are. Look, Max—"

But whatever he was about to say never got said, because they were interrupted by a shout in a familiar voice.

"Petal! Found them!"

Max and Riley exchanged a look as Émile came winding through the tables towards them. He looked out of breath, panicked and wild-eyed.

"Thank God I found you, chéries! I've been all over

this hideous swamp looking for you."

"Clearly we need to move on," Riley said to Max.

"You have to help us," Émile said, and Riley snorted out a laugh as he lifted his drink to his lips.

"We really don't."

"Chér, please. Can we talk, somewhere quiet?"

Riley glanced around at the crowded tavern, the fighting and the fucking and the music and the shouting, then looked back at Émile and said, "What, this isn't quiet enough for you?"

"Please," said Petal, arriving at the other side of the table.

Max looked her over contemptuously. "My leg is getting better, in case you were wondering."

"I'm sorry about that," Petal said, then spoiled it by adding, "Can I have my knife back?"

Max's lip curled into a snarl. "You can have it," she said, "everywhere I put my hands the other night."

Petal looked as if she was about to spit something back at that, but Émile silenced her with a look, and instead she raised her micro and started tapping out a text.

"Look, in the interests of saving everyone time, why don't you tell us what it is you want us to do, so we can say no and you can fuck off?" Riley said.

Entirely seriously, Émile replied, "Orpheus and Justine have been kidnapped by Madam Savidge and we need you to rescue them."

Max's jaw dropped open. Riley stared.

Then he started laughing.

"Yes, all right, it's very funny," Émile said, hands on hips.

Max found herself laughing too. "What were they kidnapped for?" she asked.

"Ransom," Petal growled.

That only made Riley laugh even harder. "I mean

what did they do?" Max managed.

"Chérie, we can't talk about this here."

Riley slapped his hand on the table. "Oh, this is brilliant. I almost want to go and see what she's doing to them."

"D'you think she has a whip?" Max asked him, and he wiped at his eyes.

"Bloody hope so. And a pet—"

"—mosasaur!" Max finished for him, and they both set off into fresh peals.

"I told you this was a waste of time," Petal said to Émile.

"Chér please," he said again. "We can't go in there after them. She knows us all. She'll kill us."

"Tell her to use throwing knives," Max snorted.

"It has to be you."

Riley was crying with laughter now. He didn't seem able to stop.

"This is pointless," Petal said.

"Petal, are you actually serious?" Max asked between giggles. She didn't think she'd ever giggled before. "He had us tortured. She whipped us. Have you ever been whipped?"

Petal narrowed her eyes. "He is my brother."

Max stared at tiny little Petal, with her huge eyes and snub nose and rosebud mouth, and thought of Orpheus, whip-thin with a face like a hawk and eyes you could never see into, and burst into fresh laughter.

"Not biological," Petal said, rolling her eyes.

"Justine is my sister," Émile said. "Chérie, I never hurt you."

Max glanced at Riley, who was trying to get himself under control, and failing. "Then I might come and save you," she said. "But I got no love for Justine and Orpheus. Madam Savidge can feed them to the mosasaurs for all I care."

157

"Bitch," whispered Petal, and this time she looked more upset than angry.

"Then do it for him," Émile said, nodding at Riley.

Max looked Riley over, all two metres of him, still quaking with laughter and trying to wipe tears from his eyes. His hand swiped his nose, still cut across the bridge where she'd apparently thumped him while she was unconscious. He seemed to have forgiven her for that.

"Trust me, mate, he's even less love for them than I have." She picked up her drink, still giggling a bit.

"You'll regret it if you don't," Émile insisted.

"That a threat?" said Max. She looked over Émile, then Riley, who gave a sort of shrug. He had marvellously expressive shoulders, did Riley.

Ooh, his shoulders said. *I'm so fucking scared.*

Émile glanced at Petal, and appeared to come to a decision. He leaned in so he could speak in a low voice. "Justine started testing those samples on board the ship. She was looking for a common thread, somewhere to link them back to. She used our blood samples as a starting point."

Max shrugged. "So?"

"So, she found a link. A strong one. To Riley."

Max frowned at him, but Riley seemed to have heard, because he very abruptly sobered.

"What?"

"You're genetically linked to some of those samples. Can't say how close until we get more accurate testing equipment, but—"

"Riley, don't listen to him. He's just messing with you."

Riley held up a hand to her. "Are you saying I'm… related to those…samples?"

"Yes, chér. Closely."

Riley's eyes met Max's, distracted and troubled. All

the mirth had drained out of him. Abruptly, he stood. "A word?"

He pulled her over to the other side of the bar, a dark corner where Max was fairly sure people were actually having sex.

"You can't trust what he says," she said urgently. "Not for a minute. He'll say anything to get us to help."

In the low light, Riley's big honest face was anxious. "But what if it's true?"

"Why would it be true? Look, a close genetic match could mean anything. Just that they came from the same, I dunno, town as you. Maybe a distant relative. It doesn't —"

"But why is the Service transporting samples and… and embryos from my distant relative? Max, some of those had gone beyond embryos. A few more months and they'll be people. Babies. Human beings."

"Yeah, and that sucks for them, but you can't seriously be suggesting…Riley, he's manipulating you."

He scrubbed at his shorn hair, looked out across the bar at Petal and Émile, then back at Max. There was guilt in those baby blue eyes of his.

"What?" Max said flatly.

He leaned in close, hesitated, then said, "Do you know how many medicals I've gone through with the Service? How many samples they've taken from me?"

"Yeah, but I don't reckon you can create an embryo from a blood sample," Max said, and Riley gave her a look. "Oh. *Oh*. Really?" She couldn't help glancing down. *So he does know what it's for.* "Weren't you suspicious? Why did they want a sperm sample?"

"I don't know, I didn't ask! You don't ask," he said anxiously.

"Besides, I don't suppose there's any reasonable answer to that," Max said thoughtfully. "Why is the Service harvesting sperm from its members? Do you think they were taking eggs, too?"

He threw up his hands. "It wasn't the sort of conversation we had over the mess table."

She looked back at Émile and Petal, who'd now been joined by Murtaugh and Hide. Then back up at Riley. Tall, strong, clever, honest Riley. Exactly the type of DNA you'd want to reproduce. If someone had been stealing samples, it made sense to take his.

"I don't suppose," she said, "there's any way we could steal those samples and get them tested ourselves?"

He shrugged. "Do you know anything about genetics?"

"I know I've got a chip in my arm that prevents conception and that's all I've ever wanted to know," Max replied gloomily. "And before you ask, I'm up to date with my shots. Clean as a whistle."

Riley ignored that. "We don't have a ship either. Or any contacts."

"Oh, fuck," Max said. "We're going to rescue them, aren't we?"

"Looks like it."

Resignedly, they started back across the bar to the Eurydice crew. "We ain't doing this for nothing," Max said. "How much do you get out of each haul the ship takes?"

"An equal share. Captain gets double, so that means the rest of us get an eighth."

"Well, that's bollocks," Max said, and squared up to Émile. "For one, I should have my own share, not just half his—"

"Fine—"

"I ain't done yet. We do this, we get a double share of future profits. Each."

Émile swallowed. "Chérie, that's…what, a third of gross?"

"Four shares out of eleven is more than a third," Riley said.

"Yep. Why don't we go with forty percent? It's a nice easy figure."

"Forty—?"

Max let him splutter, then said softly, "How much d'you want your sister back?"

He nodded, and then she knew he was serious. "You're right. Forty percent between you."

"And a half share of any big-ticket items. Over ten thousand bits in value and we get half of it."

"Quarter."

"Half. Items over fifteen grand."

Émile glanced nervously at Petal.

"Whatever they want," she said.

"Renege on this and I will kill the whole fucking lot of you," Max threatened.

"All right, all right, forty percent and half of everything over fifteen thou," Émile said. He held out his hand. "Anything else?"

"Yeah," said Max, and punched Petal hard on her perfect little nose.

Then she used the same hand to shake Émile's.

"Feel better now?" Riley asked, as Petal swore and Murtaugh laughed and Max shook her sore knuckles.

"Yeah," she said. "Lots."

CHAPTER TEN

"Be honest with me, Primer," Max muttered as they followed the crew through the cluttered, vertiginous streets, "do you honestly trust any of these culchies?"

"Not as far as I could throw them," Riley replied. Round here, the streets were lit with torches and lanterns, throwing ghastly shadows over Hide's bulk as he led the way.

"I mean they could've lied about the whole thing," Max said, as they followed Hide up a handful of steps to a bridge. "The captain and Justine could be sitting in a tavern somewhere laughing their heads off over this."

The thought had occurred to Riley too. But he'd seen the honest panic in Émile's eyes, and in Petal's, too. If they didn't believe something terrible was going on with their loved ones, then they'd wasted amazing careers as actors.

Loved ones. Émile worshipped his sister, that was clear to everyone. Theirs a relationship based on more than shared genetics. Petal and Orpheus on the other hand...they were clearly close, but they weren't related. At least not by blood. Riley had been in the

Service long enough to know that not all brothers shared the same mother.

"We'll see what we'll see," he said, crossing the dark water without looking down. "Whatever the situation, we go in loaded for bear."

"For…?"

"We take a fuckload of ammo," Riley clarified, and Max nodded.

"Although," she began, but halted when Hide did, just ahead of them at a set of imposing doors.

They'd been travelling through the Cauldron, the most dangerous part of a dangerous colony. Here, the power was unreliable, the darkness impenetrable, the trouble magnified. Riley had had his hand on his weapon from the moment they left the inn at the sign of the raven. Every street—well, street was pushing it. Most of the streets were filthy little alleys, overbuilt by groaning, lurching buildings, half lit and seething with desperation.

And now here was a grand set of doors, flanked with carriage lanterns and a pair of bouncers. A man and a woman, both tall and imposing, both tattooed and lethal. They nodded to the crew, gave Riley and Max suspicious looks, and let them pass.

"Where are we?" said Max.

Riley glanced back at the doors, suspicion forming in his mind. The lobby beyond the doors was calm, well-lit and ordered.

"'Cos you said we was going somewhere to talk strategy."

"We are," Émile said. "This is the home of the Prideaux brothers."

"And…why have we come to see them?"

"They've no love for Madam Savidge," Émile began, as a set of double doors opened and the two well-dressed men they'd met after escaping the mosasaur appeared.

"Indeed we have not," said the one on the left.

"Been trying to usurp our position for years, so she has," said the one on the right.

"Then why don't you go and rescue Orpheus and Justine?" Riley asked, folding his arms across his chest.

"Oh, we couldn't get involved in politics," said one.

"Or be seen to have favourites," said the other.

"I see," said Riley. "Or is it that we're expendable? Newcomers to the place, no one knows us, we fuck up and nobody cares. Is that it?"

The brothers shared a glance. "For someone so tall he's remarkably perspicacious," said one.

"Yeah, it's amazing my brain works at this altitude," Riley said.

"Why don't you come with us for some refreshments and we can talk about plans?" the brothers offered, and the doors behind them opened by themselves.

Riley let Petal and Émile go through first, and Murtaugh and Hide bring up the rear. This whole thing had his hackles rising.

They were led into a salon that was a faded, cheapened version of the parlours of Riley's childhood, and offered seats on overstuffed velvet sofas. The silk on the walls was stained and ripped. Riley opted to stand, as did Max, her hand on the knife at her belt.

"Take some refreshments," offered one of the brothers. Max darted a glance at Riley, who shook his head incrementally.

"I'd rather get down to business," he said. "Why do you care what happens to Captain Orpheus and Justine?"

One of the brothers poured amber liquid into small glasses and passed them around. The other offered a tray of sweetmeats. It was clearly meant to be a version of the high society rituals practised by people with more time and money than sense, but the way they did it bespoke people who'd only ever heard about such things, and never even witnessed them.

Riley watched Petal pick up a small cake with her fingers and could almost hear his mother admonishing her.

Clearly they'd got one part of the ritual correct: that no business was discussed until everyone had been served. Riley was offered refreshments again, more forcibly, and this time he took them, and waited for the brothers to speak before he set them aside. Reluctantly, Max did the same.

"Captain Orpheus came to us yesterday with a fine shipment," said one of the brothers.

"Always the best offers from Captain Orpheus of the Eurydice," said the other.

"Do you know where the name comes from, Mr Thrynn?" said the first, and Riley's attention narrowed sharply on them.

"My name is Riley," he said.

"Riley David Thrynn, we hear," said one.

"Engineer First Class."

"Son of Teodore Thrynn and Varinia Einarsson. Brother to—"

Riley had his gun aimed at them before they got any further. "One more word on that sentence and I will kill you. How the fuck do you know about my family?"

"Oh, it's our business to know," said one, taking a macaron and biting it daintily.

"We trade in knowledge," said the other, sipping what was probably supposed to be sherry.

"Well, you can forget that bit," Riley said. He glanced aside, and said, "If you know so much, how do Petal and Orpheus know each other?"

"Oh, that's a very interesting story, that is," said the one with the macaron. A crumb fell onto his jacket and he brushed it fastidiously away.

"Which you're not going to tell," Petal said threateningly.

"Has its origins in the Omega system, as I recall," said the brother with the sherry.

"You want to stop talking right now," said Petal. There was a knife in her hand.

Riley looked her over, then quirked an eyebrow at the Prideaux brothers. "You going to piss off Émile next? How about telling me the story of how Murtaugh came to be on the ship?"

"No story, that. He was hired for his muscle."

"True," said Murtaugh.

"Suppose you know how I came to get that scar on my thigh," Max spat. She was beside Riley, crouched in a fighting stance, a wicked curved blade in her hand.

To Riley's eternal gratification, the brothers looked nonplussed.

"Did we just find something you don't know?" he said, and a hint of anger crossed those eerily calm faces.

"How about we put away our weapons," Émile said, "and discuss this without getting personal?"

Riley looked from one to the other of them, and slowly lowered his gun. Petal reluctantly followed, and finally Max.

"But I'm having that story from you," he said to Petal.

"Like fuck—"

"Ball's in our court now, Petal."

They all looked confused. "Ball?" Petal said.

"I think what he means," Max said slowly, "is that we're the ones with the power now. We get to say yes or no. So answer our questions, or fuck you."

"Well put," Riley said. He didn't holster his gun. "Now. Why do you want Orpheus and Justine back?"

The brothers looked him over. "Our question stands," one said.

"About the name of the ship."

Riley sighed. "Eurydice was the wife of Orpheus.

Classical myth." They seemed to be wanting more, so he continued, "When she died he went to the underworld and persuaded the gods there to return her. She had to follow him back to the waking world and he wasn't allowed to look back, but at the last moment he did, and she vanished forever."

There was a short silence, and then Max said, "Bloody hell, Primer."

"Just so," said one of the brothers. "But how did he persuade them, do you know, Mr...Riley?"

He gave them a tight smile at that use of his name. "He...I dunno, was a silver-tongued charmer. Can't remember."

The brothers nodded in tandem. "He played to them the lyre."

"So sweetly they were entranced."

It was creepy the way their sentences ran on from each other. "Right, yeah. Lyre," said Riley.

"...the fuck's a lyre?" Murtaugh muttered.

"He offered them music," said one of the brothers, standing and retrieving an ornate pot from the water-stained wooden mantelpiece.

"Music?" said Max, and Riley looked at her before shrugging at the Prideaux with the pot. He glided to Riley and opened it. There was a red powder inside. It glowed faintly.

"Don't breathe in," Max said, and Riley took a step back.

"Your slave has a better knowledge of street drugs than you do," said the brother with the pot, closing the lid and stepping back.

"What is it?"

"Hallucinogen," said Max. "It's either fun or terrifying. I once spent three days thinking I was a fecking sand beast."

"You should take it purer," said the brother on the

sofa.

"Ours would give you exquisite dreams," said the other, replacing the pot and sitting back down again. He twitched his trousers into place as he did.

"I'll pass, ta."

"So Orpheus supplies you with drugs," Riley said, unsurprised.

"It's used in medicine," Émile said. "Mixed with other substances, it forms part of a treatment for various cancers, I think. But uncut, yeah, it's a street drug."

Riley frowned at the little pot. Before the train job on Zeta Secunda, they'd orchestrated a heist on a small bank at a trading post, boarded a passenger ship and held them up like highwaymen, and robbed the governor of one of Secunda's moons. He'd been under no illusions that the crew were anything other than criminals, but he hadn't expected them to be stealing drugs that could save lives.

He closed his eyes, seeing those stacks of Service crates in the carriage of the land train. "That's why we hit the train," he sighed. "It wasn't about the money."

"Well, partly it was about the money," Hide rumbled.

"Right. Okay. QED. Orpheus supplies you with this Music, and…what, no one else does?"

"His is the best."

"Service supplies."

"Which must tickle you some."

Riley gave up on trying to work out which of the brothers was speaking. "Yeah, it's hilarious. Why are you telling me this? Why are we," he gestured to himself and Max, "here?"

Petal let her gaze settle on the fairly standard gun Riley carried. "That all you're packing, Primer?"

"I've another one or two I can lay my hands on."

"Likewise," said Max. "And some knives," she added with a smile at Petal.

"You know how to use them?"

"Never met a weapon I didn't know how to."

"Primer?"

"Service training," he said impatiently. "Look, do you have anything else to offer, or are we just going to stand here dick-swinging at each other all day? I was under the impression that this Madam Savidge was the type to return hostages on the instalment plan."

Petal flinched. Émile looked a shade paler.

The Prideaux brothers, on the other hand, exchanged a glance and said, "Oh, we have something to offer you, Mr Riley."

If the Prideaux brothers' establishment was a tribute to Primer glories, Madam Savidge's was a one-fingered salute to them.

The place was entered across a bridge lined with flaming torches. One way out, one way in, Max guessed the message to be, although she'd bet her left buttock there were plenty of secret passages around the place.

She limped along behind Riley, a choke chain around her neck. Where the hell Émile had found that, she didn't want to know. She'd kept on her short shorts, swapped her shirt for a see-through top of Petal's, which was too tight and did somewhat obscene things to her breasts, and taken off her boots to walk barefoot along the filthy streets.

Back at the shuttle, where they'd transferred their gear for a quick getaway, Riley had asked Max what she wanted to do about the slave cuff. "Do you want to disguise it or go with it?"

She shook her head. "You're asking the wrong question. When we go in there, do you want me to be an obvious asset or not? Do you want me showing strength, or not?"

He tilted his head and waited for her to give him the

right answer.

"I can fight the shit out of anyone Madam Savidge throws at us," she explained, "but do you want her knowing that?"

"You'd rather she underestimated you?"

"If she thinks I'm weak and submissive, she probably won't even look at me."

Riley looked her over with a look that asked if she was kidding.

"I could be weak and submissive," Max insisted, and Riley snorted.

"Yeah, and suns revolve around moons," he said. "Go on. Surprise me."

She pulled off all the bandages he'd so carefully applied, and teased apart the skinglue which had begun to knit the wounds back together again. Pinching them, she even got a few to bleed. A bit of rummaging around the mechanical parts of the engine got her some grease to smear on her face and body.

Then she said to Riley, "Hit me."

He'd been watching with detached amusement, but now he looked confused. "I'm sorry, that sounded like you asked me to hit you."

"I did. In the mouth. Or the eye. Hard as you like."

He gave her the same look he had when she said could be submissive.

"D'you want this to work or not?" Max said. "I'll get Murtaugh to do it—"

"All right. All right."

"Don't hold back," Max said, and braced herself.

His left fist hit her jaw, catching her lip and jamming it into her teeth. Almost instantly, his right fist caught her cheekbone and the bridge of her nose.

"Fuck!" Max gasped, and Riley caught her as she staggered. He peered at her uncertainly.

"Too much?"

Gingerly, she touched her lip, which was beginning to swell. Her nose throbbed, and she knew that her eye would be turning a nice purple quite soon.

"I did tell you not to hold back," she muttered, spitting out blood.

Riley screwed up his face. "I did a bit," he confessed.

She looked up at him, his earnest blue eyes and reddening ears, and told herself that nice wasn't the same as harmless.

"Remind me not to get on your bad side," she said, and he gave her a bit of a smile.

Now they were approaching Madam Savidge's establishment, which towered above them like an ancient ship, all elaborate carving and tiny windows. Max had visited earlier, and part of her desire for physical transformation was to stop anyone recognising her.

It had started to rain, but the huge flaming torches outside the door burned with a greenish light when the water hit them.

You'd better be a bloody good actor, Max thought as she followed Riley in past the bouncer. Inside, there was a dark tunnel with various small slits in the walls and ceiling. You could hold back a siege in this place. There was even a portcullis to pass under before they got to the courtyard, and when they did Max held her breath, half expecting it to slam down on them.

Savidge's was like the Brazen Head in that there was a central courtyard surrounded by higher buildings, but there the similarity ended. There was no friendly camaraderie here, nobody drunkenly playing a fiddle or a flute in the corner. Here the music was loud, pounding and composed mostly of people moaning in a vaguely orgasmic fashion.

There were various platforms on which scantily clad girls and boys gyrated for the benefit of eager punters. In the middle of the courtyard was a raised section surrounded by ropes, in which there seemed to be a permanent live sex show. Max wasn't honestly sure if the participants were customers or staff or a mixture of both. There were at least four of them up there now. At least, that's how it seemed when she squinted through her one good eye. The other had half-closed now, and throbbed with every heartbeat.

She waited for Riley's reaction, and was impressed when he stood for a moment, then jerked his head arrogantly at a girl. She turned a smile on him and slinked her way over.

Like the girls Max had seen on her previous visit, her clothing was minimal, yet not overtly sexual. She was barefoot and tousle-haired, as if she'd just stepped from someone's bed. Her face was skilfully made-up, turning a pretty girl into a glorious creature. Her hair was a shade of red that looked almost natural.

"Welcome to Savidge's," she purred. "What's your pleasure?"

"A drink," Riley said. "And a table close to the show."

He caressed the girl's hand, and if Max hadn't been watching she wouldn't have seen the money pass from his palm to hers.

"Sure thing, darling," said the girl, and sashayed her way to a table two rows back from the arena.

Riley looked down at it, then back up at her, and said chidingly, "You can do better than that."

"How about," she said, pushing forward her breasts so they just brushed his chest, "I throw in a little extra?"

"What kind of extra?"

She pushed him down into a chair and opened her bodice. Her breasts were full and pink-tipped, and she took Riley's hand and placed it full over one creamy globe.

Neither of them had even looked at Max the whole

time. She stood as meekly as possible, not meeting anyone's gaze, trying to suss out the layout of the place and trying not to look at Riley feeling up one of Madam Savidge's whores.

"I'll think about it," Riley said, his expression unimpressed. "First I want a drink. Champagne."

That seemed to surprise her, but she gestured to someone else and pressed her breasts closer to Riley. "You're celebrating, darling?"

"Fucking right I'm celebrating. The cuntweasel I've been working for has finally got his comeuppance."

"Which cuntweasel would that be, darling?"

Riley brushed her red hair back from her face and seemed to be considering the softness of her neck. "Captain Orpheus, of the Eurydice."

The girl straightened up. "You're the engineer?"

Riley shrugged.

"I heard he had you whipped!"

Riley jerked his head at Max, the first time he'd acknowledged her. "He had my slave whipped. Which is a fucking cowardly thing to do, if you ask me."

The girl glanced dismissively at Max. "What for? Does it know something?"

It.

"No, but he thought if he whipped her, I'd tell him what he wanted to know." He caressed the girl's bare shoulder in a way that made Max irrationally jealous.

"Did you?"

Riley gave her a contemptuous look. "Do I look stupid to you?" He glanced at Max as if she was extremely unimportant.

"No, darling, you look hot to me."

Riley's mouth curved in a smile Max would kill to have aimed at herself.

As the champagne arrived, he poured some for the girl and himself, and completely ignored Max, who was starting to get annoyed at how good his acting skills were.

Or maybe this is the real Riley and he's just been acting with you.

No.

No, surely not.

The girl slid her long legs either side of Riley's and pressed her bare breasts against his shirt. "If you really wanted to celebrate," she murmured throatily, "we could go upstairs."

"Mmm," said Riley. "What did you have in mind?"

She leaned in and whispered in his ear, caressing his chest and giggling a little. Riley raised one brow as if considering what she suggested, and then he said, "That sounds good to me. Come on," and to Max's astonishment he stood up, the girl clinging to him and giggling as she wrapped her legs around his waist.

What the hell was he playing at? All he'd actually told her of his plan was that he was still working on it and she should follow his lead. Now she watched him swat the redhead's backside and let her slide down his body to the ground.

"What should I call you, sweetheart?"

"Whatever you like," she murmured, rubbing herself all over him like a shameless kitten.

"What's your name?" he chided, pulling up her skirt and slapping her bare buttock. Max tried not to stare.

The redhead bit her lip in enjoyment and pouted. "Angharad," she said.

"Angharad? Hmm. Haven't had one of those before. Come on, Angharad, you can show me what you meant by 'pop like hot champagne'."

He started towing her away, and Max stood, almost choking on her own shock. Then she was choking on the leash around her neck, as Riley tugged on it. "Come on," he said, the picture of annoyance. "And bring the champagne."

Too shocked to do anything but what she was told, Max scooped up the bottle and glasses, fumbling them as Riley tugged on the lead and dropping one. It smashed audibly, and he whipped round and glared at her.

"Fucking moron! What the fuck is wrong with you? Jesus Christ, come on."

He dragged her after him, and Max stumbled, yelping as the broken glass cut into her foot. Someone laughed, and she hopped on by, trying to get her breath back.

Riley towed her up the stairs, and as she watched Angharad drape herself all over him she wondered if this was payback for the night she'd taken half the Eurydice crew up the steps of the Brazen Head.

The girl led them down a corridor and unlocked a room. It was draped with fabrics and soft lighting, and the bed was big enough to hold Riley and probably half a dozen bedmates of his choosing.

The girl Angharad pushed him down on it and shook back her hair as she climbed on top of him. Riley tossed Max's leash over the bedpost and growled, "Sit," at her. Max did, hard on the floor.

Angharad giggled. "Do you really want your dog in the room for this?" she asked.

"Yeah," Riley said. "The little whore fucked Orpheus. Hey, you know what?"

"What?" said Angharad, nuzzling his neck, and as her face was turned away, Riley shot Max a look of agonised apology.

Suddenly she felt like laughing. He was acting after all.

Then the glorious red hair parted to reveal that perfect face once more, and Riley's expression turned devilish again.

"Well," he said, smoothing his hand over the generous curve of her breast, "I heard your boss had my old boss here, locked up somewhere."

Angharad's face switched to wariness. "Did you?"

"Yeah. Crew tried to convince me to get him back for them. Like I'm a fucking moron or something. He tied me up, fucked my slave and had her whipped. I'm the only person who gets to do that."

"Really?" said Angharad, looking Max over with an expression that questioned why anybody would want to fuck her. Max forced her gaze to the floor and bit her tongue.

"Yeah. So you know what I'd like? What would really," he walked his fingers up to her collarbone, "really turn me on?"

She squirmed in his lap and cooed, "I'd say you're already turned on, darling."

"Even more," Riley murmured, close to her ear. He flicked a glance at Max and said, "I'd like to fuck you while he watches. And if," he bit gently on her earlobe, "you had a whip handy I could use on him, so much the better."

Angharad sat back, regarding Riley thoughtfully.

"What d'you think? I'll pay you extra."

"How much do engineers make?" Angharad asked.

"Not as much as engineers on the make," Riley said. "I've been whoring her out, too."

Angharad looked at Max again, and then she slid to her feet. "I'll see what I can do," she said, and exited the room, hips swaying.

The second the door closed, Riley turned to Max, and she shook her head, eyes pleading. "No, please, I'm sorry about the glass, sir, let me bring you the bottle..."

He watched her with narrowed eyes as she shuffled forward on her knees and presented him the bottle, her gaze flicking towards the picture on the wall. Riley froze, and she saw the understanding come over his face. There was no way they weren't being watched.

"How about I fuck you in front of the captain?" he said.

"Whatever you want, sir," she murmured.

He pulled her in close, and said right against her mouth, "If she's bringing Savidge, we take her out first. Then the girl. Use the chain when I say."

Max jerked her chin in understanding, and Riley pushed her away to wander to the window at the front, twitching the curtain aside and looking out at the courtyard below. Max took the opportunity to check the cut in her foot. Small, and no glass stuck in it. So long as she got the dirt out, it'd be all right.

After a few minutes, the door opened, and Angharad was back with an imposing woman in a red dress. She wasn't as old as Max had expected, maybe around Max's own age—

No, wait. You ain't a kid any more, Max. Depressed, she realised she could probably give the Savidge creature a few years.

Madam Savidge was handsome rather than beautiful, with a certainty about her that said she was used to being in charge.

"Well well," she said, looking Riley over and paying a little more attention to Max than she liked. "Orpheus's deserter. I heard all about the mosasaur."

"He's a fucking animal," Riley said. "Madam Savidge, I assume?"

He held out his hand, and after a moment, she took it and shook.

"I heard he had you whipped too," said Madam Savidge, and quick as a snake her hand was tugging down the front of his shirt.

"So much for keeping that quiet," he said with a shrug. "You see now why I'd like to get my revenge on him."

"Fucking one of my girls in front of him is a fitting

revenge? How about you fuck his girl in front of him?"

"His girl?"

"The dark one. You know he's in love with her."

Max's gaze darted to Riley. She couldn't help it. He looked as if he was considering the prospect. "Makes sense," he said. "Hmm. Maybe. Can I see them?"

Madam Savidge looked him over, then, worryingly, did the same to Max. She tried her best to look small and helpless, which wasn't easy when you were taller than the average man and had spent the previous morning demonstrating how to arm-wrestle them into submission. *Really hope Savidge hasn't heard about that.*

"Give the girl your weapons," she said, and Riley began unstrapping the two baldrics fastened crosswise over his chest. He handed the first belt to Max, but Savidge just laughed and said, "No, my girl. I'm not stupid."

He shrugged and handed them over as if it made no nevermind to him, and then they set off, the four of them, down the dimly lit corridor.

"Don't forget the champagne," Riley said, and Max picked it up with the remaining glass.

"You know," said Madam Savidge. "It's almost a shame about these two. I mean, she's a beauty, and so haughty. She'd make a great girl. And him—did I hear you say you've fucked him, dear?" she said to Max, who nodded rapidly, surprised to be addressed. *Don't underestimate her.* "Hung like a stallion, isn't he? I did hear a rumour he used to be a whore, back in the day. Shame I'm going to have to kill them both."

"Why, when you could profit from them?" asked Riley.

"Well, the crew aren't going to ransom them, dear. They've already sold everything to those Prideaux bastards."

"Ah," said Riley, as if he didn't really care, "is that

why you've kidnapped these two?"

"They've done me out of such profit," Savidge complained. "The Music goes to the Prideauxs, of course, they're obsessed with the stuff. But human life? That's mine, dear."

"Human life?" Riley said, glancing at Max. "The slave is mine—"

"Oh no, I don't want that. What they've got is fresher and younger than that," Madam Savidge said, and if Riley hadn't turned his face away right then she'd have seen what Max did: the flare of his nostrils that said he knew exactly what she was talking about.

Ahead of them was a door with several locks on it. The Prideaux brothers had told them about this place, where Madam Savidge kept people and things she didn't want the world knowing about.

She unlocked it with her thumbprint. "After you, dear."

Riley tugged Max after him, and she put her hand up to the collar as it tightened. And as she did so her fingers tapped out a sequence on the surface of the micro hidden in the studs of the chain.

Riley's micro was right there on his wrist, where any command he gave it would be visible and audible to anyone in the room. But no one expected a slave to have such a device. At least, she really hoped they didn't.

Madam Savidge and Angharad followed them in, and Max allowed herself to look up as she heard the door locking behind them.

There were various crates and boxes in the room, and a few cages too. One of them contained something very large and furry that growled softly in its sleep. And two of them, side by side but not touching, contained Orpheus and Justine. They'd both been bound hand and foot, and both were covered in bruises. Orpheus was naked, tied to a chair, and Justine was topless, her wrists chained to the roof of the cage.

"Jesus," Riley said, admiringly. Moving closer, he peered at them both, and held out his hand for the champagne bottle. "Did they whip you?" he asked, voice all mock sympathy. "Did it hurt?"

Orpheus's head came up. His face was as swollen as Max's. "Fuck you," he said.

"No thanks. I might fuck her though," he said, pointing the bottle at Justine. Then he considered the bottle and added, "Maybe with this."

He glanced back at Madam Savidge, who shrugged. "Fine by me, dear."

"I'll kill you," Justine snarled, and Riley's eyelid flickered in a wink.

"You've already tried that."

He turned back to Savidge and Angharad and swigged from the bottle. It was probably only Max who noticed how he changed his grip on it.

"Think I'll have you warm me up first, though. Get on your knees."

He swaggered over to them, and as Angharad went to her knees, Max lifted her hand to the clasp that would undo the chain from around her neck and turn it into a weapon.

And froze, as she saw Savidge watching her intently. Fuck. She turned the gesture into a pained rub of the scar across her chest instead, but the other woman wasn't fooled.

"Angh—" Savidge began, but then Riley smashed the champagne bottle into her face and followed it with his fist. Savidge went down, and Max fumbled with the clasp on her chain.

"Now," she said into the micro, "now, but *not* the south corner. Go north."

She was already turning towards the girl on her knees, but Angharad was quicker, and had Riley's pistol out of its holster. Max tensed, not knowing whether she or Riley would be the target, but then the girl turned the gun on Madam Savidge and fired.

Riley, his fist raised, stared at her. But only for a second, then he grabbed for the gun.

"Take me with you," she said, holding out the gun and weapons belts. Somewhere, a siren sounded, and her eyes went wide with fear. "That's because a gun was fired in here. Her security will be here in seconds. Please! Take me with you."

Riley flicked a glance at Max, then shrugged and nodded and turned to fire on the cages holding Orpheus and Justine. He threw the other belt at Max, who slung it on and backed towards Orpheus's cage with a second pistol aimed at Angharad.

"Hello, lover," she said, and began dragging Orpheus's chair out of the cage. When it tilted, she saw that the bottom of it had been cut out and by the look of it, someone had been whipping him from beneath.

"Jesus, they're worse than you are," she grunted, and had just got him clear of the cage when the ceiling exploded and a chain link ladder was thrown down. Angharad wasted no time in climbing up it, much to the consternation of Émile at the top of the ladder.

"Keep a gun on her," yelled Riley, dragging a stumbling Justine towards the ladder. He'd cut the ropes at her wrists and ankles and she had to make a visible effort to haul herself up the ladder, but she made it. Riley motioned to Max to go next and moved to cut Orpheus's ropes with his knife, but then they both heard someone hammering at the vault door and exchanged a look.

"Take his arms," said Riley, and Max hooked the chain through them and slung it over her shoulder as she began to climb. Orpheus's weight dragged, and then was lifted as Riley got his shoulder under it and began to climb after her.

"Go, go," Max screamed, and Émile bawled the order on, and just as Madam Savidge's men poured through the vault door, the shuttle lurched away. Max hooked both her arms around the ladder, clinging on for dear life as they swung higher, away from the shots being fired from the eviscerated vault.

"Climb, climb," Riley yelled from beneath her, and she made it another rung, straining with Orpheus's extra weight and the terrifying drop beneath.

"I can't," she gasped, but then the ladder began to rise of its own accord, and she looked up to see Murtaugh and Hide hauling it up into the shuttle.

The relief she felt at crawling onto the cold metal floor of the vehicle almost had her sobbing, but she made herself turn back and help to bring the other two in.

"Fuck me," Murtaugh muttered as Hide pressed the button to close the hatch. They were both wide-eyed at the state of Orpheus, on his side, buck naked and still tied to the chair.

Max made it to her knees and saw Riley, chest heaving, get to his feet. He stood looking down at Orpheus for a moment, as the other man glared up at him.

Then he kicked the captain in his abused balls and watched him cringe and shake in agony.

"Fuck you," he said.

CHAPTER ELEVEN

They made it back to the Eurydice too quickly to do much more than catch their breath. Émile untied Orpheus, who lay panting in a ball on the floor as Petal screamed the shuttle towards the Eurydice in her floating bay. The girl Angharad cowered in a corner under the eye of Riley's pistol. Justine took her brother's jacket to cover her nakedness and sat glowering at everyone.

Then Riley said, "Max. Cubby under the enviro. Disable it."

"What?"

"The incendiary I fixed there. Disable it."

Everyone started shouting, but Max shouldered them aside and prised open the cubby door. The bomb wasn't immediately obvious, but when she forced herself to focus she could see how the wires had been hooked up to a tiny device that was turning red hot and would, before much longer, overheat and fire sparks into the oxygen packs of the enviro unit.

The wires were already orange.

Max reached out, her fingertips burning, and was about to seize them barehanded when Angharad said, "Here," and handed her a strip of fabric torn from her bodice. Gratefully, Max used it to protect herself from the heat as she gently, carefully, moved the wires apart and pushed them back into their correct housings.

The shuttle shook, and her heart nearly stopped, but the wires were protected by that strip of fabric. She finished disabling the makeshift bomb, and closed the housing.

Riley nodded to her, ignoring the death stares from the rest of the crew.

"You sabotaged the shuttle?" Justine said.

Max put her hand on her gun.

"Couldn't take the chance they might leave us," Riley said. He flicked his wrist, with the micro attached to it, and glanced at Max. "I put it into your call sequence."

Max was so impressed she stopped shaking.

A moment later, the shuttle locked onto Eurydice and they all piled out of the airlock. Petal paused only to pull Orpheus to his feet and kiss his cheek, before she ran hell for leather for the cockpit, followed by Justine.

Orpheus gave them all a black look, and limped off towards his quarters. Murtaugh sniggered a bit, but not very much, and followed them all to the communal area of the ship, where Max shoved Angharad into a chair and waited for the jolt of takeoff and the recriminations of the crew.

She didn't let her muscles relax until the ship's docking clamps had released and they were hurtling towards the mesosphere. Then she leaned against the bulkhead in the mess, suddenly unable to stay upright.

Riley, his back to the wall, kept his gun trained on Angharad, but she could see the strain in his face.

"You can put the gun away," the redhead said, raising her palms. "I'm not planning anything."

"So you say," said Max.

"You could have been planted here by Madam Savidge," Riley said.

"Wait, we've got one of Savidge's girls on board?" Murtaugh said, his eyes lighting up.

"I shot her," Angharad said, big green eyes pleading. "I was desperate to get away from her!"

"Handy we were planning an escape attempt then, isn't it?" Max said.

"All right, calm down," Riley said. He glanced around, and Max realised he'd just sort of assumed charge of them all in the absence of Orpheus and Justine. "How about we put Angharad here in the brig, and Max," he added, over the protest Max began to voice, "Max, you can stay with me."

"Oh, like that, is it?" Murtaugh jeered, and they both cut him a look that had him shutting up pretty quickly.

"Sure," she said, stifling a yawn. "Uh. Hope the sickbay's well stocked."

"It is, chérie," Émile said, and she nodded and stumbled after them to reconfigure the lock on the cell door as Angharad was shut in.

Then she followed Riley to his quarters and let herself in to wash quickly while he raided Justine's sickbay. When he came back she was more or less clean and dressed in clean clothes. Well, underclothes at any rate. She was still wearing more than Angharad.

For a moment he stood in the doorway, big and looming, looking down at her with an expression she couldn't read. Then he came in and the door cycled shut behind him.

"I'm sorry," he said.

Max was pulling down the neck of her undershirt and poking at the cuts she'd re-opened on her chest. "What for? Did you get any skinglue? I'm going to be made of this stuff soon."

He held up a tube of it, then gestured for her to sit down so he could apply it to her. There was nowhere to sit but the bed, which was so big it took up most of the small room.

"What for?" he said, sitting beside her and peering at her chest with absolutely none of the interest he'd paid to Angharad. "For the things I said back there. And did. You know I didn't mean them, right?"

"Course," she said. "Gotta tell you though, Primer, you've been holding out on me. Who knew you could act that well?"

He glanced up at her, and when he looked back down he was smiling slightly.

"Who says I was acting? She's a very attractive girl," he said, and grinned as she shoved his shoulder. "You might want to wash your hands," he added. "I can't believe I've had Orpheus's balls up against my neck."

Max laughed so much at that he had to pause in glueing her skin back together. "That makes two of us," she said, and wiped tears from her eyes. "Oh God, Primer, how'd we end up back on this ship again?"

"Yeah, and probably with Madam Savidge's friends in pursuit," he said.

"You think?"

He shrugged as he finished with the last cut and reached for a dressing. "Angharad might have shot her, but did any of us check she was dead?"

Max rubbed at her face, which hurt. Then she tapped the micro she'd fastened back on her wrist and texted Murtaugh. "Did you scan the girl for a tracker chip?"

"No. Sickbay's a bit busy." She could almost see his eyebrows waggling. "I'll do a physical check though."

"Whatever. Just remember she's one of Savidge's girls. We don't know where her loyalties lie."

"Sure. How you doing, Max?"

She shrugged, but his concern was quite nice really. "Surviving."

She swiped the micro into standby and looked down at Riley, who was inspecting the cut on her foot.

"It's not bad," he said. "I'll clean it up, should be fine. Oh," he handed her a tub of something. "For your face."

She touched her cheekbone, then her jaw. "You've got a punch like a freight train, you know that?"

He quirked his eyebrows at that but said nothing. Max watched him as he gently disinfected the cut on her foot and put a dressing on it. The tub of ointment he'd given her was to bring down bruising and numb pain, and right now she felt like bathing in it. Instead she smeared it on her swollen face.

"No wonder you preferred that girl to me," she said gloomily, grateful she couldn't see her reflection.

Riley stood up and shrugged out of his jacket, rolling his shoulders tiredly. "What d'you mean?"

"Well, she doesn't look like the back end of an air crash, does she?" He frowned at bit at that. Max shook her head. "Never mind. D'you want me to take the floor?"

Riley scrubbed his hand over his face, and looked down at her. "Look, the bed's big enough. Promise not to molest me or try to kill me in my sleep and we can probably share it."

"What an invitation," Max said drily. Riley went into the tiny cubbyhole that passed for a bathroom and shut the door.

Max was asleep before he left the shower.

He had no interest in sleeping. The bed might have been big enough for the both of them, but Max's long bare limbs took up too much of it for Riley's liking. His hormones were raging, adrenaline pumping through him, and he knew he had to do something more productive with it than just lie there next to her all night trying to pretend he was unmoved.

Because he was fucking moved. Even a saint would

have been tempted by a woman like Angharad, but all she'd felt like was a kind of warmup. And even thought part of him had wanted to show Max what he could do—

No. You wouldn't. Angharad was a bought and sold whore, and even if he hadn't actually paid her for anything above a table and a drink, she was still a whore and he still had principles, damn them. And Max didn't deserve that kind of treatment.

If he couldn't have her, he shouldn't have anyone. *Control, Riley.*

He dressed silently, left Max sleeping, and went on up to the mess. Émile was there, half-heartedly cooking something in a big pan. "I figure everyone must be hungry," he said.

"Well, we'll all need to eat," Riley said. "Have you taken the girl anything?"

"Not yet." Émile gave him a knowing look. "You seem to be making a habit of collecting them, chér."

"Don't." Riley helped himself to a bowl and leaned against the counter as he ate it. *Your mother would be horrified.* "How's Justine?"

Émile gave a philosophical shrug. "Angry."

"At?"

"Eh. Herself. You. Madam Savidge. Me. The world. You know."

"Good to know I'm in there somewhere."

"Chér, not many people would be happy to know my sister is angry at them."

"I'd get upset if she'd forgotten me," Riley said loftily, and Émile smiled. "How's Orpheus?"

Émile made a so-so motion with his hand. "Comme-çi, comme-ça. He wouldn't let anyone see him, so I had to fix up Justine enough to fly this thing so Petal could go down there."

Riley thought about how he'd felt after Justine had spent the afternoon whipping him, and said, "Er, should she be in charge of a spaceship?"

"Hide is keeping an eye on her. To be honest, chér, she and Petal are the only ones who know what they are doing in the cockpit. Orpheus and I can help out, but…"

"I'll go," said Riley, finishing his stew. "Take Angharad some food, will you? Even if she's a spy we should still feed her."

"You've a soft heart, Primer."

"Tell me about it." As Riley left, he paused and said, "Petal and the captain?"

Émile just shrugged. "They've known each other since childhood. That's really all I know."

Riley grunted, and made his way forward to the cockpit. Hide sat in the copilot's seat, apparently reading something on his tablet, while Justine took the nav, her fingers gripping the heavy-air controls even though they were in space. She wore a thick sweater and had a dressing on her forehead. Her hair was damp.

"Justine," he said, and she looked up warily. Hide, he noticed, never let his hand stray far from his weapon. "You should get some rest."

"Someone has to fly this thing."

"I will." At her expression, he sighed and said, "Service, remember? It's been a while, but I don't suppose things have changed that much."

Her lovely eyes narrowed. "How do I know I can trust you, Primer?"

He stared. "Am I on Music, or did I just save your life?"

"You also rigged a bomb on my shuttle."

"What do you care? If the bomb had gone off, it meant that the crew hadn't come and you'd be dead anyway. I saw that creature in the vault with you. What was it, a tigon or something? Big fucker. Probably bored. It'd enjoy playing with you."

She glared at him. Riley compared it to one of Max's

glares, and found it wanting.

"Don't you play the injured party with me," he said softly. "Don't you fucking dare. Now go and get some rest, and I'll take care of the ship."

She looked up at him mutinously.

"If he was going to kill you he'd have done it by now," Hide rumbled, and they both looked at him in surprise. Justine narrowed her eyes. Riley winked at her.

Justine stood up, carefully, clearly still in pain. She made her way to the door, and Riley called after her, "Oh, I'd avoid Max if I were you. She still might beat the shit out of you."

"She'd try," Justine said.

Riley laughed. "No, she'd succeed. Night, Justine."

Petal had set a course for the Epsilon system, and the ship was running on autopilot. All Riley needed to do was be aware of any obstacles in their path, or anyone who might be chasing them.

He checked the settings, made sure the proximity sensors were at their most sensitive, and sat back in his seat, feet up on the desk.

"I don't really need you babysitting me," he said to Hide.

"Two sets of eyes are better than one."

"Which I'm translating to mean that you and the crew still don't trust me."

Hide just grunted.

Riley was just wondering if he should fetch his own tablet and catch up on the news of the day when Hide said, "She yours now then?"

"What? Who?" Then he caught himself and said, "No one's mine."

"Max. We all know she belongs to you, but she's sleeping in your quarters now. She your girl?"

Riley put his head in his hands.

"'Cos I don't want to tread on no toes," Hide went

on. "Don't want to end up fighting you, Primer."

"Nobody's fighting anybody." Riley paused to consider the truth of this. "Well actually, I reckon Max might still have a score to settle with Orpheus and Justine, but I'm not fighting anybody."

Hide nodded thoughtfully, then said, "Why not?"

"What d'you mean, why not?"

"I mean, if Max was mine I'd fight for her. Little bloody firecracker, that one. Hell of a woman. You really saying you'd share her?"

"You did," Riley pointed out.

Hide smiled nostalgically. "Aye, but that was just for one night. She never made no pretence it was for any longer."

Riley sighed.

"I see that jealousy, there. You can't stop her fucking other people, but you want to, am I right?"

Yes. "It's none of my business—"

"Primer, she's sleeping in your bed. Of course it's your fucking business."

Riley took a deep breath and let it out.

"Me and Murtaugh, we kind of assumed that was why you brought the other girl with you. So you could have Max to yourself."

Riley looked at him, this big hulk of a man who'd had what Riley couldn't, and nearly growled in frustration. "What is it about her? How is it she's got everyone on this ship trying to get into her knickers? I'm half expecting to find Émile in bed with her next."

Hide snorted at that. "You tell me, Primer. I've seen the way you look at her."

Riley felt his cheeks heat. "No you haven't. Have you? What way?"

Hide gave him a knowing look, and Riley felt like banging his head on the console.

"I don't know what it is. I mean, Angharad, who

came on board with us this evening. You saw her, right? Beautiful girl. Very beautiful. Charming, sexy, tits like you wouldn't believe. I know, because I spent half the evening with her rubbing them in my face. And yet I felt...nothing. But one look from Max..."

"Yep," said Hide. "Why're you holding out on yourself, Primer? She wants you."

She's made that abundantly clear. "It's complicated."

"Only if you make it that way." Hide stood up and stretched. "Right. This Angharad of the amazing tits. You got any claim on her?"

"No," Riley said wearily.

"You mind if I have a go?"

"For Christ's sake," Riley muttered. "If she says no, she means no, all right?"

"I ain't a fool," said Hide, and lumbered off.

No, thought Riley, but I might be.

Max woke alone in a strange bed. This was something of an occupational hazard, so it didn't bother her that much, but this time she knew where she was immediately. Riley's quarters were perfectly clean and tidy, and entirely empty of his presence. Literally: she couldn't see anything personal around the place.

She sat up in the large bed that was all to distinguish his room from anyone else's, and looked around. No personal items anywhere, no pictures or holos of loved ones, no keepsakes or ornaments. No, of course Riley wasn't really an ornament kind of person, but...

...he wore those things round his neck. They weren't useful or necessary, and she doubted he was as superstitious as most of the people who wore charms and the like.

Last night, all his possessions and hers had been in a few bags on the floor. While she slept, he appeared to have put all his clothes away, folded nearly in drawers and cupboards. Military precision. Even his boots were lined up perfectly straight.

She shook her head. Must be painful being that straight-laced.

According to her micro it was morning, so she got herself ready for the day and wandered up to the mess, where most of the rest of them were sitting around eating. Conversation dipped as she entered, then resumed, awkwardly, as she helped herself to breakfast. More sedate-like, these days, since Riley really hadn't been kidding about the indigestion.

"Anything occur overnight?" she asked, taking a seat next to Émile.

"Not really. We're still waiting to see what the fallout from last night's escapade is going to be."

She nodded, and looked around the table while she ate. Riley wasn't there, and neither was Petal. Orpheus slouched in his seat, watching her with his narrowed cat eyes. Aside from a few new cuts and bruises, he looked exactly the same as ever.

"Morning Captain," she said, grinning at him. "How you doing today?"

"Fine," he growled.

"Really? Don't need a cushion or anything to sit on?"

"Drop it," Justine snarled. She looked paler than usual, drawn around the eyes.

"Ooh, someone got her tits whipped. Hurts, don't it?"

Justine glowered at her. Max let it roll right over her like a wave, and ate some more food. "Anyone seen Riley?"

"He's in the cockpit," said Émile after a pause. "Sleeping, last I saw."

She rolled her eyes. She'd never met such a stupidly self-denying person in her life.

"And the new girl? Anyone checked on her?"

This time the pause was more awkward.

"What?" Max said, looking around them all.

"Petal's with her," said Émile.

"I see," said Max, who didn't.

"Apparently they're old friends," said Murtaugh, and something in the way he said it pushed a cog into place in Max's brain.

"I *see*," she said.

"If I hadn't got in fast I'd never have got in," said Hide, and Max looked at him, just for a moment seeing herself as she saw Angharad.

"Looks like you've been usurped," Justine said, and Max let her spoon fall into her bowl with an unnecessarily loud clatter. She stood up.

"Look," she said, planting her hands on the table. "I don't like you and you don't like me, although why the fuck that is I don't know. Maybe 'cos I've had a taste of him," she jerked her head at Orpheus, "even when I look like this, and you haven't, even when you look like that. Or maybe you're just a bitch. Now, you've just been beaten and humiliated and that tickles me some, but don't you think for a fucking second that makes us even."

She heard a noise from the door and looked up to see Riley standing there, looking somewhat pained, and shoved back her chair to head in his direction.

Justine looked as if she was going to swipe at Max as she passed, but Orpheus caught her wrist and gave her a look.

"And I ain't finished with you, either," Max told him, and shoved past Riley towards the cockpit.

He followed her a minute or so later, a bowl of food in his hands, and sat down at the nav to eat it, watching her wordlessly the whole time.

"Oh, what, like you didn't kick him in the bollocks yesterday."

Riley said nothing, but his eyes gleamed with

amusement.

"She just really pisses me off."

"No, really?"

"She's so...you know what, she's so beautiful, and she just...like, gets away with it."

Riley looked puzzled. "What, with being beautiful?"

"Yeah. I was only ever a bit pretty and I never got a second's bloody peace from it. Look at Angharad. Face like that, body like that, so of course she's everyone's fuck toy. She's been on this ship ten hours and already Hide's had a go and now Petal's cosying up with her. I mean..."

She'd been flicking through data on the comm console as she ranted, changing the access codes to the camera in the brig. Then her screen and Riley's filled with images of Angharad and Petal, naked and writhing sensuously.

"Jesus!" Riley spluttered through his food. "Bloody warn me next time, will you?"

Max watched them dispassionately. It didn't bother her that Petal had found a new playmate so soon, and it probably wouldn't have bothered her even without that knife to the leg. She could watch the two of them together, and even admire Angharad's technique.

"She really is good."

Riley flicked his screen off and gave her a pissy look.

"What? Professional opinion." Max closed the image and changed the access codes again. Her fingers continued to hover over the screen for a moment.

"What?" Riley said.

"Nothing." She looked at him, then back at her own fingers. "I mean, is that how the crew sees me?"

"Erm." Riley cleared his throat. "Through a camera, you mean?" he said, the joke falling flat.

"Just as...I dunno. As a toy."

He was silent a long time. It took Max longer than it

should have done to get up the courage to look at him.

"Isn't that how you wanted to be seen?" he said eventually.

Was it? She stared at her hands again, the scarred knuckles and torn-down nails, the myriad small marks under the skin from burns and cuts and grazes. They were the hands of a fighter, but that wasn't what she'd been using them for since Riley pulled her off the land train.

"I'm sorry," Riley said. "Shouldn't have said that. It's not how I see you."

"Isn't it?"

"Max. Hey." He wheeled his chair closer to hers and touched her arm. His fingers were warm against her bare skin, the skin rough but the pressure gentle. "I told you from the start you don't have to do anything you don't want to."

"I did want to," she said. "I mean…at least I think I did. It's…"

He waited, big and warm and close, the first man she'd met who wanted her and hadn't tried to take her.

"It's all I know, really," she said. "It's always been fight or flight or fuck for me. Fucking's easier. Usually. Thought it would be here, anyway."

"Seem to recall you had a decent go at fighting when we first brought you on board."

"Did I?"

Riley touched the bridge of his nose, smiling a little, and Max smiled a little back.

"I was unconscious at the time," she reminded him.

"Right. Remind me not to get into a fight with you when you're conscious."

She smiled properly then. "Too bloody right. I'd have you."

"Oh yeah?"

"Yeah."

Riley smiled at her and scooted his chair back to the nav as it pinged. "Just an asteroid on the long-range sensors. Path doesn't coincide with us."

Max nodded, and straightened up in her seat.

"Just for the record," Riley said, not looking up. "I didn't think Angharad was all that."

"Liar."

He shrugged. The tips of his ears were red again. "Not my type."

Max didn't believe him, but she was smiling as she looked back at her screen.

The rest of the day passed without much incident, and although Riley spent it upgrading the Eurydice's weapons array, he had half an eye on the expectation that at any moment he'd have to break up a fight between Max and Justine. From the way the captain eyed Max, he suspected that whatever had been between them both wasn't over, either.

With all that going on, and the prospect of Madam Savidge sending retribution, Riley focused his efforts on the weapons the Prideaux brothers had bestowed upon them. Concentrating on mechanics meant he didn't have to think about Max, or how they were stuck on this ship again, or about that crate of samples that might or might not be related to him.

Petal and Angharad finally emerged, pink and smiling, and Petal told them all Angharad was an old friend of hers from the Golden Butterfly before Madam Savidge seized her for her own.

"Never thought I'd see her again," she said happily.

"You going to vouch for her, then?" Orpheus said.

"Of course. Angharad isn't a spy for Madam Savidge, are you love?"

Angharad looked at them all with her wide green eyes. "What? Is that what you think? I hate that woman.

The things she made me do…"

"You didn't seem that unhappy to me," Riley said, and Max snorted.

"She had me well-trained," Angharad said helplessly. "And, well, forgive me, but you're a lot, um…nicer-looking than most of my customers."

"Yeah," said Petal. "I mean if I did guys I'd totally do you."

"Good to know. Not to change the subject completely now, but where exactly are we headed?"

"Epsilon Decimus. It's not too far and we need to restock. Oh…Max, I implemented that new nav file system. It's working really well. So much more efficient."

"Fantastic," said Max, who still didn't seem to have forgiven Petal for the knife in her calf.

"I was wondering if you wanted to take a look at the rest of the ship's systems?"

Riley watched the two of them carefully. This looked very much like an olive branch.

"S'pose," said Max. She straightened away from the wall where she'd been leaning and said, "Angharad, are you moving in with Petal now?"

"Well, I…er…yes?" said the gorgeous redhead, and Petal beamed.

"So I can have my room back? Ta."

She headed out of the mess, towards the crew quarters, and Riley followed, aware of everyone's eyes on him.

"You don't have to go back to that cell," he said.

"Don't want to impose on you anymore," she said, not looking back.

Okay, this wasn't good. "What's wrong?"

"Nothing. You deserve your space is all. So do I."

"Of course you do. But…"

"What? Did you want to keep me in your room,

Primer?"

He didn't really know how to answer that, so he followed her to his cabin, unlocked it and let her pick up her things. The bed was unmade, her clothes were scattered around and one of the drawers wasn't shut properly. Riley, who'd had Service discipline beaten into him, itched to right it all. But he stood and watched her instead, and when she turned to leave the room, he blocked the doorway with his shoulders.

"What?" Max said.

"Talk to me."

"I am talking. Never stopped talking to you."

"Talk to me about what's wrong. This time yesterday you couldn't wait to get in my bed. You've never stopped flirting with me. Now you're..."

Max rubbed the back of her neck and looked away.

"What's changed?"

Max shrugged. "You didn't want me in your bed. I mean, you slept in the cockpit to avoid me."

"I was trying to be polite," said Riley, which was more or less the story of his life.

She blew out a sigh, and then her brown eyes met his. Just for a moment, and then her gaze skittered away, uncomfortable for the first time since he'd met her. "I just...saw myself like they see me. And I guess I didn't like it."

Right then, he kind of wanted to put his arms around her. "Max. How do you see yourself?"

She looked surprised. "I...never really thought about it."

Riley waited, but nothing else seemed forthcoming. He shrugged, stood back to let her out, and she walked a few paces, then stopped and turned back.

"I see myself as...mine," she said. "Not yours, not theirs. And...that's why I can't stay in your room. 'Cos then that just makes me yours."

Riley nodded. "Good answer."

She smiled at him, and then the ship bleated an alarm and Max threw her things back in Riley's room and bolted after him to the cockpit.

"What is it?"

"Proximity alert," Petal said, focused on the nav. "We're being followed."

"Are you sure?"

"Trail, ion signature, all following our exact path," said Justine at the comm.

"Who is it?" Orpheus said.

"Not sure. ID is masked. Takoba by the looks of it."

Max was already leaning over Justine, fingers flying so fast Riley couldn't even see them.

"Hey!"

"Fuck off," Max mumbled, hardly paying attention. "It's Takoba class, but the ion sig is of a bigger ship."

"It's been modded?" Riley said, craning to see. Justine glared at him and was ignored.

"Yeah. Probably a second engine. Faster. But it's not going as fast as a ship with two ion thrusters..."

"At least a Takoba isn't as manoeuvrable as we are."

"No," Max said, only half paying attention. "It's got like half a dozen IDs. But the one it's broadcasting is... oh fuck."

"What?"

She looked back at him, fearful, as Orpheus leaned over Justine's other side to see. Justine threw her hands up and shoved her chair back out of the way.

"It's the Savidge Beauty," Orpheus said.

Everybody swore.

"How far back?" Riley said.

"Half a day," said Petal. "But they're closing on us."

Max was still searching data. "They have a fuck ton of weapons," she said. "That's why the ion sig is so strong. Half of it's going to the weapons. There's...I can't tell, might be a plasma cannon…"

Riley pushed past Orpheus to see, but the data only made half the sense to him it did to Max. Hell, he knew his ship configurations like the good little Service officer he'd been trained as, but Max was reading raw data and translating it into facts faster than he could think.

"We have one of those. Give me an hour, we'll have two."

"Will we?" Orpheus rasped, shooting him a sideways look.

"We obtained a few upgrades while you were gone," Riley said. "The Prideaux brothers are very invested in the Music you bring them."

"The shuttle has a plasma cannon now," Petal added.

"And we've all got more sidearms than we can carry," rumbled Hide.

Orpheus very nearly raised his eyebrows.

"We weren't totally helpless without you," Émile said.

"Right." Orpheus looked around at them all, crammed into the cockpit, and nodded. "Petal, give me an ETA for Epsilon Decimus and ETC for the Beauty."

"They're both about the same. Seven hours."

"Then that's seven hours to prepare for battle. Primer. You and Max go fit whatever you can to the weapons array. Fit out the shuttle and the HAV's too, if you have time. Émile, stocks and supplies. Make sure the shuttle has plenty of ammo too. Justine, sickbay. We might need it. Murtaugh, Hide, find a way to carry those sidearms. Petal…find us somewhere habitable, but not too close to a settlement and get us the fuck there ASAP. Everyone clear? Go."

CHAPTER TWELVE

They'd just hit atmo when the Beauty caught up with them. She wasn't aptly named, being a bug-like shape with far too many weapons welded on, but she was fast. She screamed out of the sky right behind Eurydice as she made her descent towards a landmass near the equator of Epsilon Decimus, and if it hadn't been for the instability of the planet's upper layers of atmosphere Max knew they'd be under fire already. But only fool loosed a plasma cannon in a stratosphere.

Then they were through it, down to the troposphere, and the land was clearly visible below them as the sun came up.

"Looks like a beautiful day," Riley said beside her, and Max could only admire his chutzpah.

"Yeah. And look at that. Trees, beaches, sea, it's almost a holiday."

"It's just a shame we don't have cocktails."

They were ready for combat, or as ready as anyone ever could be in Max's experience. She'd accepted a certain amount of weaponry and protection from Hide, but there was too much on offer and it had started to weigh her down. Max knew all too well that sometimes in a fight, you just needed to run for it.

Riley had taken on more weapons than she had, including a kind of cutlass someone had rustled up from the armoury.

"Who fights with a sword?" Max had asked as she saw him testing the weight and heft of the blade.

"People who aren't afraid to get up close," he replied, not looking at her.

She'd selected a few extras from the frighteningly complete collection of murderous devices in the armoury, one of which was a set of knuckle-dusters. There was no way of knowing what would happen when they hit the ground, but Max knew she was better in a hand-to-hand fight than farting about with plasma rifles.

"Ready?" Riley said to her now, and Max was more or less lying when she nodded. He grasped her shoulder briefly, and then fired up the Vector's engine as the Eurydice's hold door opened.

Beside them, the brand new Hades containing Orpheus and Hide rose elegantly, then shot out of the hold into the heavy air of Epsilon Decimus. The Vector followed it, and dropped low until it was out of range of the Eurydice's engines.

When Max twisted around she could see the shuttle detaching from the ship and seeming to shoot up into the air. Seconds later, a plasma burst arced out towards the Savidge Beauty as it pursued them.

"That should surprise them," Max said.

Riley grinned as he aimed the Vector down towards the surface, spiralling and changing patterns to make them harder to hit. The plan was to get quickly to the ground, then set up a surface-to-air gun and fire away at the Beauty as she approached. The big cannon, partially assembled behind them, wouldn't take out a light air ship like the Beauty, but it could do some serious damage to her weapons array, if targeted properly.

Right then something green lanced past the window, seemingly centimetres away, making Max jump.

"Stupid," Riley muttered. "Better off targeting the ship." He glanced at Max. "At least we know they're idiots."

She attempted a smile.

"Come on, Max. I know you're a fighter. You got arrested for brawling."

"Sure. But that was on the ground. I've never been in an air fight."

"Interesting," said Riley, sweeping them out over a wide bay, blue waves lapping at white sands on a palm-lined beach. "That's mostly what I've done."

She stared in mounting horror. "Please tell me you can fight hand to hand."

"Probably," he said, and grinned at her. "We'll be fine."

"Oh God, I wish I was with Orpheus," Max moaned.

"No you don't. You'd spend all your time fighting him."

This was true, and the reason why she'd ended up paired with Riley in the first place. "Of the four of us who can fly these things," Riley had said to her, "you're still inclined to attack three of them." She hadn't argued. Petal remained flying the Eurydice, swooping her around in the heavy air as if she were a wheeling bird, whilst Justine, the second best experienced pilot on board, took the shuttle with Murtaugh to fire the cannon.

Max looked back up at the three light air vehicles firing beams of energy at each other, and felt a bit sick.

"We should have stayed in Nassau," she groaned, clutching her safety straps as the Vector zoomed towards the beach.

"Shoulda, woulda, coulda," Riley said, making for a textbook landing on the white sands. But as they approached, something shook the vehicle and it lurched to one side.

"We're hit," said Riley, somewhat unnecessarily. "Fuck. Brace for crash landing."

Max did, every muscle in her body tensing as the HAV spun sideways and dropped several metres, taking her stomach with it. As they headed not for the beach but the jungle behind it, she saw Riley's hand briefly leave the controls and touch one of the pendants around his neck. Maybe there was something he was superstitious about.

Then they hit the ground, the vehicle careening onto its side, smashing into trees and plants and ploughing a furrow into the earth as it lost momentum. A window shattered, showering them with shards of toughened glass. It lasted seconds and felt like hours, and Max found her arm clutched by Riley's strong hand as the Vector screamed its way to a halt.

She kept her eyes on his, tried a tight smile, and saw him clutch that pendant in relief as the Vector finally stopped moving and rocked to a stop up against a large rock, then thudded heavily down on all fours.

"You okay?" Riley said into the sudden silence, and she nodded. "Right. Good. Let's..." he sucked in a deep breath, "let's get that cannon assembled."

They hauled it out of the back of the Vector and set it up on top, bolting the sections into place and aiming it at the sky. The Eurydice was playing a game of cat and mouse with the Savidge Beauty, swooping away from her and playfully firing back, while the shuttle darted in and attacked like an irritating insect.

From the shoreline came a boom as Orpheus's anti-aircraft gun fired at the Beauty. It scored a hit on the underside, where the Takoba class had its weapons array.

"Our turn," Riley said, and Max rested her hand over the trigger as Riley aimed it. "Target set. Fire."

She did, and the recoil nearly knocked her over. Shading her eyes against the brightness of the morning, she watched their missile arc towards the Beauty, scoring a hit close to where Orpheus's gun had attacked her.

"Reload," said Riley, and she chambered another massive round.

They fired three more shots, four coming from Orpheus's gun, and the Savidge Beauty looked like she was beginning to fail. But then something small detached from the back of her, and Riley, squinting up at the ship, swore.

"Is that a shuttle?"

"A HAV, big one. Let's hope it's not armed."

"Yeah, but the people in it will be."

Suddenly, with two targets, the four-pronged attack seemed less effective. Riley continued aiming at the main ship, but Eurydice didn't seem to know what to do. Max realised that whilst Petal was a brilliant pilot, her crew now consisted of Émile and Angharad, who were probably the least combat-experienced people they had. Justine and Murtaugh fared better, continuing to hit the Beauty whilst dodging her HAV. Orpheus fired one more shot at the Beauty, then realising the HAV was untargeted, shifted his aim.

But it was too late. The HAV, bigger than either of Eurydice's heavy-air vehicles, zoomed towards the ground with augmented speed. Trails of fire flew behind it. Even as the Beauty faltered in the air, the HAV was coming right at the beach.

"Change target, change target!" Max screamed, and Riley stared at it for what was probably second but felt like an hour, before he nodded and got behind the autosight.

"Fire," he yelled over the approaching roar of the HAV, and Max did, her arms aching from riding out the recoil.

It was the last shot they got before the HAV plummeted down behind the tree line and their cannon couldn't dip any lower. Max stepped back, drawing her projectile rifle. It was less deadly than the laser pistol she also carried, but better at long range, and it could be reloaded. Laser weapons ran out notoriously quickly without a power pack, and there hadn't been enough to go around.

Riley leapt off the Vector's roof and she followed, waiting. They would come down the furrow left by the crashing vehicle, if they had any sense at all. Half the team would attack Orpheus's gun and the other would come for her and Riley.

Her heart pounded in time with her breath.

"She's falling," Riley murmured, and Max looked up to see the Savidge Beauty turning over like a dying fish and falling gracelessly from the sky.

"She'll hit the sea," Max said.

"Yeah, and probably cause a wave. With any luck it'll drown some of them," Riley said, flashing his white teeth at her.

"Reckon there's any mosasaurs in this sea?" Max said.

"I damn well hope so," he said, as the Savidge Beauty hit the water with an almighty slap and vanished from their sight.

"Think she's sunk?"

"Dunno. Look," he pointed off to their left, where Orpheus's HAV had risen in the air. On top of it, clinging to the cannon, was Hide, firing down at the beach. It was an incredibly risky manoeuvre with a gun not properly mounted and fired at the wrong angle. It was only Hide's strength that kept it up there.

"They're mad!"

"It's that or drowning." They could hear the roar of the wave approaching, but it never came over the top of the beach. What came instead were men, figures in a mismatch of outfits, screaming and waving weaponry. Maybe a dozen of them.

Hide's gun remained aimed at the beach, not targeting the men coming their way. They had their own problems. As did Eurydice and the shuttle, still firing at the sea where the Beauty appeared to still be floating.

"Just you and me, Max," Riley said, shouldering his gun. Max did the same, and as she did began to feel a kind of calm come over her. Riley might be the strategist, he might be the one with all the fancy Service training, but Max knew that next to sex, fighting was the thing she was best at. Maybe even better than sex.

"I've got this," she said, and Riley glanced at her as she started firing.

One man fell, then another, but then they began returning fire and she had to duck behind the Vector for cover. Riley followed, firing like mad at the oncoming men. She heard their screams, war-cries turning to agonised pain, and kept shooting, blindly, until her rifle ran out of ammo and she ducked to reload.

It seemed they hid there forever, ducking and reloading, firing over and over, and then suddenly there was no more ammo and she was down to her laser pistol and knives.

"The hell with this," she snarled, leaping out from the safety of the battered Vector as Riley cried her name. She ignored him, slicing out with the the laser pistol at the first man she saw. It cut him through the arm and the torso, and he went down with a cry. Then they all turned, maybe seven or eight of them, and Max fired her pistol in a wide arc, her teeth bared.

More fell, but not from her weapon. Riley had leapt out from behind the Vector and was firing on them too. They staggered and fell, but regained ground and kept coming. Max realised they were nearly out of ammo too, and she started laughing, dropping the stupid laser pistol and running at them. This was what she understood. Not hiding behind a weapon but running towards danger, meeting it full on and punching it hard in the face.

Her knuckledusters seemed to come as a surprise to the first man she hit, and the knife she had in her other hand certainly did. She thrust it up under his ribs, but he had some kind of body armour on and it didn't go deep enough.

"Fuck you," he spat, through bloodied lips, and Max laughed and punched him again. His right arm was tangled in the straps of his rifle and his left fell under the repeated stabs of her knife. He shoved at her, but Max came back with her knee in his groin, and as he staggered, she thrust the knife down into his neck.

But even as he fell, someone else was there, at her back, and she barely saw his shadow falling before she swung back with her fist, catching him on the jaw. She spun, kicked and whirled her knife around into his face. He fell back, screaming, but not before he dragged her with him. His hand clamped around her wrist, slamming it into the ground at an angle that would have broken it if not for the convict cuff there. Max screamed in fury and reached back economically to drive her fist into his stomach, but he was there with a knife, jabbing up at her, and she lost momentum as she rolled to the side away from it.

He shifted his grip on his knife, which gave her just enough time to figure out his vulnerabilities. If she went for her knee in his groin he'd stab her in the leg. Already the arm under her was trying to pull her off and he was bringing the knife around in a stabbing motion.

But his neck was right there in front of her, and Max launched herself at it, stabbing with her knife and tearing with her teeth. He screamed, his knife thudding down against her back and sliding uselessly off the empty ammo casings on her weapons belt. Feral now, she worried at his jugular like an animal, feeling his hot blood spurt into her mouth, salty and coppery. She roared in triumph.

But he hadn't even stopped twitching when a weight hit her back and the breath was knocked out of her, along with a mouthful of blood. Trying to roll, she saw a knife flash in front of her, darting up towards her throat. Panicked, she grabbed her attacker's wrist and tried to yank him forward over her head, but she couldn't seem to suck in a breath and her hands were slippery with blood.

She wormed like an eel, ducking the blade so it slashed into her ear and scalp instead of her neck, and shoved backward with her foot and elbow at the same time. The man grunted, but didn't let go of the grip he had about her waist. Max bucked her head back sharply, felt the satisfying crunch of bone as her skull broke his nose, and she took advantage of that to twist out of his grip and shove him up against a half-uprooted tree.

But the bastard was quick and he was armed, and he halted her turn, jamming his hand into her neck and slamming them both sideways against the tree. The bark tore into her left arm and she raised her right, still gripping its knife tightly.

"Fucking cunt," he grunted through bloodied teeth, and this time it was his skull that hit her nose. Max bellowed with the pain of it and struck blindly with her knife.

Then a whoosh of air came from above and a sword hacked into the top of her attacker's head, narrowly missing Max.

The body jolted forward onto her as Riley shoved with his foot and tugged back his sword. His teeth were red with blood, his eyes bright white against the mud and gore on his face. But the relief was short-lived, as another man rushed Riley's back, a wicked blade raised to strike just as Riley's had done.

"Behind you," Max gasped, or tried to. There was no air in her lungs. But Riley must have seen her face, because he jinked to one side and the killing blow fell on his right shoulder, biting so deep Max could almost feel the pain herself.

Riley simply swivelled the cutlass in his left hand and stabbed backwards with it, impaling his attacker, then he spun and sliced into him with the knife in his right hand.

The deep cut in his shoulder didn't even seem to have registered.

Max, struggling for breath, watched in horror as Riley turned back to the two remaining men, his fist already outstretched with the knife blade clenched in it. He didn't need to stab. His fist smashed into one man's face, once, twice, and then he stabbed down into what was left. Without looking, his left arm swung back in a wide arc, catching the last man across the chest. It wasn't enough to kill him, but it bought Riley time to finish off the man with the ruined face.

Two punches, and the guy only had half a skull left. Max watched in horrified fascination as Riley turned on the last man, his lips peeled back in a snarl, as unstoppable as a land train. The man charged him, and Riley simply drove his fist forward into the guy's face as his sword arm came up and stabbed, again and again. She watched him drive the man backwards, against the edge of the ravine the Vector had created, stabbing and punching until all that was left was a bloody mess.

Max clung to the tree, unable to move, unable to breathe, unable to believe what she was seeing.

Finally, Riley lifted his head, like a lion from a kill, and turned his blood-red visage in her direction. Max gripped her knife so hard it hurt, her whole hand shaking as he approached. His eyes, stark white against his face, never left her.

"Max," he said, lifting one bloodied hand to her. His sword clattered to the ground and he grasped her jaw, tilting it up towards him. "Max..."

His grip gentled, his palm flattening over her cheek, and Max dropped her knife, her hand going to his neck, the back of his head, both of them wet with blood as he kissed her.

Suddenly she needed to touch all of him, her fingers clutching into his scalp, her body arching against him. His mouth was harsh, demanding, tongue invading. Max took it all and gave back as good as she got.

His hands were everywhere, grasping at her body, her breast, gripping her thigh as she hitched it over his hip and moaned to feel him where she wanted him. His fingers slid under the edge of her shorts and she made a guttural sound as he touched her. Then he was tearing at her belt, tugging down her shorts and freeing himself and with a thrust he was inside her.

Shocked, she stared up at him, this man she knew and didn't know, and then his mouth was on hers again as he fucked her, hard and fast. Her bare thigh slid over his leg, his hip, and she hitched herself higher, wrapping both legs around him and holding on for dear life as he hammered her against the tree. His lips left hers, found her neck and bit into her, just painful enough to make her gasp and clutch him tighter.

It was fast and brutal, and it made a beast of Max, her fingers digging into his scalp and his shoulder, sliding in his blood and that of the men he'd killed, she'd killed. Primal and unstoppable, they rutted like animals and she revelled in the glory of it. And when she shuddered out her climax, shouting wordlessly, he was right there with her.

She gripped him tight as the aftershocks ran through her, gasping for breath with his face pressed against her neck.

And when he finally lifted his head to look at her, she leaned in for a kiss and he suddenly jolted back, away from her.

"Riley?"

He stumbled back, and as Max tried to hold onto him he pushed her limbs back, shoved her feet to the ground, tripped over his own feet in his haste to retreat.

"Oh Jesus," he was whispering, his eyes wide with white and blue in his dark red face as he fumbled his clothes back into order. "Oh Jesus, Max."

Hardly able to comprehend what had just happened, Max reached for him, but he just shook his head and stumbled away, gaining speed as he leapt over corpses and bolted from the furrow.

Max stood alone, looked around at the devastation surrounding her, and touched her trembling hands to her bruised lips.

"Well, fuck," she said.

She made herself act rationally, righting her clothes and grabbing Riley's sword to check all their attackers were really dead. Some of them were so dead she couldn't make out their features. Her stomach rebelled as she checked them methodically for anything of use, collected their weapons and stored them in the crashed Vector, then climbed out of the furrow using what felt like the last of her strength.

She kept one hand on the laser pistol she'd retrieved and the other on the hilt of the cutlass she'd jammed into her belt, and forced herself to put one foot in front of the other as she made her way back to the beach. There were more bodies there, the men they'd gunned down. One was still moving, and Max aimed her laser pistol at it and fired until it stopped twitching. As she passed the corpse she saw it had been a woman. Probably quite a few of them had been.

The sky was empty of either the Eurydice or her shuttle, and as Max approached the tree line she could see what remained of the Savidge Beauty slowly disappearing beneath the sea. A few people were trying to swim away from it, but none of them got far before someone on the beach shot them down. Before long, the corpses were dragged down by some giant fish or other.

Mosasaurs, thought Max, and wondered if this was what delirium felt like.

She peered in the direction of the shooter, and saw Murtaugh standing with a long-range rifle, grinning as he picked off the survivors. Behind him, parked at a rakish angle on the sloping beach, was Eurydice, the shuttle beside her and Orpheus's Hades not far away. The anti-aircraft cannon lay on its side in the sand, near a heap of bodies Émile and Angharad were compiling. Approaching the groove in the earth closer to the shoreline were Orpheus and Petal, both carrying large weapons.

Justine stood picking at something in Hide's arm while he pretended that it didn't hurt him. "If you will go standing on the top of a moving HAV," she chided, and broke off as she followed his gaze towards Max.

"She's here," Justine called, and Orpheus and Petal changed course as they saw her.

Max waved somewhat half-heartedly, gaze darting about for the one figure she couldn't see.

Petal came loping up, fresh as a daisy. "Any survivors?"

Max shook her head.

"Max!" Émile waved at her and came over, clearly happy to escape the pile of bodies for a while. "You all right, chérie?"

She nodded, although it felt like a lie. "Have you seen Riley?"

"Sure. Ran through here like a bat out of hell five, ten

minutes ago," Émile said.

"What the fuck did you do to him?" said Justine, looking Max over like she smelled bad. Which she probably did.

She stared at them, trying to work it out. Her head felt like an anvil.

"Well," she said. "I had sex with him."

Émile burst out laughing. Petal exchanged a glance with Angharad, and then held out a roll of money.

"Told you," said the redhead, tucking it into her bodice.

"Most men don't react like that after you fuck them," said Orpheus, eyeing Max.

"No," she said, adjusting the sword at her hip. "Which way did he go?"

"You sure you want to follow him, chérie?"

"Yeah," said Max. "Which way?"

Justine jerked her head at a stream emptying itself onto the beach. "That way. The west side of the water. He looked fucking feral."

"I bet," said Max. "You got a medkit?"

One was procured for her, in a backpack Max slung on over the empty ammo belts. Justine offered, somewhat half-heartedly, to come with her, but Max shook her head.

"Better if I go alone. He's…I dunno."

"I think you fucked all the sense out of him," Murtaugh laughed, and Max turned, tiredly rolling her shoulders, and kicked him hard in the groin.

"The fuck?" he roared, staggering backwards.

"There's eight dead men by that HAV," Max said, pointing back the way she'd come. "And I only killed two of them. Next time you punch a man's skull into a fucking pancake, come and tell me how much sense you have left, all right?"

Then she turned, and began to trudge toward the

stream.

She wasn't sure how far she walked. The land behind the beach quickly turned into tropical forest, trees and bushes all alive with birds and insects. The floral life was abundant, huge bright flowers drugging the air with their scent, and Max was grateful for its cover from the burning sun.

She thought about sending Riley a text, but decided against it. If he knew she was coming he might bolt. Instead, she configured her micro to track his down. She hardly needed it, with the flattened path through the jungle he'd left behind, but without it she thought she might have walked forever. Instead she found his signal staying in place up ahead, where she could hear rushing water.

"If he's drowned himself I'll fucking kill him," she muttered as she approached a waterfall. It wasn't particularly tall or wide, but it formed a curtain over a cave, from where his signal was broadcasting.

Taking a deep breath, Max climbed the rocks and ducked behind the water.

The light was eerie here, dappled and filtered through the constantly moving water. The cave was darker at one end, but as her eyes adjusted Max could see something moving.

"Now, if it turns out you're some wild beast and you've just eaten Riley, I'm going to be really pissed off," she said, unholstering the laser pistol and aiming it as she approached, slowly.

"I am a wild beast," the shadows whispered hoarsely, and Max let out her breath in one long go.

"Riley. Thank God." She lowered the pistol, but didn't holster it. She kept moving forward, his form coming gradually into view.

"You shouldn't be here," he said, as she made him out, huddled against the rock wall.

"Yeah, and why's that?"

"It's not safe. I'm not safe."

He looked up at her, his eyes about all she could make out in the gloom. His face was caked with dried blood, but she didn't imagine she looked much better.

"Not safe from who?"

"You're not safe," he said, eyes big and pleading. "From me."

Max looked him over, curled wretchedly against the wall with his arms wrapped around his knees. The closer she looked, the more she could see. Like the cuts on his face and scalp, the terrible gaping wound on his shoulder, and the tracks of tears around his eyes.

"Oh Riley," she sighed, holstering the gun and dropping to her haunches in front of him. "Course I am. Look at you."

He swiped at his face with his hand. "You should leave."

"Not gonna do that." She unstrapped the pack with the medkit and set it down with relief, nodding towards the dreadful cut on his shoulder. "That needs some work."

She moved closer, and he flinched like a wounded animal.

"We won the fight, by the way. The Savidge Beauty is sinking into the bay, which no doubt the local authorities will be delighted about, and Murtaugh is picking off survivors with great relish."

"Any casualties?" He whispered it without looking at her.

"Not on our side, no. The plan worked. Apart from the part where we got shot down and had to fight our way out. I'd say we make a great team," she said, almost close enough to touch him now, "except that you did most of the work. Mind you, I would like to point out that I tore out a man's jugular with my teeth, which I reckon ought to give me extra points."

Riley's white-eyed gaze flickered over her. He swallowed.

"I know, and me so innocent-looking," Max said.

He looked up at her warily. "You come to do that to me?"

"No, Riley." She touched his arm, felt the fabric sodden with blood, felt him flinch away. "I've come to help."

"I'd deserve it."

She sat back on her haunches and swiped the sweat from her brow with the back of her arm. It stung, and she realised there was a cut there. There were probably more than she realised.

"Why in the name of all that is holy would you deserve to have your throat ripped out by me?"

Riley's gaze skittered away. He was trembling. "Because…because…what I did in that gully. To you. It was…inexcusable. I don't know what came over me."

Max found laughter bubbling up in her throat. "Not to put too fine a point on it, Riley, but I did."

He looked at her uncomprehendingly.

"You saved my life, I saved yours, we fucked. By the way," her gaze darted downwards, "I'm very glad to find you're in proportion."

Riley stared. "How can you joke about it?"

"'Cos you're taking it so seriously, that's how."

"I raped you," he whispered brokenly.

At that Max looked up sharply. "So that's it," she said. "Oh, sweet Jesus. Riley, honey, you didn't rape me. Trust me, I know rape and that wasn't it. Just…next time a bit gentler, yeah?"

"But I…it was…"

She waited, watching his throat work as he tried to find the words. Poor thing was in shock. That couldn't possibly have been his first time, could it?

"…brutal," he finished eventually, voice breaking, and Max reached out gently to stroke his head. If his hair had been any longer it would have been matted with gore.

Fresh tears were leaking from his eyes. Max stroked her hand down to the back of his neck, pulled his resisting body closer, and wrapped her arms around him.

"Just because it was brutal doesn't mean it was bad," she said. "It was what we both needed. What I wanted. You've got nothing to feel bad about."

Slowly, she felt him give against her, his rigid body yielding until he could look up at her.

"But," he began. "I don't know if I could have stopped. If you'd said no. If I'd even have noticed."

His eyes, stark white against his face, never leaving her. The way his grip had gentled on her face. He might have been beside himself in that gully, but he was still Riley on the inside. The same Riley who'd felt so bad about punching her even when she'd told him to.

"Well," she said. "You're a fucking berserker, but you never hurt me. And besides, I promise you, Primer, if I'd thought you were going to, I'd have ripped your fucking balls off."

His eyes were so blue, so frightened. For a man who held himself in such rigid control, he must be terrified right now.

"Trust me on this," she whispered, and Riley gave a great shudder and pressed himself into her arms.

Max leaned her cheek against his head and held him like that for a while, until the shaking stopped, and Riley looked up and said, "I'm a fucking idiot, aren't I?"

She kissed his temple and said, "Not really. Most people aren't really equipped to deal with this shit."

He looked at her with those big blue eyes so full of sorrow, and her heart grew a couple of sizes.

"I don't deserve you," he said.

"Course you don't deserve me, Primer," Max said breezily, shaking away the sentiment and getting to her feet. "But I'm probably exactly what you need. Come on, on your feet, soldier. You're a bloody mess and there is, for once, an overabundance of water hereabouts."

He let her pull him to his feet, grimacing in pain at the tear in his shoulder, and Max flipped open the medkit. There was a water safety tester there, and she held it under the running water until it beeped to tell her it was safe. No sense in risking it and finding out it was secretly sulphuric acid or full of cattle dung.

Then she led Riley down the rocks to the edge of the waterfall pool and helped him out of his clothes, dipping them into a shallow pool at the edge of the water. It might help to clean them a bit, she reasoned, stripping off her own, smiling at the way he avoided her nakedness.

"Come on," she said, leading him down into the water, which was cool and clear and a blessed relief after the heat and sweat and blood of the morning. It seemed to wake Riley up a bit, and he washed himself more or less clean whilst darting shy looks at her.

Christ, you're adorable, Max thought, swimming closer and splashing him.

"Hey!"

"Like you're not wet already."

He splashed her back, and Max laughed and sent more water at him.

"I'm gonna get you for that," he said, and she shrieked and tumbled back into the water as he came after her, catching her in his arms. She splashed him again and he laughed, and then her bare leg brushed his hip and her breasts touched his chest, and she kissed him, tasting the smile on his lips.

He was hesitant, stilling against her, and then he kissed her back, slowly at first and then with more passion. Her body slid against his, all that lovely nakedness hers to enjoy, and she sighed and relaxed into his kiss as the water rained down beside them.

It was only when her arm, winding around his neck, caught the deep cut on his shoulder that he flinched and broke the kiss.

"Shit," she winced. "Sorry."

"It's okay." He looked down at her, his hands at her waist under the water, fingers gently caressing, and started to say something twice before he came out with, "You mentioned a next time?"

She smiled and brushed her lips up to his ear, whispering, "Definitely a next time. But first," she said, stepping back, and he reluctantly released her. "I need to look at that cut."

They sat naked on rocks by the waterfall, skin drying in the heat of the day. Max found a thin blanket rolled in the bottom of the backpack and spread it out on the hot stone, "because there are some places you really don't want to get burned," while she tended to the gash on his shoulder.

Max, as ever, seemed totally unselfconscious about her nudity. Riley, who'd been raised in the strict belief that a gentleman was half naked without a cravat, tried not to let his discomfort show.

From the looks Max kept giving him, she wasn't fooled.

"Your clothes are soaked through," she said. "If you think wet bloody rags are better than being naked, be my guest. But I've gotta tell you, I ain't complaining about the view."

Riley's cheeks heated.

"You are adorable when you blush," she said.

"I'm not blushing. It's the heat. I have fair skin."

"Yeah, sure." She finished injecting anaesthetic into

the wound—the needle having disappeared deeper than Riley liked to think about—and busied herself with a needle and thread. That in itself was a bad sign: he'd rarely had an injury too deep for skinglue.

"Primer?"

He sighed. They'd killed together and survived together and even had sex together, and she was still calling him Primer.

He waited, until she clucked her tongue and tried again.

"Riley?"

He smiled. "Yep?"

"Where you come from...does everyone look like you?"

He cut her a look. "My family looks like me. Not the whole planet."

"I mean...are there so many people so...yellow?"

At that he laughed. "Yellow?"

She gestured to her buzzcut hair, he touched his, and then rolled his eyes so hard they nearly fell out.

"Blond, Max. I know you know that."

"And blue eyes, too."

"What are you getting at?"

She seemed to be thinking about how to say it, then just said, "I've never seen someone as white as you."

Riley laughed, and realised she was serious. "And here's me thinking I have a tan. You know, there are people on Sigma Prime even whiter than me."

"You're fucking with me."

"Swear to god. Even redheads. Some of them have freckles."

She snorted. "Don't make stuff up."

"Well, look at Angharad."

"Yeah, but...I figured that hair ain't natural, and she has been living on a planet without sunlight." She bent her head to his shoulder and dipped the curved needle

225

deep into the cut. "Hold still."

Riley looked down at her as she concentrated on sewing a deep layer of stitches. True, he was more fair-skinned than most, especially once you left the rarified enclaves of Sigma Prime. Where he came from, people clung ferociously to their bloodlines, assessing future mates on their probability of creating suitably complexioned children. He knew families who proudly traced their ancestry to very specific areas of what used to be called Earth, going to greater and greater extremes to preserve a skintone the colour of night, or an eye without an epicanthic fold.

Max would probably have given them a collective heart attack.

"I'll take you there some day," Riley said, and Max snorted.

"No you won't. You wouldn't have the nerve."

"Why?"

"There's a price on your head, remember?"

His smile faltered. "Sure. Never mind."

"Besides, look at me. I'm like them dogs, you know. The ones you can't tell what breed they are."

"Don't say that."

She looked up. "I am what I am," she said without rancour. "You got enough racial purity to be naturally blond. I got so little I'm the colour of mud."

"Yeah, but…who cares, really? I never understood why it was important." Max was tall, strong, smart and lethal. Riley would have to go a long way down his list of descriptions for her before he started thinking about skintone.

"That's cos no one ever treated you as unimportant because of the way you look. C'mon, Riley, you're like the end result of a breeding programme to create the best humanity has to offer."

Is that how you really see me? A thing created for a

purpose?

Max appeared to hear what he hadn't said, because she looked up and winced. "Sorry."

"Can we change the subject?"

She looked back down at his shoulder, where the first layer of stitches still wasn't complete. "You could always tell me what got you so fucked up about sex."

"Christ. What is, this, Pick On Riley Day?"

"Maybe it's Try To Understand Riley Day. Let me put it this way," Max said, rethreading the needle. "I'd quite like to fuck you again, but I need to know if you're going to run away that time too."

"I won't."

"Why not?"

"Because..." Oh hell, he was going to have to tell her. "Because you want to be with me."

She frowned. "Um...?"

Riley took a deep breath and let it out again. It hurt. Everything hurt, apart from his shoulder, and that was probably going to give him hell when the anaesthetic wore off.

"You asked me for her name. That day at the Brazen Head."

Her gaze darted to his, wary.

"The girl who fucked me over. I might as well tell you."

She gave him an assessing look. "You don't have to," she said, in tones that made it clear he'd never hear the end of it if he didn't.

"Yeah. I do." He blew out a sigh as she bent to his shoulder again. It was easier when she wasn't looking at him.

"Look, you have to understand a few things about Sigma Prime. The area of it I came from, anyway. The things that are considered important are...well, kind of bizarre, to be honest. Manners. Rules. Bloodlines. I can tell you eighteen generations of my ancestors' names, and which part of old Earth they came from, and even the names of the properties they held there. It's true," he said when she looked up disbelievingly.

"But...why?"

"Dunno. It's just how I was raised. Bloodlines are incredibly important. That racial purity you mentioned," he added. "See, I'm blond and blue-eyed. So my future wife had to match that, so we could have perfect blond, blue-eyed children. Elandra," he said, pushing down the nausea, "was a perfect match. Beautiful. Intelligent. Petite; because I'm so tall, and we had to breed that out, you see."

Max looked bewildered. "Like...with dogs? Or cattle?"

"Exactly. Anyway, she was considered to be quite the catch. Lots of suitors. Every party or ball or dinner I went to, she'd be surrounded by a crowd of men. And my parents had put a lot of effort into me, they wanted to see it pay off, so—"

"Effort?" Max said.

"Yep. Schooling. Training. I spent half my childhood learning which fork to use with which meal, and how to dance, and how to address a president."

Max shook her head in amazement. "You dance?"

"Well, how d'you think I learned to fight? It's just dancing with weapons."

Max appeared to consider this, then she shrugged and nodded.

"Anyway," he said, because he didn't really want to go into a detailed discussion of the finer points of a waltz, "they were determined I would succeed. Now the thing is, I didn't really want to do any of this stuff in the first place. I liked messing around with machines. I didn't really see the point of all the...fripperies. I wasn't even allowed to talk to Elandra until we'd been introduced formally, and even then we were always in company. Had to find something innocuous to talk about. Something suitable. Machines, by the way, were not deemed suitable. None of my interests were. We talked about nothing. It was excruciating. But finally..." he took a deep breath and tried not to remember the details too much, "finally, I got to the stage where I was invited to a house party."

His hands were beginning to shake. Max glanced at them, but said nothing.

"And I knew this was my big opportunity. That I'd never have such a good chance to catch Elandra. So... one night, I waited until everyone else had gone to bed and I...went to her room. I thought I'd declare myself. Maybe even steal a kiss."

"Ooh, a kiss, Primer. Check you out being all racy."

Riley tried to think of a comeback to that, but the nausea was rising again and he had to concentrate on keeping it down. Yes; a kiss. That was all he'd dared hope for, and it still seemed an insurmountable goal.

He could remember it all, despite himself. The creak of the floorboard that was so shockingly loud he thought it would wake up the whole house. The words he'd rehearsed in his head. The agonising wait after he knocked on the door. The musky perfume rising from Elandra's hot skin, revealed by her silken robe. The artful tousling of her hair.

"She let me in. She knew why I was there; after all, you don't go knocking on people's doors in the middle of the night to have a chat about the weather."

Max snorted at that.

"And...I asked if I could kiss her. She said yes, and...well, it got...it went a bit further than I was expecting."

He could still recall the wonder of it, the thrill of the realisation that it was actually happening. The softness of her hair, the satin of her skin, the fullness of her breasts as she pressed her body against his. The lavender water scenting the sheets.

"You fucked her?" Max said, yanking him back to the present.

"I...we...yes. And it was..."

"Magical, marvellous, you were in love, hearts and flowers," Max said briskly. "Was it your first time?"

He nodded.

"Bless. How old were you?"

"Why is that important?"

She shrugged. "Just wondered."

He'd been twenty-two. Fresh out of university, staring into a future with a promising career in engineering and a beautiful woman by his side.

"And the next day," Riley began, and the bile rose in his throat. He started again. "The next day I went to her father and asked for her hand."

"Her hand?"

"In marriage. I asked to marry her."

Sweat broke out on his brow, and it wasn't because of the sun. He felt sick remembering it.

Max finished that layer of stitches and sat back, squinting up at him. "Take it that didn't go well?"

Riley let out a bark of laughter. "No. I think it's safe to say nothing has ever gone worse. I did it publicly. I was so damn sure of myself." Smug. Cocksure, that was the word. "I thought he'd say yes, that she'd say yes, that everything would be..."

He stared out at the jungle, focusing on one bright red flower. It was glossy and bright, something that would never have been allowed in Elandra's father's house.

"She said no," he managed.

Max waved her hand in a 'tell me more' gesture. "Don't tell me all this is because someone once turned you down?"

He shook his head, breathing hard. "I took it badly," he said, which was something of an understatement. "I demanded to know why. I started…shouting, and people looked over, and then I…I…"

His throat closed over. Max watched him, frowning.

"You…what? Screamed abuse at them? Started punching people? Went mad like you did in the gully and massacred everyone?"

He flinched. "Worse. I told everyone we'd slept together." It came out as a whisper. "I said we'd lain together like man and wife and now we must become man and wife."

"So? I mean, nice choice of language there, Primer, but—"

"But what? Max, I just told everyone we'd had sex." She raised her palms uncomprehendingly, and he struggled to explain. "In a world where you don't speak to someone without a formal introduction and don't dance together until you've known each other a month and everyone wears gloves and nobody even touches each other with bare skin? Where men and women are never alone together unless they're actually married? Where sex was something I had to learn about from books, because nobody ever talked about it? And then I went and yelled it to the entire house party?"

"I can see how that would've been a bit awkward," she conceded.

"Awkward?" Riley shook his head at the understatement. "It was the stupidest thing I could have done. I felt like a fool, but I'd underestimated just how far Elandra would go to protect her reputation."

He felt hot and cold all over. He was going to be sick. Max peered worriedly at him and hurriedly filled a cup with water. Riley spilled half of it on himself, his hands shaking terribly.

"What did she do?" Max asked softly.

"She said…she said I'd forced her," he managed. "That I'd gone to her room and made her lie with me. She said I'd raped her."

"Did you?"

His head jerked round so fast it hurt. "What kind of question is that? Of course I didn't! She let me in, she said I could kiss her, I asked…"

"Yeah, well, kissing isn't sex," Max said.

"Whose bloody side are you on?"

"Calm down." Her hand touched his arm. "I'm just playing devil's advocate. Are you sure she actually wanted it at the time?"

"Yes." He set down the cup, hands still shaking. "I'd stake my life on it. She was the one who…she took it further. Max, you don't know how often I've gone over and over it in my mind. Did I get it wrong, did I misunderstand? Misread her signals?" He made himself drink a bit more water, trying to banish the memory of the shouting, the screaming, the panic and shame.

What gives you the right, boy?

"She said I was so big and I overpowered her. She was crying and everyone was shouting. Her father hit me. I thought I deserved it."

"Didn't you tell people the truth?"

"Well yeah, of course, I tried…but no one listened. People I'd known my whole life were condemning me. They all believed Elandra. And mud sticks. Even if I could conclusively prove it, which of course I couldn't… my reputation was destroyed. And reputation is everything on Sigma fucking Prime."

Max sat back. "So what did you do?"

He shrugged. "Got very, very drunk. Woke up on a Service transport."

Understanding came over her face. "I see."

"Yeah." Riley took a deep breath and let it out. Now he'd told her, he felt a bit better.

"That's why you're so obsessed with consent."

He nearly laughed at that. "I suppose that might have something to do with it."

Max cleaned her hands and picked up the needle again. "What d'you think it was, then? That she just changed her mind? Or maybe you were a lousy lay and she didn't want to be stuck with you," she said, eyebrows waggling.

"Cheers, thanks for that," Riley said, saluting her with the empty water cup. "I don't know what her problem was. For all I know she'd done this to half a dozen other men."

"Was she a virgin, too?"

"How the hell should I know? I wasn't exactly drowning in experience."

"S'pose not."

"Although," he hesitated, "I've kind of wondered if...maybe she wasn't. With a bit of hindsight, I've wondered if she, um, maybe..."

"Had shagged a load of other blokes on the quiet and panicked when she thought she might be found out?"

Riley met her knowing gaze. He felt his cheeks heat. "Well, yes."

"Bitch. I mean, she can fuck who she likes, but that's a shitty thing to do. I mean...do you think she knew, really *knew* what she was accusing you of?"

"What do you mean?"

Her face went dark for moment. "If she knew what rape really was. If she understood what a violation it is. If she had any comprehension, any at all, of what a terrible thing she'd accused you of. 'Cos it's not something you can brush off lightly. It ain't something you can just...get over."

She stopped abruptly, her fingers flexing, and looked away. Riley both wanted to ask and really didn't.

Max made another stitch and tied it off, then said,

"You have been with other women since, right?"

"One or two. My CO on the Valiant made a play I couldn't refuse. Like, literally couldn't. She threatened to have me demoted."

Max frowned up at him. "She made you fuck her?"

Riley shrugged. "I'm aware of the irony."

"Christ. And men? You said you'd tried it with men."

"Yeah. Wasn't having any luck with women."

"And?"

He shrugged. "It was okay, I guess. Not really my thing."

Max finished another stitch. "What is your thing?"

You. You're my thing. "Don't really know."

She flashed a smile at him. "Won't we have fun finding out?"

Riley laughed at that, relief overwhelming him. She was so brazen. His former friends and family would have a collective apoplexy if they met her. He tried to imagine Elandra kneeling there naked, sewing up a wound he'd received trying to defend her. She'd probably rather let him die than get her hands so dirty.

"There," Max said after a while, finishing the second row of stitches and applying skinglue over the top. "It ain't fancy embroidery but it's a damn sight more useful."

Riley craned his neck to see. The row of stitches stuck up, black against his pale skin. Max applied a dressing and looked him over. "What next?"

He didn't even know. If Max hadn't told him about that cut he wasn't sure he'd have even noticed it.

"Your leg, I think," she said, and he looked down to see a wound on his thigh that he really didn't remember getting. Max prepared the anaesthetic and got to work again. He'd have to return the favour, when his hands stopped shaking. That cut on her scalp looked nasty and there was an evil graze on her left shoulder where that bastard had slammed her up against the tree.

That was when he'd really started seeing red. After that…it had all become something of a blur.

"What a state we're both in," he said softly, and she looked up.

"We're alive, Riley. The rest of it is just cosmetic."

He smiled at that, and she went back to sewing up his leg.

"Oh, and Riley?"

"Yeah?"

"She didn't screw you over because you're a lousy lay. Trust me on this."

And Riley laughed.

CHAPTER THIRTEEN

He woke to the sound of water and the ache the anaesthetic had left behind. According to his micro, he'd been asleep for hours, there in the cave behind the waterfall. Max had laid out the thin blanket and fallen asleep almost instantly, while he lay beside her, marvelling.

He'd fixed up the cut that notched into her ear and ran across her scalp. A nasty wound. Any deeper and she'd have been in real trouble. "Good job I don't care about being pretty," she'd said, and he hadn't known what to say.

Max wasn't pretty. She was glorious. 'Pretty' wouldn't have fought off those murderous bastards Madam Savidge sent. 'Pretty' wouldn't have tracked him down in the middle of the jungle, out of his mind with fear and rage. 'Pretty' wouldn't have talked him off a ledge.

Max was a warrior, her body lean and scarred, her attitude fearless. What good was 'pretty' compared with that?

Her micro buzzed, and she stirred sleepily, grunting

KATE JOHNSON

as it buzzed again. "Yeah?" she said, yawning, and Émile's face appeared on the small screen.

"Did you find him?"

"Oh. Yeah. Sorry. Forgot to tell you."

She swivelled the screen so it was facing Riley, who tried not blush.

"I see. You both okay?"

"Yeah. Mostly. D'you need us back there?"

"Not at present. We're just clearing up, although there will be some repair work to do and we could use you for that. Also we captured one of the survivors alive. You probably don't want to be around for what Orpheus is doing to him."

Max made a face. "No. Look, we'll be back sometime soon. Need some rest."

Émile's chuckle was pure filth. "Don't wear him out, chérie."

Max winked at him and ended the call. Then she sat up, and froze.

"Ow," she said, her eyes going wide. "Jesus. Fuck. There's not a bit of me doesn't hurt."

"Yep," said Riley. "Feel like I've been hit by a train."

"Christ on a bike." She stretched gingerly. "Been a while since I've been in a fight like that."

Riley watched her move, admiring her long lean muscles, and she glanced down at him, one eyebrow raised.

"Sorry. Didn't mean to stare."

"Stare all you like. I mean I'm doing quite a lot of perving from here, too."

She swung down on top of him, her strong body covering his, and kissed his mouth. Her fingers gently brushed his sore shoulder, slid over his arm, reached down for his hand and placed it on her breast.

"You know that next time we were talking about?" she breathed against his lips. Riley nodded, daring to let himself hope. "How about now?"

"Now sounds good," he said very quickly, and she laughed softly and kissed him again.

Her hands were everywhere, caressing him, and it was all he could do to keep up. She gently kissed a small cut on his cheek, then moved down, feathering delicate kisses over his face and neck. Her teeth grazed his skin, then she lapped at the small sting she'd created. When she reached his nipple and sucked on it, Riley couldn't help groaning.

"You like that?" She sat up and looked down at him, her fingers delicately tracing the thick scar on his chest he'd made such a mess of fixing up. "Christ, look at you. You're like a feast."

Riley, who'd spent most of his life being told he was too tall, too broad, too big, shook his head. The women of Sigma Prime wanted slender, elegant men, with delicate hands and smooth, unblemished skin, not giants too big to dance with who hadn't shaved in days and had ugly, badly mended scars.

"Shut up," said Max, despite him saying nothing, and leaned down to rub herself against him, shameless as a kitten. "You're fucking gorgeous." She bit her lip, and then she bit his, and murmured, "What do you want?"

"You," Riley said honestly.

Max laughed, a low dirty chuckle, and smoothed her hands over his chest. "What do you want to do with me?"

Everything. God, it was too much. Riley slid his hands slowly up her thighs, over her hips, circled her waist. She looked down at his progress, her small breasts moving as she breathed. Riley caressed his way up her back, over the healing scars from Justine's whip, and gently pulled her down to lie against him, finding her mouth with his and enjoying it. His fingers feathered over the soft stubble at her scalp, and he smiled as she touched him the same way.

Max rolled to her side, tugging him with her, sliding her leg over his and undulating against him. She was wet down there, hot and slick against his hip, and Riley's hands clenched with the desire to touch her. But before he could make a move she was ahead of him, taking his right hand and guiding it between her legs.

"Yes," she murmured, her eyes closing as he touched her, followed her direction, explored her with his fingertips. "Oh yes. Oh, Riley…"

She grasped the back of his head and kissed him, open-mouthed and dirty, laughing and gasping as he stroked her. Then the hand guiding his between her legs left him to his own devices and grasped his hot, hard length.

Christ, nothing had ever felt this good. Lying with her, stroking and kissing, feeling her gasp and shudder in his arms. Those fast fingers he'd admired so much when she worked could be slow, too, delicate and just as clever. It was almost too much.

"Max," he breathed, as her teeth delicately worried at his lip. "I want to—to kiss you."

"You are kissing me," she sighed against his lips.

"No. Yes. Here," he said, and flexed his fingers inside her.

Max moaned. "Oh yes. Please."

He made himself slow down, taking the time to kiss his way down her body, following the line of the scar across her chest that had been such torture to tend to. How did one remain a gentleman when one was manhandling someone's breast?

He laughed softly to himself as he kissed her nipple. As if Max had ever cared about him being a gentleman.

The muscles in her stomach jumped and tensed as he tasted her bellybutton, her hip, her thigh. The curved, puckered scar high up on the inside of her leg. Her breath came in shallow pants even before he put his mouth where he wanted it to be, and when he did she let out low, guttural moan.

"You might have to direct me," he mumbled.

"No I won't," she groaned, her fingers splaying on the back of his head as he settled in. Her thigh brushed his injured shoulder, but before he could worry about the logistics of what they were about to do she'd pulled her knee up to her chest and pressed him closer with her other hand.

It turned out they'd both been right. Riley figured out what he was doing without much direction, but that didn't stop Max yelping, "Yes, don't stop, there!" when he got something particularly right. He settled in to enjoy himself, and to his surprise it wasn't long before she started pressing herself closer, her breath coming faster, her fingers digging into his scalp.

"Riley, don't stop don't—oh! Fuck, Riley, fuck!"

She shook and writhed, her whole body convulsing with orgasm. Riley kept on doing what he was doing, revelling in her high-pitched cries and desperate gasps, until eventually she pushed him away, lying there panting and twitching.

Then she lifted her head and breathed raggedly, "What are you waiting for?"

She nudged him with her leg, pushing him on his back and swinging herself over him as if he was a stallion she intended to ride. Which it seemed she did. Riley let her guide him into her, felt the aftershocks of her orgasm rippling through her as she took him all, looked up at the pleasure flushing her face and thought with immeasurable pride, *I did that.*

"Oh Riley," she said, her voice low and throaty. "We're going to be doing this a lot."

Then she leaned down and kissed him again, and began to move, and Riley was lost. Her strong lean body felt so perfect, rocking against him, around him, her breath fast and hot against his neck as she took what she wanted. He grasped her tight buttocks and thrust up, and Max let out a sob.

"Yes. God yes. Harder."

He did what she wanted, what they both wanted, until he could barely breathe, delirious with pleasure, and when he thought he couldn't stand it any more Max let out a sharp cry and convulsed in his arms again. The ripples and pulses of her orgasm were more than Riley could withstand, and pleasure flooded him as he came with her, clutching her desperately and gasping out her name.

Max lay on top of him, biting and sucking at his neck and shuddering pleasurably. Tears came to his eyes, and he nearly sobbed with the perfection of it. This was what he'd been missing, what he'd always wanted and never found. *Max. Oh Max.*

Eventually she lifted her head and nuzzled his cheek. Her lips were swollen, her eyes heavy-lidded. "Good?" she murmured.

Good? Was she insane? "It was amazing," he managed.

"Yeah," Max said, smiling lazily. "I know."

He laughed at that, and she grinned and eased herself away from him, lying beside him in the cool dark cave. Riley rolled his head to look at her. *Wouldn't it be nice to just stay here, doing this, and never go back to the real world?*

Max stretched and yawned, and then her hand bashed his chest and she said, "I've gotta tell you though. You're a fucking idiot."

It was as if she'd punched him. Stricken, he turned to her. "What?"

"You kept saying no for—how long?—and it's *this* good. Just think of all the sex we could have been having."

Riley stared. She *was* insane. "That's the most backhanded compliment I've ever had." Max winked at him, and he let out his breath in a laugh. "You're mad."

"Yeah, but you like me anyway."

Riley looked her over, the polar opposite of all the women he'd grown up with, the women he'd been so afraid of, the women he'd thought he'd have to choose from.

"I do," he said. "I really do."

They made it back to the shore just before sunset. On the beach was a large, charred pile of ashes and the scent of burning meat.

"That's not Émile's cooking, is it?" Riley said, looking at the remains in horror.

"I'm guessing that's the bastards who attacked us," Max replied, "so I do hope not." Here and there, if she looked, she could make out a hand or foot or a bit of a skull.

She stopped looking.

"Christ, what happened to you?" Murtaugh said, looking Riley over.

"Well, they did," Riley said, gesturing to the burnt bodies.

"I meant your neck, laddie," Murtaugh said, and Riley's ears went red as he touched the small marks Max had left behind with her mouth. "Some kind of nasty insects there inland?"

By the gleam in his eye he knew exactly what had made them. "Yeah, you don't want to get on the wrong side of them," Max told him solemnly, and he laughed.

"We counted eight bodies by the Vector and another seven at the far end," said Hide. He looked impressed. "Another dozen who attacked us, but we still had the cannon working."

We killed fifteen people. Max glanced up at Riley and saw his face shut down. He'd killed most of them.

She made a show of looking up at Eurydice where she rested on the sand. "Looks like we'll need to replace a few panels," she said, and Riley followed her gaze, suddenly appalled.

"Endless night, what did they do to you?" he cried, rushing over and stroking the ship as if it were a beloved pet.

"Tried to shoot her down," said Justine. She was peering at the ship and making notes on her tablet. "Don't worry, Primer. The men who did this are sharkmeat now."

"Poor girl," Riley cooed, and Max wondered if he'd ever look at her like that.

"Émile said you had a prisoner?" she said.

"We had. He's dead now," Justine said dispassionately.

"Did he tell you anything useful?"

Petal shrugged. "Madam Savidge sent them. You should have killed her when you had the chance."

"Angharad did shoot her," Riley said, giving the girl a narrow-eyed look.

"I'm sorry, I don't really know how these things work!" Angharad protested. To Petal, she added, "And I thought you said there were no native mammals on these islands?"

"There aren't. At least according to the data we have. Why?"

"Something had been chewing at one of those corpses. It wasn't a knife wound or a gun or a laser. Something ripped its throat out!"

Max couldn't look at anyone.

"Yeah, you've gotta watch out for those insects," said Riley with a straight face. "Speaking of, is there anything to eat?"

There was a short silence, as the rest of them decided whether to believe him or not. Then Émile cleared his throat and said, "Yeah, a fish we caught. Big as you are. Doesn't register as poisonous…"

"Sounds delicious," Riley said pleasantly. "Now, if you'll excuse me, I'd quite like to put on some clothes that aren't caked with blood."

"Can tell you're a Primer," Murtaugh teased.

Max followed Riley onto the ship and to his quarters, where her few belongings still sat in a bag on the floor. She stripped off her shirt, wincing, and dropped it. Riley stood watching her.

"What? Ain't you getting changed?"

"Sure. I just…wondered if you wanted to stay here. I mean, tonight. And, um. Keep your stuff here."

Max tilted her head at him.

"It's just, yesterday you said you didn't, and I totally understand that, but given, um…" he gestured between them, and Max fought a smile.

"That we're fucking now? Riley, if you can do it, you can say it."

His ears went very red.

"Do you want me to stay?"

"Well. Kind of. Yes. It's just you said you didn't want to be seen as mine. As my…possession."

Max looked down at the cuff on her right wrist. It had acquired a distinctly battered look in the last twenty-four hours, and the skin around it was dull with bruising.

"Because if you're my possession, how can you want to…to fuck me? How can you choose it?"

Christ, after all they'd done together, after that amazing session in the waterfall cave, he was still being uptight about this. As if getting back onto the ship had reminded him of the real world.

"You think we need to be equals to be fuck?"

"Well, yes. Don't you?"

She sighed. "Thing is, Primer, you own me, so we're never going to be equal."

"But I don't want you to be...Max, you're not my slave. It's just a—"

"—technicality, yeah. Look, if we was just friends, shipmates, whatever, you wouldn't have to keep asking if things was okay with me. If we was equal you wouldn't have to ask. But we ain't, and even without this cuff we never would be, so don't you fucking patronise me by pretending we are."

He was silent a moment. Then he nodded once, sharply, and moved to pick up her bag.

"On the other hand," Max said, holding out her wrist with its slave cuff. Riley stilled, watching her carefully.

"D'you know," she said slowly, "one of them culchies this morning tried to break my wrist. Just kept slamming it into the ground over and over. If it hadn't been for this, he'd probably have succeeded. And I don't know if I'd have been able to fight on without my right hand working properly." *Let alone without you whacking that cutlass into the head of the bastard attacking me.*

"Max." Riley came closer, took her right hand and turned it over in his own. "I'm pretty sure you'd be able to fight on if both your arms and legs were cut off. After all," he added with half a smile, "I've seen what you can do with your teeth."

She looked up at him. "And you still want to sleep with me?"

"Very much. But I'm not going to make you. You want your space, you can have it."

It wasn't much of a choice. The cell with its bare mattress, or Riley's large bed with, and this was the crucial aspect, Riley in it.

"You said if you stayed in my room, they'd see you as mine," he said.

Max tried to shut down the little voice inside her that answered, *I already am.*

"It's complicated, isn't it?" she said.

"So complicated," he said wearily.

She slid her arms around his neck and kissed him, slow and deep, until he pressed her tight against his wonderful body and kissed her back with just the same intensity.

"But this is simple," she whispered against his lips.

"I guess it is."

"So...I'll be staying, then?"

"I'd like that."

She started to kiss him again, but then Riley's micro buzzed and he answered with the sigh of the long-suffering. "Yeah?"

It was Émile. "Primer. You learn any diplomacy in the Service?"

He exchanged a look with Max, and stepped back. "Why? Who's trying to kill who?"

"Nobody, yet. But the locals have just turned up. Apparently crashing a spaceship into the ocean isn't considered good manners around here."

"What d'you expect me to do?" Riley pulled off his shirt and reached for a clean one, as Max finished putting on clean clothes.

"Come out and talk to them. Let's face it, you have a more honest face than the captain."

Max snorted, and Riley said, "Mosasaurs have more honest faces than the captain. Give us a minute."

"Yes, please do get dressed first," Émile said, laughing, and ended the call.

Max peered out of the porthole as she fastened her boots. "They're not there yet. I can see lights approaching though."

"Do they look angry?"

"Can't tell, from here." There were half a dozen of

them, including men who looked very much of the armed variety. "What are you going to say to them?"

"No idea." He shoved his feet into his boots. "You ready?"

Max smoothed down her shirt and shrugged. "S'pose. Gotta tell you, Riley," she said as she followed him out, "you don't look much like a diplomat."

"Known a lot of them, have you?"

"No, but I don't suppose they're meant to look like they just fell out of someone's bed."

He grinned at her, and swung through the hatch to the hold, and the open door to the beach. Max followed him down, and glanced at his suddenly stoic face.

"Forgot about your shoulder there, didn't you?"

"Little bit," he admitted, wincing.

She hopped off the loading bay onto the sand after him. "Yeah. The worst ones are the ones that don't hurt so much. You forget about them until you do something you shouldn't, and then it's, bam, like your leg's going to fall off."

Riley raised his eyebrows.

"Or arm," Max amended hastily, but he wasn't fooled.

"That scar on your leg? Inside your thigh?"

"Yeah."

"You want to tell me how you got it?"

"Oh," Max said airily, "there was this fight with like, six, twelve, large, big lads. You should see what I did to them."

"I've seen what you can do to large, big lads," Riley said, quirking his eyebrows at her, and Max thought he almost might be teasing her.

Orpheus was gathered with the others near the fire-pit on which Émile was roasting a very large fish. Someone had collected a bunch of leaves and fruit, which Max sincerely hoped they'd checked for edibility on the ship's databases.

"Are the natives friendly?" asked Riley as they watched the delegation arrive.

"Thought you knew everything about every planet," Orpheus replied.

"Just the ones I was ordered to know about," Riley said evenly. "We never came to Epsilon. I'm hoping that means they're not troublemakers."

The group of people stopped fifty or so metres away. There were armed men there, but they had a rather civilian look about them. A peacekeeping force. Their uniforms had a somewhat cheerful tropical print. There were two women in beachwear, and a man and women in linen suits. They looked tanned, healthy, and a bit wary.

Riley glanced around at the assembled crew, none of whom looked tanned, healthy or remotely trustworthy. Sighing, he said, "All right, Angharad. Petal. With me."

"Why them?" rasped Orpheus.

"They're the least threatening-looking," Riley muttered, untangling his weapons belt and passing it to Max.

He set off across the sand, the two women following him.

"Does he know what he's doing?" Justine said, and Max made a so-so motion with her hand.

"He grew up being taught how to talk to presidents," she said.

"What fucking use is that?"

None of them could hear the conversation that went on between Riley, who was gesturing expansively around at the scenery, and the local islanders, but nobody seemed to be coming to blows. He pointed out at the water, where the Savidge Beauty had completely disappeared, and gave a rueful shake of his head. The woman in the suit pressed her hand to her chest in concern.

"Forgot to tell you he's a really good actor," Max added.

"Had me fooled at Savidge's," Justine muttered with obvious reluctance.

"Hmm. Well, I'm not sure he really was acting. He does kind of hate you. He's just too much of a gentleman to beat the shit out of you."

"Ladies," Orpheus murmured. He'd never taken his eyes off Riley.

"I don't see no ladies here," Max growled under her breath.

"If you two are gonna fight, can we watch?" said Murtaugh.

"Yeah. There could be mud of some kind," Hide added, eyes gleaming.

"Cannot believe I fucked you," Max muttered.

"Technically speaking—"

"Oh thank God, they're coming back," said Émile loudly.

They were being followed by the islanders, who were all smiles. "I told our good friends here about our misfortunes," Riley said. "What's it coming to when honest merchants are set upon by pirates, eh?"

"What indeed," growled Orpheus.

"Should we have any particular items we require to fix the ship and be on our way, they'll see if they can get them for us. And the governor of the islands, Madam Kaipo, has even offered a recipe for cooking the lalakea fish. Apparently we should cook it in the fire-pit, not on a spit."

"My daughter is an accomplished cook," said the woman in the suit, as one of the girls came forward. Her clothing was minimal even by Max's standards, her body toned and browned by the sun. Murtaugh's eyes went out on stalks, and Max gripped his wrist hard.

"We're all very grateful for your help," Orpheus rasped.

Riley beamed at them all. "And we promise not to outstay our welcome," he said, a glint in his eye as he turned his gaze on Orpheus.

"Not a day longer than necessary," said the captain, and that seemed to placate the governor.

They sat around a campfire on the beach that evening, something Riley had never done before. To his amusement, Max had taken Murtaugh and Hide aside and threatened to castrate them if they made a move on Madam Kaipo's daughters, and they'd settled instead for watching the two beautiful young women as if they were made of gold.

"Seriously," Riley said, watching them drool. "They're grown men!"

"Grown men without the opportunity or social skills to actually get ordinary women to sleep with them. Come on, Riley, you never drooled after a woman during those long years of celibacy?"

He felt his cheeks heat. "Not so visibly," he muttered.

He wasn't sure how much the crew knew about his sudden relationship with Max, but he should have realised they'd figure it out. Every single person teased them both, even when all they were doing was talking.

Of course, it became a lot harder to stay cool about it when Max announced she was going to bed and followed it by hooking her finger into Riley's shirt to physically drag him after her. The catcalls followed them into the ship, but she didn't seem to care and within a few minutes, neither did he.

She was there when he woke in the morning, and he followed her to breakfast on the beach, where the teasing was beginning to get a bit tiresome. But then Max caught his eye and looked him over in a manner that had him remembering all the extremely wonderful things they'd done last night.

He smiled and looked down at his plate, trying not to blush and failing.

"Primer finally popped his cherry!" crowed Murtaugh.

"All right, enough," Riley said. "Can we not have some privacy?"

"On this crew?" said Petal.

"Oh, fuck the lot of you," Max said.

"You more or less have," replied Orpheus.

"Well, let's be honest," Max said, standing, "show of hands who got laid last night?" Petal shoved Angharad's hand in the air as the redhead blushed. Max put her own up, and Riley shook his head at her, torn between laughter and embarrassment. She draped herself over him and kissed him extravagantly, before turning back to the crew and telling them, "Besides, he's got a bigger dick than the rest of you put together."

With that, she wandered off, leaving Riley to wonder if a person actually could die of embarrassment. He leapt up from the driftwood log and followed her, to jeers and whoops and a very speculative look from Émile.

He found her in the hold, going over some data on a tablet. "I can't believe you just said that."

"What?" She seemed totally unmoved. "They were pissing me off. Don't you get tired of all the teasing?"

"Well, yeah, but…" Rise above it. That was what he'd always been told.

"And it was true anyway. But look, Riley," she went on before he could react to that, "they'll forget about it soon enough, and besides, there's one really important question you haven't asked since we came back on board."

"What's that?" he asked, distracted. Max was wearing her short shorts today and a sleeveless top that revealed more than it concealed. Goddamn, she had a lovely body.

She waved the data at him. "Whether Émile was telling the truth about those samples being yours."

Riley's lust abruptly evaporated. He looked down at the data on her tablet but it was meaningless, just lines and lines of code. "How do we tell?"

"We spend many boring hours analysing code."

He looked at the scrolling lists of letters, then back at her. "How did you get these codes?"

"Hacked Justine's system," Max said, as if it was obvious. "Riley, there are whole databases of this stuff in government facilities. If we wanted to, we could find out which planet it had come from, which region, which family, maybe even which person. Aren't you just in the least bit curious?"

The crate with the Service insignia was sitting on the other side of the hold. It sucked at Riley's gaze like a black hole.

"All right," he said. "Yes."

"Cool." Max folded the tablet into the pocket of her shorts. "And if it turns out she's lying, can I cut her?"

"If you find out she's lying, we both will."

CHAPTER FOURTEEN

They spent several days on Epsilon Decimus, repairing the ship and shuttle and trying to salvage the Vector. Riley cottoned on that the governor wanted them gone quickly, especially since she'd seen the way Murtaugh eyed up her daughters, and casually mentioned once or twice that a few spare parts for the Vector would get them off-world that much quicker. They arrived the next morning.

He spent his days working on the ship, supervising the repairs that even Angharad got involved in. The girl surprised him, apparently willing to do most of what she was asked without complaint. Not that this meant he trusted her at all.

He spent his nights with Max: hot, wild and eye-opening nights. And not just nights. There was one especially memorable incident in the hot afternoon sun, involving the wreck of the Vector, a dropped spanner, and a little bit more kissing-it-better than was strictly necessary.

Eventually the crew got bored of teasing them and accepted what apparently everyone but Riley had known to be inevitable. Only Orpheus didn't seem wholly happy, but then he never did. Riley sometimes caught him watching Max in a way he couldn't quite fathom, but definitely didn't like.

Then there was Justine, who watched him climb down from the top of the Eurydice one afternoon, frowning, and nodded at his bare shoulder.

"I should probably take a look at that."

"It's fine." It wasn't remotely, the strain of the day's hard work and Max's relentless nights taking its toll.

"Don't lie to me."

"Max stitched it. It's fine."

Justine eyed him beadily, and Riley wished he'd kept his shirt on, despite the heat. "No offence to Max, but how many years of medical school does she have?"

"How many do you have?"

"Six," Justine said. "Come on. At least let me scan it."

It was something of an olive branch, so he took it, following her into the coolness of the ship and up to the sickbay. Like Justine, it was neat, controlled and full of things he didn't understand. He took a seat on the reclining bed.

"The lash cuts are healing quite well, in case you're interested," he said as she peered at his stitches. Her gaze flickered down to said lash marks. "But there's a slight scarring issue, which will probably remain since it's been...ooh..." He began counting on his fingers.

Justine gave no reaction.

"...five, six, seven, eight whole days." He watched for her response, but those beautiful eyes showed no remorse. "Since you *whipped* me."

"It had to be done," she replied, her gaze flickering over the messy double lash scar he'd had to fix himself.

"Did it? Did it really? Whatever happened to 'first do no harm'?"

256

Justine fixed him with a look that might have frightened a man not used to Max's ferocity, and turned her attention to the stitches in his shoulder.

"How deep did it go?" she asked, her attention on the handheld scanner.

"Dunno. About a cutlass-width."

"Doubt it," Justine said. "That would have caused more obvious damage. The shoulder is a complex joint, full of bones, muscles, blood vessels…"

Riley stared up at the ceiling and waited.

"…which you'd know since you've broken your clavicle at one point." She peered closely at the scanner's output. "Two points."

"Yep. Dislocated it too. Actually that might have been the other side now I think of it."

"You can't remember?"

"Lost track," he said, which was more or less true. "No, it was the left. Had to do everything right-handed for a while. Drove me mad. How do the rest of you manage?"

Justine ignored that. "I had no idea being an engineer was so dangerous," she drawled.

"Engines are big, heavy things full of components that go 'boom'," Riley pointed out. "But actually I did that one getting thrown off a horse."

"You Primers and your quaint hobbies," Justine murmured.

"That was Service. We were encouraged to do sports," he added at her questioning look. "Pentathlon was popular." The five disciplines were archaic for the modern Service, but Riley for one was glad to have been taught to use a sword.

"How impressive." Her beautiful face was devoid of expression. "There's a slight chip in your clavicle—"

"Wait, did you just tell me there's a chip on *my* shoulder?" Riley said, grinning.

She ignored that. "I don't really want to open it up again now it's started healing, but I might be able to inject it with filler. You'll have to keep it immobile for forty-eight hours as it sets."

"I've got a ship to fix!"

"Then delegate," said Justine dispassionately, turning away to start assembling what looked like a terrifyingly large syringe.

He watched for a few moments, then said, "How come you only have six years of medical school?"

"Because then I got married."

"And you can't be a doctor and married at the same time?"

"Not according to my husband."

She had her back to him, her posture giving nothing away.

"And where's he now?"

"A cemetery, I should imagine."

"I'm sorry."

She turned back, carrying a sling which she arranged loosely in place before injecting his shoulder with anaesthetic. "Don't be. I'm not."

"Not a love match, then?"

"You could say that."

Christ, it was like pulling teeth. "My parents tried to arrange a marriage for me," he told her. "Didn't work out so well."

"Did you bash her head against the wall until she stopped twitching?" Justine asked, her voice calm, her expression impassive.

"Um. No." Although he had a strong suspicion Max would, if she ever got the chance.

"Can't have been so bad, then."

Riley watched her as she set the scanner on a bracket and positioned it over his shoulder. Then she picked up the very large needle.

"Hold still."

He felt the needle go in, that disconcerting sensation which ought to bring pain with it but didn't, and watched Justine as she kept her attention on the scanner. The needle moved, even more disturbingly, inside his shoulder.

"There," she said eventually, withdrawing the needle and pressing a swab over the site. "Stay still."

He did, and she tightened the sling, fastening his arm snugly to his chest and setting a brace over the top of it. "Keep that on for forty-eight hours. No exceptions. Move your shoulder at all and you'll have a deformed lump there."

Riley saluted her with his left hand. "Yes ma'am."

Justine didn't look impressed at that as she turned away to tidy her implements.

"While I have you," Riley said, and she tensed and glanced back. "Those samples, in the crate."

"Yes?"

"Whose are they, really?"

"The Service's," Justine said tonelessly.

"And whose were they before they were bottled and frozen and put into test tubes?"

She sighed, and turned back to him. "Émile told you, didn't he?"

"He told me something. I don't know if it's true."

Justine folded her arms. "I don't really have the equipment to do more than a basic analysis here," she said, "and I strongly suspect there's a lot of data we're not seeing. But if what Émile told you was that some of those samples are yours, he was right."

She crossed to a cabinet and took out a small container. The label printed on it had several codes and numbers. One of them was 592-246-094.

Riley went cold. That was his Service number. All it lacked was his name.

"Pretty damning," Justine said, as Riley tried to think of something to say.

"Could be coincidence," he managed.

"Sure it could. Which is why I ran it against your DNA. It's on file from the slave tab. It's yours, Riley. There are two more in the crate. But here's something you might be able to help me with. They all begin with 592. What does that denote?"

"That's Engineering Corps," he mumbled.

That caused one perfect brow to rise. "Then the whole box is full of engineers' sperm. Wouldn't you like to tell me why that is?"

Riley stared at the tiny container. "I really, really would," he said.

"She's right," said Max that night, lolling in his bed with a tablet balanced on her knees. "I looked up the DNA matching. It's identical. Not even, like, a degree of removal."

"But…why?"

She frowned. "She said it was all engineers?"

"I looked at the labels. All engineering numbers."

"And the…embryos?"

He showed her a copy of one of the labels on his tablet. "Likewise, but with two numbers. Presumably the parents. None of them were me."

"Well, there's a relief, at least. Right, Riley?"

He shrugged his left shoulder. "I suppose so."

He looked so dejected, sitting on the bed with his back against the wall, arm trussed up in that stupid sling.

"Don't tell me, you wanted to find out you had dozens of secret children?"

"Dozens?"

"Come on. How many sperm are there in one sample? Hundreds? Thousands?"

"Oh God!" Riley planted his free hand over his face.

"But they don't seem to have used yours. I wonder why? I mean, look at you, Primer."

He peeked at her from between his fingers.

"You look like a pretty good prospect to me, and I ain't even sure I want kids."

He sighed, and she crawled over to sit beside him, leaning against his good shoulder.

"You know what's depressing," he said, "is that I totally understand why Orpheus had us whipped now. Well, me at any rate."

"'Cos he's a twat," Max opined.

"Because if someone came on board my ship who had just left the Service, and then they helped me liberate a crate of samples that just happened to be their own, from what looks like a secret Service programme...I reckon I'd be suspicious."

"Yeah, suspicious. You don't whip people when you're suspicious."

"Well, I don't. But Orpheus clearly does."

"Like I said. He's a twat."

"You're the one who slept with him."

"*Before* he had me tortured," Max stressed.

Riley looked as if he was going to say something else, but changed his mind. "Did you hear what Madam Savidge said about him?"

She snuggled closer to him, reassuringly, and slipped her hand over his groin. "Yes, but trust me, you're much more impressive."

There was a pause, then Riley gave a strangled laugh. "I meant when she said he'd been a whore. When he was younger."

"Oh." She considered this for a moment. "Well, if you're asking for my professional opinion, it's not unlikely. I mean he's—" she glanced up, remembered who she was talking to, and made a lip-zipping gesture. "Right. You don't want to know that."

"I'd be happier without the knowledge, yeah. I just thought, what with him and Petal…"

"Which we still haven't got to the bottom of," Max said. Then she realised she'd just called herself and Riley 'we' and had to catch her breath.

"Right, and then Justine." He'd told her the story about Justine's unfortunate husband. "I mean none of them are what you might call normal."

"Define normal," Max said, looking up at him. "I've got a bit of metal wrapped around my radial artery, you're on the run from the Service, Justine beat her husband to death, Orpheus hasn't smiled for so long the muscles in his face might break if he tried, Petal has named all her knives, and Émile—no actually, Émile might be normal. Relatively."

Riley laughed at that. "Don't forget, we're space pirates."

"How could I?"

She rested her hand on his bare stomach, her head on his shoulder. It felt so comfortable it kind of disturbed her. Max wasn't used to comfort.

She was about to straighten up when her micro buzzed with a text. The name on the screen was Justine's. "Max, I need to talk to you."

Max frowned, but replied anyway. "He's resting," she texted back. "Hasn't moved that shoulder a millimetre. I swear."

This time Justine called. Her face on the micro screen was serious. "It's not about Riley. It's about you."

Max rolled her eyes. "Yeah, no offence but the last time you said you needed to talk to me I ended up getting whipped, stabbed and nearly fed to a prehistoric —"

"Max, please. It's important. I think. Serious."

She exchanged a look with Riley. Justine wasn't exactly known for her cheerful disposition, but right now she looked more troubled than Max had ever seen her. "What's it about?"

"The embryos in the crate. You're related to some of them too."

"All right, you've got my attention," Max said, strolling into the mess with a nonchalance she didn't feel. To her surprise, Petal was there too, and Orpheus.

The fuck with nonchalance. "What's going on?" Max said, hand going to her knife. She glanced back over her shoulder at Riley, shirtless and splinted in the doorway, his weapons belt back in their cabin. He couldn't be more out of action if he tried.

"You can put the knife away," Justine said. "Take a seat."

Unconvinced, Max nodded at Petal and Orpheus. "What are they doing here?"

"It concerns Petal too."

"And where Petal goes, Orpheus goes," Max said. "Are you sure you're not sleeping together?"

"Positive," Petal said, fiddling with the beads in her hair. "What's going on, Justine?"

Justine tapped at her tablet and the screen in the middle of the table popped up. "When I first started testing these samples I used our own DNA as control," she explained. "Riley's was the first to make a match. Now, I don't have designated software for this, so it's been a bit of a slow process, but even manually, you can see the samples match."

Riley took a seat, glancing back at Max. Neither of them had said much since Justine dropped her bombshell. The implications flowing through Max's mind were too much to take.

"Plus it had my Service number on it," he said. "Bit of a giveaway."

"That too. The rest of them…" she showed them the

list of numbers. "As you can see they're all 592 numbers. Riley tells me that's Engineering Corps."

"So someone's been collecting the sperm of Service engineers," Petal said, making a face.

"And then using them to make live embryos," Justine said, switching the data again. This was a list of the embryo labels. They had a case ID, and then two Service numbers. Max knew she wasn't the only one scanning them for Riley's.

"Now, being that the Service doesn't exactly publish lists of Service numbers and matching names, Riley's is the only one we have to go on. The only other DNA I have on file is the crew's. So I started running that against the samples, just to see if there was any correlation. Two came up."

"But I'm not Service," Petal said. She glanced at Orpheus. "You know I'm not Service."

"But one of your parents might have been," Justine said, and Max let out a relieved laugh.

"So what? Dunno about you, Petal, but I always kind of knew that." When they all stared, she explained, "I grew up in an orphanage. Most of the kids there were the unwanted babies of soldiers and whores. Not every orphan is the long-lost heir to a kingdom, despite what the stories say."

She looked around, but none of them seemed as relieved as she was.

"What?"

"Max," Riley said gently, "this can't all be a coincidence."

"And even if it is," Orpheus said, "the question still remains: why do the Service have these embryos?"

Silence fell for a moment. Max's head felt like a thunderstorm as she held out her hand to Justine for the tablet, and started scrolling through the data. Part of what she was good at was making connections, seeking pathways and deciphering code. And what was DNA but code?

"You can see the conclusions I came to," Justine was saying as Max found her own data and the matches Justine had drawn up against it. "They're not full matches, but they're close enough to indicate a blood relation. Perhaps an aunt, niece or half-sister."

"You found two for me," Max said, feeling a bit dizzy. "Two at a quarter match."

"Yes, and one for Petal. Not the same match."

"There's more. Lower incidence. Maybe…an eighth match. A sixteenth. Christ, look at them…"

Beside her, Riley leaned over to look. Max didn't even remember sitting down next to him.

Max's fingers flew, mostly of their own accord. Data flashed by almost too fast to read. "Slow down, will you?" Petal said, peering at the central screen. But Max couldn't. Her heart thundered.

"Petal," she said eventually, "you and I are related to half the embryos in that crate. One way or another."

Her eyes met Petal's. "Are we related to each other?" the other girl asked, looking faintly sick.

Max cross-referenced their two strands. That was a match, and there…but there were so few…

"If we are, it's distant," she said, exhaling with relief.

"Thank fuck for that," Petal said.

"Right?" Max found a smile from somewhere. Then she felt Riley shift beside her, and her blood ran even colder. Her fingers flew. Then she slumped in relief. "You neither, Riley," she said, and felt the tension go out of him. "Don't worry, you haven't been fucking your sister or anything."

Everyone shuddered. Even Orpheus looked mildly disgusted.

"While that is a relief," Riley said, as Max laid down the tablet with shaking hands, "what does it actually mean? That…Max and Petal share a common ancestor?"

"Possibly," said Justine. "Genetics really aren't my forte, but…"

"You're asking the wrong question," Orpheus rasped.

"Enlighten us," Max said.

"The question is," he paused just long enough for Max's fingers to twitch towards her knife, "what do you two have in common?"

Max threw up her hands. "Do you really want me to answer that?"

He gave her a look of amusement. "Where were you born, Max?"

"Haven't we been through this? Omega Septimus Sei. Dunno where exactly I was born, but I was raised in an orphanage. I didn't leave until—well, the day I met you."

"Petal?"

Petal had gone somewhat pale. "Septimus Sei," she said. "An orphanage."

Max eyed her. She'd swear she'd never met Petal before arriving on the ship, but then moons were big places.

"Reservoir Colony," she said slowly.

"Mine Base," Petal replied. A difference of several hundred miles. She looked hard at Max for a moment, then glanced back at Orpheus. "How did you say you'd met Max, again?"

If Orpheus thought his slow perusal of Max was going to make her blush, he was mistaken.

"Remember that ship we skivvied on?" he said to Petal. "The Yellow Dawn?" She nodded. "Remember how they made a supplies stop at Reservoir Colony and you were too scared to leave the ship? I wasn't."

Petal had been there too? Wait—Orpheus and Petal had skivvied on a ship? They'd cleaned and tidied a ship?

Petal's hand clutched Orpheus's. "We'd only been on the ship a day and a half. I thought someone would recognise you. Us. Orph, I was so scared."

"But no one did," he said gently. "And we never had to go back. I promised you that."

She nodded tearfully.

"But now I might have to break that promise." Orpheus looked around them. "Looks like Septimus Sei is where we'll find our answers."

CHAPTER FIFTEEN

Riley woke to an empty bed. It was the middle of the night, little light coming through the porthole or from the ship's systems. No light came from the tiny cubbyhole of a bathroom either.

"Max?" he said, sitting up, trying to get his eyes to adjust. There weren't exactly a lot of places to hide in a cabin this size.

No reply. He got up, pushed at the door to the head. Empty.

After such a disturbing evening, where would she have gone? Why? They'd come back to the cabin after agreeing to leave Epsilon Decimus in the morning, and he'd expected Max to just want to get to sleep. But almost as if she didn't know what else to do, she'd begun kissing him, pulled him into bed, and started having sex with him.

But her heart clearly wasn't in it. Riley wanted to say something as she rocked above him, going through the motions, but how the hell did you bring that up in conversation? It hadn't exactly been covered in Sigma Prime etiquette lessons. *Should I interrupt my lover in the middle of sex to ask whether she's just fucking me out of habit, or stay silent and pretend everything is fine?*

Eventually, as Max's gaze dimmed and went distant, he stilled and waited for her to notice. It took a disturbingly long time.

"Riley?"

He gave her a wave. "I'm still here."

She looked confused. "Where else would you be?"

"Dunno. Not where you were. Max," he put his hand on her thigh, "are you okay?"

"Of course," she said, which was a lie too outrageous to bother contesting.

"Look, I know it's been a shock, but…"

"I'm fine." She forced a laugh. "What, you think finding out I'm related to a dozen Service brats has upset me? There's probably millions of us scattered across the universe."

"It doesn't bother you that you're involved in some kind of Service breeding programme?"

A muscle twitched in her cheek. "No," she said, and climbed off him, turning her back and getting under the blanket. "I'm tired though. Early start tomorrow. Night."

Riley lay there, shocked. Max had never turned down sex, much less stopped halfway through. He turned his head to look at her, or rather the back of her head.

"Max," he began, and she sighed and looked over her shoulder.

"You want me to finish you off?"

"No," he said, ignoring his body's demands to the contrary. "I want you to talk to me."

She turned back away from him. "I ain't got anything to say."

He reached out, but she was on his right side, and with his arm bound up in its sling all he could do was reach across himself to touch her back. She shied away, and he let his hand fall.

"All right. Night then," he said, and lay back, feeling like hell.

Also not covered in etiquette classes: lying naked beside a woman who'd decided she didn't want to have sex after all and also didn't want to talk about it.

Yeah but thank God I know what the tines of a fork mean, eh?

Apparently at some point he'd finally fallen asleep, because he woke alone.

Where was she? Had she left to look at more data, to sit and think, or to...

Oh God. She hadn't gone to Orpheus, had she?

Riley struggled into his trousers, which with only one hand wasn't as easy as it should have been, and was out the door as quickly as he could. The corridor was silent, no sound coming from anywhere, and he suddenly felt foolish. What was he going to do, hammer on Orpheus's door and demand to know if he had Max in there?

She's not really yours, you know.

He shook his head, and instead used his micro to locate hers. She was outside, on the beach. What the hell was she doing there?

The night was mild as the passenger door opened to let him out, and he glanced around, frowning as he heard the sound of fists hitting something. It was dark out here after the brightness of the hold, only a little light coming from the dying campfire, and it took him a few moments to locate the source of the sound.

Max had dragged the boxing stand out from the hold and set it in the sand. She was pummelling it, crosses and hooks and uppercuts, occasionally spinning her foot into the strike bag. She was fast, fierce and unpredictable —all of which he knew about her, of course, but it was something of a joy to watch her fight.

Then she saw him standing there, and stopped, wary

as a cat.

Riley stepped forward, the door swishing shut behind him. "You're good."

She grunted, and as she swiped the sweat from her forehead he realised she hadn't even wrapped her hands. Her knuckles were dark with blood and fresh bruises.

"Not that I should be surprised," he added, moving forwards. "I've seen you in action after all."

Max said nothing, and moved to the speed-bag, rapidly hammering her fists into it.

"Look," Riley said, taking another few steps. "I know it's been a hell of a day. All this stuff about the Service is a lot to take. But we've got to get the ship off the ground tomorrow, and—"

"I'll be there."

"I know you will. I'm just saying, maybe we should be getting some sleep."

"I'm not tired." She paused, and stepped back from the speed-bag to amend, "I couldn't sleep."

"Neither could I. Got used to having you next to me," Riley said, realising it was true.

Max began hammering her fists into the speed-bag again, faster and faster, her teeth clenching, hitting the damn thing so hard he thought it'd break. "Max—"

She fell back, panting, and Riley might have convinced himself the wetness on her face was just sweat, had it not been for the way she sniffed.

"I'm not your teddy bear," she lashed out. "You can sleep without me."

Riley had very little idea what the hell was going on. "But I don't want to. Max...I thought you and I...I thought..."

She stood with her bloody hands on her hips and glared at him. "What? That because we're fucking you get to keep tabs on me all the time?"

"No," he said, stung.

"Or is it because of this?" She raised the slave cuff. "You own me, Primer. Can't let me forget it, can you?"

He stared. "Max, I don't know what's brought this on, but—"

"You don't know? Were you there in the mess this evening?"

Her voice broke a little and she turned away, wrapping her arms around herself. Riley took a few steps toward her, his hand outstretched, then stopped.

"Of course I was there. Look, this is a lot to take in. I'm freaked out by it. I don't know where it's going to lead. What we're going to find."

She was still.

"Come back to bed," he said softly, "and we'll talk about it in the morning."

"Back to bed?" she said, on a bitter laugh, turning. "For what? More sex where I'll leave you hanging?"

"We don't have to have sex," he said. "We can just sleep."

The breeze blew through the trees, making them rustle. Some insect buzzed in the darkness.

"What is it you want from me, Riley?" Max asked, arms still wrapped around herself. "A fuck-buddy? A girlfriend? A wife?"

His throat worked a few times as he tried to think of his answer. He'd never really had the option for any of those things with anyone but Elandra, and look how that had turned out.

"I just want you," he said, and it was true. He wanted to wake up with her and go to sleep with her, he wanted to work with her and laugh with her and be embarrassed by her.

"You want me to be what? 'Cos I'm down with the fucking, but the rest...Riley, look at me. I ain't wife material."

"I'm not asking for that. Just...to be with you."

"Do you even know how?" Max said, and Riley reared back, wounded.

Did he know how? After all, what was his experience of being in a relationship? Of what was acceptable and what wasn't?

Because after all, he was the one who'd followed her out here in the night, he was the one who'd reached for her and been rejected. Should he have...not done that? After all, this was Max, who talked with her fists and had really only shown any tenderness when she was in bed with him.

He'd pushed her too far.

"I..." he began, and horror infused him. "I..."

Oh God, was that how she saw him? So clueless in a relationship that he was making these basic mistakes? Max wanted to have sex with him, sure, but she'd never made any pretence it was any more than that. And here he was, trying to...what, to trap her? Was that what she thought?

You own me, Primer.

That old panic swamped him. Nausea rose in his throat. "I'm sorry," he murmured. "I didn't mean to..."

"To what, Riley?"

To jump in this deep, this fast, again. To mistake lust and admiration for something more. He wasn't in love with her, was he? No. He wasn't that stupid any more.

Was he?

"To push you into something you didn't want," he said, stumbling back over the sand. "It...I went too fast. Made presumptions. I'm sorry, Max." He turned so she wouldn't see his tears. "I'm new to this and clearly I misunderstood what was appropriate. I apologise. Maybe we should just...forget about the whole thing."

Max watched him walk away, and opened her mouth at least twice to call after him, but she still wasn't sure what the hell had just happened.

She'd lain awake, staring at the bulkhead in Riley's cabin, trying to process the night's news and trying not to think about it all at the same time. *I am what I am. A nobody, a whore and a slave.* She could run all she wanted, but she'd never escape who she was.

Max wasn't very good at introspection. She was much better at beating the shit out of her problems. And then Riley had gone all...*relationshippy* on her, and her head felt like it was full of thorns.

"Forget about it?" she said eventually, and he paused. "You're ending it?"

Without turning back, he said, "We want different things. I don't want to get it even more wrong."

Max watched the best thing that ever happened to her walk away and tried to figure out what had gone so disastrously wrong so quickly. He was too bloody sensitive, that was his problem. So the sex was good, and he was sweet and kind, but this was too much bullshit to put up with.

"The fuck is wrong with you?" she yelled after him. "Coward."

His shoulders hunched, but he didn't stop.

Fucking Primer. Never had to grow a thick skin. And all that formal language! "Clearly I misunderstood what was appropriate." One tiny rejection and—

Wait.

Riley's formative experience of sex was basically one big, brutal rejection. Sure, he should've grown out of it, but he was a sensitive soul, and...oh fuck. And she'd mentioned marriage.

Talk about a trigger warning.

"Oh fuck," Max said, and ran after him. "Riley, wait. *Wait.* That's not what I meant. We can figure this out. It doesn't have to be over."

He stopped, but didn't turn back. "I don't know how

to be with someone," he said, shoulders stiff. "With you."

"I don't know either," said Max, touching his bare shoulder. When he didn't move away she left her hand there, resting against his warm skin. His muscles were hard with tension.

"Look," she said. "I didn't mean what I said. Most of it. I just don't know what I'm doing, either. All men have ever wanted me for is sex, and then you came along and you actually, I dunno, *like* me, and treat me like a person and, and respect me, like…you want me for what's between my ears not just between my legs, and I'm not…used to that. No one ever respected me before."

Riley made a sound she couldn't decipher, but he wasn't moving away or shrugging her off, so she took a breath, put her arms around him and laid her face against his back.

"And…then I left you hanging in there and you didn't *mind*, and…I don't know. On top of everything else, it freaked me out."

"I'm sorry," he whispered.

"I don't know how to be with anyone either," she said. "But I still want to be with you."

His hand covered hers where it rested on his stomach.

"No one's ever treated me like you do," she said quietly. "Like I'm worth something. I guess I'd started to think…"

"Think what?"

"That I was worth something. And then Justine went and reminded me that I'm…I'm just an orphan, and a whore, and a criminal."

His hand tightened on hers. "Max, no. Not to me you're not. Don't you know that?"

She sniffed. "Like you know you're not just some useless Primer who doesn't know what to do with a woman."

Riley made a sound that might have been a sob or a laugh and turned in her arms, holding her close. When he pressed his face to the top of her head she felt the wetness of tears there.

"I just want to get this right," he said. "You matter to me."

"I'm not used to mattering to anyone," she said. "Shit, I'm crying. I never cry!"

"Neither do I. Must be important, then."

She looked up at him, tears shining in the low light, and kissed him.

"So what do we do now?" he asked.

"Buggered if I know."

"What do you want?" Riley asked, and a gravelly voice answered from behind them.

"I know what I want. For you two to shut the fuck up and go back to bed."

Riley froze in horror. Max grimaced and looked up at Orpheus as he emerged from the shadows by the shore.

"How long have you been there?"

He shrugged. "Long enough. Noise travels. Now go off and 'matter' to each other somewhere else, yeah? Early start tomorrow."

With that he slunk silently back into the ship.

Riley clutched at her with his free hand. "Oh God," he moaned, and she rubbed his back as he buried his face against hers. "How much do you think he heard?"

Enough to embarrass us both if he chose, Max thought, but what she said, firmly, was, "Enough to know I'm definitely going on sleeping with you." She turned her head and kissed his jaw. "Come on, then. Early start tomorrow."

He nodded, sighed, and slipped his arm about her shoulders to walk back with her into the ship. And when they reached his quarters, their quarters, she helped him undress and slid into bed with him, curling up against his side, letting herself be comforted by him.

Her right hand rested against his side, the metal of her slave cuff warmed by his skin. *You own me.*

"Only technically," Riley murmured, and she realised she'd spoken out loud. "But I'm yours too, you know that?"

"Yeah," said Max, closing her eyes. "I do."

By midday the Eurydice was ready to depart Epsilon Decimus, much to the ill-disguised relief of the governor. Her daughters seemed disappointed, neither of them able to take their eyes off Orpheus as he helped manoeuvre the wreck of the Vector back into the hold. Riley was pretty sure he'd stripped to the waist for just that reason.

Max hopped down from the hold and held out her hand for the water bottle Riley carried. She followed his gaze and smiled.

"So that's where he was last night."

Riley looked down at her in surprise, and then at the two attractive, scantily-clad young women. "Really? How can you tell?" Max looked at him scornfully. "Right, what am I saying."

He regarded them both, posing and pouting for the captain's attention. Orpheus ignored them, although the way his muscles bunched and strained as he carried a crate into the hold was probably not necessary.

"Which one?"

Max waggled her tongue at the two girls, who gave her a look of disgust. "Both, I'd say."

"What? Not at the same time?"

"Probably."

"But…"

She patted his cheek. "So much to learn. Come on, help me with some of these supplies."

Riley stared at the two sisters, their long hair blowing

in the breeze, and tried to stop his imagination running wild.

"Stop gawking," said Max, and he shook himself and took one handle of a large crate full of fruit.

The ship took to the air, and Riley stood with the others in the observation deck, watching the islands grow smaller. The two girls Orpheus had spent the night with ran forward, waving madly.

"One day," Justine said from her position at the comm, "you'll learn to keep it in your pants, Orpheus."

"Today is not that day," said Petal. "Course set. I'll fly heavy-air until we're on the other side of the world, just in case Madam Savidge has anyone watching us. Should hit atmo in about an hour."

"Where exactly are we going?" Émile asked.

"For now, the Theta system. It'll take us a week or so. We'll pick up supplies and scout for info."

"Info on what?"

There was a pause. Riley looked at Max, then at the captain.

"On the Service's secret breeding programme."

It took a while to explain their findings to the crew, half of whom only knew that Riley was involved. Everyone had a different theory, from Petal being the daughter of a top assassin to Max being the mother of a hundred children.

"Like that's not terrifying," Max muttered to Riley. "Come on. I need a drink."

"We do have work to do," he reminded her.

"I didn't say what kind of drink," she chided, but when they got to the mess she poured herself a beer anyway.

"We have the Vector to restore," he told her, "and the ship's systems could all use some work. Plus the shuttle and the Hades took a bit of damage I haven't got around to fixing. You and Émile will have to be my work crew for now," he added, gesturing to his sling.

"Sure. But once that's done I want to spend some time on tech."

"Sorting the ship's files? Sure—"

"No." Max wiped the foam from her lip and set down her glass. "I'm going to hack the Service's system."

Riley opened his mouth to ask if she was mad, then closed it again. He kind of knew the answer to that. "Max, I know you're good, but the Service is impenetrable. I mean even the ship's techs are only allowed access to small parts of it—" She held up her hand, and he sighed. "Like that makes any difference to you. All right."

"You don't think I can do it, do you?" she said.

"If anyone can, you can," he said, and she rolled her eyes.

"That's not quite the same thing, is it?" She sauntered closer, a look in her eye he didn't like.

"What?" he said guardedly.

"Bet you I can do it."

"Bet me what?"

Her eyes gleamed. "If I do," her fingers trailed down his chest, and he swallowed involuntarily. "I get to do whatever I want with you in bed."

She did that anyway. Riley shrugged one shoulder. "And?"

Max smiled, a slow, seductive curve of her lips that had all his blood rushing south. "Oh Riley," she said huskily. "You have no idea what you don't know."

Suddenly he remembered a few of the things Angharad had whispered in his ear at Madam Savidge's, and he felt his cheeks heating.

"Oh, there it goes," Max purred.

He laughed, embarrassed, and she grinned at him. "What do you want?" she said. "If you win?"

Riley considered this. "Maybe I get to do whatever I

want to you in bed."

"Don't you already?"

He let his eyes travel over her body, most of which he was pretty well acquainted with now, and let her think about it a while.

"Oh, I'm sure I can think of something," he said.

Max laughed and drained her beer. "All right. What's first on the to-do list?"

By the time they hit light air, he had her up on the catwalks of the hold with Émile, welding a new piece of flooring into place. It wasn't essential, but it would make maintenance much easier, since access to the enviro units was up there. Standing below the hole a falling light-fitting had caused, he called up directions to the pair of them through headsets.

"I am sweating like a fucking pig," said the woman he shared his bed with. "Christ, Primer, how'd you cope with this?"

"Guess I'm tougher than you are," he said, and she flipped her finger at him while Émile laughed.

Riley leaned back against a crate and sipped a mug of tea, watching her. Even in overalls and a heavy face mask she was all long, lean lines, her face animated as she teased Émile about the poor quality of his welding.

"You've got it bad," said a voice beside him, and he nearly spilled his tea all over Angharad in his haste to close the channel to Max. Thank God, she didn't seem to have heard.

"What do you want?"

She nodded up at Max. "You're totally in love with her."

"Jesus, Angharad! Keep your fucking voice down."

She grinned. "It's true, then?"

"No," he said scornfully, heart pounding.

"You're not that good an actor," she said. Her gaze on Max, she shrugged. "I wouldn't blame you. She's very impressive."

"You think so?"

"Sure. I mean, I've seen her fight. I've seen her kissing you. And I saw her come out of that gully, all covered in blood and guts, and go into the jungle to bring you back. She's a hell of a woman. You're a lucky man."

Riley looked up at Max, her mask in place as she concentrated on a join in the metal. Hell of a woman.

"Please don't say anything," he said.

"Why not? Man like you, Riley, any woman would love to have you in love with her." He glanced down at her doubtfully. "I'm just saying. I didn't have to act with you at Savidge's."

He felt his ears go red, and Angharad grinned.

"Don't tell Petal," she stage-whispered.

Trying to distract her, he said, "Did you know Max slept with Petal too?"

"From what I hear, Max has slept with more people than not on this crew."

Riley sighed.

"But no one else since she started sleeping with you. Got to be significant, don't you think?"

"I think," Riley said slowly, "it's none of your business. I also think a warning might be due to you."

"A warning?"

"Yeah." Riley looked at Angharad, looked at her properly. Her skin was creamy and white even under the ugly lights of the hold, her hair soft and kinky, her lips full enough to tempt a saint. She wore some skimpy excuse for a dress, probably half-inched from the girls on the beach, which managed to leave plenty to the imagination. She was beautiful, alluring, a vision of perfection, and she undoubtedly knew it.

On this crew, where grubby and scarred was the order of the day, she was like an exotic bloom in a garbage heap.

"You've been with us…what, six days now? Seven?"

She nodded, her lovely green eyes questioning. Riley, who hadn't bothered to put on a shirt since Justine had told him to keep his shoulder immobile, gestured to the whip scars across his chest and stomach. "Six days after I brought Max on board, Orpheus did this to me. And Max. He strung us upside down, had Justine whip us, and left us to be eaten by those prehistoric bastards swimming around the waters of London."

Her eyes were wide.

"And all that was, apparently, because he was a tad suspicious about our link to that evil little crate. Just a test of loyalty, apparently. Now, I might be ex-Service, but I'd been on board three months then, so you'd have thought any lingering doubts about that might have faded. And as for Max, I don't know how in the hell a railroad slave can be considered a Service spy. But that's Orpheus for you."

Angharad's hand reached out to the pink line of scar tissue on his stomach. Riley, unamused, took hold of her wrist, and her gaze darted guiltily to his.

"I wouldn't," he said softly. "For one thing, it might make Max jealous."

Angharad swallowed nervously, her gaze darting up to Max with her arc welder, and kept her hands to herself.

"But the fact is, you're one of Madam Savidge's girls, and none of us can really trust that you're not still working for her."

"I hated her," Angharad said vehemently.

"Don't we all? She kidnapped the captain and Justine, and believe me, they're the type to hold a grudge."

"So is she!"

"Really?" Riley said, widening his eyes innocently.

"Because I thought those bastards with swords on the beach were there to offer us a free fuck and a glass of champagne."

Angharad's eyes pleaded with his so prettily. "I'm not working for her. I promise you. I just wanted to escape!"

"And I just wanted to escape the Service," Riley told her.

"But…they wouldn't. I mean, Petal wouldn't let them hurt me…would she?"

Riley laughed at that, and started counting on his fingers. "I'm trying to work out how many hours it was between Petal fucking Max, and throwing a knife at her," he explained.

Angharad went the colour of milk.

"And don't forget, Max was still shagging the captain at that point. If you think either of them are going to confuse lust with mercy, you're an idiot. And something tells me, Angharad," he leaned in conspiratorially, "you're not remotely an idiot."

Her lips parted, she stared up at him in fear. Riley straightened up, and turned his attention back to Max. "Just something to think about," he said, and flipped the comm channel to Max back open. "How's it going up there?"

"Almost done. What's the next thing on the list?"

Riley consulted his tablet, and when he looked round, Angharad had gone.

CHAPTER SIXTEEN

"It's been a week," Justine said to Riley at breakfast. "I'll take those stitches out."

"What about the ones inside?" Max asked.

Justine shrugged. "Won't kill you to have a bit of thread inside you."

"Lovely," said Riley, and followed her to the sickbay. Having the stitches taken out was a disconcerting sensation, each thread sliding through his skin as she pulled.

Justine clocked his expression. "Be grateful you don't have to do it yourself."

"I'm sure that day will come," Riley said, because he'd never been more beaten up than since he'd joined this crew.

She'd nearly finished when Orpheus appeared silently in the doorway.

"Is the shuttle in any shape to fly?"

Riley considered it. "Yeah, pretty much. Why, where're you going?"

Orpheus ignored him and tapped his micro. "Set course. We'll have them."

"Set," came Petal's voice.

"Sails?" asked Justine.

"Sails," Orpheus confirmed, and disappeared.

Justine wordlessly bent her head to his stitches again.

"Okay, what?" said Riley.

"Sails," repeated Justine, and when he waved his hand for elaboration, she said, "It used to be that ships were things that floated on water, and they were propelled by wind and sails made of cloth."

"I know what a sailing ship is," said Riley, who had spent half his summers yachting.

"Of course you do." Justine pulled the last stitch out and swabbed his shoulder with antiseptic. "They used to be pretty tall, those ships. Sails would be the first thing you'd spy in the distance. If you were on the hunt, that is."

Hunt? "Ah," said Riley. "We're hunting?"

"Orpheus is never one to pass up an opportunity." She prodded at his shoulder, frowning.

"Ow," he said pointedly.

"Don't go swinging a sword," she said. "Stick to projectile weapons. No hand-to-hand."

"Is there likely to be hand-to-hand?"

Justine shrugged. "What am I, the oracle of Delphi? Go and get your weapons. And your dog."

He cut her a look as he stood. "Don't call her that."

"You knew who I meant."

"Dogs bite," he reminded her.

"In the jugular, so I hear," said Justine, unperturbed. Riley nodded, and left to find Max.

Orpheus outlined the plan as they piled into the shuttle. The ship they were targeting was a merchantman, broadcasting a nice legal signal about where it was going and where it had come from. Epsilon Tertia, apparently, which a planet rich in minerals and ore.

"Not sexy, but worth a fuckload," was how Murtaugh put it.

"Crew is likely to be about ten. See if they'll go quietly. If not, you know what to do. Secure the ship, load the goods into the shuttle, and get out. Primer, your job is to disable their engines long enough for us to get away."

"What if they're all dead?" asked Max.

"Then we take the helm, fly her to the nearest planet and sell her on." Orpheus paused to consider this. "Actually, we do that anyway. I don't care if you kill them or not."

Max shrugged as if this was fair enough.

As the shuttle neared the merchantman, Orpheus opened the comm. "This is the pirate ship Eurydice. We will be boarding you shortly. Give up your goods and nobody needs to get hurt. If you put up a fight we don't mind killing you all. Your choice."

"Succinct," Riley murmured.

He expected them to fire on the shuttle, but nothing happened. As they latched on, he drew his gun, and beside him, Max did the same.

"Don't go fucking that shoulder up again," she said.

"Not you too."

"I've just been thinking of all the fun things we can do now the sling's off. Don't spoil my plans."

"Wouldn't dream of it," Riley said, and she gave him a saucy wink.

The airlock cycled open, and Riley resisted the urge to press Max behind him for protection. But instead of weapons fire, there were two people standing with a datapad.

"Ship's manifest," said one, a nervous-looking man. "So you know we're not hiding anything."

"Very sensible," said Orpheus, not sheathing his sword.

"Please don't hurt anyone," said the woman beside him.

"We're well insured," said the man. "Just take what you want and leave us alone."

"Aw, I was looking forward to a fight," complained Murtaugh.

"Show us the goods," said Orpheus, and the crew followed the two merchants into the hold of the ship. It was huge, stacked neatly with large crates.

"We can't get this on the shuttle," Max muttered.

"We won't need to," Orpheus said, flicking through the manifest. "Rhodium, gold—is it stamped?" They nodded. "Worthless to us. Methamphetamine. Clean?"

"Medical grade," said the woman, twisting her hands.

Orpheus nodded to Hide. "Crates 24-324, 325 and 326. Get it on Eurydice. Taaffeite? The fuck is that?"

"A rare gemstone. Epsilon Tertia is the only place to have any left."

"We'll pay them a visit. Crate 49-678," he said to Murtaugh. "All right. Diamonds."

"Yes please," said Petal, looking over his shoulder. "I'll take those."

As she skipped off to find them, Riley said, "Émile did tell you our new deal, didn't he?"

Orpheus glared daggers at him. "Yes."

"Forty percent and half of everything over fifteen thou," Max reminded him helpfully.

"The fuck do you need all that money for?"

"What do you need it for?" Riley countered. "We could just contact Madam Savidge's people and tell her where you are…"

"You'd be dead before you finished," Orpheus said.

"Yeah, but you'd be dead too, so it works out all right. Come on Orpheus, old chum, we saved your lives."

It was worth it to see the look on Orpheus's face at

being called 'old chum'. "Californium," he growled. "Crate 58-285."

Californium was one of the rarest substances in the known universe. Riley nodded approvingly to Max. "Half of that's ours."

"Bang tidy," she said. "Let's go."

By Riley's estimation, the contents of the shuttle could probably buy a whole new ship. Not that they needed to, because by the time they'd loaded half a dozen crates each, Orpheus was collecting the rest of the merchantman's crew in the hold and tying them up so he could take the ship. To Riley's horror, half of them were children.

"You can't tie up children!"

"Already have," said Petal. There were four of them, none older than about twelve, huddled close to the woman who'd brought the manifest. Two of them were crying.

"Please don't hurt them," the woman begged.

"Keep 'em quiet and we won't. Don't look so shocked, Primer. Bit of rope won't hurt them."

Riley shook his head helplessly. The oldest of the children looked up at him with big, big eyes.

"Try anything and I'll kill you," Max said to him, and he shrank back against his mother.

"Max!"

"What? D'you know how much trouble I could've caused at that age?"

Christ. It didn't bear thinking about. "I don't doubt it," he said, "but…"

"Plus, threaten the kids and the parents'll stay in line. Simple. And we've got a half share in this lovely big ship," she added, looking around in delight. "We're gonna be rich!"

Riley looked around critically. It wasn't a particularly large ship, and nor was it in particularly good shape. It wouldn't make them terribly rich; but then again, to someone like Max, for whom getting fed three times a day was wealth beyond reason, it represented great glory and riches.

"Do you have any Service goods on board?" he asked the captain of the merchantman.

"No. Civilian trade only."

"Anything refrigerated?"

"We have some organs. Grown, not harvested," he added quickly.

"Worth a few," Max said, and saw Riley's face. "But of course we ain't stealing them."

"People's lives depend on them," Riley said, and she sighed.

He checked the crates listed as artificial human organs, and the first two contained just that. The third, however, did not.

Riley stood looking at the grimly familiar sight of neatly-labelled tubes. His eye sought out Service numbers, found them, catalogued them in his mind.

"Pilots," he said to Max, as she stood silently beside him. "And those, Medical Corps."

"They're cross-breeding them?"

"Fuck knows." He turned back to the merchantman's crew. "Did you know about this?"

"No! Trafficking in humans is illegal in most of the systems!"

"Certainly is in Epsilon," Riley said. "Where were you taking these?"

But he already knew the answer. "Omega," the captain said. "Septimus Sei."

They stopped in the Theta system a week later to sell their purloined goods and take on supplies. Orpheus sold the merchantman and ordered her crew to unload the heavy goods before he let them go. He spent a day as happy as Riley had ever seen him, finding buyers for the crystal meth and rare minerals.

Riley had to force Max to concentrate on the list of things he needed for the ship before she dragged him off to a succession of bars and clubs. Waking the next morning with a feather boa around his neck and what appeared to be a tattoo of a peacock on his arm, he looked around for Max.

She was sitting up, half dressed and fiddling with something on her tablet. "Morning."

Riley unwound the feather boa on the second try. His head felt like the fuel tank of the Zeta Secunda land train. "What the fuck happened last night?"

She glanced up. "You don't remember? That club. The one with the pink drinks. I didn't know something could be over a hundred percent vodka."

Riley groaned. "Tell me that's not a real tattoo."

"Nah. They said it'd wash off."

He rubbed at it, but it didn't come loose. Unimpressed, he looked her over. "How come you're so fresh?"

"Good constitution. Look, I had an idea. There were some Service boys in there last night—"

"There were?"

"Yeah. You really did have a lot to drink, didn't you?"

Riley just moaned and closed his eyes.

"Anyway. I figured, we just go out and get them really drunk, and see what they know."

"About what? The embryos?" Justine had tested the new samples, and found more matches to Petal and Max. None, Riley was relieved beyond measure to be told, seemed to have come from him.

"Well...I wasn't going to ask about that right off. I meant about the security systems. There's got to be a database of DNA somewhere we can use to cross-reference."

"Why the hell would they know that? And what use would it be anyway?"

"A database of DNA, when we have all those samples to check? I don't believe you just said that."

His head was pounding. "Sorry. Not thinking straight."

He heard her stand up. "I'll get you some breakfast. Well." She checked her micro. "Lunch."

Riley peeled open one eye to see her heading for the door. He didn't even remember getting to this room last night, let alone where it was, but it looked much more salubrious than the last room they'd shared dirtside.

"Thanks Max," he said, and she clicked her tongue at him, winking, as she left.

The food she brought him was as unidentifiable as it was delicious. He gave her a questioning look, and she wrinkled her nose.

"Probably best not to ask. Have some tea."

He eyed the steaming mug doubtfully. "Real tea?"

"Well. Close enough."

"Don't mess with a Primer's tea," he warned her, and took a tentative sip. Well, it wasn't that bad.

"Did you just call yourself a Primer?" Max teased, taking a chunk of something fried off his plate and eating it with relish.

Surprised, he realised he had. "Well, it's all you lot call me."

"I mean it affectionately," Max said, and he grinned.

The last week seemed to have gone suspiciously well between them. She spent her nights in his bed, and her days helping him fix the damage to the ship and her vehicles. The two, he recalled with a slight flush, often coincided. There was that one time he'd leaned over her to grab a panel slipping from her hands, and they'd fixed it together, and she'd pressed back against him and given a provocative little wiggle, and—

"You all right?" Max said.

"Yep. Yeah. Fine. So. Plan for today, we go out and get some proper cold-weather gear, because I heard Petal say that the next port of call would be in Kappa, and all they've got there is ice. Should be somewhere around here selling it, one of the ports, maybe. And I'm still missing a multiport repeater for the shuttle's comm. Damn thing's so old no one has the right…what?"

She was smiling faintly at him.

"You're cute when you're all organised," she said.

"Don't call me cute. I'm not cute."

"Yes you are, you're adorable." She leaned over the bed to kiss him, and Riley let her. He could probably cope with 'adorable' if he had to.

Her fingertips trailed over his bare shoulder, the newly-healed scar there, and he shivered with pleasure. Christ, one kiss, one touch, and he was undone.

"Riley," she murmured, playfulness gone, her brown eyes big and dark with desire.

"How do you do this to me?" he said, heart hammering.

She let her fingers play with his nipple, making him gasp, then drew back. Riley followed her hungrily.

"You need to eat your breakfast," she said, and he shoved the plate aside.

"Screw breakfast."

"I'd rather screw you."

"Deal," he said, and wrestled her down onto the mattress.

Later, cold food finally eaten, they went out to face the day. The port town in the southern hemisphere of Theta Tertia was prosperous and busy with trade from the ships passing by on their way from Epsilon to Kappa, and the day before a trader had boasted that there was nothing you couldn't buy there. The streets were busy with traffic, HAVs and small personal skimmers darting chaotically around. The tuktuk cabs were automated, and if Riley paid attention he could see the carefully demarcated routes they took, separating them from the piloted traffic.

Riley found the remaining components he needed for the ship, the cold weather clothing he thought they might need, and spent the rest of the afternoon browsing with Max. She was fascinated by everything for sale under the neon lights of the market.

"What's that?"

"It's a skull."

"Yes, fathead, I can see that."

A passerby looked startled at that, and Riley hid a grin. He supposed not many slaves called their master 'fathead'.

"It's probably a...I don't know. Some kind of bison, maybe. Look at the horns."

"What's a bison?"

"Big cow thing. Extinct in a lot of places."

Her attention had already wandered. "Oh. What're they?"

"Er..." Riley squinted at the squares of colourful material. "Prayer flags, I think. They use them in the Tau system a lot."

"They're pretty. We had to pray on our knees in a freezing cold chapel. It was so... grey."

"Yeah, it wasn't much different where I came from. Chilliness is apparently next to godliness."

"Only if you have a really shit dictionary. Hey look, they've got them pendants like you have."

Riley's hand went involuntarily to the cross at his throat. "Yeah, so they have," he said. For a second his parents' faces swam into his mind, blurred with time and distance.

"What's it for?"

"For?" He blinked, and focused on her inquisitive face. "It's…well, it's not technically *for* anything…"

"Why d'you wear it, then?"

He opened his mouth and closed it a few times. "I guess…it reminds me of home."

"Aw, Primer. Check you out being all sentimental. Only thing that'd remind me of home would be a smack on the arse. Don't suppose they sell those here."

"I don't know, if you found the right kind of establishment," Riley said, and Max laughed and linked her arm with his.

"And you didn't even blush," she said. "Come on, I'm starving."

"You ate half my lunch."

"Yeah, well, I worked up an appetite," Max said, biting her lip and winking at him. "Hey look, those beads are nice…"

Later that evening, Max in a new coat she kept swishing around as if it were a ballgown, they made their way to the bar where she'd seen the Service guys the night before.

"No more pink drinks," Riley warned her. His head still throbbed a little at the memory.

"Not for you, anyway," she agreed. Her brow furrowed a bit, and Riley waited, because he knew that look. "Riley…?"

"Yeah?"

"You know that stuff round your neck?"

"Yes," he said patiently.

"What actually is it? You said the cross thing was from home. But when we was coming down on Epsilon Dec with those culchies firing at us, you touched it for… what, luck? Were you praying?"

"You're not very curious, are you?"

"And those beads. What're they for? Cos you're not

the type of guy to wear something like that just because he thinks it's pretty."

He couldn't help touching the beads, the cross. "They're from my family," he said. Max looked up at him expectantly as she walked. "You said you prayed in a chapel, and you're really not above taking the Lord's name in vain, but you don't know what a crucifix is?"

Max shrugged. "They never told us the why. Just some prayers to memorise. Pointless if you ask me."

Riley, who'd gone to church every Sunday like a good boy, sighed. "It's a symbol of faith. Not that I believe in God over science, but...well, we all have them in my family. This was a present from my parents when I was eighteen. I guess it's more tradition than belief."

She nodded thoughtfully. "And the beads?"

His throat got a bit tight. "My sister," he said. "I haven't seen her since...since I left Sigma Prime. I thought the scandal would have been...but she got married anyway, apparently, and had children. She sent me these for each of their births. Service censored most communications, but they let me have these."

Max watched his fingers caress them. A niece and two nephews he'd never met. Would probably never meet. He wondered if they even knew who Uncle Riley was, or if he was simply never mentioned.

"And the red thing? The little...what is it, a cat or something?"

"A maneki neko," Riley said. The little glass tchotchke was warm against his skin. "It's for good luck. A little girl gave it to me. We were helping with this flooded town in...can't remember, one of the outer planets in the Chi system. I got her down off a roof. And her cat," he added, smiling a little at the memory. "She gave me this as thanks."

"That's cute."

He shrugged as carelessly as he could, but Max

wasn't near fooled.

"It's nice you have them. I ain't got anything from my past, 'cept a few scars."

He nodded, and said, "And then there's this one."

Max glanced at the slave tab resting casually against his palm.

"Well, you can't help that one," she said airily.

"I keep it with the things that matter," Riley said quietly, and the look Max gave him was unguarded and raw.

"Shit, don't say things like that," she said, clearing her throat.

He slung his arm around her shoulders and squeezed her tight for a moment, then let go. Max might be up for a world of snogging and semi-public shagging, but she wasn't very good with displays of real affection, even in private.

She cleared her throat. "Right, so. This bar. I asked the girls to meet us there and help us get these guys drunk. I mean not Justine, because...yeesh, but Petal and Angharad. I mean she should be good at getting secrets out of men, right?"

"Yeah," said Riley doubtfully. That was one of the reasons he didn't trust her. "Petal?"

Max grinned. "Come on, Primer, they see a bit of girl-on-girl, they'll tell us anything."

"I bow to your superior knowledge," he said, and followed her down the side-street. It was lit up with bright signs and images, holograms winking saucily at him, marquees promising exotic delights. Max pushed open a door under the sign of an eye-wateringly pink cocktail, and he followed her in.

The bar was dark and thrumming with music. Men and women danced, alone and in groups and pairs, surrounded by high tables cluttered with sticky-looking glasses.

Riley purely hated places like this. He must have been half cut to even come here last night with Max. But then, given the state of him lately, if she'd suggested a cocktail on the roof of Eurydice while she was in deep space, he'd probably have said yes.

"Max, Max," someone called, and there was the rest of the crew, occupying a corner booth that most people would have had to pay a lot for. With Orpheus on your side, however, a lot of things came for free.

She sauntered over, improbably sexy in her big boots and swishy coat. Surrounded by men and women who were all trying just that bit too hard to look good, Max's swagger made her the hottest thing in the room. Or maybe that was just how Riley saw her.

You've got it bad.

She certainly caught the eye of the bunch of Service men and women drinking at another booth. Sending them a saucy wink, she continued on to the Eurydice crew, picked up a glass at random and took a deep swig.

"Help yourself," said Orpheus, and Riley tensed. But the captain, as ever, just seemed mildly amused with Max.

Max waved for the attention of the waitress in her skimpy uniform. "Can I get one of them pink things, please? The ones that are like nine hundred percent alcohol?"

"One Annihilator coming up. Sir?"

"Beer," Riley said firmly, and she wiggled her way back to the bar.

"Too manly for a pink drink, Primer?" said Émile, who seemed to be enjoying his.

"Too hungover," Riley said. He took a seat, watching Max shifting foot to foot in time with the music. "Max has some mad plan to flirt secrets out of the Service boys over there. One of us needs to stay sensible."

"I can take care of myself," Max told him scornfully.

"I know you can," he replied calmly. "Just…don't get too drunk, yeah?"

She rolled her eyes at him and downed the pink drink in one as soon as it came. Riley shook his head and sat back to watch her work.

It was something of an education, he had to admit. For someone who utterly rejected conventional standards of beauty, Max could get a room full of men—and women—begging for her attention. She started dancing, and it didn't take long for her to be surrounded by admirers. Riley could see why. The way Max danced was like she was already having sex.

He hadn't even finished his second beer when she laughingly collapsed in the lap of one of the uniformed men, and allowed him to pour some of that vile pink stuff down her throat.

"Christ, she's fast," said Émile admiringly. Angharad, beautiful sensual Angharad, was still dancing and Petal had given up to watch.

Riley raised his palms, and caught Orpheus's eye. The captain almost looked pitying.

"Jealous, Primer?" he rasped.

"No," Riley lied, because the Lieutenant Commander on whose lap she was sitting was getting far too bloody handsy for his liking.

"How far did you licence her to go?" Justine asked.

"Licence? I didn't licence her to do anything. I don't —"

"—own her, yes, we've all memorised that tune."

"Don't suppose you'll mind when she fucks that guy, then," said Murtaugh.

I'll skin him alive. "I'm not biting," Riley said, and took a sip of beer to cover the shaking of his hands.

It was tortuous, but he forced himself to stay the whole evening and watch Max get drunker and drunker, more flirtatious with every downed cocktail, more brazen with every innuendo.

The bar didn't seem to actually have closing hours, which was disastrous in Riley's opinion, given that a single day cycle on this planet lasted four standard weeks. But as on many worlds with a non-standard calendar, people regulated themselves and the custom began to thin out sometime in what his body clock told him was the early hours of the morning.

The Service boys were some of the last to leave, and Riley knew they'd try to take Max with them. The rest of the Eurydice crew had wandered off ages ago, with the exception of Orpheus who'd disappeared upstairs with one of the waitresses, so it was left to Riley to retrieve Max.

Reluctant to approach a table full of people who could potentially recognise him and send him back to the Service, he texted her. "Time to go."

She comm'd back a minute later. "What? No! I'm having too much fun!"

"It's late. We have to leave early tomorrow. Captain just told me," Riley lied.

"Fucking captain!" Max roared.

"Stay with us, darling," said a voice off-screen, and Riley used every ounce of control he had to stay in his seat. "We won't make you leave in the morning."

"See, they're much more fun," Max slurred.

"Max. It's not a suggestion."

"That your owner, darling?" said the other guy.

"He's so boring," Max sing-songed. "He's a Primer with a stick up his arse."

"And your shock tab in his hand," Riley said, mostly for the benefit of the listeners. And partly because of something he didn't want to think about. "I'm going outside. I want you to be there in five minutes or don't expect a place on the ship tomorrow."

With that, he ended the comm and sat back to finish

his drink. Slouched in the shadows, he knew Max couldn't really see him. And even if she could her vision was likely to be pretty damn blurred by now.

She can take care of herself.

Nonetheless, she got to her feet and stared around wildly, as if trying to remember where he'd gone. The Lieutenant Commander tried to tug her back down, but she shook her head and said something to him with a clownish expression of regret on her face.

It took three tries for her to get away from them, and Riley's fists clenched with the need to run over there and beat the shit out of the guys holding onto her, groping her, slobbering all over her. At about the point where his jealousy was about to simmer over, she got away and stumbled off outside. Unfortunately, her admirer followed.

Riley blew out a long breath, got up, and made his way after them. At least there was only one guy now, not a whole table of them. And their insignia had them as crew of the Pursuant, a ship on which he didn't think he knew anyone. But still…

Outside in the uncaring street, the Lieutenant Commander was groping at Max, who was putting up a somewhat blurry resistance. Stumbling and slurring, she pushed at him as he came in for a kiss.

"No, my owner…" Max, despite being too inebriated to stand, had her fists loosely curled. Riley both wanted her to hit him, and didn't.

"Fuck your owner," the officer said, yanking her to him.

"She does," said Riley. "But only when she wants to."

The man squinted up at Riley, as if he was hard to see. "Who the fuck are you?"

He sighed. "I can see the Service are promoting the finest brains. Let her go. Now."

"Or what?"

"Or he punches your lights out," Max giggled, stumbling. Riley held out his hand and she grabbed onto it, wobbling a bit. Yes, me. Hold on to me.

"Assaulting an officer of the Service is—" began the Lieutenant Commander, and Riley lost his patience and hit him anyway, first in the in the stomach and then an uppercut to the chin as he doubled up.

"—quite fun, actually," he finished.

To give him credit, the officer tried to reach for his weapon, but Riley wasn't an idiot and had it thrown across the alley before the man knew what had happened.

"Come on," he said to Max while the guy was still reeling, and tugged her away. She kept twisting to look back, losing her balance as she did.

"He fell over," she giggled.

"Good. Wasn't in a puddle or anything, was it?"

He had to hold onto Max as she nearly fell over whilst looking back.

"No. Just the ground."

"Shame."

She clung to his arm, nearly dragging him over as she swerved to avoid a small skimmer zooming past with a group of hollering youths on it. "I like it when you hit people," she slurred.

"Do you? That's worrying."

"It's hot," she insisted.

"If you say so."

"I like your arms. They're awesome arms," Max proclaimed, wrapping both hands around his bicep and swinging off it.

"I'm pleased to hear it."

"They're like iron bars. Like iron fucking bars," Max told him, nodding vehemently and tripping over her own feet.

"They're iron bars holding you up at the moment," he said, reaching a junction and mentally calculating how much further their room was. At this rate they'd still be here at midnight, and on this planet that would be two weeks away. He was tired, a bit drunk, and wanted nothing more than to lie down and go to sleep, with Max in his arms. Giving in, he tapped his micro to broadcast a summons for a cab.

Seconds later, a tuktuk landed. To Riley's slight discomfiture, it was automated. He loaded Max in, tapped the address of their boarding house, and fed money into the meter. The tuktuk lurched into the air.

"I'm gonna hurl," Max groaned.

"Then do it over the side, or this'll cost us a fortune in cleaning," Riley said.

She leaned out, far too quickly and precariously, and Riley had to grab her to keep her inside. To his relief, she didn't shower anyone below with pink vomit, but when she flopped back against the seat again her face was shiny with sweat.

"I don't like those pink drinks," she hiccupped.

"There's a reason they call them Annihilators," Riley agreed. "Come on, nearly there. I've probably got some rehydration sachets left over from this morning."

She leaned against him, and Riley, not exactly sober himself, put his arm around her and kissed the top of her head.

"Mmf," she said.

"Are you falling asleep on me?"

"No. Yeah. Dunno."

"Come on, stay awake until we get back. Tell me what those guys were saying to you."

Max giggled sleepily. "They wanted to fuck me."

"Apart from that. Did they say anything about stolen samples, or embryos? Is there a lab or anything we need to look for?"

Max yawned and snuggled against him. "I'unno," she said, and Riley sighed. Well, this had been a waste of time.

But then she said, "Lot of people gone missing though. High death rate, they said. People who shouldn't've died. Like, too competent. Midshipman from the Sentinel on away mission. Stable planet. Eaten by bears or summat. Girl with, like, four engineering degrees fixing an engine on the Intrepid, engine blows up, she's dead. Two from the Pursuant 'reassigned'," she made inverted commas with her fingers, "to the arse-end of the universe and never seen again. They thought it was mysterious. And that I was too stupid to pay attention," she added, giggling sleepily.

Riley blinked at her, impressed. "The last thing you are is stupid," he murmured. He was about to say more, when the tuktuk rolled to a stop and informed them they had reached their destination.

He hauled a semi-conscious Max out of the automated cab and got her inside. "I don't feel so good," she moaned.

"I know, I know. Nearly there. Sleep it off."

He got a few lascivious looks from other patrons of the boarding house. "Few drinks and she's anybody's, eh?" said one, and Riley would have hit him if it wouldn't have resulted in Max sliding to the floor.

He got her to bed, and she was asleep as soon as she got horizontal. Riley tugged off her boots, poured out some water, and settled down beside her to make notes on what she'd said before he forgot it.

Then he sat and looked at Max for a while, sprawled on her back with her mouth open, snoring. Would she pull this same trick next time they made landfall? Would he have to watch her in a different bar every night, flirting and writhing on some other man's lap? Would he keep going on punching the people who touched her, groped her, kissed her?

He didn't want anyone else touching her, ever. He wanted her to be his and only his. But that just wasn't... Max.

He touched the soft stubble of her scalp. If she were any different he'd never have fallen for her this hard. And because she wasn't any different, he could never keep her.

Riley blew out a sigh, turned off his tablet, and lay down beside the biggest conundrum he'd ever faced.

CHAPTER SEVENTEEN

They stopped for supplies on the frozen planet of Kappa Sixtus, inhabited mostly by scientists and Service engineers. Max thought she'd have been happy to get back off the ship, but the planet seemed to be in the grip of a permanent blizzard and after a minute or two her eyelids were stuck together with ice and her breath froze inside her scarf. Retreating to a bar to continue trying to crack the Service's internal systems on her tablet, she listened with half an ear to the conversations around her.

"There was some mention a while back of a project called the Big Freeze," said one woman, who specialised in some kind of rocks that sounded impossibly dull to Max. "A bunch of us tried to find out more but they said it wasn't in any of our specialist areas."

"You don't know what it was about?" Riley asked.

"No. But given the name we thought it'd be right up our street. I mean...there's not much about ice we don't know between us."

Back on the ship, a blizzard howling around them, they compared notes. "The Big Freeze, and we have a container of frozen humanity," said Justine.

"No wonder they were keeping it quiet. Anything more?"

"Service harassment, pirates, the usual."

"Well, this was a fucking waste of time," Max said.

"You wouldn't say that if you knew how much engine oil I've just bought," said Riley, never happier than when covered in grease. "Just comes out of the ground around here. It's paradise."

The rest of them looked out of the porthole at the ice storm battering the ship, then back at Riley.

"For engineering," he said defensively. "Where are we going next?"

Next was the Tau system, and a port known for its stunning beauty and incessant rain. While Angharad flirted her way through the Service officers staying in a smart hotel, Max headed out to meet the enlisted men. They got so enthusiastic she had to text Riley, who once more intervened.

"Told them I'd been with a guy who mentioned the Big Freeze," she said as they ran through the hot tropical rain to a hut by the beach, "and a couple of them had heard of it but no one knew what it was."

"And if they did, would they have said?"

"I asked them if it was true they all had to donate samples," she explained. "They said it was but they had no idea what happened to them."

"Well, that's a lot of use." Riley pushed the door shut and swiped the rain from his face.

"I did ask if they didn't think it was weird, and what if they were being used in some secret breeding programme, and they just laughed and told me if I wanted to breed with them I only had to ask."

Riley's gaze darted over her as if he couldn't help the motion. "You didn't take them up on the offer?"

Sometimes, she wished he'd just come out and say he hated her being with other men. But he was so bloody hung up on her having her own freedom he was sabotaging his own happiness. Max wondered what he'd do if she actually did go to bed with someone else. Probably go and beat the crap out of the punchbag and never mention it. Bloody Primers and their repressed emotions.

"Nah. They were all fucking ugly," she said, and he managed some sort of smile. "C'mon, Riley. Why would I fuck someone else when I've got you here, all innocent and corruptible?"

"Innocent?" Riley said, as she draped her arms over his shoulders. "We've been sleeping together for weeks and you're still calling me innocent?"

"Comparatively," Max said, nuzzling his ear.

"Even after what we did the other day?" Riley said, his ears going red, and Max smiled slowly as she recalled it.

"Mmm, I don't remember," she murmured, and he looked surprised until he realised she was joking. Then he tackled her, laughing, down onto the bed, and proceeded to remind her.

Or at least, he started to. The door crashed open, and Justine stood there with her modded pistol in her hand. "Come with me now," she said.

"Er, kind of busy here," said Max, as Riley tried to shield her with his body.

"Fine, then they can kill you."

That got her attention, and Riley's too. He stumbled to his feet, grabbing for the weapons belt he'd only just discarded. His shirt was on the floor, where it stayed as he jammed his feet into his boots.

"Who can?" said Max, reaching for her own weapons and throwing her rucksack on her back. In seconds they were out the door after Justine.

"I don't know. Service. They followed Angharad. Attacked us." Justine paused as she peered around the next hut. "Hide is dead."

"What?" Hide was a ferocious fighter, and not the type to let his guard down.

"Back of the head as he looked out of the rain shelter. Stupid fuckers. If they hadn't shot him we wouldn't've known they were coming."

Max glanced at Riley, appalled at Justine's coldness even when she knew she shouldn't be surprised. Hide was crew, he was a friend, sort of. "But—shouldn't we —"

"You want to sit around and dig a fucking grave, Max, you can join him in it," Justine snapped. "There's no time. Come on. This way."

Heart pounding, they followed her through the cluster of huts on the edge of the dark beach. The rain still came down, pattering on the leaf roofs of the huts and shelters. Max had her sword drawn, and Riley had both sword and gun. The flickering flames coming from under the open-sided structures on the beach cast unreliable shadows, tricking them into stopping far too often.

Then Justine held up her hand, and Max made out four people in dark clothing, their faces and weapons darkened, creeping past just a few feet away.

The three of them held their breath, and Max was just about to suggest shooting all of them when Justine jerked her head in the opposite direction.

The Hades was hovering at the edge of the beach. They ran for it, and the door had just opened when the first shots were fired.

Max scrambled inside, reaching back for Riley and yanking him after her. Justine was still clinging to the door as the Hades soared into the air, and might have fallen if Max hadn't grabbed her wrist.

Justine looked surprised, but she nodded sharply as she was hauled inside. Riley slammed the door shut and immediately went forward to lean over Orpheus at the controls.

"The others?"

"Ran the other way. We'll meet them at the ship." He paused. "Apart from Hide."

"Justine told us."

"Bastards," Max spat. Granted, she hadn't known Hide that well, but he'd always been decent to her and at the end of the day, they were part of the same crew. The thought of him lying rotting and unmourned on some beach bothered her for reasons she didn't want to think about. Is that how I'm going to die someday?

Nobody said anything as they flew through the rain. Riley touched her hand, and she nodded to tell him she was all right. Justine methodically checked over all her weapons, and something in the tightness around her mouth gave Max pause. She might be too efficient to mourn when there was a job to do, but for the first time Max looked at Justine and saw a woman who actually felt emotion, even if she didn't show it.

Orpheus only spoke to comm Petal, who was already back at the ship with the others. "We're in the air. Hold door open in three."

Max's knuckles tightened on the handle of her sword as Orpheus flew the Hades right into the open hold of the hovering Eurydice. She didn't let go until they bumped down onto the metal floor, and then she was the first out of the HAV.

"Are you guys—" began Angharad, and then Max punched her hard in her pretty mouth.

"The fuck?" Émile yelped, catching her. Petal was, presumably, flying the ship, and so didn't see her girlfriend go down.

"What the hell, Angharad?" Max snarled. "You just led a bunch of fucking black-ops Service to us?"

"I didn't know!" Angharad protested, gingerly touching her swelling lip. Her big green eyes swam with tears.

"Why were they following you?" Justine demanded.

"I don't know!"

"You're not that stupid," Max said, her lip curling. "Who were you fucking?"

"I wasn't," she began, looking around wildly at them. Orpheus looked mostly relaxed, but his hands weren't far from his weapons and his eyes were narrowed to slits. Murtaugh had his gun pointed at the girl. Even Émile was looking suspicious by this point.

And Riley stood there with his face like granite, his bare arms folded across his chest, muscles gleaming.

"Okay, but please don't tell Petal," Angharad pleaded.

"That you just betrayed us to the Service?" Max shifted her grip on her sword. "That Hide is dead because of you? Not sure I can keep that promise."

"I didn't betray anyone! I swear! There was just this guy...a higher-up, an admiral I think, and I thought I'd see what I could find out from him. I didn't ask him anything suspicious. I didn't! I thought he hadn't suspected anything! I was going to wait until he fell asleep and then check his tech for clues, but he didn't sleep, so I just...left, and then when I got back to the beach...I didn't know why they were following! I still don't!"

Max glanced at Justine, who said, "I don't think I believe you."

"Please!"

"Justine doesn't respond to pleas," Max said. "Trust me on this."

"But it's the truth!"

"So?"

"What was his name?" Riley asked softly. Max glanced back at him. He was being feline again, quiet and ready to pounce. If she hadn't known for sure he

312

didn't have one, she'd have expected to see a tail twitching behind him.

"Naz—Nazarine. No. Something like that?"

"Nazario?" Riley said.

"Yes! No. Nazarian. That was it. Admiral Nazarian. First initial was B, I think."

Riley's eyes narrowed fractionally.

"That mean anything to you, Primer?" Justine said.

"Not sure," he said. "Which ship was he with?"

"Didn't say. The men with him were from the Redoubtable and the Intrepid, and...there was a third one but I didn't know the badge and no one said."

"Describe it."

"Uh, it had wings. It was blue. And some letters I couldn't make out. I didn't know it would be important!"

Max waited for Riley's reaction. They all did.

"Put her in the brig. Max, come with me. We've got work to do."

He strode off, and Max went with him, and then nearly bumped into his back as he stopped abruptly and seemed to remember he wasn't actually the person in charge of the ship. He jerked a questioning look at Orpheus, who nodded, and Riley started walking again.

"Where are we going? What work?"

Riley put his finger to his lips until they were in his quarters with the door shut. "Admiral Nazarian. He was a Rear Admiral when I knew him. Commanded the Valiant. Efficient, cold-hearted bastard. Eyes like a fucking lizard."

"You called him Nazario down there," Max said, and Riley gave her a look that told her not to be so stupid.

"And if she'd agreed I'd've known she was lying. Nazarian, Nazarian. Balthazar, or something like that. He's from the Rho system, I think." He started unstrapping the baldrics holding his weapons. "If he was with men from the Redoubtable and Intrepid, that means he's part of the…wait, Redoubtable was Hawk Squadron and Intrepid was Panther so…that third ship might have been the Nike, which was with the Hawk…"

She sat on the bed and watched him pull off his boots as she waited for his train of thought to come into the station.

"This doesn't make sense," he said eventually.

"Maybe she's lying."

"Maybe. Listen, Service ships are arranged into squadrons, and then they're part of fleets. A rear admiral controls the squadron and an admiral the fleet. They vary depending on what's needed in that area, and they get reformed all the time. But the Panther and Hawk squadrons were never part of the same fleet. Do you see?"

Max watched him unfasten his trousers. "Could they have merged them into one?"

"No. I mean, it hasn't been that long since I left, and major restructures take time, so I'd have heard…"

Standing in his underwear, apparently unaware of the effect that had on her, Riley frowned and opened one of the drawers in the dresser. And as he turned away she noticed what she hadn't before.

"You're hurt!"

The muscles of his outer thigh were scorched with what looked like a laser wound. It must have been a glancing blow, or one from a distance, because at close range it would have hamstrung him.

"Jesus, Riley, why didn't you say?"

"Hmm? I was preoccupied. Nazarian, for fuck's sake. I heard he'd gone into an administrative role after he left…the…Valiant…"

Her eyes met his as he took a medkit out of the drawer. "Administrating a secret programme, maybe?"

His eyes got the faraway look they did when he was thinking, then he shook his head. "No, it's too much of a coincidence."

"What, your former CO running this programme? I mean, it'd explain why your samples were in the box."

Riley moved to sit beside her, and she noticed for the first time he was limping slightly.

"You think they're all from the Valiant's crew?"

Max got to her knees before him to examine the burn on his leg. "Well...how many engineers did you have?" she asked, manoeuvring him to sit sideways.

"It was a big ship. Maybe...twenty in the engine room, thirty more ship-wide, half a dozen specialised techs..."

"I don't suppose you remember their service numbers?"

"No, but there must be a database of them somewhere." He flinched as she poked at the wound. It wasn't deep, and would probably heal fairly well. "How are you getting on cracking it?"

She shrugged. "I'd probably get on better if I were on a ship or a base. Then at least I'd be able to get an in to the system. Crack that and I could probably get past any internal firewalls."

"A ship or a base? Max," he said chidingly.

"I know. Do you know where we're heading next?"

"Upsilon, probably. Uh..." He screwed up his face. "Prime, Tertia, and Quintus are all inhabited there. And both of Tertia's moons, I think, although that might just be mining colonies."

"Cool. Haven't been to Upsilon."

Riley lapsed into silence for a while as she worked, then asked for his tablet so he could review the service numbers assigned to the samples in the crate.

"Don't suppose any part of that number tells you what ship the person is assigned to?" Max asked.

"Only the first ship, or base. So if they've never moved...I mean all the guys I trained with were sent to different ships, and we were all moved on pretty quickly after that. We need that data."

"I'll work on it," Max said. She finished cleaning and dressing the wound, and smoothed her hand over the dressing. Riley had amazing thighs, rock hard with muscle like the rest of him, gilded with light gold hairs, sensitive to the brush of her fingers.

He let out a breath, and she looked up at him. "Did that hurt?"

He shook his head, his eyes on her. So blue, so honest. So unfulfilled after Justine had interrupted them on the beach.

"Does this?" Her fingertips trailed over the top of his thigh. The muscles twitched and tensed under his hot skin.

"No."

Her hand ran slowly up the inside of his leg. "Want me to stop?"

Riley's voice broke on a whisper. "No."

She slid her fingers under his underwear, felt the shape of him and smiled as he made a noise like a man trying not to make a noise. He was beautifully sensitive, and while Max had a whole load of tricks up her sleeve when it came to pleasing men, she'd hardly needed to use any when it came to Riley.

She sat back and pulled off her shirt. Riley looked at her as if he was burning to death and she was made of ice, and when she went into his arms he held her tight against him as he kissed her.

"They could have killed you tonight," he whispered.

"Could have killed both of us."

Big blue eyes, full of tears. "Yes, but…"

"Shh," she said, pushing him back down onto the bed and stripping off his prim underwear. She palmed his generous length, then bent to put her mouth to it.

Riley loved this—well, she'd never met a man who

didn't—but he never asked for it. Most of the time, he was so preoccupied with pleasing her that his own pleasure seemed incidental. Now she luxuriated in the taste and feel of him, the way his body writhed, his powerful thigh against her bare breasts. His hand reached out, caressed her scalp, stroked her in time with her own movements.

And the sounds he made. She'd barely got started and he was like a man dying of ecstasy.

Eventually she lifted her head, paid some attention to the line of muscle running over his hip, investigated his splendid abs, and generally moseyed her way up to his mouth.

"Hey lover," she murmured.

Riley looked as if he wanted to say something but couldn't, so he kissed her instead, and Max kissed him back enthusiastically, before moving away and unfastening her weapons belt.

"No," he said, and she looked up, surprised. "Leave it on," he said, ears reddening.

Max felt her lips curve into a smile. "Have I just discovered a kink?"

"I like," he began, and had to clear his throat, his cheeks going pink. "I like how fierce you are."

Max kicked off her boots and shoved off her trousers. "Oh, I want to do such bad things to you," she moaned, throwing herself onto the bed with him and rubbing herself all over his lovely body.

"Do them," he whispered.

"We might neither of us survive," Max said, wriggling around in his arms so her back was to him. She pressed her backside against his groin, making him groan as she writhed, the leather of her belt chafing between them. When she reached down to guide him into her, he tensed, holding his breath, and then his lips were on her neck and he began to thrust into her.

"Oh Max," he breathed into her ear. "Oh God, Max…"

Her foot slid over his calf, the crisp golden hairs there tickling her sole, and she reached back to clutch and release his muscular buttock. He stroked her, one hand on her breast and the other tight over her belly, wrist against her weapons belt as his fingers slid between her legs.

It was fierce, hot and hard, and Max gave herself over to the delirium of it. With Riley she could abandon herself, knowing he'd never just get his end away then roll over and leave her unfulfilled.

And he didn't this time, pushing her over the edge before he allowed himself to fall. Such delicious discipline, such control. How had she ever thought him prim? The words he gasped in her ear certainly weren't.

His arm was tight about her shoulders, holding her back against him. His heart hammered against her spine, his breath rasping hot against her neck. Max arched her back and he loosened his grip on her.

"Christ," he said. "I never knew it could be like that. Before you."

She eased away from him and took off her belt, before wriggling back where she'd been and pulling his arm over her.

"Makes a difference, who you're with," she said.

"Too right." He kissed the back of her neck, and she felt him hesitate. "And how you feel about them."

Max's hand had been wandering back over his hip, but now she laid her arm over his and laced their fingers together while she tried to think about how to respond to that. Riley was the sort of person who felt deeply, whether it was anger or hate or, well, love; no matter how hard he tried to repress his emotions. Hell, look at what had happened in that gully on Epsilon Decimus. Once he unleashed the beast it went insane.

She didn't know if he actually loved her, and thinking about it scared the life out of her. Because it came with one obvious question: did she love him back?

"Sorry," he said behind her. "Too much?"

"No. Yeah. I don't know. Riley," she said, her thumb caressing his, "I don't...I've never felt..."

She'd never had the luxury of feeling. Not soft, sweet emotions like love, anyway. Max had learned early on that giving a shit about other people was a surefire way to get hurt. Most of the kids at the orphanage, the girls at the brothel, they'd have thrown Max into moving traffic if it gave them the chance to escape. She'd always supposed she wasn't any different. You looked out for yourself because no bugger else was going to do it.

But now...now she was part of a crew. She'd dragged Justine into the Hades without thinking about it, even though the bitch had whipped her, because they were on the same crew. She had a hollow ache inside her at the loss of Hide, and not just because they'd once spent an afternoon getting sweaty together.

And she was lying here with Riley, cuddled into the warmth of his body, thinking soft thoughts about love.

"I've never felt like this either," said Riley softly. "Thought I had, but...I...care," he said slowly, as if choosing his words very carefully, "very deeply about you."

"I care very deeply about you," she whispered back, glad she wasn't facing him because her eyes suddenly stung with tears.

Riley said nothing to that, just squeezed his arm a bit tighter around her waist.

"I mean," she said, trying to lighten the moment, "I've never slept with any one person this much. Thought I'd have got bored of you by now to be honest."

"Well, thanks."

"No, I mean of only being with one person. Plus you

are kind of square."

He said nothing, just nudged her buttocks from behind, and she glanced back at him, smiling.

"Although I reckon I've knocked some of that out of you. I mean I thought I'd get bored and go off and fuck Murtaugh or someone."

Riley growled at that, and she craned backwards to rub her nose against his, then kiss him.

"Suppose I'll have to try and keep you interested, then."

"S'pose you will." Max hesitated, then wormed onto her back so she could look at him without getting a crick in her neck.

"What?" he asked softly.

"If I did, would you hate me? If I went off with someone else?"

The look on his face told her everything she needed to know.

"I mean, not that I'm planning to," she rushed to assure him. "I don't want anyone else. It's just...I saw how uncomfortable you were with me flirting with those other guys. What if it went further? What if I met someone like this Nazarian guy and got a really good shot at finding out what we need?"

"You wouldn't get it. Not from him. Man's obsessed with security and protocol."

"Riley," she said, cupping his cheek. "If I got him naked, he'd give me the keys to every ship in the fleet. That Angharad might be good in bed but she's no idea how to get a secret out of someone."

"And you have?"

She leaned forward, and whispered, "Elandra," in his ear. Riley shot her a dirty look.

"Cheap trick."

"True though. Riley...just say it, if you don't want me sleeping with other men."

His fingers traced the scars Justine's whip had left. "I don't want you sleeping with other men," he said, his gaze following his fingers, and her heart thumped. "But I can't tell you not to."

Well, that was something anyway. "If it becomes necessary—"

"If, Max. If. It's unlikely we'll come across someone that high up the command structure again. Not outside of actual Service bases." His strong hand curved over her ribs and pulled her to him, her leg slipping comfortably over his hip and her hand caressing the muscles of his back.

"Let's not talk about this now," he whispered, and she nodded, and kissed him, and was silent.

Later, they went up to the mess, where Émile had made some supper and Petal was conspicuous by her absence.

"She thinks Angharad is innocent and we're all being a bit mean," Émile explained.

"Walk a mile on these paws," Max replied, taking a dish he assured her was cassava pearls.

"The girl gave me a few more details," Justine said, tossing the data down in front of them. Max didn't ask how she'd got it.

"He's heading back to base. Could mean anything," Riley said, eating right-handed as his left fingers scrolled through the information.

"Look further down. He mentioned Omega Septimus, she thinks."

"Well, sure, but there's a training base on Septimus Otto. She didn't say what squadron or fleet he was with?"

"Said she didn't understand the insignias. The ship's names were just things other people mentioned."

Max snorted.

"Wait, what's this? Someone called him Admiral Nowhere?"

"Yeah," Justine said. "Apparently he didn't like that. Angharad asked him what it meant and he got quite angry, she said."

"Do you believe her?"

Justine shrugged. "Do you? You're the one with the Service knowledge, Primer."

Riley exchanged a look with Max, then said, "Right. And a lot of the stuff she said made no sense. Not from an operational point of view." He explained about the fleet and squadron structure. "But if he actually had gone into an administrative role, then he might well be meeting with officers from more than one area. Question is why."

"You think he has something to do with this programme?"

Riley shrugged. "Admiral Nowhere? A secret programme?"

"The base could be on Septimus Otto," Émile said.

Riley opened his mouth, then he sat back, switching the fork to his left hand and twirling it. Max bit back a smile, because it was the same way she twirled a pen when she was thinking.

"What?"

"Well...I was going to say it was a stupid place for a secret base, because the place is stuffed full of Service personnel, but the thing with the Service is that you don't really know much about what's going on outside your own department, especially when you're training. There's a few bullshit open-info things they tell everyone just to stop you getting paranoid, but now I think of it I never even left the training area on the moon. Didn't go outside the compound until the day I was assigned to the Vanguard. We were always just told there was nothing else out there. And...I did notice the shuttle approached from an unlikely angle…"

"…as if to hide something on another part of the moon?" Max finished for him.

"Yeah. And…you and Petal both being from the neighbouring moon…"

There was a pause.

"So we're going to the Omega system, then," Émile said eventually to Riley.

"Looks like."

"I'll set a course," Justine said, taking back her tablet. "We'll have to stop somewhere on the way, since we didn't pick up much today…"

Orpheus cleared his throat, and Max winced as she and the rest of the crew turned to him.

"Last I checked," he said, "this was still my ship."

They waited. Riley's ears went pink.

"We've come this far," he said, standing up. "We've lost Hide. Might as well make it for something. Set a course for Omega."

CHAPTER EIGHTEEN

The days ticked by. Max spent most of her spare time hunched over a screen, trying to find a way in to the Service's systems. Riley didn't see her for the half day she spent with Justine, attempting to construct a sort of table of likelihood of relationship between the embryos in the crate, but it was too shaky to rely upon. At least they'd managed to work together without resorting to violence.

They gathered in the mess one morning to hold a memorial for Hide, but it turned out no one really knew all that much about him. Even Murtaugh, who spent most time with him, could only give up the information that his friend had probably come from the Beta system and had once mentioned having a younger sister.

"He was quite good in bed," Max volunteered, somewhat sadly, and that seemed to be about it.

Angharad was allowed out of the brig, somewhat tearful, still maintaining her innocence. She appeared to have moved back in with Petal, but the two of them weren't half as cosy as they had been.

Riley concentrated on maintaining both the ship and

his relationship with Max, who had become so obsessed with hacking the Service that she was forgetting to eat, let alone talk to him. Tearing her away from her tablet to assist him with vital repairs of the ship was like depriving a small child of her sweeties.

"But the enviro needs regular maintenance," he told her as she traipsed after him, sulkily, to the back of the ship where the life support systems ran. It wasn't his favourite job either, the life support compartment cramped and blisteringly hot, but it had to be done.

"We still got oxygen, ain't we? Still got gravity?"

"I need you to check the programming. It's basic maintenance," he repeated. "Check it once a month and you'll know before a problem develops. Because I don't know about you," he opened the hatch, "but I quite like oxygen in my lungs."

Max muttered under her breath as she followed him, but she did what he asked, laser pen twirling in her fingers, while he checked the chloroplast packs that recycled the air on the ship. The ones at base level were fine, but there were a bunch of photosensitiser packs in the ceiling linked to the outer part of the hull that collected solar energy whenever possible and used that to synthesise fresh air and water.

"Programming's fine," Max said, flipping the access hatch shut. "Could probably make it more efficient, but I ain't gonna start messing with it while we're in space. Even I'm not that stupid."

"You're not remotely stupid," Riley murmured, glancing up at the ladders leading to the upper packs. Running between them was the gravitomagnet, heat pouring off its casing. "Okay, you take left and I'll take right, and we'll get these packs checked twice as fast. Here," he chucked some gloves and a safety harness at her. There were no catwalks around the top of the unit, since they'd just overheat and be unsafe to use.

Max got into the harness without much enthusiasm, hooked it to the safety line, and began climbing with a satchel of spare packs over her shoulder.

Riley watched her for a few moments, her strong limbs taking her quickly up the ladder, then he connected his own line and started climbing.

Christ, it was hot up here. Twice he had to wipe the sweat from his eyes as he checked the line of packs set into the hull. He was halfway round when he heard a clatter, and then a sudden loud clang.

"Max, you okay?"

She didn't reply.

"Max?"

Riley turned, but he couldn't see her for the gravitomagnet. He reached for the hand hold to his right and climbed sideway once, then another step.

Then his heart nearly flew out of his mouth as he saw Max hanging in her harness, body limp, dangling mere centimetres from the burning hot gravitomagnet.

"Max!"

It seemed an age before he could reach her, taking liberties with his own safety as he climbed sideways, going cold when he saw the red blistered skin on her bare arm. She must have hit the magnet as she fell. Or maybe it had caused her to fall?

There was blood on her face too. Riley swiped at his micro with shaking, sweating fingers, and comm'd Justine.

"Max is hurt. Unconscious. Think she hit the gravitomagnet."

"I'll meet you in sickbay."

Max seemed to come round when he he touched her, pulled her against him and clipped her safety line to his. She stirred, frowning, as he rappelled quickly down to the floor and unhooked her so he could carry her out of the compartment.

"Riley? What...?"

"You fell. Or fainted. Or something. I don't know." His heart was pounding, his words tumbling over themselves.

"I never faint," she mumbled, struggling against him. "Put me down."

"Like hell I will." He was through engineering now, running past the shuttle hatch and down the steps toward the sickbay.

"Riley—"

Justine was there, snapping on gloves as he burst through the door. She watched him lay Max carefully on the table, ran her eyes over the burn on her arm and the contusion on her scalp, then looked back up at Riley.

"Thank heavens you ran," she said flatly, "she only has minutes to live."

"What? No. Not funny," he snapped. "She fainted."

"I didn't faint. I never faint. I'm fine."

"You have a head wound," Justine said, pushing Max down as she tried to sit up. "Could be a concussion. What's the last thing you remember?"

Max blinked a couple of times. She looked tired, confused. "Uh...we were in life support. I was checking the packs, the solar thingy packs. It was hot up there, I'm thirsty, that's all it was. Heat."

"When's the last time you ate?" said Justine, peering at Max's eyes.

"I dunno, this morning?"

"You just had tea," Riley said. "You were working on your tablet."

"All right then, I hadn't eaten enough. Happy now? Just one of them things."

Justine didn't look convinced, but she turned her attention to the swelling cut on Max's temple. "Good job your hair is short," she murmured, examining it. "Hmm. Looks like you hit your head as you fainted, and...I'm assuming it was the gravitomagnet that caused the burn."

"Yeah, probably. That thing's like eight thousand degrees."

"It's less than two hundred," Riley corrected, distracted. "Is it bad?"

"The contusion itself isn't. Hold on."

She ran the scanner over it, and seemed satisfied with the results. "There's no sign of brain injury. You should still rest though."

She fixed up the cut and the burn, gave Max stern instructions to eat and drink properly— "No alcohol"— and let them go.

"Here," Riley said holding out his arm to support Max, but she gave him a scornful look and stalked off by herself.

He nodded his thanks to Justine, who gave him a wry look. "You're as nervous as a new father," she said. "If your hair was any longer you'd have torn it out by now."

"She fainted," he said. "What was I supposed to do, tell her to walk it off?"

"She'll be fine," Justine said, but added, "just make sure she rests, okay?"

Riley nodded wearily, because making Max do anything was like forcing a cat into a box, and making her rest would be the worst task of all. He found her in the mess, sulkily scooping out some leftover tagine and poking it around on her plate.

"I'm eating, see?"

"Good. Drink something too." He poured her some water and watched her sip at it.

"I really am fine," she said, not looking at him.

Riley let his gaze wander over the dressing on her head and the one on her arm—more silver on her burns, just like when she'd first come on board—and took a seat opposite her.

"Want to talk about it?"

"Nothing to talk about."

"Sure?" Riley said, because this was a woman who'd survived several months working in the furnace compartment of a land train, and if starvation and heat were ever going to affect her, that would have been the time.

"Sure," Max said, as Orpheus came in, narrow-eyeing them both. "Why don't you go finish those packs and I'll get back to the Service hacks."

Because I need to watch you. I need to be sure you're all right. But he couldn't say that to her, especially not with Orpheus standing there, so he got to his feet instead.

"If you're sure you're okay. Comm me if you need anything," he said, and left.

He ate lunch on the fly, no sign of Max, and when Émile texted him that dinner was ready, she wasn't there either. Riley excused himself and went down to their quarters, where he found her naked and asleep on the bed, tablet resting beside her. The screen was full of data he hadn't a hope of understanding. Kind of like Max herself.

His gaze strayed down to her arm, past the dressing, to the unmarked skin just below the crook of her elbow.

Oh Max. I hope I'm wrong.

He left her where she was, told everyone she'd just been working too hard, and took her a plate of food when he'd finished.

This time she was awake, tapping at her tablet, and he didn't let on he knew she'd been sleeping. She'd pulled on one of his shirts, which looked absurdly sexy on her, and terribly intimate.

"Room service," he said, holding out the plate with a flourish.

"Oh. Why didn't you tell me food was ready?"

So much for that. "You were asleep. Figured you

needed it."

She rubbed at her face, frowned when she found a sore spot, and sighed. "I'm just trying to get into these systems. I need something to pull all this data together because it's…it's there and it's really nagging at me that I can't find it."

"You will. We will."

She looked up at him with an unreadable expression. "What?"

"Nothing." She took the plate and started eating. "It's just…if I could get into their systems, if I just had a…a key… You said all the Service tech is bio-engineered, right?"

"Retina and handprint, plus code. Some of the higher-level stuff requires two codes from two people."

"How high-level?"

Riley took a seat on the bed. "Well, the dangerous stuff. Self-destruct is the most obvious," he explained when she waved him on. "And the more devastating weapons, the ones that could do damage to a planet's surface. Uh. Confidential orders, I guess. I wasn't really high enough up the food chain for that kind of thing. Only time I needed a second code was when I was accessing a major engine component or system during flight, because it's much more dangerous."

"You do it all the time on this ship."

He smiled. "Well, yeah, but that's because there's not much choice. And Orpheus isn't really a health-and-safety man, is he?"

"I guess not."

He watched her eat for a while, shoving the food in any old how, and thought of all those endless childhood lessons, of the hunger and frustration when his food was taken away for some imagined slight or minor infraction.

"What?" said Max.

"Just thinking, my mother would have conniptions if

she ever saw you eat."

Max paused, and looked at the fork she was holding like a dagger. "I'm using cutlery, ain't I?"

"Indeed you are." He sighed. "All that bollocks about the right fork, and what bloody good did it ever do me?"

"If you hold it like this," Max said helpfully, "and some culchie tries to steal your food, you can stab them with it."

His smile faded as he thought about a young Max, food so precious she was ready to do physical violence to defend it.

"I think it's quite possible I'll never forget you said that," he said, and Max wrinkled her nose at him. She wore one of his shirts and apparently nothing else, her legs long and brown as she sat cross-legged and shovelled food into her face. The scar on her inner thigh, L-shaped and puckered, stood out pale against her smooth skin.

"How did you get that?" he asked, nodding at it. "And don't tell me you were fighting off a dozen large, big lads who were after your supper."

Max looked down at the scar, and shrugged. "But the made up stories are much more exciting. It's really pretty boring."

"I'd like to hear it, anyway." Riley showed her his elbow, where there was a scar so old and faded no one ever really noticed it. "I used to pretend I got this in a knife fight, when actually it came from an engine I'd taken apart and put together again. Incorrectly, as it turned out."

She peered closer and grinned. "Stick with the knife fight. People'll think you're a crummy engineer elsewise."

"Well, I was about ten at the time."

Max leaned back against the cabin wall and finished the food, then said, "It's not what you think. I'd have been about seven, eight, nine. Not really sure. Left there at twelve, so younger than that. I think Fanty was still with us, so…"

"Left where?"

"Orphanage. Well. They called it that, but…we was hired out to work. Not strictly legal, but if they'd got us working then it was easier to get us into nice legal apprenticeships when we were twelve. They're supposed to keep you 'til you're sixteen, only that costs and they get paid for apprenticeships, so. I was apprenticed to a brothelkeeper. As a 'housemaid', you understand." She gave him a wry look.

Riley's mouth was dry. "When you were twelve?"

"Yep." For a moment her gaze hardened, then she shook herself. "Anyway. The scar, right? It was before that. We was working in town. I was skivvying for a tech —s'where I started to learn—but I was never what you might call an ideal worker." She paused, but Riley was too shocked by what she'd just told him to comment. "I skived off one afternoon and found some local kids playing with a bicycle. You know what that is?" Distracted, he nodded. "Of course you do, Primer. Anyway, I wanted to play and they bet me I couldn't ride it without falling off, and of course I did fall off, and the pedal jammed into my leg. Christ, it hurt. I was crying and crying and all they did was laugh at me. Got beaten black and blue for that, I did."

She was waiting for a response. All Riley could manage was, "When you were twelve?" again.

"No, younger than that, 'cos I was still at the orphanage, weren't you listening? And don't tell anyone it was an accident when I was a kid. Tell 'em I was fighting off four, six, great big lads, right?"

She smiled, but it didn't show in her eyes.

"Twelve."

She sighed. "Yeah, all right, twelve. I mean, I

wasn't…not straight away. And it wasn't so bad, really. One of the house lads broke me in. Men say they want a virgin but they really want experience, not some lassie who cries all the time. Anyway, virginity can be faked. I did that for years."

Riley reached for her hand. "Max—"

She shook her head, drawing back sharply. "Don't do that. Don't you dare pity me, Primer."

Jesus. When he was twelve he'd been playing around with engines, worrying about grades at school, being forced into dance lessons he despised, and really only just swinging around to the idea that girls might not be as icky as he'd thought. On Sigma Prime, childhood was celebrated and fetishised and made to last as long as possible. At twelve, very few of his contemporaries would have even known what a brothel was.

He wanted to cry, for Max and the childhood she'd never had, for the growing-up she'd had to do so quickly, so young. For the way she was looking at him now, wary as a cat, daring him to cosset her.

"I'm sorry," he said eventually, and she gave a tight little shrug.

"What for? Wasn't your fault."

"I'm sorry anyway." He didn't know what else to say.

"Primer guilt now, is it? Look, it's fine. I survived."

At that, Riley let out a choked laugh. "Max, I think I could throw a bomb at you and you'd survive. Sometimes I think you're completely bulletproof."

"See, that's where you're wrong," she said, looking down at herself and frowning. "I got shot…mmm…no, it was here, look." She showed him a small wound on her calf. "That was a bullet. Went right in and everything. And I gotta tell you, them bastards in the Zeta Secunda prison system ain't gentle about yanking 'em out."

Riley leaned over and put his arms around her, holding her close, desperate to feel the heat and strength of her body and reassure himself she was all right. That she would be all right.

"You getting sentimental on me now, Primer?" Max said, her voice muffled against his shoulder.

"Something like that," he muttered, and released her to lean back and look into her face. "Look. Something occurred to me earlier. And I don't know if it's just me being paranoid, or fanciful, or..."

Max looked as if she was going to say something, then read his face and decided not to. "What kind of something?"

He swallowed, looked away and gathered his courage.

"That chip in your arm. How long have you had it?"

Max looked perplexed. "Longer'n I can remember. Basically it's made me functionally sterile. It don't track me anymore, though, I managed to disable that bit."

"Just that bit Are you sure?"

"Ain't got knocked up yet."

"Are you sure?" Riley repeated.

"Well, I think I'd remember," she said on a laugh, which petered out when she saw his expression. Her lip trembled slightly, and fear flashed behind her eyes. "What're you trying to say?"

The words wouldn't come. All the muscles tightened in his arms, wanting to hold her tighter and not daring to.

"Riley, I can't be. I'm not...I can't..."

"'Don't want to' isn't the same as 'can't'," he managed.

Max's eyes widened, her head shaking. "But—no, but...I know I didn't disable that bit. I know."

And she would know. Max wasn't careless with tech. Especially not with something so important. "Maybe it degraded?"

"But...why would they put in a chip that degraded like that?"

335

Riley shrugged helplessly. "Everything wears out. Maybe it was supposed to be replaced. Maybe…"

"What, maybe they wanted to breed from me once I'd outlived my usefulness as a whore, is that it?"

"I don't know, Max, I don't. And I might be wrong anyway. But you said it yourself, you never faint. You survived all that time on the land-train, and the conditions were much worse than the enviro today. It's just…a thought…"

Appalled, she wormed away from him, her hands going to her belly. "I can't be. I can't be anyone's parent, Riley, look at me! I can't even take care of myself! I ended up with a fucking convict cuff, I'm so bad at taking care of myself!"

But I'm here to take care of you now, Riley thought, and didn't dare say it.

"Look, don't panic. Don't panic now. In the morning you can go and see Justine—"

"Like buggery I will!"

"Or, *or*," Riley went on desperately, "next time we make landfall you can go and see a doctor. Someone who doesn't know you or me or anyone on the crew. And they can, you know. Advise."

Max huddled her knees in close, wrapping her arms around them. He'd never seen her so scared. In point of fact, apart from when she thought she was going to be eaten by a prehistoric monster, he'd never seen her scared at all.

"It'll be okay," he said, reaching out to her, and she looked up at him like an animal who's been kicked too many times to trust a friendly hand.

"How? How will it be okay?"

"We'll make it okay," he amended. "You're not alone in this, Max."

He kept his hand held towards her, palm up, and eventually, slowly, she put hers in it, and allowed him to hold her close. He thought he felt wetness against the fabric of his shirt, but he wasn't stupid enough to ask Max if she was crying.

Eventually she fell asleep, and he carefully laid her down, moved that plate out of the way, made himself ready for bed and slid in beside her. He wanted to hold her tight, but Max really wasn't a cuddler. If she ever woke to find his arms around her she'd wriggle away to sleep by herself, usually flat on her back and snoring.

But this time, she opened her eyes, made a small distressed noise and sat up, pulling his shirt off and tossing it away. Then she curled naked against his chest, looking smaller and more vulnerable than he'd have believed possible.

Riley let his hands stroke her back, feeling the faint ridges of the whip marks, the bones of her spine, the muscles of her back as she relaxed back into sleep.

How will it be okay? He had no idea, but he was determined it would be.

"Where's the next stop?" Riley asked at breakfast the next morning, and Petal and Orpheus exchanged glances.

"What?" he said suspiciously.

"Sigma Prime," said Petal, and as Riley began to object, vociferously, Orpheus talked over him.

"Sigma is the closest system and we need supplies. Prime offers us the best chance of picking up Service information: there are seven bases on the planet."

"I know there are seven fucking bases on the planet," Riley ground out. "I could give you directions to all of them."

"How useful," purred Orpheus, and Riley glared daggers at him.

"Yeah, but we don't have to go to the exact place you grew up," Max said from beside him. She'd insisted on coming to breakfast, despite sitting there eating virtually nothing and looking like she might be sick at any moment.

"Actually," said Petal, biting her lip.

"No. There's a base in the southern hemisphere. Very remote. I won't know anyone there—"

"Too remote. Hardly any ships arrive there and none of the ones we want."

"The ones we want?"

"The captains Narazian was talking with on Tau. Captain Powell of the Redoubtable, Captain Hauer of the Intrepid and Commander Moreau of the Nike. If any of them are heading back to the base on Omega Septimus Otto, it stands to reason they'll call in at Sigma Prime on the way."

"Not necessarily. The Redoubtable is a patrol ship; they can go for weeks, months even without refuelling. The Intrepid is a Destroyer; it's probably heading off somewhere more unstable to blast the hell out of a few unlucky insurgents. The Nike...all right, she's Admiralty class, so she's short range, luxury, and..."

He looked up. Apparently Orpheus and Petal had come to the same conclusion.

"Albion Base is our best bet."

"No. So much no. A world of no." Riley tried to compose an argument as to why. "Gallia Base. Gallia is beautiful, all right, amazing food, lots of nice wine, the women are very beautiful and welcoming." Murtaugh's ears pricked up at that, the most cheerful he'd been since Hide died, but no one else seemed impressed. "Khalkata, right, big sea port, lots of trade, so many people going in and out no one will even notice us. Petropolis, big seat of power, some very influential people there. Uh. Or there's Novo Eboracum, huge city, massive Service base, everything you could ever want, so they tell me. And Jincheng, I hear the tech advancements coming out of there are just amazing. And the food is to die for. Like, really amazing."

He looked around the table of expectant faces, every one of whom turned from him to Orpheus.

And Orpheus spake: "We're going to Albion."

"Are you fucking kidding me?" Riley shouted.

"That's where the Nike is headed, according to Angharad."

Riley made a mental note to kill Angharad later.

"Come on, Primer, it can't be that bad." Max put her hand on his arm, and he flung his fork down on his plate.

"Oh, sure, can't be that bad. It's not like I had a price on my fucking head before I joined the fucking Service, is it? Or that I've gone AWOL since? Or that, I dunno, everyone I grew up with still bloody lives there?"

He folded his arms, aware he was sulking and even more annoyed with himself for it. The only possible upside was that Albion medical care was second to none, so whatever was wrong with Max they could fix it. Even if he had to send her off alone while he skulked around on the ship, remaining unseen.

"And it rains all the time," he added, and Max let out a weak laugh.

"We're not made of rice paper," Orpheus said. "Albion it is."

"Course is already set," said Petal.

"Marvellous."

"Why did you have a price on your head in Albion?" Émile asked, and Riley shoved back his chair and stood.

"No," he said.

"Aw, come on—"

"No. No way. Never. In that order. Max, we have work to do," Riley snapped, and stalked out before he accidentally punched anyone.

CHAPTER NINETEEN

Sigma Prime grew from the distance, a delicate swirl of green and blue and white. As they neared the planet, Max could make out the different shades of the landmasses, more green than brown. The clouds drifted, wispy and white.

"Thought you said it always rained?" she said to Riley, who'd had a face like granite since Orpheus had made his pronouncement.

"Does in Albion," he said, and heaved his seventeenth sigh of the morning.

"Cheer up, Primer," said Murtaugh. "You're coming home!"

"Yes, that's precisely why I'm unhappy," Riley said, and jerked his head at Max to follow him out of the cockpit.

"You've got the list of parts and supplies?" he said as they loitered in the corridor, and Max nodded. "When it comes to the rotator, don't pay more than sixty bits. Seventy if it's absolutely pristine. They'll try and con you but that's all one is actually worth. And for God's sake don't get anything with a CalTech stamp on it, or we'll all explode in a ball of flame."

She put his hand on his arm. His muscles were so tense she thought they might shatter.

"And the best doctors...they're in the Chenistone district, traditionally. I looked up a few, um, specialists, I'll send you the list—" He fiddled with his micro, not looking at her.

"Riley."

"They'll cost, but that's okay, I've just about got enough from that last score. You probably can't haggle with them, so—"

"Riley."

Her micro beeped with info. "Go to see one of these. No one cheap. Get the best, you hear?"

"I hear," she said, and lifted his chin with her finger. "Riley, look at me. Stop worrying."

He gave her a totally unconvincing smile. "Right. Yeah. Who's worrying?"

She snaked her arm around his neck and kissed him, and he held her a bit too tight, the way he'd been holding her ever since that episode in the enviro unit. It was weird, having someone worry about her that much. She wasn't sure she liked it.

They went back into the cockpit as the ship made her final descent. The landing process seemed to be pretty complex, requiring much dialogue between Petal and the control team on the ground, and as they neared the city Max could see why.

The place wasn't just huge, it was insanely busy. A constant stream of medium-sized ships descended towards a large port with a stacking system for parking. The larger ships were being directed away to somewhere out of sight, and a strictly-controlled river of shuttles coursed between the sites and the city. There appeared to be several mass-transport systems running into the city from the port, pods flying by every few seconds and splitting off into various directions.

"How does nothing crash?" asked Max in amazement.

"It's strictly controlled," Riley said. "By man as well as machine." He watched the traffic for a few moments. "Like a ballet, isn't it? Beautiful."

"Only you would find traffic beautiful," Max teased, and he found a smile from somewhere for her.

"Okay, the thing to remember about Prime planets— well, this one anyway—is to be polite. A man can do anything in the privacy of his own home and no one will much care if he's eating babies, so long as he says hello in the right way and doesn't forget to bow to a lady."

"You people are fucked up," said Murtaugh.

"Tell me about it. Begin every conversation, transaction, instruction, whatever, with 'good morning' and you'll get a much better reception. Allow ladies to go ahead of you through doors. And…" he peered through the viewscreen as Petal brought them down into a cradle and it began manoeuvring the Eurydice into her parking bay. "Don't stare at them."

"We can probably manage to restrain ourselves," Orpheus said.

"They can't be that beautiful," said Murtaugh.

"That wasn't quite what I meant," said Riley, and nodded at something passing by on a walkway across the terminal. Max peered, focused, and recoiled.

"The fuck is that?"

It looked like a huge beetle, all long spindly legs and shiny, iridescent carapace. As she watched, it was joined by another, and they leaned towards each other as if in greeting.

"What the hell is up with your insect life, Primer?" said Justine.

"They're not insects," Riley said. He folded his arms, looking the most amused he had in days. "Look."

They all did, even Petal as she took off her headset and turned off the engine. The beetles had four legs, multi-jointed but still somehow stiff, as if the bottom metre or so were totally rigid. Their bodies reared upwards, multi-coloured and quite small compared to the legs. And the heads—

"Jesus fucking Christ," Max breathed, as she got a better look.

"Yep," said Riley.

"Is that…did that used to be…"

"…human?" Orpheus finished. He sounded disgusted.

"Still is," Riley said, "technically. You're looking at the latest stare."

Max waited, glanced at the others and saw the same blank incomprehension in their faces.

"The latest what, Primer?" said Petal.

"The latest stare. Of fashion." He looked surprised, then a little embarrassed. Sometimes, he forgot he wasn't a pirate. "You don't say that? Well, okay. It's what's in style, apparently."

"Well, fair enough, I'm fucking staring," said Murtaugh.

"That's a woman," Riley said. "A fashionable one."

They all stared, stupefied into silence.

"Heels were getting higher and higher as I left," he explained. "Men kept complaining, you see, because it's not considered the thing for a woman to be taller than a man, and the ideal height for a chap around here is about one metre seventy, so it's not as if there's a big margin. But younger women kept rebelling, and fashion is designed to be ludicrous, so far as I can tell…so they just got higher. Someone was warning that before long you'd need a cane to balance with. Looks like they were right."

Max gaped at the women in shoes so long and pointed they looked like claws, bent over pairs of sticks clutched in gloved hands. Some of them wore stupid little hats that made them look even more insectile.

"It's grotesque," Max breathed.

"Where we came from," Émile said, his voice sounding distant, "the fashionable ladies used to have birdcages in their hair. With real birds."

"Or lizards," Justine said. "I had a frog once."

"And the men were all corseted. They used to break ribs."

"Or even have them removed."

Another woman scuttled past the ship, close enough to see the giant lashes pasted onto her eyelids. Max fancied that if she blinked, she'd change the weather system.

"I saw a woman once, Theta or somewhere, she'd had diamonds put into her skin," Murtaugh volunteered. "Like, this crush of fine diamonds, just under the surface, so she shone. It was kind of gross. Like she was made of shiny sandpaper."

"They paint themselves with gold here," said Riley. "Or they used to. Probably that's over now. Right, anyway, enough gawping, don't you lot have jobs to do?"

Max roused herself and looked curiously at Riley. Were these the women he'd pursued in his youth? Was this what his Elandra had looked like?

Was this what he considered to be beautiful?

As the rest of the crew filed out on their assigned tasks, Riley trailed after her like a puppy. "You've got everything? The list? Money? Émile will have the Vector, call him if you've anything heavy to load. Don't, um, strain yourself," he added with a sudden flash of panic, taking her hand.

From the corner of her eye, Max saw Orpheus pause.

"Riley," she said, "chill. I can take care of myself." Before he could say anything else, she stretched up and kissed his cheek. "I'll see you later."

She hustled off, not looking back. Out in the terminal, Orpheus gave her a long, impenetrable look.

Max glared rudely back at him. "What?"

He just shook his head and loped away. Max shrugged, and followed the others to get on the mass transit into the city. To her relief, there were none of the insect women here, although there were plenty dressed bloody weirdly. The fashion seemed to be for gigantic sleeves and tiny waists, skirts that made you look as if you were incubating a hive under your bum, and hair that defied gravity. Each woman took up twice the space she needed to, and they seemed to be regarding the plainly-dressed Eurydice crew with scorn.

Max caught Justine's eye. *I had a frog once.* It figured she'd been some kind of society lady, wherever she came from.

The men here were dressed with immense impracticality, too. They carried canes and hats, wore coats that were practically dresses—and, yes, they too had on high heels. Max found herself studying one as if he were an exotic animal. He appeared to be wearing purple frosted lipstick, and sported strange little gold rings looping in a chain from ear to ear.

All of a sudden Petal started laughing. She whispered something in Angharad's ear, and the redhead immediately covered her mouth. Both of them darted glances at Max.

"What?"

"D'you think," Petal giggled, "Riley dressed up like this?"

Max thought her eyes might fall out. She looked at the men in their lipstick and curled wigs and frilled coat dresses, and nearly choked on her own laughter. "Christ, if he wore the heels he'd never get through a door!"

Even Justine smiled at that.

"I think he'd look just darling in magenta," said Angharad.

"And with a twirly moustache?" said Murtaugh.

"Stop it, I might piss myself," Max gasped, and instantly all the Primers moved away from her. That only made her laugh harder.

By the time they reached the industrial section of the city she'd managed to compose herself, and ran through Riley's shopping list fairly easily. Émile arrived with the Vector and she comm'd Riley to tell him his things were on the way.

"Have you been to see—" he began, and she shook her head rapidly, because Émile was not very far away.

"Still one or two things to do," she said quickly, and he nodded. Before she signed off, she said, "Riley, did you dress like this when you lived here?"

"Um," he said, his ears going red.

"Please say yes," she said.

"Fashion has moved on a bit," he said desperately.

"Did you wear the frock coat things? And ribbons? And make-up?"

"Um."

"Oh, sweet Jesus." Max pressed her lips together.

"Only for big occasions! I was much more sober. Everyone else did it," he said, words tripping over each other.

"Sure, sure. Did you have a twirly moustache?"

"No," he said, so vehemently she knew the rest was true. "Or the heels."

"Well, duh." Max tried to stop herself giggling. It was hard. She'd never giggled much before.

"Get yourself to Chenistone," Riley said. "Should take you twenty minutes or so on the Fleet line. D'you want me to make you an appointment?"

Taking a deep breath, laughter fading at the prospect of what she'd be doing once she got to Chenistone, Max shook her head. "No. It's fine. You don't want to be recognised. I'll see you later, okay?"

Suddenly less cheerful, she got on the Fleet line of mass transit pods and took herself to the well-to-do district of Chenistone, where people were indeed more soberly dressed. There were no women stalking around on insect legs here, and whilst the big sleeves and bustles persisted, the wigs and beribboned coats had been vastly toned down.

Still, she wasn't sure she could see Riley in a pair of knee breeches with a skirt over the top.

The thought gave her enough cheer to begin approaching medics. The first had a receptionist who looked like a wasp and was about as friendly. The second was nicer but had no appointments. The third had a cancellation for two hours' time. Max took it, and wandered back outside, a thought having occurred to her as she'd been watching those extraordinary insect women from the mass transit's windows.

She looked up a name and address on her micro, and started walking. This in itself was enough to gather her looks of consternation, since it seemed walking in Albion was something one only did over very short distances, not a few kilometres. Then again, maybe it was the cigarette she'd just lit up. Primers probably didn't smoke.

Elandra Zola Daniels had become Elandra Zola Larsen, and lived in a mansion with her husband and three children. Max stood looking at the huge gates guarding the property from the street, decided there was no way she'd be allowed in by legitimate means, and started scouting for vulnerabilities.

It didn't take her long to find a way in. Housebreaking was amongst the earliest skills she'd ever learnt. She trotted over the pointlessly large expanse of lawn, flicked her spent ciggy into a regimented flower bed tended by automated systems, and let herself in by a door that had 'servants entrance' written all over it.

The house was dead fancy. Max's dirty boots wandered through marble halls, panelled chambers, and her fingers kind of helped themselves to more than one tiny trinket. Well, she had an expensive doctor to pay for, didn't she?

The house appeared empty, but as she passed through a room decorated entirely in blue, Max heard the unmistakeable sounds of someone having sex.

Her eyebrows went up. Elandra's husband did something highfaluting for the government, and was unlikely to be home at this time of day. And even if he was…

She crept forward to a set of double doors which weren't entirely closed, and peered through the gap. Yep, there was Elandra, naked and in the sort of pose a woman like her would never have adopted with her husband. Especially since her husband was, presumably, just one man, and the lady in front of her was being pleasured by two.

Max hadn't really made any sort of plan for what she'd do in Elandra's house. Nick a few things, obviously, and maybe look around for something to disgrace the woman with. After all, didn't they say revenge was a dish best served cold? She still didn't know whether Elandra had led Riley on, had planned to humiliate him, or had just panicked and reacted badly, but she'd scarred the poor bastard for life, and she ought to pay.

And here, in this uptight, sexless Primer society, she'd just given Max the perfect opportunity for vengeance.

Max grinned to herself, set her micro to record, and hung out enjoying the show for a few minutes. She wondered whether to identify herself, but decided not to, and crept out the way she'd come. She had an appointment to keep, after all.

It was dark outside by the time Max returned to the ship, and it had inevitably started to rain. Émile had brought back a few loads of supplies and Riley had busied himself organising them and beginning on the next set of repairs on his endless list. And whenever his micro buzzed and it was Émile asking for a hand with some of the crates, or Justine checking his opinion on which dissolute government minister was richer—he didn't ask why—or Murtaugh enquiring where the red light district was, Riley braced himself for Max's news.

But in the end she just wandered up as he was fitting a new sodium bulb to the fuel warning system, and tapped him on the shoulder.

"Max!"

Her face was calm. "Need a hand?"

"Need a...?" He nearly dropped the old bulb, which would have made a hell of a mess, and made himself set it down carefully before closing the engine bay door and hustling her inside.

"Well?"

She shrugged. "It's an interesting city."

"*Max*." He took both her hands and held them a bit too tight. He was trembling. "Did you see a doctor?"

She nodded. He couldn't read her expression.

"And? What did...is there..." he made himself say it, desperately unsure what he wanted the answer to be. "What about the baby?"

There was a beat before she answered. "There is no baby."

All his breath came out in a rush. "You're sure? Really sure?"

"Really sure," Max said quietly, firmly. "I'm not pregnant. And I got a new chip. Should last decades.

Until I'm too old for it anyway."

He couldn't help wrapping his arms around her, crushing her tight against him. "Jesus, Max."

After a moment, she put her arms around his waist, let her head rest against his shoulder. "Are you okay?"

"Am *I* okay? Christ." Was he? "Yeah. Of course. It's a relief."

"Yeah. A relief. Dunno about you but I'd be a crap parent."

"I'm sure everyone thinks that," Riley began, looking down at her, and she gave him a frank look in reply. "Well. I guess…it's for the best, isn't it?"

"Yeah. For the best."

He held onto her for a few minutes, until she writhed away. "So, anyway. You know your old friend Elandra?"

Bloody hell, she was putting him through it today. "By what possible measure could she be considered my friend?"

Max shrugged as if to concede this was true. "She's got married."

"Doesn't surprise me."

"Children, too. Perfect little poppets. They're in, like, lifestyle magazines and shit."

"How nice for them," Riley said, watching her carefully to see if this would upset her. But she seemed to be fighting a smile. "What?"

"Her husband is in government. Look, this is him. Minister for the Third Moon."

Riley looked at the image she showed him, of a distinguished man somewhat older than himself. It figured Elandra had married up. "So…what? She got over the scandal? The concept of a trophy wife is alive and well in Albion? Not really a surprise." Elandra, he had realised eventually, was the sort of woman who always got what she wanted in the end.

"Interestingly," Max said, "there didn't seem to be

much of a scandal. She didn't ever press charges. Whatever accusations she made against you at that party stayed at that party."

He stared at her.

"She just wanted to make you go away," Max said. "And it worked. When I looked up mentions of you, there were hardly any. Just that you'd joined the Service eleven years ago and been promoted a couple of times."

Riley leaned back against the wall, feeling somewhat dizzy. This whole time, there had been nothing to run away from? He'd abandoned his family, run away with his tail between his legs like a bloody coward, and for what? So Elandra could marry someone grander, someone richer, someone with a fancy title?

"When I read that I wanted to fucking kill her," Max admitted, and he looked up to see her watching him carefully. "But instead I broke into her house, nicked a few things, and as a nice bonus, filmed this." She tapped at her micro, then looked up and added wickedly, "I'm warning you this time, Primer. Explicit content."

"I really don't want to see—" Riley began, because the thought of Elandra having sex was probably going to give him nightmares.

"Trust me," Max said, as the sound of gasping filled the engine bay. "You do."

He peered unwillingly at the screen, blinked, and frowned. What the hell was—oh. *Oh.*

"Oh," he said out loud, just for good measure. There were three people on the screen, one of whom was Elandra, and none of whom were her husband. The two muscular young men servicing her were being issued a stream of increasingly explicit instructions, and struggling to comply. The filth coming out of Elandra's elegant mouth was enough to make even Max's eyebrows go up.

"Jesus," he said, as the clip ended.

"Yep."

"Fuck."

"Yep."

Riley surprised himself by laughing. "What a fucking bitch," he said, and Max smiled.

"Yep."

He drew her towards him and kissed her mouth. "That's the best thing I've seen since...well, since last time I was on this miserable planet," he said.

"Thought you'd like it. Come on. I brought some food back. We'll get something to eat and discuss whether to send that clip to Minister Larsen. What d'you think we could get for it? Few million?"

He slung his arm around her shoulders as they left the engine bay. "Or we could send it to everyone else in the government. Destroy them both."

"Riley, I never knew you were so vindictive." Max sounded admiring.

"She destroyed my life. But then...if I'd married her, I'd have a cheating bitch of a wife and, moreover, I'd never have met you. Maybe I should send her flowers," he said, and Max laughed.

They went back out that evening, Riley's confidence boosted by Max's discovery that he wasn't actually wanted on a rape charge. Sure, there were still people around who might recognise him, but Albion was a bloody large place and the bars they were targeting were quite dimly lit.

They were all around the Service base, down in the south of the city. Like most bars favoured by Service personnel, they were loud, dark, and cheap. A soldier with a day's shore leave wasn't going to waste it staying sober.

As before, he took a seat in a dim corner, nursed a beer and watched Max flirting. She danced, drank, chatted, moved on. He knew she'd found someone promising when she hung around for more than one drink. None of the lads were wearing their uniform caps, so it was harder to work out which ship they were from, but when he ordered another drink he asked the waiter.

"Those lads, sir? The Kratos, I believe." The young man looked him over. "You want to watch out, sir. They still have the power to impress people they think look likely."

"So I've heard," Riley said drily, and took his beer. Interesting that these guys were from the Kratos. It had always been the sister ship to the Nike. They'd travelled together so much it was unusual to see one crew here without the other.

When he looked back around for Max, he couldn't see her. Dammit, and she was easy to pick out of a crowd, taller than most men and with that shaved head. Where the hell had she gone? Please not upstairs or outside or whatever. Not with someone else. He couldn't stand it.

No, wait, there she was, dancing with someone who...looked a lot like...Orpheus? Well, how many other whip-thin men could there be with long braided hair and features like a hawk?

What the fuck was he doing dancing with Max?

Quite apart from anything else, Riley reasoned, trying to tamp down his jealousy, he was cock-blocking all those other men she could be getting information out of. What the fuck did he think he was doing, grinding his hips against her like that, nuzzling her ear as if they were lovers? He knew Max belonged to Riley!

The bottle stopped halfway to Riley's mouth. Shit. He'd just thought that, hadn't he? Max belonged to him. Well, technically, legally, sure, but she was a person in her own right and he firmly believed people couldn't be owned. But...

But…

But Max was his. It was as simple as that.

As he watched, Orpheus said or did something that made Max freeze. Her head snapped round and and she glared daggers at him.

Riley was on his feet before he really knew what he was doing, pushing through the crowd, reaching them just as Orpheus gave a cocky little smile and straightened away from Max.

"He bothering you?" Riley said, and she looked up, something flashing across her features he didn't like. But it was gone before he could comprehend it.

"He was just leaving," she said coldly, and Orpheus looked Riley over contemptuously before he slunk away to harass someone else.

"What did he want?" Riley asked, as Max pressed herself against him, writhing in time to the music.

"He was just being a twat. You know Orpheus."

"Not as well as you do," Riley said bitterly.

She tilted her head. "None of that. You got me." Her lips brushed his jaw, then his ear. "I might be flirting secrets out of this lot, but it's you I'm going home with."

Because you're mine. He turned his head, found her mouth with his and kissed her possessively. Max kissed him back, her arms going round his neck, her hips undulating against his. He moved in time with her, finding the rhythm of the music, sinking into the heat and sensuality of the woman in his arms.

"Speaking of going home," she murmured against his lips, her deep brown eyes burning up at him.

"I'm not sure we'll even make it that far," Riley said, and Max gave him a wicked smile. "Did you learn anything useful?" he asked reluctantly.

"Mmm. I'll tell you later," she said, and towed him out of the bar.

Riley was right, and they didn't make it back to the ship before she found herself with her pants around her ankles. They'd at least found a dark corner round the back of the mass transit stop, which to be honest was still not the least salubrious place she'd had sex.

They stumbled back to the ship in a warm glow despite the drizzle, stopping every now and then for a quick snog on a street corner. But once they reached the brightly-lit terminal, a change came over Riley. The arm he had around her waist suddenly stiffened, and his footsteps lost sync with hers.

"What?" she said, and followed his gaze. A group of people were alighting from a pleasure cruiser opposite, all of them dressed in the sober, expensive styles she'd seen around the Chenistone area. Riley seemed riveted by one dark-haired man, extending his hand to help a lady down from the gangplank.

"Handsome man," she said, and Riley seemed to remember she was there.

"What? No. The guy there. I used to know him."

"Friend or foe?"

As if drawn by Riley's gaze, the man turned his head, and their eyes locked. After what felt like an age, he lifted a hand in greeting. Irrational jealousy shot through Max.

Riley's left hand was like stone against her waist. Eventually, with agonising slowness, he raised his right hand to the other man.

"Friend," he murmured. "My best friend, once."

Once. "Do you want to go and talk to him?"

"What?" He glanced down at himself in horror, then at her. "Looking like this? Are you kidding? I'm amazed he even recognised me."

"You are pretty distinctive," Max said, because Riley hadn't been joking when he'd said he was thirty centimetres taller than the Primers' ideal height for a man. "I'm sure if he's your friend he won't care what you look like."

"We should go in," Riley said, turning abruptly and dragging her towards Eurydice. "I'm tired. Early start tomorrow."

"Is there?"

"Probably."

She let him haul her at double speed into the ship, but as the door closed he stood looking out, almost longingly.

Riley missed his life here, whatever he said. The luxurious living, the frivolous clothes, the dance of politeness. He made a pretty good fist of fitting in on a pirate ship, but he was a sheep in wolf's clothing, and always would be.

He could never talk to an old friend with you at his side, said a treacherous little voice inside her, and Max caught her reflection in the polished side of the refrigerated crate they'd taken from the merchantman. Too tall, too brawny, too shaven-headed and scarred to ever be introduced to a Primer, even as someone's slave. *Imagine if he had to admit you were his lover.*

She turned away from the image she'd never minded before, but then her gaze fell on that crate, *the* crate, the one that held a piece of Riley and parts of her. Those embryos, her cousins or nephews or whatever, that were probably as close as she'd ever get to having a child.

Her eyes closed as she remembered Orpheus's awful words in that bar.

Then Riley turned from the closed door, his face shuttered, and she found a smile from somewhere. "You're right," she said. "We should go to bed."

CHAPTER TWENTY

In the morning, Angharad and Petal shared the news they'd gleaned, from the considerably more salubrious surroundings of the officer's club on Albion Base. It tallied with what Max had learned from the Kratos's men: that the Nike would be taking Admiral Nazarian back to Omega Septimus, and thence to one of the moons. No one had been forthcoming about which moon, but only three of them were inhabited and the crew were all pretty sure they could rule out Quattro, which was mostly used for farming.

"Yeah, but farming what?" said Max gloomily.

She'd been in a strange mood all morning; in fact, ever since they got in last night. Riley was still shaken from seeing his old friend Jyoti, once his confidante and the only person to try to talk to him after the Elandra disaster. A friend he'd left behind with the rest of his life when he let the Service take him.

That pleasure cruiser, those prettily-dressed, smiling people with their servants and their careful hairstyles and their absolute certainty of their place in the world. Had he ever felt like that? Had he ever been part of that crowd?

He was so preoccupied with his thoughts that he hadn't really noticed how subdued Max was until Orpheus started outlining their new plan to trail the Nike wherever she was headed, probably back to the moon where he, Max and Petal had all been born.

"Scared?" Riley said to Max as they left the table to tune the ship's sensors into the Nike's broadcast wave. "Nervous?"

"Nah, I've hacked into comms a million times."

"I meant about Septimus Sei."

Her shrug wasn't half as carefree as she'd probably intended it to be. "Bunch o'fucking culchies," was all she said.

It was later, after they'd followed the Nike into light air, keeping a decent distance so as not to look suspicious, that he discovered what was wrong. He found her talking quietly to Angharad in the mess, which was unusual since Max didn't usually have any time for the redhead.

They both glanced up guiltily as he came in, and then Max got to her feet and said, "There's cards in the drawer."

"Ace is high?" asked Angharad as Max crossed to the storage area and unlatched the drawer.

Riley folded his arms and watched, nonplussed, as instead of playing cards they both shuffled the pack.

"Highest card, highest rank?" Max said, and Angharad nodded. Riley frowned.

Angharad cut first, holding up a queen. Hard to beat. Max drew a seven.

They both looked at it, then Max took a breath and nodded. "Okay," she said. "Okay."

"If you want to swap—"

"What was the point in cutting cards if we're gonna swap?" Max said, exasperated.

"I suppose. Just…" Angharad glanced at Riley, and stopped. "I'll tell you later."

Max nodded again, and Angharad rose gracefully and left the room, dipping her gaze as she passed Riley.

"Okay," he said when it was just him and Max. "What was that about?"

"Nothing. Doesn't matter."

"You know, for a thief and a pirate you're a rotten liar."

She shoved the cards back in their drawer. "It's nothing. Just a strategy for when we get to Omega."

"What kind of strategy?"

"Christ, you ain't very curious, are you?" She pushed past him, heading for the crew quarters. Riley watched her move for a moment, the long stride she got into when she was annoyed, and then went after her.

"Max, this isn't a very big crew and these really aren't very big quarters," he said, following her into their cabin. "Don't keep secrets from me. What are you planning?"

She rolled her shoulders as if preparing for a fight, then turned to him. Her face had a cat-like wariness to it that instantly put him on edge.

"All this sneaking around, flirting and drinking and playing poker, what's it really got us? A ship to chase. A name that might be involved. We're getting nowhere. Flirting is getting me nowhere."

His mouth went suddenly dry. "So…?"

"What do we need? To get into their systems. Access codes, hand and retina prints. Even I can't flirt that out of someone."

"So get one of them really drunk and wait til he passes out," Riley began, but she was shaking her head.

"What, some sub-lieutenant? Think he'll have access to the level of shit we need? Riley, those crates in the hold have your sperm and the embryos of my close

361

relatives in them. There's this Big Freeze that no one seems to know any details about. And people have been disappearing. Every crew we've spoken to has said it. People who've gone asking the wrong questions."

"We don't know that."

She looked at him as if he was mentally subnormal. "If anyone knows what's going on, they'll be high up the food chain. Commanders, admirals. Like the ones on the Nike."

Riley's heart started beating faster. He took a step towards Max. "They're not going to give up that information easily."

"No. I'd need to be..." her gaze skittered away. "On a ship. Or a base. Somewhere they're using those access codes. Somewhere I can actually get the right hand on the right scanner. Somehow a man won't notice. Or mind."

Riley concentrated on breathing. "And how would that be?"

Her gaze met his, dark brown and serious. "You know how," she said. "Riley, I know you don't like to think about it, but I was a whore for quite a few years, and I was a good one. Men came to that brothel with money in their hands and secrets in their head and left with less of both. Find the right way in and you can get anything out of a man in bed."

His eyes closed. His fingers clenched. "Please don't."

"There isn't any other way. If we miss this chance then what can we do?"

"We'll think of something," Riley said desperately, taking her hands and holding them tight. "You and me, we're smart, Max, we can figure this out together."

"We've had weeks and haven't come up with owt else. Look, I know you hate the idea of me being with other people. I try to picture you with another woman and I want to stab her fucking eyeballs out. But I've got to do it."

His fingers gripped hers so tightly he couldn't believe she didn't pull away.

"You said it yourself, you don't want me to but you can't stop me, either."

Riley rested his forehead against hers, choking back tears.

"And hey, look on the bright side. I've got this shiny new chip, so it ain't like I'm going to get knocked up again."

He felt her go still as she realised what she'd said. And then he realised it too.

"Again?" he said into the sudden, deafening silence.

Max had gone entirely rigid. When he drew back a few inches, she remained like a statue, eyes wide, hardly breathing.

"You said," he began, his voice cracking, "there was no baby."

She sobbed in a sudden breath, and gasped, "Well, there isn't now."

Riley didn't know what to think or believe, let alone say. His head began shaking of its own accord, and his hands released hers as if they were made of poison.

"I wanted her to say no, it was a mistake, I thought she would," Max began babbling, "and just tell me to eat right and take some supplements or something, but she didn't, she told me…and I knew I couldn't go through with it, couldn't keep it, Riley look at me, I can't be anyone's fucking mother!"

He stepped back, away from her trembling hands and huge damp eyes. Back again, and again, until his back hit the wall. It really wasn't a big cabin.

"So you just…got it done?" he said, his voice coming from far away.

She nodded jerkily. "They can do it real quick these days. Hardly any bleeding. Your Primer medicine is amazing. Far cry from the girls at the brothel. Used to take all kinds of shit. Bled for days. I'd stopped by the time I left the clinic."

"You," Riley began, and had to start again. His mouth felt like it was full of sawdust. "You had an abortion?"

"Yes. I did."

"And," his fists were shaking, and he hadn't even realised he'd made fists, "and you didn't even ask me?"

"Not your fucking body, is it?" Max snapped, tears starting to spill down her cheeks.

"It was my fucking baby!" he snapped back.

"How do you know?"

He stared at her, horrified. "What do you mean how do I know?"

"How do you know it's not Orpheus's?"

Riley's fists came up. They shook with the effort of not lashing out. "You've been fucking Orpheus?"

"No, not for weeks. But there was only a few days between you," she added nastily. "Could've been his."

He thought he might be sick. "Or Murtaugh's, or Hide's—"

"No. Not them."

Disgusted, he scraped his gaze over her. "How do you know?"

"Do I need to draw you a fucking diagram, Primer? There's other kinds of sex than that."

Bile rose in his throat. The memory of Elandra and those two men rose in his mind, only now it wasn't her elfin features he saw but Max's, and it was Max begging them to do those depraved things to her.

He stumbled backwards, and she said his name, the way she said it when he was making love to her, the way she cried and gasped as she clutched at him and shuddered, but now all he could think of was Orpheus naked with her, Orpheus with his hands on her body and his lips on her skin and Orpheus inside her—

"I'll fucking kill him—"

"Riley," Max said, grabbing for him, and he clutched at her slave tab and deliberately pressed it, watching her convulse and fall to the floor, in a fraction of the pain he was feeling.

He didn't remember leaving the cabin or even how he found Orpheus. The first thing he remembered after Max was smashing his fist into the captain's face.

"The fuck?" roared Orpheus, staggering under the blow.

Riley couldn't even think of words. His fist flew again, and again, making such a satisfying sound as it hit Orpheus's disgusting, rotten flesh. He got the man on the floor and made to kick him, but Orpheus grabbed his leg and shoved him off balance, going sprawling into something hard. Before he could regain his feet Orpheus was on him, his fist unbelievably fast on Riley's face, getting in two punches before Riley grabbed his right arm and twisted it back.

But Orpheus still had one hand free and it went for Riley's throat. Riley punched him hard in the face and shoved hard with his left arm, rolling Orpheus off him and to the floor, coming up to his knees and rearing back for another blow.

He'd reckoned without the captain's catlike speed and grace. Even as his fist powered forward into the other man's gut, Orpheus had produced a knife from somewhere and jammed it into Riley's thigh.

He barely felt it, punching the captain in the ribs, hearing something crack, then seeing the knife rear back again. He grabbed Orpheus's arm but the captain was quicker, dropping the knife and using Riley's momentum against him, shoving his own fist back into his nose then twisting him at lightning speed down onto his face, knee in his back, his arm wrenched back at an angle it shouldn't ever reach.

"Yield," Orpheus hissed.

"Fuck you," Riley spat, and slammed his head back, hearing more than feeling the crunch of his skull against the other man's face. He tried to shove back, roll Orpheus off him, but his arm was yanked back at an angle it wouldn't tolerate, and with a popping sensation it suddenly stopped co-operating.

He roared in frustration, shoving back with his elbow and getting nothing but a dark chuckle in response.

"Now," Orpheus began, as Riley spat blood onto the cold metal of the hold floor, but he didn't get any further.

A shot rang out, then another one, and the pressure on his back suddenly eased. He spun on his back, or at least tried to. All of a sudden his body was screaming at him that it was in pain.

Before he could catalogue it, Max's voice reached him, and he looked up to see her standing with her gun trained on them both, hands steady as anything.

"Hands where I can see them or I swear the next two shots will go in your empty-as-fuck heads. *Hands!*"

Riley managed to get himself onto his back, his right shoulder in absolute agony, his leg a world of pain, and did his best to raise his hands. Beside him, on his knees, Orpheus lifted his.

"Drop the knife," Max said, and the captain did, tossing it a metre or two away.

"Are you insane?" he rasped. "If you'd hit the coolant—"

"Are *you* fucking insane?" Max snarled. The gun didn't waver, even as the rest of the crew rushed in behind her. "What are you *doing*?"

"He attacked me," Orpheus began.

"Oh, and I see how you responded rationally and calmly," she snapped back. "Riley, what the fuck is wrong with you?"

He lay there breathing hard, pain radiating through

him from Orpheus's blows and Max's bloody gun, and rolled his head to look up at her. "You are, Max. You fucking are."

Justine was as disgusted with the two of them as Max.

"Children," she said witheringly, hands on her hips as she stood over them in the hold. "Get yourselves to sickbay. I'm not helping you."

Max left them to it, turning on her heel and heading for the mess, where she poured out a large measure of the gin Émile had picked up on Sigma Prime, and downing it one. Then she poured another.

They'd live. She'd shot them both in the leg, figuring if that didn't get their attention she could always aim a bit higher.

"I suppose it's flattering," Angharad said from behind her, "to have men fighting over you."

Max drank more gin. "You'd think," she said. Fuck, she really wanted a cigarette, but only a moron lit up inside a pressurised ship in deep space.

"Dare I ask why?"

"You probably do, but that don't guarantee I'll answer."

All of a sudden Max felt like a puppet with its strings cut. Flopping onto a chair, she poured more gin, and didn't look up as Angharad sat down across from her.

"Was it about what we decided earlier?"

The girl probably wouldn't go away until Max told her. "That's how it started."

"Want to talk about it?"

"Nope."

Angharad tilted her pretty head. Her lip was still swollen from its close encounter with Max's fist a few days ago, but somehow she even managed to make that look sexy. "You don't like me very much, do you?"

"Don't take it personal. I don't like a lot of people."

"You like Riley."

"Not right now I don't."

"He's just jealous."

Max rubbed at her arm above the slave cuff. It still ached, an ache she thought she'd left behind on the land train. "Look, Angharad, not that I don't enjoy our little chats, but is there any chance you might fuck off soon?"

Angharad quirked her eyebrows. "I've been where you are. Two men who thought they both had a claim on me."

"For the love of God, Orpheus doesn't."

"But you still spent the night with him several times, right?"

Max lost the little patience she had left. "I also fucked your girlfriend. Want me to get her into a fight with Riley, too?"

"She'd win," Angharad said complacently. "Don't you want to know how I resolved the situation? With the men fighting?"

"No," said Max.

"You like them fighting over you?"

"No."

"Then—"

"Look, just drop it, all right?"

Angharad sighed. She did it beautifully, just like she did everything else. She was really starting to get on Max's tits.

Then she said something that surprised Max. "Are you sure you're all right with taking Moreau?"

She stared at her gin. "Why wouldn't I be?"

"I've heard...he has particular tastes."

Max looked up suspiciously. "You ain't talking hair and eye colour, are you?"

"No." Angharad looked uneasy. "They say he likes pain."

"Taking or giving?"

"Giving."

"Figures."

"Aren't you worried?"

Max gave her a look. "Less than you would be. I don't have a pretty face to ruin," she said, and drank some more gin.

Angharad frowned a little and regarded Max. "Why do you shave your head?" she asked.

Max looked at her drink, which was mysteriously empty again, and refilled it. Truth was, she didn't know why. It was practical, and it annoyed people, so there were two good reasons. But the girl wanted a story, so she might as well give her one.

"Years ago," she said. "Some shitty backwater planet. First place I got to after I hopped a flight from Septimus Sei, so...well, anyway, it doesn't matter. I'd been surviving. Getting from place to place. Doing bits of work. Then one day...well, night actually. Used to get dark as anything out there, cos there was a bigger planet blocking out the sun. Great for a thief, o'course."

"You were a thief?"

Max saluted with her glass. "I've been lots of things, love. So anyway, I'm out in this lane somewhere, looking at these pigs and wondering if I can nick one, 'cos I'm hungry and I like bacon, but what the fuck do I know about butchery? And I turn a corner, and there's these three lads. Not all that big, or all that mean, but... kind of desperate looking. Long story short, they thought they could take what they wanted from me. And I didn't want to give it. I know that'll come as some surprise to you. But it wasn't long after I'd left the brothel and I'd told myself I didn't have to fuck anyone I didn't want to."

Angharad said nothing. Max supposed this was one bit she didn't need to explain.

369

"So I fought them. Didn't know my own strength. Used my teeth on the first one, like with that culchie on the beach. The second one I got with my knife, right across his ankles," her fist made the motion, slicing across the table. "Cut his heels, you know, the tendon at the back. The other one pissed himself and ran away. But I was still stuck there, under the first one, all covered in blood. I didn't know if he was dead. Never killed anyone before."

Max paused. She had killed someone in that pig lane. The smell of blood and shit and fear was only a memory away.

"And I managed to get free of him, and ran, but I was covered in shit. I mean, actual shit, cos it was a pig lane. And blood, and…" Remember the story, Max. "Well anyway. I washed and washed but I couldn't get my hair clean. Couldn't get any of me clean, but I could nick a pair of shears and cut my hair off. And…well, I get some clippers every now and then and that's all I need to do to it. Simple, innit."

Angharad stared, eyes huge.

Max poured some more gin. It was beginning to blunt the edges of a day that had gone to shit far too early.

"On the beach," Angharad whispered. "That was you? With the teeth?"

Max gnashed her teeth at the girl, who jumped. "Who the fuck d'you think it was?"

"I…I suppose I…didn't want to think about it. But why? Didn't you have weapons? Wasn't Riley protecting you?"

Max gave her a look so black it might have killed someone less dense.

"I mean—"

Since the girl wasn't shutting up or going away, Max pushed herself to her feet. "You're back in Petal's room, right?"

"Yes—"

"Good." She scooped up the gin bottle, left the glass, and went to get her things from Riley's cabin before he came back. It didn't take her long. A few clothes, weapons, and her tablet were about all she owned, which was depressing as hell.

There was Hide's old cabin, of course, but it felt far too soon to take that over. Besides, going back where she'd started felt vaguely appropriate.

Max helped herself to some spare bedding from the laundry compartment, then trailed the lot down to the hold which was, thankfully, empty of stupid men beating the shit out of each other. There was some blood on the floor, which she'd bet her left buttock Orpheus wouldn't clear up and Riley would make a mess of. After all, it looked like Orpheus had done something awful to Riley's shoulder, which would mean another brace on it. Damn, and they could really use him fighting fit when they got to Septimus Sei.

Max supposed she probably shouldn't have shot him in that case, but she'd needed to do something, and anyway, it was only the flesh of his calf she hit.

She more or less settled into the old cell, marvelling that it hadn't really been that long since Riley had locked her in here in the first place. She supposed it had been weeks. Hard to keep track out here in the black.

She was on her third attempt of counting them up when the doorbell she'd forgotten about chimed.

Hmm. Had she synced her micro to it? No, apparently not. That meant getting to her feet and doing it the old fashioned way, pressing the intercom button.

"Whoever it is, I really don't want to talk."

"It's Justine," said the voice, "and you probably ought to hear this."

Dammit. The woman was irritating as hell but she was clever and she was a good medic, and if Riley had—

Oh shit! What if Riley was really badly hurt?

She had the door open in seconds.

"Love what you've done with the place," Justine said, and Max gave her the finger as she tramped back to her mattress on the floor and picked up her gin.

"Did you have something actually important to say, or is this another 'let's pretend to give shitty advice to Max in the guise of gawping over her latest stupid misfortune' thing? 'Cos I've gotta tell you, I never had no patience for lectures in the first place and today really ain't a good day."

"No," said Justine, looking down at her. "The day after a miscarriage rarely is."

Max nearly smacked her own teeth out with the gin bottle. "What? How did—" Oh fuck, Riley must have told her. She'd bloody kill him—

But Justine just rolled her eyes. "Firstly, because I am a medical professional. Secondly, because I've been through it. And thirdly, because I made Riley tell me why he was trying to kill the captain."

She waited for that to sink in. Max rolled her head back against the wall and squinted up. "You've been through it?"

"Three times. And not voluntarily or cleanly in a clinic, either. They can do marvellous things these days," she went on, as if that wasn't a bombshell and a half, "although I believe you're still advised to wait a few days before having sex again. Not that I suppose there's much to stop you and Riley going at it like rabbits."

Max gaped at her.

"He does have a dislocated shoulder, however, and I've had to reset his nose for the second time in as many months, so I'd advise you go easy on him for now. And just in case you're wondering, the bullet came out of his leg quite cleanly."

"What," Max said, finding her voice, "makes you

think I'd want to sleep with him after a stunt like that?"

Justine shrugged as if to concede the point. "It was monumentally stupid," she said. "Only a fool attacks Orpheus. Or a madman." She sighed. "I suppose that's love for you."

Max flinched. "What would you know about it?"

"I'm not blind, Max."

At that she laughed. "Yes, you fucking are. Orpheus is crazy in love with you and you've got no fucking clue. Unless you have, and you're just being a bitch."

Justine went very still for a moment, and then she took a breath and said, as if Max hadn't spoken, "I suppose any man in his position would be upset, looking to lash out. It's just unfortunate he picked on Orpheus."

"There weren't any other candidates," Max muttered.

"That's truer than you know." She hesitated. "Orpheus doesn't talk about his past much, but you can take whatever inference you like from this: at some time in his youth he was sterilised."

"Yeah, well," Max began, displaying the pink skin on her inner arm.

"I don't mean a chip. I mean surgery. Permanent." She made a snipping motion with her fingers, and Max made a face.

"Really? But I never noticed...uh...you know what, never mind."

Then the implication of what Justine had said sunk in, and she groaned. "Oh, for fuck's sake. All that and there was no way it could've been Orpheus's?"

Justine nodded.

"Does Riley know this?"

She nodded again. "Halfway through his explanation Orpheus started laughing, so I asked him what was so funny, and, well."

"Orpheus laughs?" Max muttered.

"Interestingly, they seem to have shaken hands over

the incident. I suppose that's men for you. They're like boys getting into a fight in the playground."

Justine straightened up and brushed some imaginary dust off her shirt. "Now all we need is for you and Riley to kiss and make up and we might be able to see this thing through without any more fatalities."

Max thought about what she was going to have to do when they reached the Omega system and laughed bleakly.

"Wouldn't bet on it," she said.

CHAPTER TWENTY ONE

Max lay awake and stared at the ceiling. She'd forgotten how much less comfortable the mattress on the floor of the brig was, compared to Riley's big bed. And how much lonelier. Even if Max didn't like being held as she slept, it was just somehow…reassuring to have his big body beside her.

How the fuck do I fix this?

Quite apart from Riley's insane jealousy and apparent berserker tendencies, there was the unavoidable fact that he'd used her slave cuff against her yesterday.

She looked down at her wrist, which looked just the same as it always had. There was no visible sign of his betrayal.

Eventually, unable to lie awake any longer, she got up and dressed, heading up to the mess in the hope of finding some coffee. Not tea. Tea was Riley's drink, and that felt…wrong, this morning.

What she found was Orpheus, sitting with his feet up on the table and what looked like a glass of whiskey beside him. His face bore several small cuts, most noticeably across his nose, and the skin under his eyes was black with bruising.

"Morning," she said, warily.

"Is it?"

"Technically." She started some coffee going and leaned back against the counter. "Couldn't sleep?"

He shrugged.

"*Do* you sleep?"

"Everyone sleeps."

"Hmm." Her gaze strayed down to his long legs, crossed at the ankle. "You okay this morning?"

"Probably better than your boyfriend."

Max flinched. "Yeah. Well."

"I notice," he said, "you shot us both."

"Had to get your attention somehow."

"You could have shouted."

"You wouldn't have heard me."

Orpheus shrugged as if that was a moot point. "He's a fucking maniac when his blood is up."

"You should've seen him in that gully," Max said with feeling. "I thought he was going to kill me."

"And instead he fucked you. Would have been better all round if you could have gone in that direction yesterday."

Max stared at him incredulously.

"Just saying," Orpheus said. He looked down at his tablet. "We're set to arrive in the Omega system in five days. Maybe another day to reach Septimus. We start at Sei, see what we can find out from who. We won't get onto Otto unless we have access codes." He looked up at her, and she noticed for the first time how green his eyes were. "Angharad tells me you two have a plan for that."

Max took a deep breath. This kind of plan wouldn't have bothered her before, but now...

Pull your fucking self together, Max.

"Yes," she said. "We do."

"You cut cards for them."

She nodded.

"She tells me Moreau is an evil bastard."

"Kink isn't evil."

Orpheus gave her a knowing look. "There's kink, and then there's inflicting pain," he said.

"Yes," said Max. "Speaking of, you can save me looking. Does anyone have an electroshock gun I can borrow? And possibly a rubber sheet."

Riley was awake when she let herself into his cabin. "Well, bollocks," she said, glaring at the door as it swooshed gently closed. "I wish these things slammed."

He lay on his back, right arm strapped to his chest, face dark with bruises. She couldn't see his legs, but from the state of him yesterday she expected they'd be in a fine mess, too. He looked like hell, in short, and when he turned his head and saw her, his eyes contained all the pain in the world.

"Max," he murmured, and tried to sit up. But it didn't work very well, and he laid back with a grimace.

"Does it hurt?" she asked.

"Everything hurts."

"Good."

He looked up at her, blue eyes swimming with sorrow.

"What the fuck," she asked, "were you thinking? Orpheus, for fuck's bloody sake. He could kill you with his little finger."

Riley closed his eyes. "I know."

"You weren't even bloody armed!"

"Yeah."

"I've half a mind to shoot you again."

"I'd deserve it."

Oh God, not this again. He was going all remorseful, like he had in that cave. Well, at least this time he had something to be remorseful about.

"Get up," she said, and he opened his eyes. "Come

on, get up. Out of bed."

She held out her hand, and tried not to react to the feel of his as she pulled him upright. He stood with all his weight on one leg, the other swathed in bandages from where Orpheus had stabbed him and she'd shot him.

Refusing to let herself pity him, she shook the waterproof sheeting over the bed. They hadn't had anything rubber, but the sickbay had several protective mattress covers, so she was making do. Max had heard that fancy houses and Primer hospitals had bedlinen that cleaned itself, but the Eurydice wasn't that sophisticated. If it didn't go in the laundry compartment, it didn't get washed.

"Um?" said Riley.

"Sit down," she said.

"Why have you just covered the bed in sheeting? Are you going to stab me?"

"Sit."

He did, looking up at her uncertainly.

"Give me your hand."

Obediently, he held out his left hand, and she unfastened the leather vambrace from it. Then she produced the electroshock gun from her weapons belt, and without warning, jammed it on full blast against his inner wrist.

He jerked and writhed, but Max's grip was strong and she didn't let him pull away. She kept her eyes on him the whole time, watched the waves of pain swamp his face, the muscles in his arm contract and ripple uncontrollably, the lids of his eyes peel right back to show white all around.

When he bit down on his lip hard enough to cause blood to mix with the drool, she let go. He twitched like a fish out of water, flopping around on the bed, curling into a ball and gasping.

"Hurts, doesn't it?" she said.

Riley stared up at her in shock.

"Still, at least you didn't piss yourself. Lot of people do. Fucking stank in that land train. Then again, we were shovelling shit, so it was hard to pick all the smells apart."

Slowly, Riley uncurled, and used his abused left arm to push himself into a sitting position. His wrist was red and blistered.

"Is that what I did to you?" he asked, voice broken, staring at the wound.

"Pretty much, yeah."

"Max, I…"

"You're sorry. Yeah. I know. I'm sorry too. You know what, you should've just hit me. Punched me, or slapped me, or broke my arm or something. Cut me. Shot me. Because that's what you'd have done if we was equal. If I wasn't your slave. But the one thing you could do to me no one else could…the one thing you could do to remind me you own me? That's what you did."

She put the electroshock gun back into its holster, then let her hand rest on the hilt of her gun.

"You ever pull that shit again and I will shoot you. And not with electricity, either."

"I won't. Ever."

"How'm I supposed to believe you? I never thought you would in the first place, but, here we are."

"Max, please." He edged closer, wincing. "I'm sorry. I don't know what else to say."

"I don't think there is anything."

He looked utterly defeated, sitting there staring up at her like a kicked puppy.

"At the end of the day, you own me. And I was a fucking idiot to forget about it."

"I've never treated you like a slave."

She looked at the cuff on her wrist. Then she looked

back at him.

"You just did," she said, and left.

The next few days were the most miserable of Riley's life, even worse than the day Elandra had made her terrible accusation. Max remained sleeping in the brig, ignoring him as much as possible when she saw him around the ship, turning her gaze away from him when they ate at the same table. Pretending he didn't exist. More than once he tried to talk to her, but she pushed past him and walked away.

Not that he really blamed her. He'd like to walk away from himself right now. Whilst Orpheus seemed to consider that they were even, Max clearly didn't, and probably never would. What she'd said to him hurt even more than the wounds he already had.

The one thing you could do to remind me you own me? That's what you did.

He could try explaining that he hadn't been in his right mind, that he was hurt and in shock and angry and all the rest of it, but that still didn't excuse what he'd done.

The rest of the crew was giving them both a wide berth, especially after Murtaugh had made a comment about a lovers' tiff and Max had punched him hard enough to break his cheekbone.

Worse, he knew she and Angharad were planning something when they arrived at Omega Septimus, and he knew he was going to hate it. And that he could do nothing to stop it.

Justine worked on his shoulder, using some muscle-mending stuff she'd picked up on Sigma Prime that made it heal a hell of a lot faster, but by the time they made landfall on Omega Septimus Sei, he was still wearing the damn sling. The bullet wound in his calf was healing well, but the effects of Orpheus's knife were still making themselves known. If they ended up in another fight, he knew he'd be less than useful.

"All right," said Petal, shaking the rain from her newly pink and purple hair as she came back into the hold. "The Nike landed yesterday, and the crew are taking their ease here for two days. Moreau and Nazarian are staying at a place in Reservoir Colony, the Service officers' club. Apparently it's where they always stay when they're visiting, because they don't like the facilities at the base on Otto."

"Can civilians get in?" asked Max. She was in a skinny vest and shorts, her feet bare on the cold hold floor.

"For a fee. But," Petal went on, glancing at Angharad, "they do have 'guests'. Usually brought in from the local brothels. Get in with them and that's how you do it."

"Fine," Max said. "I'm ready whenever you are."

"Best get yourselves to the brothels and offer your services. They did say it was hard to get girls for Moreau," Petal added, glancing at Max.

"Then I'm sure they'll be glad to have me. Angharad, you got much to do yourself?"

"Oh, a quick tidy-up," said Angharad, who looked utterly perfect, as usual. "Half an hour?"

Max nodded and went to her quarters in the brig, walking past Riley as if he wasn't there.

Angharad noticed his expression, and patted his arm. "She'll come round," she said.

"You know nothing about it," he replied, and turned away.

The officers' club was located on one of the few respectable streets in the sprawling, hopeless Reservoir Colony. Most of the people there worked for the water company, pumping supplies to the rest of the moon. It was a dangerous job, and created plenty of orphans, who usually ended up in the same place Max had apparently been born.

Except that Max seemed to be part of this Service breeding programme, and who the hell knew where she'd really come from?

Riley looked up Commander Avilius Philon Moreau's public profile again, but saw nothing more than he had the last ten times. Exemplary record, promotions, mentioned in dispatches, yada yada yada. No mention of a secret programme to steal reproductive cells from Service personnel and use them to create a secret race. Funny, that.

He was waiting for Max and Angharad as they left. Every part of him wanted to grab her and pull her back and beg her not to go. But he didn't. He let her go, and then he took off his sling and put on his coat and walked out of the hold without talking to anyone.

The officer's club was house in an imposing building, one of the few in this one-horse town that stood over two storeys high. On the corner opposite was a saloon, and Riley sat on the verandah outside it, nursing a beer and watching the club.

He'd been there for nearly an hour, a damp chilly hour, when a group of people approached the club, mostly women but with a few young men mixed in. They were led by a blowsy-looking woman wearing too much make-up. She knocked on the door, and thrust her bosom at the young officer who opened it. He smiled, and beckoned her in.

Max and Angharad were towards the back, Angharad in a skimpy dress with her hair in crimson waves. Max looked like a woman going to her execution.

Don't do it, please don't do it...

But she went in, and the door closed, and all Riley could do was watch and wait. People came in and out of the saloon, and in and out of the club, but no one else sat outside on this dull, drizzly evening. The bartender seemed to think Riley was mad.

After a while, a small cat jumped up onto the wooden verandah. It was skinny, black and wary with huge eyes, and it nosed up to his table. Riley put out a hand, and the cat approached with agonising slowness.

"I might call you Max," he said, and the cat twitched its ears at him.

"She'll love you for that," came Orpheus's gravelly voice, and Riley looked up to see him detaching himself from the shadows.

"Yeah, well, it's not like I can go any lower in her estimation."

Orpheus leaned down to the cat, who let him stroke its head. Fickle bastards, cats. Mind you, Orpheus was probably half feline.

"Probably not," he said, and straightened up to go inside. When he came back he had a packet of pork scratchings, and tossed one down to the cat. It gobbled it up, just as fast as Max.

He fed it another, then a third, and then he looked up and said to Riley, "There's no need for you to be here."

"Yeah, there is."

"She can handle herself." He lit a cigarette.

"Yeah, she can."

"She currently hates your guts."

"Yeah, she does." Riley took a swig of his beer and shrugged his good shoulder. "Your point being?"

Orpheus shook his head slowly. "I've seen a lot of men fall in love with whores. Women too. Never seen it work out all happy ever after. It ain't going to for Petal and Angharad, and it was never going to for you."

"Oh, and you know all about it, do you?"

Orpheus blew out a cloud of smoke. "More than you do. Face it, Primer, she'd fucked four other people on the crew before she got round to you. We take on someone else she fancies, she'll probably fuck them too."

"You want to walk away right now," Riley said, fists clenching.

"No I don't." Orpheus's bloody Sphinx gaze flickered over him. "You're going nowhere, are you?"

Riley fixed his gaze hard on the redbrick opposite, and folded his arms. "I'll be here."

Orpheus flicked his cigarette on the ground. "Poor bastard," was all he said, before he went back inside.

Riley reached down, scooped up the cat, and held it close. It sank its teeth into his hand, and he swore and released it. Nonchalant, the cat perched on the table, eating the rest of the pork scratchings.

"You really are like Max," he said.

The cat ignored him.

"Uncannily so."

The club door opened a few times, but it was more than an hour before Max was the one who came out. She was huddled into her coat, looking neither left nor right as she stumbled down the steps and along the street.

Riley was on his feet in seconds. His leg ached at the sudden movement after sitting out in the damp for so long, but he ignored it.

"No," said Orpheus behind him. "I'll go."

"Like fuck—"

"Primer. Give her space."

He watched Orpheus saunter after Max, who glanced back and saw him, hesitated, then let him walk with her. Riley waited, agonised, until they'd turned the corner, and then he hustled after them.

The ship's passenger door was just closing behind them as he approached. He tapped in his code with shaking fingers, darted inside, and nearly ran into Petal. She sat on one of the crates, twisting her fingers and looking miserable.

"Oh, it's you," she said. She watched him hurry past,

and called after him, "Sucks, doesn't it?"

He paused, glanced back. *Never seen it work out all happy ever after.* "She'll be fine," he said shortly, and headed to Max's room in the brig.

"She's not there. Orpheus took her upstairs," Petal said.

"Christ, can't he wait five minutes for a debrief?"

But as he reached the corridor leading to the mess and crew quarters, voices made him hesitate. They came from the sickbay.

Riley's blood turned to ice. His feet moved of their own accord, running, propelling him fast towards sickbay, and when he got there he had to grip the doorframe to keep from collapsing in shock.

Max lay on one of the beds, naked and covered in bruises. Her thighs and breasts were smeared with blood. Her neck wore a ring of purple. There were burn marks on her skin, just like the one on his wrist.

She wasn't moving.

Orpheus and Justine looked up as he hung there, scarcely able to breathe.

"I've sedated her," Justine said, reading his face, and Riley's heart restarted.

"Max," he whispered, stumbling into the room. Her clothes lay on the counter, torn and filthy. "Oh Christ."

"Do you think he knew?" Justine said, as Riley's horrified gaze catalogued the damage. Her lip was swollen to a cut, her arms chafed as if they'd been bound. Her breasts had electroshock burns on them.

"Angharad said he likes pain. That's why it's difficult to find girls for him."

He likes pain, does he? I'll show him fucking pain. Riley's hands shook with rage.

"And I suppose if he thought she knew something, he'd have killed her."

"Could have sent her back as a message."

There was a bite mark on her thigh. Human teeth had broken the skin.

"I'll kill him," Riley heard someone say. It sounded like his own voice.

"Primer—"

"I'll fucking *dismember* him."

"Riley, be rational."

"*Rational*?" He wanted to tear Moreau limb from limb with his bare hands.

"If he's killed, we'll never get the info we need. Even if Max managed to steal his access codes, they'll be blocked as soon as he's found."

"You think I care about access codes?" Riley roared.

"Don't let this be in vain," Justine said. She was carefully, gently, cleaning the blood from Max's face. When she glanced up, her dark eyes were solemn.

Riley shook his head. "Tell Max I love her," he said, and turned on his heel.

He made it to his cabin and strapped on his weapons belts. When he came out, Orpheus was waiting.

"Get in my way and I'll kill you," Riley said.

"I'm coming with you."

Riley stopped, looked the captain over. His face was nearly as impassive as ever, but there was fire behind his eyes.

In the myth, the lyre player descended to into hell to bargain for the woman he loved. If Riley had been in his place he'd have ripped out the jugular of the king of the underworld and turned his kingdom into flames.

He nodded, and they set out into the dark night.

Riley had no plan, except perhaps to storm in there and kill anyone who got in his way. But when they reached the club there was a crowd outside. Junior officers were herding civilians away, several barely-dressed women amongst them. One of them spied Riley and Orpheus and rushed over. It was Angharad.

"Turn around and walk away," she said in a low voice. "Do it. Now."

"Like fuck—"

"Moreau is dead," Angharad said, and both men stared at her. "Now, unless you want to become a person of interest to the Service, I suggest you walk away."

And don't look back, or you'll lose her forever.

She started back towards the landing area, and Riley hurried after her. "What do you mean, dead?" Who the fuck had cheated him of his revenge?

"I mean life is fucking extinct, Primer. He was found by one of his men. I heard," she lowered her voice even more, and it was hard to hear her over the rain, "he was electrocuted. One of those devices, you know, an electroshock, right to the balls."

Orpheus winced. Riley stumbled over his own feet. "Seriously?"

"It's what I heard. I don't know. Where's Max?"

"On the ship," Orpheus said, as Riley's mind whirled. Max had done it. She had to. A fitting revenge for the torture Moreau had inflicted on her. Or maybe it had been an accident?

No. Max wouldn't have done something like that accidentally.

His gaze met Orpheus's. "We need to get the fuck out of here," he said, and the captain nodded sharply.

CHAPTER TWENTY TWO

Max's dreams were full of blood.

She was covered in it, running from it, chased by a tidal wave of crimson. The blue spark of electricity shot at her, from eyes as cold as ice. She screamed, tripped, fell and fell. The abyss was endless.

"Max?"

She kept running, away from that voice, away from the hand patiently reaching out to her. She ran, and she survived. She always survived. But no matter how far she ran the hand was still there, the voice still called her name, and eventually she grabbed that hand and it swung her to safety.

She woke with a gasp to the sound of the ship's engines and the clinical scent of the sickbay. The room was dark, just a few low lights to illuminate the door and the figure sitting in a chair, watching her. She didn't need light to tell her it was Riley. Nobody else was that size.

"What," she began, coughed, and started again. Her throat felt like sandpaper. Silently, Riley held out a cup of water and she took it without touching his fingers.

"What are you doing here?"

He shrugged. His arm was bound into its sling, his face drawn and tired under its fading bruises.

"Thought you might need something. Justine said you can have another painkiller in...oh, an hour or so. Unless it's really bad and I can give you another sedative."

She shook her head. She hurt, by God she hurt, but she didn't want to be pushed back into unconsciousness again.

"How long...?"

He looked at his micro. "Eight hours, fifty-seven minutes, and thirty-four seconds. Thirty-five. Thirty-six."

"You haven't been here all that time?"

He nodded. He looked like hell. He'd looked like hell all week, miserable and guilty, but this was even worse.

"Why?"

Riley sighed. "Why d'you think?"

Max eased herself into a sitting position. Riley reached out to her, just as he'd been reaching out in her dreams, and she flinched back, just like she had then. His hand fell back into his lap.

"Honestly, Riley, I don't know what I think. And right now I feel like shit run over twice, so don't make me do any heavy thinking, all right?"

"All right," he said softly.

She wore one of his shirts, the fabric soft and smelling of him. Under it, she was covered with dressings. Had Justine applied them? She must have done, she wouldn't have let anyone else use her sickbay.

So she knew, and so did Orpheus, because he'd walked her back to the ship and seen how hard it was for her to even put one foot in front of the other, and taken her straight up to sickbay without even asking.

And Petal had seen her come in, although she was so

wrapped up in her own concern for Angharad that she probably wouldn't have noticed if Max had grown another head.

"Is Angharad all right?" she asked, and Riley nodded. "Did she get anything from Nazarian?"

"That's what you're asking?" Riley said, incredulous. "That's your concern?"

"I'll be buggered if all this was for nothing," Max said. Damn, unfortunate choice of words. "Do you have a tablet? I want to check something."

He handed one over, watching her carefully. He almost certainly knew the extent of what Moreau had done to her.

"And don't look at me like that," she said, without glancing up. "I knew what I was getting myself into."

"Did you? Really? The extent of it?"

She hesitated, and shot him a guilty look. "I didn't exactly foresee the cattle prod. I suppose there's a symmetry to it."

Riley stared. "How can you joke about it? Max, he tortured you. I know you've explained to me about kink but that's just fucking torture, plain and simple."

"And you know all about torture, do you? How's your wrist?"

"Not half as bad as the rest of you," he shot back.

She glared at him, and turned her attention back to the tablet. "Anyway, he's dead now. I electrocuted him."

"Right in the balls, so I heard."

"Good news travels fast." The data on the tablet blurred. "Thought he'd like a taste of his own medicine. He never thought I'd fight back, you see. I let him think I was weak. That he'd broken me. He thought he could leave me lying there covered in my own snot and blood and tears while he just got up and fannied about with Service business. He never saw me coming. I held that fucking electric gun there until there was smoke coming off him and the only reason he was still twitching was that I was sending ten million volts into his bollocks. Still. Figured safe is better than sorry, so I smothered him with the pillow for good measure." She blinked her eyes clear. "Trust me, that fucker is dead."

She didn't look up to see Riley's reaction. He was probably staring at her in horror, like a shocked little boy.

"That's my girl," he said, his voice rough, and then she did look up. There were tears in Riley's eyes, but he was smiling.

"And I'm sorry, I know him being dead means we can't use his codes and shit, but—"

"Are you kidding me? Sorry? Max, I want to bring him back to life so I can kill him again. I was ready to murder him. I wanted to rip him apart with my bare hands for what he did to you." He reached out and grabbed her wrist, her hand, held it tight. "You never have to do that again, you know that, don't you?"

Max looked down at his fingers wrapped around hers, the knuckles scarred, the nails torn down, and she squeezed his hand with her own.

"I know," she said, and felt herself start to smile. "Because…"

He frowned, sliding his chair closer to take the tablet she held out.

And then his expression cleared, and he looked up at her in astonishment.

"You're in?"

Max grinned. "He'd already logged in, the stupid bastard. I used his account to add myself to the system. My hand, my eye, my codes. As far as the system is concerned, I'm a fucking high-level Service officer."

Riley's eyes were wide, glued to the screen, his head shaking in wonder.

"Jesus, Max. You're serious? You're not fucking with

me?"

She shook her head. "So it was worth it," she said, and the joy drained from his face.

"No. Nothing's worth...this. Nothing is worth you being hurt like this."

Something turned over inside her at that, at his earnest expression. "I'm all right," she said gruffly. "I'll survive. I always do."

"I know you do," he said, voice cracking a little. "Still can't bear you being hurt. Max, I—"

But whatever he was going to say was interrupted by the buzz of his micro. Sighing, he answered it.

"Yeah, she's awake. And," he glanced up at her. "There's some good news."

Later, after he'd helped Max dress and walked her, shaky and determined, down to the mess; after Angharad had attempted to hug Max and been rebuffed—"I'm too fucking sore, but I appreciate the sentiment"—and they'd shared the news that they had access to the Service systems; after they'd eaten and Riley had escorted Max back to her room in the brig; after all that, he lay in his bed, staring at the ceiling and fantasising about all the things he'd do to Moreau if he'd had the chance.

The little black cat, who'd apparently crept onto the ship while no one was looking, curled asleep by his feet, occasionally batting at his toes through the covers if he accidentally disturbed it. He'd have to talk to Justine about de-fleaing it, or it'd infest the whole ship.

Then his door opened with a soft hiss, and he turned his head to see Max standing there wrapped in a blanket, her eyes huge and dark, bandages standing out pale against her skin.

She said nothing, but dropped the blanket and climbed into bed beside him. Her head nestled on his shoulder, the soft fuzz of her hair brushing the scar there. Her hand crept inside his sling and her fingers twined with his.

Riley turned his head, kissed her forehead, and held her as she fell asleep.

"Can't make head nor tail of this data," said Émile as Riley took a seat at breakfast. "None of it makes any sense. Can't work out what I'm looking at."

Riley took the tablet and scanned it. He was right, it was basically gobbledegook. "It's encrypted."

"Well, duh," said Justine. "Are all Service files encrypted?"

"Depends on the content. And the encryption changes every day. A rolling cipher."

"Do we have the cipher?" Orpheus asked.

"No. But we have the next best thing." He put down the tablet, and looked round at them expectantly. "Max," he reminded them.

"She up to this?" Émile asked.

Riley thought of Max lying asleep in his bed, her face shadowed with bruises. That she had to rest physically was obvious; that she was rubbish at resting was equally obvious.

"Pretty sure she'll be up to it, yeah," he said. And when he went back to his cabin he found her awake and playing with the cat.

"So fucking bored already," she said. "Also, where did this flea bitten little bastard come from?"

"Followed me aboard," said Riley, reaching out to the cat, who batted at his hand. "Kept me company while I was waiting for you."

Max eyed him as suspiciously as the cat, and Riley winced. "Waiting?"

"Um." He rubbed the back of his neck. "I just wanted to make sure you were okay."

Max cocked her head. "Orpheus wasn't there by accident, was he?"

"Do you think Orpheus does anything by accident?" Riley sighed. "I wanted to walk with you, but I didn't think you'd let me."

I'd walk into hell for you.

Max looked down at the cat for a while, drumming her fingers for it to chase, and eventually Riley cleared his throat and held out the tablet. "So anyway, I wondered—"

But he didn't get any further, because Max took the tablet, tossed it aside, and pulled him close for a kiss. Her hands were firm on his arms, her touch gentling as she brushed his dislocated shoulder. Riley held her carefully, desperate not to hurt her.

"You know what I want?" she said against his lips.

"What?"

"I want you to make love to me. I want you to remind me how it's supposed to be."

His breath caught in his throat.

"If you still want me, that is," she added, and Riley fought the urge to laugh. He'd have thought there would never come a day when he'd turn down Max's sexual advances, but it looked like today was it.

"Of course I want you. I could be dead and still want you. But—"

"But," she agreed, smiling a little. "Maybe give it a day or so, yeah? I'm not quite…um, up to it, yet."

He kissed her again and held her as tight as he dared. "Wait as long as you want," he said. "I'll be here."

"Okay," Max said, after hours of staring at data and getting nowhere, "none of this makes sense."

"It's a cipher," Riley reminded her. "Isn't that the point?"

Her shoulders felt like they were glued to her ears.

395

She tried to force them down, rolled the joints, winced as the muscles made cracking noises. She'd been sitting in his bed all day, because there were fewer distractions than in the public areas of the ship. Riley insisted on interrupting her every few hours to force food into her mouth and make her drink sips of tea, which, all right, she probably needed, but couldn't he tell she was trying to concentrate?

"No, that's not it. I thought I'd got something, like… look. Here. I'm looking for patterns, right? Simple key words, that's how you crack a cipher. Found a few that worked."

She transferred the data to his tablet so he could see. "Here…I was looking for words like 'donor' 'sample' 'subject' and things like that. And I found them."

Riley was staring like it was written in ancient Aramaic. "You did?"

"Yes," Max began.

"How?"

She considered trying to explain a rolling cipher to him, then gave up and said, "I'm clever, all right?"

He cracked a smile. "You are. But look, if you deciphered those words, then what's the problem?"

"The problem is that only about a third of the words make sense. Now, it might be that there are different ciphers going on here, which will make slow going, or, it might be that these words just don't make sense."

Riley was looking at her expectantly. "Or?"

"How did you know there was an 'or'?"

He raised his brows. "Max."

She couldn't help smiling at that, even though it hurt her bruised lip. "All right. There's a lot of stuff in here that might just be jargon. Service terms, medical stuff, I don't know. Does anything look familiar to you?"

"No…wait. Yes. Hang on. You've got Greek letters. Does your cipher allow for punctuation?"

"Some, why?"

"Because Service jargon is full of the bloody stuff. Here, look, change this to a forward slash and...and this to an em dash—"

Max did, wondering why the hell the type of dash made any difference.

"It does," Riley said, apparently reading her face. "Now, that's...enlisted Tau Secundus, 61719, so...ten years-ish, background in bio-engineering...basic training...transferred to...612, that's R&D, I think, maybe? Promotion, OR-7, OR-9, OFD...OF-2..."

"This makes sense to you?" Max said, as he reeled off the gobbledegook.

Riley nodded, absorbed. "DSM, MCM, BFP. BFP?" he repeated.

"Big Fucking Prick," Max said, throwing up her hands. "The rest?"

"Right. The rest. We're looking at a Lieutenant Salwar Moser, enlisted about ten years ago—Service runs its own calendar—and worked through the ranks, sent to research and development on Omega Septimus Sei, awarded a Distinguished Service Medal and a Medical Corps Medal, which are basically for good service. The BFP—"

"Big Freeze Project," Max suddenly realised.

"Yes! This is a scientist who worked on the project. Until a year or so ago. See? Termination."

Max looked at that word, one of the words she'd been able to translate, if not actually decode. "Do you think that means employment, or life?" she asked as dispassionately as she could.

Riley chewed his lip. He sighed. "Well, I'd like to say employment, but all those people who've gone missing..."

"They're getting rid of people who...what, know too much? Ask the wrong questions?"

Riley shrugged. "Don't suppose we'll know until we talk to Nazarian."

"You think that's likely?"

"I think it's the only way to find out what's going on." He hesitated, looking at the data. "Did you find me on the system?"

Max nodded. She'd remembered his Service number, used it to find him. Now she understood some of the code the Service used, she could work out his record.

"What's IPR?" she asked.

"Impressed," said Riley distractedly, scanning the data. "Press-ganged."

"Right." Pressed into Service, following an advanced degree in engineering from Albion University, and then…what she assumed was the shorthand for his training and placements on the various ships he'd mentioned, ending with the J26, which he'd called the Dauntless. According to the Service, he'd then gone AWOL and was still wanted.

"What's all these? Distinguished Service Medal I get, but what's the rest?"

"Medals," Riley muttered.

"What for?"

"Just…stuff. Service. Doing my job."

"CB? You got three of those."

"Commendation for Bravery."

"CBM?"

"Conspicuous Bravery Medal."

Her brows went up as she read the list, which went on for quite a while. "CGM?"

"Same, but for gallantry."

"What's the difference?"

"I don't know, is it important?"

She looked up at him, jaw tight as he scanned the data attached to his file. All these awards for bravery and gallantry, when most of the Service men she'd met would laugh at a beggar in the street.

She reached for Riley's hand, the same way she'd reached for it all those weeks ago on the land train. And he'd reached back. Conspicuous gallantry, indeed.

"Yes, it's important." She touched the little cat on its ribbon around his neck.

"It's not. Just chunks of metal on a uniform I don't wear any more."

He kept his attention on the data, obviously avoiding her gaze. She knew what he was going to find. That since he was promoted to Engineer First Class, the Service had started taking regular samples from him for their programme. That several had already been used, without success.

That at least three had been used, with success.

She'd looked up the women he'd been matched with. All of them came from tech and mech backgrounds. All of them were highly decorated and promoted.

She put down her tablet and slid her arms around his waist, resting her head on his shoulder as he read. Presently, he put down his own tablet and pressed his cheek against her head.

"You've read this?"

"Yeah."

"There's three of them."

"Yeah."

"In labs or something. Petri dishes. I didn't understand the medical stuff."

"Neither did I."

He angled his arm around her, and as he held her close she felt his pulse thudding in his neck.

"How do you think they do it?" he asked, and she thought he was trying to go for matter-of-fact. "In lab conditions, like...tanks or something? Or do they implant the embryos in real women? What's the word, surrogates?"

"Don't know," Max said.

He was quiet a while, holding her, then he said, "Did you find yourself?"

She sighed, and untangled herself to pick up the tablet. "Not really. I searched for my number, the one I had from the orphanage, but I didn't get much. Everyone has their own labelling systems, apparently. I started searching back from those embryos and the labels on them, to see who their parents were, and who else they might have been, um, used for, but it's slow going." She yawned. "I need to build an algorithm for that. Like, genealogy software or something."

Riley took the tablet from her and set it down. "Not now, you don't," he said. "You need to sleep."

"I'm tired of sleeping."

His mouth tugged in a small smile. "Me too. There are much more fun things to do in bed. But unless we both rest, we can't do them."

Max scowled, and he kissed her gently. "When d'you get that sling off?" she asked.

"Few days, hopefully. Give us time to work out what to do about what we've found out."

"What do you want to do?"

Riley shrugged. Even with that sling on, he had very expressive shoulders. "I don't know. On a general level…well, how big is this thing? How many people are involved?"

She nodded at her tablet. "Thousands. And it potentially goes back years. Chances are I'm a product of it."

His hand rested on her shoulder, and squeezed gently.

"And on a personal level?" she asked, more quietly.

"On a personal level? Fuck me Max, I could have three children out there. I don't know what to do with that information."

He looked so forlorn. "Come on," Max said, tugging

him down to lie in her arms. "If I have to rest, you'll have to rest with me."

He gave her a smile, one that didn't convince her much, and let her snuggle against him, but she knew he didn't get a lot of sleep that night.

"It's a breeding programme," said Justine the next day. The information appeared on the central screen in the mess. "Here."

To Riley, it was nonsense, but Justine and Max seemed to understand it, and so did Émile.

"Our father bred livestock," he explained. "I know a breeding programme when I see one. You discard the weakest and breed the strongest with the strongest."

"Or the smartest with the smartest," Justine said. "Most of the people selected for this programme are the best in their field. The ones who flew up the ranks, the ones who graduated early, the ones dripping with medals."

Riley felt Max's eyes on him. She sat there, fingers flying over her tablet, the black cat in her lap as if it had always lived on the ship.

"And what happens to the... er... products of the programme?" Petal asked.

"Well..." Justine glanced at Max, who'd roughed out a program for matching the records in a sort of family tree. It was glitchy and didn't cover everyone in the files, but it was enough for now.

"Looks like they're mostly sent to orphanages. At first it looked like Omega Septimus Sei was the big receptacle for them all," Max said briskly. "And then after a while they started sending them somewhere else. A couple of facilities, looks like, one in Sigma and one in Omicron. My guess is the kids are probably specially raised to suit Service life."

"Poor bastards," said Murtaugh.

401

"It gets better," Max said. "I found quite a few who were recruited back into the Service. Mostly into the field they'd been bred for…"

"Some of the early ones were cross-bred," Justine put in. "Engineers with doctors, for instance. But then they seem to have realised they were better off focusing their efforts."

"About the same time, they expanded the pool of donors," Max said.

"Donors?" Riley said. "That stuff was stolen from me."

"Think of a better word, then," Justine said. "Either way, about two thirds of the babies born under this programme were recruited back into the Service."

"And the other third?" Petal asked. Her hand clutched Angharad's.

Max took in a deep breath and let it out. "It took me a while to figure this one out," she said. "A lot of them had the code RTP added to their files. It was only when I made the genealogy prog that I put it together. These women—and they're all women, or girls really—are the mothers of the younger generation of babies created by the Big Freeze. RTP means…"

"Return To Programme," Riley said, sickened.

"They're breeders, essentially. The children who go back into the Service are mostly boys. I don't know why some of the girls, maybe they're the brighter ones or maybe their fertility was low, I don't know."

"But in the last twenty years," Justine took over, "it seems that most of the babies have been live births. There are some grown in, well, tanks, really. Artificial womb is the way they describe it. But the technology isn't reliable, mostly because there's been little chance to develop it. People don't like it. They find it unnatural."

"Oh Christ," Riley said, and they all looked at him. "I remember…we broke up riots outside a lab once. It was something to do with artificial life. I didn't pay much attention at the time…"

"They could have been growing your children in there!" Max said with brittle cheer.

"A lot of the samples were sent to R&D," Justine said. "Proportionally, more than brought to full term. Primer, it's likely a lot more of yours were used up that way."

"Not helping," he muttered, thoughts of those three potential children whirling round and round his mind, making it difficult to concentrate.

"So, what you're saying, essentially, is that most of us in that orphanage in Mine Base were just…what, sleeper agents for the Service?" Petal said. "Waiting to be activated?"

"That's about the size of it, yes."

"Christ." Petal glanced at Angharad, who'd gone even whiter than usual. "And…does it say what they intended to do with…um, me?"

Justine looked to Max, whose fingers flew over the pad in front of her. A load of data appeared on the screen. Yesterday, Riley wouldn't have known what most of it meant, but today he could read it as if it were clear text.

"You were to become a breeder," Justine said, and Petal made a noise like she'd been gutted. Angharad folded her into her arms, but Riley couldn't help thinking there was something strange in her expression.

"Your…well, parents," Justine said, "were two of the Service's top pilots."

On screen, two Service profiles popped up, a man and a woman with long strings of medals and commendations after their names. Odds were, Riley thought, they'd never met. He recognised both names, having heard them mentioned often, and with awe. Petal's father was from the Theta system, and was somewhat older than her mother, who was from Tau and had quite a strong look of Petal. She had died in action more than twenty years ago, and the man had retired with full honours only recently.

Beside Riley, Max stroked the cat and said nothing.

"Always said you were born to it," murmured Orpheus, reaching out to touch Petal's hand. She clutched it blindly. "You got out, Petal. They can't touch you now."

"If it hadn't been for you," she whispered.

"You'd have killed the fucking lot of them and escaped by yourself," he said, with one of those rare smiles. But it didn't reach his eyes, which were watching Angharad. Riley knew this, because he was watching her too.

"What about you?" he asked Max, as a distraction.

"Does it matter?" she asked, and if he hadn't known her better he'd have believed in her carelessness.

"Not to me. But don't you want to know?"

She shrugged, and Riley flicked a glance at Justine. In a moment, the screen cleared of Petal's parents to show the data belonging to the child labelled 131-10-17 by the orphanage.

There was Max's birthdate, written Service style. "We'll have to celebrate your birthday next month," he said, and she frowned.

"First time for everything," she muttered. She peered belligerently at the screen, and he knew the exact moment he read the three letters she was looking for. All the muscles in her face tightened for the briefest moment, and then she let out a grunt that was half-laugh, half-sob, and sat back in her chair.

"Figures," she said. She glanced at Orpheus. "That's two of us you've helped escape being breeders. Ain't you just a knight in shining armour?"

He shrugged, eyes narrow.

"Your parents—" Justine began.

"I don't care. Why does it matter? They ain't my real parents. They didn't want me. They don't even know I exist. What does it even matter?"

She clutched the cat fiercely and glared at everyone. The cat opened one eye, batted at her hand, and went back to sleep.

Into the silence that followed, Orpheus said, "How long has there been a cat on my ship?"

"They're supposed to be good luck," Riley said. To Max, he added, "Okay, it doesn't matter. You're right. We'll…move on."

He glared at the crew, daring them to comment. If any of them brought up Max's abortion the crew would be growing smaller pretty quickly.

Émile cleared his throat. "Right. Now that we have this information, what do we do with it?"

"Sell it," said Murtaugh.

"To who? The Service? They'd just destroy the lot of us."

"The Prideaux brothers?"

"No fucking thanks," said Petal. "Imagine the chaos they could cause."

"Amongst the Service? Who cares?"

"I care," Riley said. "They're still people, you know. They still have families."

"Bigger families than they realise," said Émile laconically.

"I mean, we could cause a political stink," Justine said thoughtfully. "Imagine the controversy."

"But controversy is about all it would be," Max said. "I mean, is any of this actually illegal?"

Silence fell. Émile started furiously searching on his tablet.

"Slavery is illegal in most systems," Orpheus said.

"Yeah, why couldn't I get arrested in one of them?"

405

Max muttered.

"But the Service operates outside system-wide laws," Petal said. It was true. Whilst they abided by individual laws within a system, their charter, agreed by all systems who enjoyed the protection of the Service, was above the law of any individual star system, planet, or country thereof.

"Slavery's illegal in the Service," Riley said. "But this isn't slavery. Not technically."

"What, breeding people for a specific purpose?"

"No one owns them," Justine said. "I suppose until they're recruited these children are, what, wards of the state?"

Max and Petal nodded.

"And God knows it's not illegal for the Service to impress anyone with the right skills," Riley sighed.

"And while a lot of people don't agree with it, artificial wombs are also not illegal," Émile put in, looking up.

"What about those samples? They've been stealing them!"

"Not really," Riley said. "Part of the Service contract is that you'll undergo regular medical tests and provide any samples they request. Far as I can recall, it doesn't stipulate what they'll do with them."

"Look it up," said Orpheus, and Émile nodded. Now they had Max's access to the system, a standard contract shouldn't be hard to find.

"There is one thing," Max said slowly, her fingers moving in the cat's fur the same way they moved when they twirled a lightpen. "The girls who grow up as wards of the state, like me and Petal. Legally, we then get apprenticeships. Legally, we work in brothels—'cos fuck knows they're illegal nowhere—and then, what? We disappear to some facility somewhere to have babies?"

A small silence fell. "What happens to those women

after they've, um, bred?" asked Riley.

"And how are they inseminated? I suppose a case could be made for rape."

"Shame you two escaped," said Murtaugh, and was glared down. "I'm just saying, if we could talk to one of them, we'd know."

"You can talk to one of them," said Angharad, and only the cat didn't turn to look at her. "Me."

CHAPTER TWENTY THREE

"I was sixteen when they came for me. I didn't have any idea, of course. I was just another whore in another brothel. Raised in an orphanage, like you two."

Petal nodded understandingly, her arms around Angharad.

Max said, "Where was this?"

"Omicron Quintus. One of the mining towns down in the south. Endless sun. I used to freckle."

"How exciting," Max said flatly. Riley shot her a look. She had one hand on the cat and one tapping away at the speed of light on her tablet, but her shoulders were rigid.

"One day, these guys came in. They were Service, but it wasn't that unusual. They asked for me, and I guess I was flattered. They wanted to take me back to their shuttle, but the madam said that wasn't allowed, unless I was chaperoned, because she wanted to make sure I was coming back. So she came with me." Angharad's pretty forehead creased. "She wasn't a bad old thing, really. I mean, once you've been under someone like Madam

Savidge…" she shuddered.

Petal cuddled her. Both of them were tearful.

Max gave Riley a bored look.

"They killed her," Angharad said. "Soon as we got to the shuttle. Shot her and dumped her body outside. And when I screamed they just hit me, and…well. There were six or seven of them and one of me, and I was a whore after all…" She dissolved into delicate sobs.

"We've all been gang-raped," Max said. "Get on with it."

Riley shouldn't have been shocked at anything Max said any more, but his mouth fell open at that. Émile shook his head. Even Murtaugh looked disapproving.

"Your compassion knows no beginning," Orpheus murmured.

"Just sayin'. You ain't so special, princess."

Riley saw Petal's hand go to her knife belt. "Max," he said, abruptly dragging her to her feet, "a word?"

As soon as the door shut he rounded on her. "What are you doing?"

"What?"

"Petal was about to throw a knife at you in there."

"Wouldn't be the first time." Max clutched at the cat, who wriggled and squirmed away. She watched it saunter off down the corridor, and sighed. "I'm sorry, all right? It's just…it's like she's the only person bad things have happened to. Ever since she came on board she's got right on my tits."

"You used to feel sorry for her. Everybody's fuck toy, I think was your phrase."

Max shrugged. "Been there, done that. It's just, she's making out like it's some big tragic thing and…"

"Um, it kind of is, Max."

"Yeah, I know, it's awful and it's cruel, and…I don't know…"

He waited impatiently for her to get her thoughts in

order.

"Look. There's me, right, and I guarantee whatever she's had done to her I've had worse. 'Cept the baby-stealing part. And there's Orpheus, who I'm increasingly sure was a brothel boy, and fuck only knows what it was he rescued Petal from, but given her preference and the number of men who think they can rape that kind of thing out of a girl, I 'spect I can figure it out. Justine, now she was some kind of society lady whose husband beat her and she lost three babies, and don't you think for a fucking second those two things are unrelated. Murtaugh kills people for fun and only had one actual friend he cared about, and he's dead now, and Émile...do you know what he said to me once? That their father thought Justine was the pinnacle of all humanity could create, and that he, Émile, was all the crap left over."

Her chest heaved. Her nostrils flared. Her hands were curled into fists.

"And then there's you," she added, looking up at him.

"And then there's me," he said, waiting to see what she'd scour him with.

"I still don't know what to make of you," Max said. "But I'm pretty sure if six or seven people gang-raped you, you wouldn't sit there like a princess and cry about it. You'd kill the fuckers." Her fists shook. "I did."

Riley didn't know what to say to that. He reached out for Max, and she let him hold her.

"Don't pity me," she said, and not for the first time. "Don't you dare pity me, Primer."

And then he understood. Max loved to tell tall tales about the fights she'd been in and the trouble she'd caused herself, but she did it defensively. If she invited people to laugh at her, then they weren't pitying her.

Things like this, she kept to herself. You couldn't laugh at gang rape. All you could do was stare, appalled, and thank whichever god you prayed to that it had never happened to you.

And then pity the victim. And realise that you'd just thought of her as a victim.

"Max," he said, and she tensed. "There's only one thing I pity you for."

"What's that?"

"Being stuck with me." She lifted her head, and he went on, "I mean, look at me. I'm a Primer who knows more about engines than women and...and I know more ballet positions than sex positions. I didn't lose my virginity 'til I was twenty-two. Now that's something to pity."

She realised he was joking, and smiled gratefully. "Twenty-two, huh?"

He hung his head. "I know. Pathetic."

"And virtually a monk for how many years after that?"

"Too many. I don't know how you can be seen with me."

Max put her arms around him and kissed his neck. "I'll manage," she said, then sighed and jerked her head at the door to the mess. "Come on, then, let's hear the Tale of Woe."

"Be nice," Riley said as she towed him back in.

"Can't promise anything."

At the table, Angharad was crying freely, and so was Petal. Murtaugh and Émile looked uncomfortable, Justine's face was like granite, and Orpheus...well, Orpheus was being a sphinx again.

"How many of you were there?" Justine asked, making notes on her tablet.

"I don't know. Ten in my wing. We weren't really allowed to leave it."

"You don't know how many wings?"

"No. The building was structured so we couldn't see much beyond our own area. But we were probably on the third or fourth floor, because we had to go down in an elevator to get to the exercise yard."

"Were you all brought to term at the same time?"

"No. We were all at different stages, all the time. Every now and then someone would leave, usually after her third."

"Did everyone have three?"

Angharad sniffed. "Well, I did, and the girls who left before me did. Apart from Cloella, she just had the one and then...I don't know. There were complications. She stayed a little while, then left."

"Where did they go?"

"I don't know! We weren't allowed to ask questions!"

"What happened if you did?" asked Max, which Riley could have guaranteed.

"They hit us," Angharad said, blinking her spiky wet lashes.

"But nowhere it'd hurt the baby, right? Face, arms, that kind of thing?" Max peered at her. "Not very hard, either?"

"Hard enough!"

"Broke any bones?" Max asked sweetly. Angharad shook her head. "Not very hard," Max repeated, and picked up her tablet.

"How long were you there?" Justine asked calmly.

"Um. Three years, I think. They let us, um, recover, in between births."

"And did you spend any time with the babies?" Justine asked, her beautiful face devoid of all expression.

Angharad shook her head tearfully. "No. They were taken away immediately. I don't even know if they were...boys or...girls," she managed, dissolving into sobs.

Riley glanced at Max, because so help him if she made fun of that he'd...well, he'd have something to say, at any rate.

But all she said was, "Do you want to know?"

Angharad looked up sharply.

"It's all right if you don't," Max said gruffly, and Riley realised that was probably as kind as she was going to get.

"Tell me," Angharad whispered.

The data flickered onto the central screen. Two boys, then a girl, born approximately a year apart. The youngest would be nearly seven years old.

Angharad let out a sob and buried her face in Petal's bosom. Riley ignored her, and watched Max, her movements so calm and precise he knew there was a storm inside. *That could have been her.* Carted off to some institution to breed babies like a farm animal. Would she be like Angharad now, weeping and desperate, or would she close it all off and pretend it had never happened? Given her horror at the very idea of motherhood, he strongly suspected the latter, but—

But what was the point in speculating? Max would have eviscerated anyone who so much as tried to do that to her.

"I think we've got as much here as we need," Orpheus said, and flicked his gaze at Petal. She nodded, and half-carried the weeping Angharad back towards their quarters.

"What'd we miss?" Max asked, and there was a slight pause.

"You hit the high points," Justine said crisply. "Mostly you missed some crying. I'd have thought," she added, "you might have shown a little compassion, Max."

"Why? That shit makes you weak. You're weak, you don't survive."

"Lass has a point," Murtaugh said.

"Yeah, but how would you feel if someone did that to you?" Émile said.

Max stood up. "Mate, it's about the only thing that hasn't been done to me, but I'm sure if I hang around long enough, someone will oblige."

She stalked out, and Riley scrubbed his face with his hand.

"Women," said Murtaugh, and the ice emanating from Justine was enough to reduce the temperature in the room.

"Leave," growled Orpheus, and Murtaugh did.

"Gosh is that the time better turn in," said Émile in a rush, standing up so fast his chair fell over.

That left Riley playing gooseberry to Orpheus and Justine.

"Sorry about Max," he began.

"Don't be," said Orpheus. He stood up and took a flask from its hatch in the galley. Poured three glasses. Riley didn't know what it was, but it smelled as strong as that pink stuff they'd been drinking in Theta.

The captain took his seat again, swung his feet up on the table, and rasped, "Question now is, what do we do?"

"No," Justine said. "The question is, do we do anything? As pointed out, very little of this is actually illegal."

"I'm fairly sure imprisoning women and forcing them to have babies against their will is illegal," Riley said. "Might need to check the finer points of law in Omicron."

"We can't prove it was Omicron where they held her," Justine pointed out. "She wasn't exactly in a position to check starcharts on the journey."

"How long did it take? What kind of vehicle?"

"She doesn't know. Most people wouldn't. Anyway, it's not relevant."

"I suppose. Well, look, taking babies from their mothers can't be legal, can it?"

Justine made a so-so gesture. "It can be, if the mothers are proved incapable. What's the betting they have a pet psychiatrist to certify that?"

Riley drummed his fingers. "Was Angharad part of the programme from birth? I mean, were her parents—?"

"Yes," said Justine. The data flashed up. "A decorated combat officer and a crewman," she frowned, and then it cleared, "who was a pentathlon champion."

Riley studied the two faces. Did this mean Angharad had latent physical abilities they knew nothing about? That she herself knew nothing about?

"Seems odd," Orpheus said, seemingly addressing his drink, "to go to all that trouble and only breed three babies from her. She was less than twenty when they let her go."

"Maybe they were going to come back for her."

"Maybe the pool of donors was too small back then," Justine said. "You don't want inbreeding."

"Either way, it's a bloody long game they're playing," Riley said. "How far back does it go?"

Justine skimmed through the data, much slower than Max would have done. "Oldest dated samples I can find are nearly forty years old. They're...hmm."

"What?"

"Well, there are seven. All the same date. Six female, one male."

"The beginning of the programme?"

"Looks like." The data spilled over the screen. Yes, those six women had gone on to have three babies each —it seemed to be the magic number—and each of their female offspring had likewise had three babies. Those second generation children would probably just be joining the Service now. Or being held in a breeding facility.

"Live births," Orpheus said.

"Maybe he was just a randy bastard," Riley said

416

absently, scanning the data for any names he knew.

And then he saw it.

He smiled.

"What're you so happy about?" said Orpheus, pouring himself another drink.

Riley stuck his finger on the screen over the name of that first man. "This one. Here. Magnus Larsen. The father of the whole project. I know what we can do."

She knew Riley wasn't happy with her. Max wasn't happy with herself. She wasn't the only one affected by this shitty programme, and she wasn't the only one hurting, so why was it bloody Angharad getting all the sympathy? Because she was fragile and pretty? Because she'd for once got the shitty end of the stick Max had been beaten with all her life?

"That's what you get for being capable," she told herself. "No fucking sympathy." She pulled up the small mirror above Riley's dresser and glared at the battered face it showed her. Not fragile. Not pretty.

Oh, for fuck's sake, was that what this was? Was she bloody *jealous* of Angharad?

"You are pathetic," she told herself, and flipped the mirror down guiltily as the cabin door opened.

"I wouldn't say pathetic," said Riley, ducking inside. "But you were…"

"Mean," Max sighed. "I shouldn't have been so… mean."

"No, you shouldn't." He drew her down with him to sit on the bed. "Look, Max, I know you've been through a whole load of shit, probably worse than I can even imagine, but you've just picked yourself up and dusted yourself off and moved on. And I can't tell you how much I admire you for that. I think you're amazing."

Max blinked at him. Was this what it felt like to be embarrassed?

"But not everyone is as strong as you. People like Angharad, they're more…breakable. And I know it's annoying, but sometimes you have to take care of people like that."

She sighed. "Yeah, I know. Which is why," she held up a hand to head him off, "I went round and apologised."

She didn't think she'd seen him this shocked since, well, since the gang rape comment, but there he was, gaping at her like a landed fish.

"Petal tried to kill me and Angharad cried a lot but I said I was sorry and they both accepted it, so," she shrugged.

Riley put his arm around her and hugged her hard. "I'm proud of you, Max," he said, and damn but his approval felt good.

"That said," she added dubiously, and he released her. "I dunno. Maybe I'm just a suspicious sod but I still don't really trust her. I mean, isn't it kind of handy that the one thing we needed was the one thing she could tell us? Like, she just happened to be an escapee from this project and she just happened to end up on this ship?"

"You and Petal did."

"Yeah, and two out of nine is enough of a coincidence. Three? Come on, Riley."

He sighed, then to her endless relief, nodded. "I did think the same thing. But why would she lie? How could she know that stuff?"

"What stuff? How can we verify any of it?"

He opened his mouth, closed it, then said, "You have a point."

"I mean, unless we go and track down other women who've survived this. And you know what else I wondered? Why do they let them go? I mean, wouldn't they talk about it? There have been hundreds of girls used this way. Surely one would have blabbed by now?"

Riley spread his hands. "I don't know."

"Letting them go doesn't make any sense. I'd just kill 'em. Well, actually, I'd get a load more babies out of them and then I'd kill them. You know," she added, as Riley shook his head, "if I was running an evil breeding programme."

"You frighten me," Riley said, but he didn't look scared. He looked adorable. He kind of always looked adorable to Max these days.

He'd followed her to that club and waited to see her home, even after she'd fucked someone else. He'd befriended a cat who seemed hell-bent on savaging him. He'd treated her with greater kindness and affection than she'd ever had from anyone in her life.

Don't go falling in love with him, Max warned herself, but she had a dreadful feeling she might be too late.

She reached out and stroked her hand over his chest, above the fabric of that damned sling. Under the open neck of his shirt, her tab was tangled up with the beads and remembrances of his home. She touched the hot skin there, felt his muscles jump and shiver under her fingertips.

She didn't need to look up to know he was watching her.

"You know what?" she said softly.

"What?"

"I'm feeling a lot better."

"Glad to hear it," Riley said, and she smiled up at him, letting her hand travel south.

"No," she said, deliberately. "I'm feeling a lot *better*."

"Ah," said Riley, as her fingers reached his groin. "I see."

He let her play with him for a moment, then tugged her towards him for a kiss. His hand on the back of her head felt huge, strong, gentle. Hands like that could crush a skull. She'd seen him do it. But they were hands that wouldn't ever hurt her.

"Get this fucking sling off," she said, pulling at it, and he obliged, stripping it away and throwing his shirt after it. Damn, he was beautiful, all long lean muscles and a scar or three.

"I want you so much," she told him, and he looked up at her like she was something precious.

"Feeling's mutual."

She pushed him down onto the bed, crawled over him, and reminded herself what it was like to be with a good man.

"Problem," said Justine.

The peace and quiet had been short-lived.

"Yeah, well, the siren kind of gave that away," said Riley. He reached out and switched the damn thing off. It had started wailing five minutes ago, and he and Max had dragged themselves out of bed to find the crew assembling in the cockpit.

"There's three of them," said Petal. "Oh, shit."

Orpheus peered over her shoulder. "Shit," he agreed.

"Somebody want to explain?" said Max.

"It's the Siri, the Bones and the Savidge Beauty—"

"Wait, what? No!" Max, Riley and Émile all began protesting at once.

"—Two," Petal finished. "She's commissioned a new one."

"Probably more like stole it," said Justine. "They're coming after us, and…"

She flicked on a screen. Madam Savidge looked out at them, no less haughty for the livid red scarring on her face and neck. Angharad turned away.

"Never send boys to do a woman's job," said Savidge. "I'm coming after you fuckers, and I'm going to destroy you. Best make peace with your lord," she said, and the transmission ended.

"It's a bigger ship this time too, and God knows the Siri is packing. Chaudhri's famous for it. The Bones I don't know…" Justine said, frantically searching data.

"Used to be McGraw's," Orpheus said. "I heard his crew mutinied."

"Great, so we have a mad bitch, a slaveowner, and a crew of mutineers."

Everybody started talking at once, trying to make plans and contingencies. Riley caught Max's eye. She shrugged.

"And it was shaping up to be such a good day," he muttered. They'd come up with a plan to expose the Big Freeze for one thing, and for another, he'd woken up to Max doing delightfully wicked things to his body. And now they were being chased by three ships with very large weapons.

"Where exactly are we?" he asked Petal.

She showed him. They were in deep orbit around Omega Septimus, probably too far to reach the surface before Savidge's fleet caught up with them. Not that being on the ground would be any good to them at all with three ships firing on them. They'd just be an easier target.

"We could try for a landing on Septimus Sei," Petal began, and Orpheus cut her off.

"Too much of a target."

"Well, we can't land on Otto. The Service controls it."

"Besides, we start firing around here, they'll probably shoot us down."

"Great, so the Service is going to be after us as well as Savidge?"

"We need to get away from Otto," Justine began.

"How much time do we have?" Riley asked. "Until

they catch up with us?"

"Not much. An hour, maybe. More if they speed up. They might send shuttles to board us—"

"Bring it on," said Max, cracking her knuckles.

"No. Worst-case scenario," said Riley, thinking fast. They'd already set plans in motion to expose the Big Freeze, now all they had to do was survive. God damn it, Savidge had to come after them now!

"Wait. Wait." He turned to Max, ignoring the others. "The facilities, the ones where the women are sent, there's one on Sei, isn't there?"

"Think so," she said, "but we may have misunderstood the code—"

"No. It makes too much sense. We aim there. Petal, take us there. Uh…southern hemisphere, it used to be a research base near the quartz reserves—"

He hadn't even finished speaking when the objections started tumbling over themselves. "Are you mad?" Petal said.

"Why the hell are we going there?" Émile demanded.

"As if those women aren't suffering enough," Justine began.

Riley fixed his gaze on Angharad. "There'll be no one else around," he said. "Am I right? No other habitations nearby?"

"I don't know. I never saw anything."

"And it'll be secure," Riley added, as Orpheus eyed him thoughtfully.

"Look, if you think Savidge will hold fire because that facility is full of civilians, you're completely—"

"And there are babies there! What are you thinking?"

"I'm thinking," Riley shouted, then let his voice drop to its normal level when they'd all shut up, "that it will be secure, so we can hole up in there and have a better chance of surviving than in the air. And," he added, holding up his hand to ward off further comments, "what do you think the Service will do when a bunch of pirates start attacking their secret facility?"

"Kill us," Justine said.

"No. Kill them. Think about it. They see Savidge's ships firing on the facility, they'll shoot them right out of the sky. All we have to do is be on the inside when that happens. Angharad. What can you tell me about the men who brought you to the facility? Were they in uniform? Was it a Service transport?"

She shrugged helplessly. "I don't know, I can't remember! I...yes, they were in uniform, but I didn't recognise the vehicle. It was a HAV of some kind. I don't think it had a Service ident."

"The Vector," Riley said, meeting Orpheus's gaze. "We hide the ship somewhere. Must be a valley or something we can land in. Take the Vector to the facility. Tell them we have a couple of new girls." He gestured to Angharad and Justine. "The rest of us in uniform—"

"We don't have uniforms," Murtaugh pointed out.

"Improvise," Riley said impatiently. "We have a fuck ton of weapons, and that usually distracts people."

"And what do we do when we've got in?" Justine said.

"Well, for one thing we film the hell out of it and broadcast it all. This is our best chance for exposing the truth."

"But the plan—"

"New plan!" Riley said. He glanced at Petal's screen. "Because if we just sit here we've got about forty-five minutes before they catch up with us. Any other bright ideas?"

There was a furious silence. Then Orpheus said, "It's half-baked, but it's the best we've got. Move."

Riley strode off to his cabin, Max following behind as he stripped off that damn sling. His shoulder was mostly healed now, and two hands would sure as hell be better than one.

"Is this going to work?" she said.

"No idea. We might all die. But if we stay up here we're dead anyway."

He stopped abruptly in the middle of the corridor and Max ran into him as he turned.

"What?"

Riley took a deep breath, then gripped Max's shoulders and looked her square in the face. "I love you, Max. I completely, madly, truly love you. In case we die today I thought you ought to know it."

She stared up at him, mouth half open.

"Just FYI," he added, and continued on to his cabin, heart pounding.

Max was in too much of a daze from Riley's declaration to really concentrate on their mad dash to the sunburnt, scabrous surface of the moon she'd been born on. She found herself in the HAV, festooned with weaponry, wearing fatigues and a Service cap Riley had unearthed from his cabin. He sat beside her, gaze intent on the sky, apparently undisturbed by pouring out his heart to her.

She honestly had no idea if she felt the same way. How the hell was a guttersnipe whore ever supposed to know if she was in love? For all she knew, her tender feelings were just the result of having someone be kind to her for once.

"Riley," she said, touching his hand. She kept her voice low so the others wouldn't hear. "I, uh. We're not going to die today."

He squinted out at the endless, scorched plains. "I certainly hope not."

"No. We can't. Because you still have a bet to make good on. Remember? If I cracked the Service systems?"

He frowned for a second, then it cleared to a smile.

He laughed. "You get to do whatever you want to me in bed."

"Yep. And there's a whole ton of stuff we haven't tried yet. So, you know. No dying."

"Duly noted," he replied, squeezing her hand.

"Also, I…" Oh hell, she couldn't say it. "I…"

I love you. I never want to be without you. I'm terrified of my feelings for you.

His brows went up a tiny fraction as he tried to read her face.

"Oh, you know," she said helplessly, and Riley slung his arm around her and hugged her to him.

"Yeah," he said. "I probably do."

"Sails," said Émile, staring up at the sky through binoculars, and they all turned to look. Max peered up from under Riley's arm and made out something moving in the clouds. She checked her micro. Yep, right on time.

"What's our ETA?" Orpheus rasped.

"Five minutes. Six," said Petal, from the controls.

"How long 'til they're in range?"

"Five minutes," Justine said. "Six."

"Fantastic," Max muttered.

"It'll be fine," Riley said, but she felt the tension in his body.

The compound loomed out of the desert, a bleak building with high walls and watchtowers all around the perimeter. The inner courtyard was covered over with what looked like a laser net, which would allow light and air in but shred anyone trying to get past it.

They zoomed up to the entrance, where a voice from a screen barked, "Yes?"

They'd tried to get Angharad to tell them more details about the arrivals procedure, but she said she'd been unconscious, so Riley had tried to make up something that sounded likely.

"Admiral Nazarian sent us. We have two new girls."

"Nazarian?"

"Yep. He likes these two." Riley shoved Justine at the camera, and she did a pretty good job of flinching from his touch.

"I don't have any record of—"

"The job number is 354-286-BFP."

"Oh," said the soldier inside. "Well, um—"

"Oh, and just so you know, we have bogeys. Check the sky."

Something started bleeping inside the control room, and a lot of swearing ensued.

"All right, all right, get in." The large door in the perimeter wall opened and they flew under the laser net.

"Job number?" Max muttered.

"354 is an order from the admiral. The rest I kind of made up."

"Risky."

Riley winked at her. He was enjoying this, the bastard.

Orpheus picked up Justine's weapons and pushed her out of the Vector. Riley prodded Angharad out with more force than was probably necessary. As the sound of the Savidge Beauty II's engines grew louder, a door opened in the side of the bleak building and they rushed the girls inside.

"Wait, where's Niko?" said a woman in a lab coat as they spilled into a utilitarian lobby. She was flanked by two soldiers in Service uniforms, and Max kept her head down, letting Riley take the lead. Even if his uniform wasn't quite correct, he radiated Service discipline and there was just so much of him that everyone else kind of faded into the background.

"Off sick," Riley said easily. "Caught something nasty from one of the brothel girls."

"I keep telling him," the woman said with a sigh. "Stop sampling the wares. Are these two clean?"

"Hope so, or we're all in trouble. Where d'you want them?"

The woman looked Justine and Angharad over as if they were livestock. "They'll need processing. Do you have the paperwork?"

"Yeah," Riley said, reaching as if for his tablet. Instead he produced a gun and shot the nearest guard. Orpheus took out the other. Max took great satisfaction in shooting the woman.

"Right, we probably only have a few minutes until someone comes," Riley said. "We need to get as many people as we can into a safe place. Inmates, that is. Angharad, is there a basement?"

She was staring in horror at the three bodies.

"Angharad! Basement?"

"I don't know," she whispered. "It's...it's not like where I was held."

"What a surprise. Okay, we—"

The building suddenly shook. Bits of concrete scattered down from the ceiling. Murtaugh grabbed for a door that didn't open, swore, and dragged up one of the dead soldiers to use his hand print.

"Cut it off," Riley said dispassionately, doing the same to the second soldier. "We might need it."

Max had never seen him like this, in soldier mode. Hadn't he just been a Service engineer? When did he get so good at giving orders?

She followed the group out of the lobby and into a corridor. There were several empty gurneys there and a couple of big service elevators. She didn't understand the code written on the walls beside them, but evidently it made some kind of sense to Riley because he used the dead soldier's hand to gain entry to the elevator and punched in a number.

The building shook again.

"Plan?" Orpheus said, apparently resigned to Riley

taking over this operation.

Riley pointed at the directory on the wall of the elevator as it began to rise. "Patient dormitories on one, sickbay and staff quarters on two, nursery on three. Basement is storage. We get as many of them as we can down there. Justine, you go rescue the women. Take Petal. Orpheus, you and Murtaugh take the staff. Is anybody good with children?"

There was a short silence. Max felt like laughing.

"Right. Great. So that's me and Max—"

"So not a baby person," she pointed out.

"—and Angharad. Émile, you get down to the basement and work out the logistics. Is there any way we can separate the staff and patients? Look for partitions."

Émile nodded.

"And get your recorders on. We'll never have another chance to broadcast this."

A siren started wailing. "There, they know we're here."

"They certainly know they're being attacked," said Justine, who looked much happier now she was tooled up.

"On two fronts. Classic." The elevator ground to a halt and the doors slid open to a grey corridor. "Nurseries. We're up."

"Wait, what happens when we're all in the basement?" Émile asked.

"Praying might help," Riley said, and strode out.

Fuck, he was sexy when he was like this.

Max and Angharad followed him, and the elevator swished shut behind them. Max glanced at Angharad, who'd accepted a gun from Petal and didn't look happy about it.

"Do we really have to do all this nursemaiding?" Max asked as they set off down the corridor, which led only to one other door at the end.

"They're the most vulnerable people here, and this is the most vulnerable place. First thing we do is subdue the staff. Try not to kill them."

"Wish we had those darts Orpheus used on us."

"That would be handy."

Riley used the dead hand to get through the door, motioning to Max to cover him as it opened. She tensed, half expecting a hail of bullets and half a wail of crying children, but all they got was a desk that looked like a nurse's station and a variety of further corridors leading off. Everything was utilitarian and grey, including the uniforms of the staff who stood, hands raised, looking terrified.

"Is this going to be easy?" asked Riley suspiciously.

"Please don't hurt us!" one cried, as the building shook again.

"What do you want?"

"What's going on?"

"Where are the babies?" said Max.

A nervous man pointed down one of the corridors. "We only have seventeen! They're down there."

"I notice nobody said, 'please don't hurt the babies'," Riley commented. "Go fetch them. Go, now! Max, you go with them."

Max did as she was told, following the four staff members with her gun. In rooms either side of the corridor were sets of cribs all laid out, although most were empty. The things latched together and wheeled along, so she told the staff to push them out as they were. Probably easier than trying to carry the poor little sods. They were tiny creatures, probably none of them over a couple of months old.

Each of them, she was chilled to see, had a fresh mark on its arm where the Service had already implanted tracker chips.

One of the little bastards woke up and started crying,

which she really didn't need. "Can't you make that thing stop?" she said, as she prodded the woman in charge with her gun.

In response, the woman started crying too.

"Oh, for fuck's sake," Max muttered, but then she came back into view of the nurse's station, and froze.

Riley and Angharad faced each other, guns out. And from the way Angharad aimed hers, utterly steady, it was clear she wasn't an amateur.

"The fuck?" Max said.

"It appears our suspicions weren't unfounded," Riley said, not taking his eyes off the redhead.

"Do you know where he is?" Angharad said.

"What—"

"Do you know," Angharad repeated, more loudly, cutting Max off, "where he is?"

"Where who is?" said Max, trying to figure out what the hell was going on.

There was a long, excruciating pause, filled in by the wail of a baby and the scream of a siren.

"No," said Riley eventually. "But I swear I'll find out."

"Oh, and how are you going to do that? You've burned all your bridges with the Service, and as soon as this crew finds out—"

"Shut the fuck up," Riley snarled.

Angharad gave him a knowing look.

"Finds out what?" Max said, dread curdling in her stomach.

"It's not important. Get those kids down to the basement. Now. Do it."

Max swung her own gun on him. "Not until you tell me what's going on."

Riley glanced at her for the first time. "Max, seriously. Trust me."

"Who is she? Who are you?" she demanded of

Angharad.

The woman didn't answer, but the look she gave Riley spoke volumes. The two of them knew something, had known it all along, and they weren't sharing.

"She's a Service agent," Riley said eventually. "Internal police, am I right? How long were you planted at Savidge's?"

"Too fucking long," Angharad said. "But I knew you'd turn up eventually."

"No, you didn't—" Riley began, shaking his head.

"Profiling, Thrynn," she snapped, almost bored. "We knew you'd take up with another crew, and there were no legal avenues so it'd be a pirate crew. And sooner or later every pirate comes to London. News like you gets around. All I had to do was wait."

"But Petal knew you from the Golden Butterfly—" Max said, trying to catch up.

"Previous mission. You're not the only one who can whore herself for a greater cause," Angharad said, her eyelashes flickering in Max's direction.

"So you were never held in a facility like this—"

"No. I stole some other bitch's data. Keep up."

"I knew you were lying!" Max said hotly. Ugh, and she'd apologised and everything. "Petal is going to kill you."

"Petal can take a number. Put down the gun, Thrynn," Angharad said. "I'm taking you in."

"Look, in case you hadn't noticed, there are seven of us on the crew, and, oh yes, we're under fucking siege," Riley snapped.

"And why do you want to take him in? He's just an engineer!" Max said, and from the pitying look Angharad gave her, immediately regretted it. "Riley?"

"I was an engineer," he said, not looking at her. "I got…promoted."

"To?"

"Doesn't matter. Angharad. Move. We're getting these children into the basement before the roof falls in." As if to demonstrate, the building shook again, and another baby started crying. "Move!" Riley yelled to the staff, who'd been standing still and shocked throughout. They quickly began moving towards the exit.

"Is there anyone else on this floor?" Riley demanded of the nearest one, who shook his head. "Sure? Then move," he snarled, and the man nearly fell over himself in an effort to do just that.

Max kept her gun on Angharad, but she couldn't help darting looks at Riley as he led the group. Who was he? What wasn't he telling her?

"But your file, it said you were an engineer," she said as they followed the staff and the cots down the corridor.

"Was," Riley said. "That's not important now."

"But...why would you lie?"

He squared his shoulders and glanced back at her. "Max, I will tell you, but not right now, okay? Because —"

He didn't get any further. The ceiling suddenly shuddered, and chunks of masonry began falling.

"Fuck, that was a plasma cannon," Riley said.

He slapped the dead hand on the elevator control panel, and Max looked around impatiently and said, "No, stairs are better if the building is coming down," and then something cold pressed against her neck and she was being held at gunpoint by Angharad.

"Right, stairs, but—" Riley began, and then went very still.

"Put the gun down," said Angharad. "You," she nodded at the staff with the cots, "get into that fucking elevator and fuck off. Go," she yelled suddenly, and they scurried to to her bidding.

Riley's gun quivered in his hand, but he didn't move until the staff had taken those screaming cots into the elevator and the doors had shut.

Then it was just the three of them, and Max was acutely aware that the gun being held to her neck could blow her head off. She wasn't going to try to disarm Angharad. It was one thing to fight off a desperate culchie with a gun and another thing entirely when it was a Service trained officer.

"What do you want?" Riley said quietly.

"Put the gun down!"

"And when I've done that, what do you want?"

"I want to take you in. You're going back to the Service. If you don't know where Jameson is—"

"I don't. He's why I left. Look, if we work together, we'll have a better chance of—"

"No!" Angharad yelled. She sounded close to tears. "You don't care about him. What have you done to look for him, this whole time? You don't care about anything but this stupid programme!"

"I know Jameson went missing because he started asking too many questions," Riley said. His voice was soothing, placating. "His brother Pherick was my friend, he was looking for Jameson too—"

"Until he vanished too," Angharad said bitterly.

"Right. Which I thought was suspicious, so I went to my CO and explained it and he told me not to pursue it. Because something was up and people who asked questions went missing. That's why I left." His steady blue gaze flickered to Max. "I left before they could make me disappear. That's the truth."

The building shook again with another huge blast. Much more of this and it would start to come down around them. Christ, Max hoped the basement was structurally sound. If she even lived long enough to get down there.

"Who's Jameson?"

Angharad said nothing, so it was up to Riley to reply.

"He was a med tech. I didn't know him but I served with his brother. He seemed to have discovered something— probably this project—and was trying to find out more, then he disappeared. Pherick started searching for him. Then he vanished too."

The gun shook against Max's neck.

"I'm guessing," Riley said softly, those blue eyes kind, "he was your lover?"

"You know nothing about it," Angharad spat.

"I know what I'd do if Max went missing," Riley said, and she had never loved him more. "Angharad, let her go. We'll go down to the basement. There's nothing to be gained from fighting each other—"

"No!" Angharad yelled, and then the building jolted and she lost her footing, and Max thought that might be the end of her, but then there was an almighty crack and the wall exploded, and Angharad suddenly fell away.

"Max!" Riley shouted, but the air was full of dust, and she couldn't see or hear properly, or move, why couldn't she move? "Come on, Max," Riley said, closer now, and then there he was, grabbing her arm, tugging her to her feet and firing blindly at the elevator doors.

She wasn't sure what was going on, but Riley grabbed her and sort of rappelled down the elevator shaft, shooting his way back out at the bottom, and they were in a basement with flickering lights and babies crying and people herded into cages, and someone shouted, "She's hurt, she's hurt, we need a doctor, now!"

"Who's hurt?" Max started to ask, but then pain knifed into her and her knees buckled.

"I've got you," Riley said, easing her down, and the pain was suddenly really intense, and she looked down to see a chunk of masonry where her ribs used to be.

"Fuck, fuck," she said, but she couldn't breathe properly and the words turned into coppery bubbles in her mouth.

"Max, don't die, stay with me," Riley ordered, and his eyes burned blue in his dusty face. Someone touched her, there where it hurt, and she cried out and it seemed to hurt Riley too.

His face in agony, he leaned down and kissed her lips. "I love you," he said, his tears salty. "I'm doing this because I love you."

Doing what? she wanted to know, but the med techs were swarming her now, and all she could do was watch as he sat back on his heels, wiped a bloody hand over his face and spoke into his micro.

"Urgent message for Admiral Orlov. This is Commander Riley Thrynn of Hawk Squadron, Sigma Fleet. We are under fire from hostiles. Do you have my location?"

There was a pause, then, "We have your location, Commander."

"Take them out. We need a medical evac. Severe injuries." His eyes never left her face. "And pregnant women and infants. Estimate thirty-five plus seventeen. Make it fast. The building is collapsing."

"On their way. Good to have you back."

He ended the comm, and took Max's hand, and if she'd been able to she'd have pulled it away. Because Riley had been lying to her this whole time.

He'd never left the Service.

CHAPTER TWENTY FOUR

"She tried to kill three of my staff," said the Dunkerque's senior doctor, a grey-haired woman with a scowl and a whole bunch of stripes on her sleeve.

"I'm sure she wasn't trying to actually kill them," Riley said as patiently as he could. "She just gets a bit feisty when she's, er, unconscious."

"One of them has a broken nose."

Riley touched his own, which was totally healed now, and nostalgia overwhelmed him. "Yeah. She does that." Something to remember her by. "She will be all right?"

The doctor sighed. "The injuries were severe. We may have to operate again. I've put in a request to transfer to a base on Omega Prime where they have specialists in trauma injuries."

"But she'll live," Riley said urgently. "She will live?"

"I believe so," said the doctor. She looked him over. Riley was filthy with dust and blood, exhausted and worried and hideously out of place in the cool, clean, efficient Service sickbay. "Have you been treated?"

He shook his head distractedly. He'd been in debrief for hours, barely paying attention to what was said. The fallout was already massive, and they weren't even halfway there yet.

He was waiting for the other shoe to drop.

"I have to go," he said. "I was supposed to be on Admiral Orlov's launch five minutes ago. Just...take care of her, all right?"

The doctor nodded, and Riley forced himself to turn away. He felt, as Max would put it, like shit run over twice, and the fact that she'd hate him when she awoke wasn't helping matters.

"It had to be done," said Admiral Orlov, falling into step with him.

"How'd you know I was here?"

Orlov laughed. "Thrynn, you broke your cover for that woman. Clearly, she's important."

You have no idea.

"I don't like leaving her here," Riley muttered, punching in the code for the elevator. The doors slid open silently, perfectly. Everything on board this bloody ship was neat and clean and perfect. It was starting to get on his nerves.

"She's in the best hands. They'll take care of her."

Riley stepped in after the admiral and watched the doors close silently. There was no indication of movement aside from the screen on the wall, silently counting down to their destination.

"You did well," Orlov said. "Did any of them suspect you?"

Riley shook his head. He was, as Max had observed, a surprisingly good actor. "Thanks for altering my record. They believed I was just an engineer." The words tasted bad in his mouth.

"Ah now," Orlov said, knowingly, "you've always been an engineer. I suspect you rather enjoyed yourself on a little Scimitar class."

More than I ever did here. He kind of wanted to cry.

"All those women are being transferred to maternity hospitals on Omega Prime," Orlov went on, "and the children are being cared for. This thing is so much bigger than we could have expected. It's going to be quite the confidence trick keeping it all quiet."

Riley knew he should have said something then, but a thought had just occurred to him. "What happened to the Eurydice?" he asked.

"The—it's still on the surface, I think."

"Was she damaged?"

"I don't know. I don't think so. Why? Surely that's none of your concern any more?"

No. It seemed terribly final. Riley rubbed the back of his neck, suddenly too exhausted to stand. "It wasn't empty. You'll have to dispatch someone on a rescue mission."

Orlov nodded sharply. He opened a comm channel and ordered somebody to send out a rescue team to the ship. "Medical evac?"

"Maybe, once they're done," said Riley, resting his head back against the wall and closing his eyes. "That little cat's a bloody spitfire."

The Service ship's sickbay was bright and clinical and deeply irritating. Slouched in an uncomfortable-looking chair, Orpheus couldn't have looked more out of place.

"What are you doing here?" Max asked.

"Someone needed to watch you."

"Don't they have staff for that?"

"You kept hitting them."

"I've only just woken up!"

He shrugged as if to ask why that made any difference. There was a cut on his cheek and dust in his hair, but otherwise he looked just as he always did.

She made to sit up, but her stomach muscles didn't

seem to work properly. That, and she appeared to have been cuffed to the bed.

"Oh, very fucking funny," she said, wriggling in the straps. They pinned her down at the chest, arms and legs.

"You kept hitting people," Orpheus repeated.

"Maybe they deserved to be hit," she said sulkily.

"They were saving your life. Good job Primer had a Service cruiser as back-up. You'd be dead otherwise."

Max turned her face away, the pain that lanced through her nothing to do with her injuries.

"Fuck him," she managed.

"He did what was right by you," Orpheus said, and she turned back, glaring viciously.

"What was right by me? He was a fucking Service officer this whole time! He could have just walked back to them whenever he wanted! All that bullshit about going AWOL? About being wanted? He's a fucking Commander!"

"And you're alive because of that."

"Fuck you," Max said, tears beginning.

Orpheus was silent for a long moment, and then he said, "Did I ever tell you how Petal and I came to be on the Eurydice?"

"What? No. You know you didn't," Max said, wondering what the fuck this had to do with anything.

"It was the first ship we found that would take a couple of runaway kids. Captain was a guy called Jonatas. Not a bad man, but unambitious. Killed in an attack by…some bunch of losers. I forget who. Petal slipped into the nav and nobody had ever seen flying like it."

"Because she was bred to it," Max said.

"We know that now. Back when I met her, she was just a street kid who was about to be turned into a whore. Skinny little thing. Looked younger than she was. That's why she'd escaped the brothels so far. But the men of the

Mine Base didn't care how old she was. They saw her kissing a girl and decided to try and...correct her inclinations."

Max couldn't suppress a shudder.

"I didn't agree with them," Orpheus explained drily. "Didn't actually intend to kill them, but once I had, we needed to get out. Hence the Eurydice. Wasn't called that then, of course."

Max frowned. "Is Orpheus really your name?"

He nodded, something like humour in his eyes. "Would I choose a name like that?"

"I guess. Look, Orphy old pal, not that this isn't terribly interesting and all the rest, but what the fuck does it have to do with anything?"

Orpheus gave her a long, considered look. Then he said, "Up until that point I'd never killed anyone. Never raised a fist in anger. The women I...serviced, they wanted gentle hands and soft voices. But there was Petal, this kid I'd known all my life, about to lose her innocence the worst way a person can, and I saw red."

"Sure, anyone would," Max said, somewhat confused.

"My point is, Max, that sometimes we have to do terrible things for the people we love."

She turned her face away again, afraid she might cry. "He doesn't love me. That was part of the lie."

"Trust me on this," said Orpheus. Then his micro pinged, and he made a sound that was almost a laugh.

Reluctantly, Max turned her head back. "What?"

"Your liar appears to have done it."

Before she could ask what he meant, the sounds of more pings came from outside the cubicle. Orpheus reached up to the screen on the wall, adjusted a few settings, and a newscaster so devoid of personality she looked like a robot appeared.

"...very shortly after this, the news was broadcast to

every outlet in the Sigma system, and from there, onwards to other systems." She paused, as if being given silent instructions. "And we have just received word that it has also been sent to every Service officer on the payroll. Do we have confirmation of this?" she asked, · her perfect veneer slipping a little in her excitement.

"Shit, it worked," Max said, forgetting her anger at Riley momentarily.

"The origin of the story appears to be a Mrs Elandra Larsen, wife of the Minister of the Third Moon of Sigma Prime. He is of course the nephew of Magnus Larsen, who appears to have been the instigator of the programme known as the Big Freeze. Details are still coming in but we understand it to have been some sort of breeding programme for super-soldiers. We go live to our Service correspondent, Gregor Guzstav. Gregor?"

Max exchanged a look with Orpheus, who pulled back the curtain around her bed to reveal a sickbay full of horrified Service staff, staring in shock at tablets and micros and screens on the walls.

She knew what they were seeing. The decrypted files, annotated and explained in layman's terms, telling them all that the Service had been stealing from them for years and that some of them had probably been genetically engineered for the positions they were currently in.

They were seeing the footage the Eurydice crew had recorded from the facility. From several dozen screens, they heard a woman saying, "They treated us like things. We are not things."

That, Max thought, that was a killer line. It was almost a shame it had been recorded by Justine before they'd ever left the Eurydice.

"I mean, this Larsen was a fucking idiot," Max said, and Orpheus let the curtain fall. "This plan he had to bio-engineer engineers…did he not notice the giant flaw in it? That one day he might engineer someone smart enough to work out his stupid plan?"

Orpheus gave her a faint smile, and glanced back at the screen, where the correspondent was explaining that they didn't currently know how Mrs Elandra Larsen had come across the Big Freeze, nor why she'd chosen to publish the information.

"Because otherwise we'd have published footage of her getting spit-roasted by two men who weren't her husband," Max said, grinning despite herself. "Point of fact, I'm still kind of tempted to publish it anyway, after what she did to…" Her smile faded. "Never mind."

Orpheus said nothing.

"The man currently in charge of the expansion of the Big Freeze Project has been revealed as Admiral Balthazar Nazarian, seen here at his recent arrest. The Service has yet to comment on the situation."

"Turn it off," said Max, who wasn't feeling as gleeful as she'd thought she would. She'd nearly been killed in the pursuit of uncovering this thing. Riley had lied to her the whole time they'd known each other.

"Where is he?" she asked after a moment. "Is he on the ship?"

Orpheus didn't bother asking who she meant. He was busy looking at his micro as he answered. "No. He left on some Service business. There's a lot of fallout from this."

"He left?" She wouldn't even get to yell at him? "Is he coming back?"

"I don't know." He nodded at her wrist. "They've neutralised the cuff. Apparently Service has the power to do that."

For a moment Max couldn't process that. And then she realised what it really meant: that Riley had severed all ties with her. And that he could have done it at any moment.

"I did get told we'd be allowed to go free," Orpheus

went on, as Max tried to free herself from her grief. "We were going to wait and see how you were doing first."

Max craned to see but the straps kept her from looking at her own body. "Is it bad?"

"Yes," said Orpheus.

"I don't feel bad..."

"Service have the good drugs." He held up his micro for her to see. "Bad news. Someone rescued that mangy cat."

For some reason her eyes filled with tears as she looked at the picture of the dusty, dirty creature clawing the shit out of some hapless junior officer. Must be the drugs.

"And the rest of the crew is fine, thanks for asking."

"What about Angharad?"

He shrugged. "Couldn't find her. The Service teams are still looking through the building, though. I'd watch your back."

"How's Petal?" Max asked, after a pause. Poor girl kept losing her lovers.

"She'll survive," Orpheus said shortly.

He stood, and Max looked up at him with interest. Strange how she'd spent several nights with this man but hardly knew him until today. If indeed she knew him at all now.

"The doctor said," he told her, "that they'd need to keep you for a while. Maybe transfer you to a specialist hospital dirtside. I've got a ship to salvage and a reputation to mend. Can't have people thinking I'm a friend of the Service now."

He paused, and looked down at her. "There's a place for you on the Eurydice whenever you're ready," he said, and left.

They found Pherick in a slave colony on Zeta Quintia, one of the few places left where slaves were allowed to be kept. Riley personally removed his friend's cuff, trying very hard not to think about Max as he did.

"What happened to Jameson?" was the first thing Pherick asked, and Riley just shook his head. "What happened to my brother?"

"I'm sorry, Pherick. A lot of the med techs were killed. Mostly the ones who started asking questions."

Pherick mourned, and Riley comforted him, or at least tried to. In the weeks and months since he'd traded Max's life for his own freedom he'd become increasingly distant from the people he used to consider his friends. Pherick was in no shape to be offering support to anyone. Admiral Orlov, the best CO he'd ever served under, had been as helpful as he had since Riley first went to him with his suspicions about Pherick and Jameson, but he was an increasingly busy man and Riley was well aware that the Service didn't care about his broken heart.

The captain of the Dauntless had got off scot free. She'd only been following procedure, after all. But Riley remembered her name.

He'd been reassigned, into the corps dealing with aftermath of the Big Freeze, and promoted too. Commodore Thrynn, now, and wouldn't Max have found that hilarious? Commander had been something of a courtesy title for a senior engineer, but Commodore? He had shiny new stripes on his sleeves and never had to get his hands dirty.

He got updates, of course. A Commodore could bully a team of doctors into passing along regular information about a patient, and so he knew that Max had been transferred to a hospital on Omega Prime and operated on by the very best doctors available.

This had in part been at his insistence, but also, he was surprised to find, at the request of one Rear Admiral

Romesh Baral, a senior intelligence officer who had created not only the rolling encryption Max had broken, but also Max herself. Baral, it turned out, was Max's biological father, and she'd been invited to recover from her injuries at his home on Sigma Prime.

A week ago, Riley had swallowed his pride and put in a call to Rear Admiral Baral. He was pretty sure Max wouldn't want to talk to him, and he was right, but Baral chatted for a few minutes about the daughter he never knew he had.

"She's not very good at relaxing, is she?" was how the older man put it, and Riley laughed for the first time in weeks. Max was never going to settle easily into a Primer's home. That this guy could joke about it was a good sign.

"Absolutely terrible, sir," he agreed. "This one time, she was supposed to be recovering from…uh, injuries," he covered, because he didn't think now was a good time to bring up Max's ordeal with Moreau, "and she was bored out of her mind from the minute she woke up. I had to give her a cipher to break to occupy her."

"Yes, she told me. My cipher. It was supposed to be unbreakable."

"Well, like father, like daughter." Riley hesitated. "Is she…okay? Are you getting on all right? I know she can be, um, an acquired taste sometimes."

Baral looked at him hard for a minute, then shook his head, smiling. "Do you know what she said when I first met her? 'To be honest, I'm just glad you're not somebody I've fucked'."

Riley spluttered with laughter. "Oh God. Yep, that's my Max." Shit. "I mean…uh, that sounds like, um, Max…"

Baral gave him a knowing look, but said nothing. Riley tried to change the subject.

"Sir? Has Max…has she met her mother?"

Baral shook his head. "They're aware of each other, but she—the woman—has expressed a preference not to meet with Max. It's becoming quite a common story."

Riley knew that all too well. These days, most of the people he met were either donors or children of the programme. In one or two cases, they'd been both. He'd spent an upsetting few days transporting the women of the Omicron facility, the one Angharad had lied about. She'd clearly got her information from somewhere, possibly the deceased Jameson, but one thing she hadn't been aware of was the mind-altering illegal drugs used on the surrogate women. The reason nobody had ever come forward was that nobody remembered it with enough accuracy to be sure it was anything but a fever dream.

The data from the programme showed that of the samples taken from Riley, one so far had resulted in a live birth, and two more were expected. He had met with the women in question. He'd thought, and cried, and eventually made formal statements to the effect that he relinquished all rights to the embryos created from his stolen DNA. An adoption had been arranged for the child who'd been living in an orphanage.

Riley had, anonymously, made sure it was a really good family. Then privately, he organised funds for the two women who were still expecting. And then he put it as far from his mind as he could, and went back to helping the many, many others.

"Three fucking years," one of them had said, staring out of the porthole at the stars. "Three years, three babies, and I thought I was just having a nightmare. For three years."

At least that hadn't happened to Max. And now she was living a safe, comfortable life with Baral's family. She'd even got that mangy cat. According to Baral, she referred to Riley as 'that fucking liar' and had instructed his younger daughters never to believe a single word that came out of a man's mouth, especially if he said he loved her.

"That was the truest thing of all," Riley said to the blank screen, then made himself get back to work.

Five minutes later, a comm pinged into his personal channel.

No, not one comm. A whole file of comms. Eleven years of comms.

Everything the Service had censored from him.

Letters from his parents. Pictures of his sister's wedding. Videos of her children.

Notes from friends. From Jyoti Patil, the only friend who'd tried to talk to him after the business with Elandra. From other friends, acquaintances, though less and less over the years. Not a word from Elandra. Not a single word.

But now he was a senior officer. And he had the confidence of the top brass. And he got personal comms.

"That's eleven years well spent," he murmured, and opened the first message.

Eleven years later, he sat back in his chair. He began a new message, and slowly, slowly typed his way into the future.

The day dawned warm and beautiful on Sigma Prime. Romesh Baral had an elegant, comfortable home in the lush hills overlooking the port of Khalkata, with spectacular views over the jungle, the city, and the ships arriving by land and sea.

Max had been given a large, airy room with a bathroom that was approximately twice the size of the Eurydice. She had every conceivable technology at her fingertips, and even some she'd never thought of. In the early days of her recovery, doctors and med techs had visited every day and even slept in a room nearby to be on call for her whenever she needed them. These days, it was physios, personal trainers, and even beauticians.

Fecking beauticians, for Christ's sake. She'd given them short shrift as soon as she was able.

She got up, and regarded herself in the mirror. Those beauticians would need to do a body of work on her today, if she hadn't told them where to fuck off to. Up until the small hours watching Omicron soap operas with a bottle of expensive gin in one hand and a tablet texting Émile in the other, she'd eventually crashed out, fully dressed, and woken with her face in Cat's fur.

At least Cat's fur was significantly cleaner and softer these days. Romesh had politely requested the services of a veterinarian, who had proclaimed the cat entirely healthy but for its army of parasites, and eventually Max had been allowed to keep it. The lazy bastard slept on her bed for all but two or three hours of the day, when it prowled around looking for things to destroy.

Cat was technically female, but Max had been called an it for long periods of her life and survived, so she supposed the feline could manage, too. And whilst her sisters badgered her to give it a name, she'd resisted. "I ain't got a name neither," she told them, "and it never did me no harm. If I catch you calling it something soppy like Midnight or fucking Sable, I'll drown it in the pond, you hear?"

They hadn't taken her threats to heart. Max had come to the depressing realisation that she wasn't even scary to teenaged girls any more.

She stroked Cat's furry head, got a half-hearted swipe for her trouble, and yawned loudly. The micro on her wrist, brand new and frighteningly advanced, beeped to tell her she was due at the country club in an hour.

"When did I become someone who attends a fucking country club?" she asked Cat, who glared at her with one yellow eye and went back to sleep.

KATE JOHNSON

"When you became a lady of quality," said Priti, who had a disconcerting habit of disabling the door chime and entering Max's room unannounced. She wore a dress that looked like a wedding cake.

"You take that back. I ain't a lady of anything," Max scolded, kicking the gin under he bed.

Priti was seventeen and beautiful, the daughter of a Service admiral and a respected diplomat. She danced and sang, did charitable works and was set to study at one of the best universities on the planet. She had been disconcertingly pleased to discover Max was the 'big sister I always wanted' and worshipped her a little bit more every time she did something other people disapproved of.

"You're a lady who goes on dates with handsome riding instructors!" Priti practically sang.

Max wrinkled her nose. There had been a reason for that gin, after all.

"He's not hiding under the bed, is he?" Priti performed an elaborately elegant movement to look.

"No, he isn't. And he's not in the dunny, either," Max said, as Priti skipped off to check. "You can look all you like, but you won't find him. Unless he's taken up stalking. In which case, you'll have an opportunity to practice them moves I showed you the other week."

Priti flowed through a stylised version of the self-defence moves Max had attempted to teach her. She made them look like ballet, which was no bleeding good. Ballet never killed anyone. Well, probably.

"So, how did it go?" Priti demanded, dancing on the spot as Max searched through the endlessly confusing automated clothing system the house insisted on. Jesus, and she'd thought Riley and his tidiness was annoying.

"Fine," she mumbled.

"Was the meal nice? I've heard that place is amazing."

"Sure. Grand."

"Did you try the—"

"Yes," said Max, stripping off yesterday's clothes and shlepping towards the shower. "Now, can I go and wash myself in peace, or do you want a blow-by-blow of that too?"

"I'll wait," said Priti, bouncing onto the bed and playing with Cat, who rolled over like a little bloody hussy and showed her belly.

The shower was hot, cold, soft, intense, scented, refreshing, and any other bleeding thing Max demanded of it. She washed matter-of-factly, then hit a button on the wall and told it to deliver her riding clothes (special clothes just for riding, for fuck's bloody sake). They arrived in moments, freshly pressed. She had no idea if a machine did this or a secret army of elves. Mandula, her new stepmother, had told her not to worry about it.

"But I want to know how it works," Max had grumbled, and never got around to it because she was being dragged off to some other event. There was always an event these days. She'd become some kind of cause célèbre, an exotic pet to be marvelled over. People with butterflies on their lashes peered at her mud-coloured skin and shaven head as if she was the strangest thing they'd ever seen.

This was her life now. And it was a good one, safe and comfortable, in the arms of her family. After a life spent running, she'd finally come home.

But maybe I liked the running...

That line of thought would do her no good. Just like Riley, back in the pristine, efficient bosom of the Service, she was where she was supposed to be. Officially. Probably.

Just for a moment, Max let herself think of Riley. Of his eyes, of his smile, of his broad shoulders and fierce tenderness. And then she made herself remember that he'd lied to her, betrayed her, and abandoned her just when she'd fallen in love with him.

Well. That had been a stupid thing to do.

Max scrubbed her hands over her face and picked up her clothes.

Dressed, she stomped back out into her bedroom, where Priti was watching four different things at once on the huge screen, and poked at the micro she'd salvaged from Metal Joe's until it promised to send her HAV round. Yeah, she had her own HAV now, a shiny sleek thing that almost drove itself. Romesh had offered her a chauffeur, but Max had been determined to drive the damn thing herself. After all, Justine could do it. Couldn't be that hard, right?

"Well?" said Priti, batting her eyelashes. They had little stars on them.

"Well what?" She scowled at the screen, where Balthazar Nazarian was being interrogated by a barrage of terrifying lawyers. "Christ, isn't he dead yet?"

"We don't have the death penalty," Priti said.

"Give me five minutes with him," Max growled, and her sister just grinned.

"You're changing the subject. How was your date?"

Max sighed. Dunstan had taken her to a fancy restaurant, been politely oblivious to her appalling table manners, told her amusing stories, listened to her own with adoring fascination, then driven her to a beauty spot overlooking the city and kissed her in a most gentlemanly fashion.

"He's...nice," she said as diplomatically as she could, and Priti's face fell.

"Coming from you that's not a compliment."

"He asked if he could kiss me. What kind of culchie *asks* to kiss you?"

Priti looked confused. "But I thought asking was the polite thing to do."

"Kissing isn't polite. Jesus, Prit, if he has to ask to kiss me then what the fuck is he going to be like in bed?"

Priti gave a shocked giggle. It was glaringly obvious to Max that she and her sister Shanti were both perfectly untouched and intended to stay that way until after they were married to safe, polite men. Men like Dunstan, in point of fact.

"Christ, the only way to get anything powerful between my thighs around here is to ride a horse," she added, glaring at her reflection. Did she look hungover? Yes. Marvellous.

"Are you going to see him again? Maybe the attraction will grow," Priti said hopefully, and started humming the theme from a popular ballad.

"Stop listening to soppy music," Max warned, as her HAV pulled up outside the verandah.

I'd have happily gone my whole life without knowing what a verandah was.

"Will you be home for supper?" asked Priti as Max climbed into the ludicrous dildo of a vehicle.

"Dunno. I'll call," she lied, and drove off.

Ugh. The thing was, her new family was just so nice. And everything here was so easy. Max had had to take up hardcore sport to keep herself from going mad with boredom. Romesh had suggested it after finding her beating the shit out of an improvised punchbag she'd made out of pillows.

"You're supposed to be taking it easy," he'd said despairingly.

"Mate, I don't know what to do with easy," she'd replied. "Keep me locked in here much longer, I'll kill myself. Serious. Isn't there even, like, a boxing gym around here?"

He'd taken her to the country club, which was full of boring twits being pretentious, but at least had decent sporting facilities. Swimming had been approved of by her doctors, and while Max found it boring, it was at least something to do. She'd been getting soft there in that big house.

The club had insisted on special clothes for swimming, however. Max had no idea why she couldn't swim naked, but that was Primers for you.

Swimming led to running, sometimes alongside the same people. Running also, for some reason she couldn't fathom, required special clothes. And then one day this kid called Braiden mentioned pentathlon, and Max had asked what it was, and he and his friends'd looked her over like the pampered bunch of Primers they were, and told her it was rigorous and elite and they'd been training for years.

Max gritted her teeth, smiled, and asked to have a go anyway.

She quickly realised that their version of shooting a gun involved a static target and no live rounds. It was… laughable. She beat them all at it, then asked what was next. They'd given her a mesh face guard and a silly thin sword and expected her to dance around pretending to fight.

"Take the fucking helmet off and fight me like you have balls," Max said after one unsuccessful bout where people had kept shouting made up terms and laughing at her.

"That's not how one does it," Braiden drawled.

"What, 'cos there's nothing between your legs? Have a special trip to the vets, did you?"

Braiden swished his sword at her, and Max attacked back, disregarding the rules of polite sport and hacking at him with the stupid thin sword until he backed off the platform and fell on his arse.

"Next time, bring a proper sword," she said, tossing hers on the floor. "What's next?"

Thankfully, next was horse riding. Max had never ridden a horse before, but the instructor was patient and calm and probably the sort of person Riley might have become if he'd never joined the Service and become a traitorous bastard.

She'd been rude to him and he'd apparently found it charming enough to ask her on a date. Even after all the men Max had known, she still couldn't fathom them sometimes.

Today she squared her shoulders as she parked the HAV and loped towards the stables. She liked it there. They were the one place on Sigma Prime you could still smell shit, for one thing.

Dunstan wasn't in attendance as she went in and selected a horse for today. Victor, a big chestnut who was slightly deaf but still loved to run. She saddled him, checked the girths as Dunstan had shown her, and was cantering before she'd even left the stableyard.

There was a proper training area set up with jumps and water features, but Max leapt Victor over the fence and headed for the jungle. She'd worked out her own circuit here, leaping fallen logs and streams, practising her shooting by targeting trees and rocks.

Victor was the perfect horse for this, unafraid of the muted noise of the gun Max kept hidden in the stables. She rode three circuits, satisfied with her performance, and scouted a new route for when this one got too easy.

Then it was back to the yard to do the stuff she was supposed to do on Victor, nice tame little jumps and all that bollocks, before she walked him back to his stable for a nice bowl of his favourite mush and a good rub down.

"Max, how many times do I have to tell you, you don't have to do that," said Dunstan's patient voice.

Max picked up the hose and tested the temperature. "At least once more, apparently."

He watched her cooling and brushing the horse. Dunstan was quite nice looking, with shiny hair and kind eyes. His shoulders were broad and his thighs were quite impressive. And when he'd kissed her it had been perfectly competent. He hadn't slobbered or groped or acted the blown gasket when she'd told him to stop.

"God save me from gentlemen," she muttered.

"Sorry?"

"Nothing. Look, I'm sorry about last night. I mean, you're nice and all, but this," she gestured with the brush between them, "it ain't happening."

Dunstan looked at her soulfully. "I understand. I mean, you're still recovering from—"

"Jesus Christ," Max threw the horse brush down, "I fucking *have* recovered, all right? All stitched up, internal organs repaired, ribs back in the right place and everything. Hardly even any fucking scars left, which is unfair if you ask me." She pulled up her shirt to demonstrate the faint lines left by the masonry that had tried to obliterate half her torso. "Injury like that should leave a decent scar or how the hell are you supposed to tell stories about it?"

Dunstan stared, eyes wide, the way Riley used to—well, he stared with wide eyes, anyway. Max looked down irritably and realised the scars from Justine's whip were still quite visible. Romesh's surgeons had offered to minimise them, but Max had declined. Some scars were worth the reminder.

"I meant, you're recovering from heartbreak," Dunstan said, and it was a damn good job Max had put the gun away.

"I am not heartbroken. I don't have a heart." She forced herself to calm down. "Did I tell you about the time I got strung up as mosasaur bait?" she said, and told Dunstan the story as she finished with the horse. Well, she told him part of the story. Mentioning Riley still hurt, so she either skimmed over his part or called him That Fucking Liar, which made her feel a bit better.

"I never know if you're just making these things up," Dunstan said, as she slapped the brush into his hand. She saw his gaze travel to the scarring on her wrist left behind by the convict cuff.

"Well, you can go on wondering. I'm going to do some fencing. You haven't seen that useless culchie Braiden around, have you?"

"No, but there was someone watching you ride," Dunstan said, and something in the way he said it gave her pause.

"Who?"

"He didn't give his name. Tall fellow. Looked familiar, but I can't quite place him."

A million newscasts of his face as the man who unmasked the Big Freeze, thought Max. No, it couldn't be. What the hell would he be doing here?

"How tall?" she asked, torturing herself.

"Oh, really big," Dunstan said guilelessly. "Easily two metres. You don't see many people that tall."

"No," Max said, sighing. "Where'd he go?"

Dunstan pointed towards the club's interior. He could be anywhere in there.

Max drummed her fingers against her leg, thinking. She could just get in the HAV and go back to Romesh's house. Or she could not be a fucking coward and go in there and practice her fencing.

After all, she'd have a weapon in her hand, which always made her feel better. Even if it was the most useless bastardisation of a weapon since the rifles they'd got out on the shooting range.

"Nice guy," Dunstan went on, as Max set off for the clubhouse. "Said he used to know you."

"Really."

"Did you used to work with him?"

"Dunstan, do you know what I used to do?" she asked, pausing at the corner of the big barn.

"Um, something to do with, um, you were on a merchant crew?" Dunstan said, his cheeks going pink.

"They were pirates," Max said. "And before that I was a slave. And before that I was a petty criminal. And before that I was a whore. So, you know. Somebody I used to work with is probably not, by definition, going to be much of a 'nice guy'. This one," she added with a roll of her eyes, "is a fucking peach."

"Well he seemed like a nice fellow," Dunstan said lamely, following her as she rounded the corner to take the shortcut over the flowerbeds.

"Dunstan, don't take this the wrong way, but you think I'm nice," Max said, and then she stopped and said, "Oh, for fuck's sake."

There was Braiden, snogging some poor unfortunate girl up behind the barn. No, wait, not snogging. She was pushing away from him, trapped between his strong body and the wall. She had on some kind of uniform. Max thought she might have been one of the club staff, most of whom were invisible to most of the patrons.

"Braiden, what the fuck are you doing?" she said loudly, and the stupid bastard turned to look at her and grinned.

"Need me to draw you a diagram, Baral?"

"My name is Max," she said, striding towards him, "Max Seventeen. I ain't got a proper name, because I was grown in a lab and raised in an orphanage, which is where I learnt to do this."

She grabbed him by his hair, yanked him backwards, and slammed her other fist into his nose. As his head went down, she kneed him in the nuts.

"Actually, I lie, that might have been at the whorehouse," she said, as he collapsed, moaning and swearing, to the ground. "You all right, love?"

The girl stared at her, wide-eyed. "Please don't hurt me!"

Max shook her head. "That was an actual protest, wasn't it? I mean, it wasn't like one of them token struggle things you Primer girls do?"

"I wanted him to stop! He wouldn't listen! I'll get in such trouble…"

Max sighed. "Dunstan, do us a favour and look after her, will you? Oh, and, next time," she added to the girl, who was quite pretty and would probably suffer a next time, "heel of your hand, like this, under his nose, hard as you can. You can break it that way. Okay?"

The girl nodded, wide-eyed, as Dunstan steered her away.

"Fucking bitch!" Braiden groaned, and Max nodded.

"Yep," she said, and kicked him in the stomach for good measure before she walked away.

CHAPTER TWENTY FIVE

Riley hadn't fenced properly for years. He'd competed as part of the Service's pentathlon team, but more recently he'd used a sword in such a different way he wasn't sure he'd remember the forms.

But it came back remarkably quickly. He fought a quick practice bout against one of the instructors, who gave him a few tips and set him to fighting one of the more skilled members of the club.

Riley won one bout, lost the second, shook the hand of his opponent and went to fetch a drink. When he came back there was someone else on the piste. He bowed to Riley.

Riley bowed back, and they both saluted.

"En—" the instructor called, but Riley's opponent was already off, lunging forward, lightning-fast.

"Foul!"

The opponent paid no attention, but continued to drive his sword at Riley, who countered with a basic parry. The attack came again, and was again parried.

"Mr—" the instructor began, and paused, unable to identify who Riley was fighting. "Stop! That is an illegal

—"

"It's fine," Riley said, beginning to fight back. This guy wasn't fighting like a sportsman. He was fighting like a swordsman, like somebody who was defending himself from an attack. Like somebody who intended to kill.

Riley found himself smiling behind his mask.

"Stop, stop!" cried the instructor, as they fought back and forth, ignoring him. Then Riley's opponent leapt off the piste and stabbed at his side.

Someone yelled for Security, but Riley grinned and fought back, thrusting and parrying. Fencing had never seemed so...well, sexual, before, but this was almost like—

Oh, bloody hell. This guy wasn't fighting like a sportsman because he wasn't a sportsman. And he also wasn't a he.

She chased him around the room and he chased back, landing some hits that would have done her some serious damage if they'd been fighting for real. She fought back harder, with less skill but more determination.

That's my girl, he thought, as she finally kicked his foot out from under him and pinned him back against the wall, her sword-tip at his throat.

"Yield," she snarled through her visor.

"Yield," he agreed, and she stepped back, ripping off her helmet. And there she was, Max, his Max, her face sheened with sweat, her eyes narrowed and her lips twisted.

"I find out you let me win, I'll fucking skin you," she said, tossed her sword on the floor, and walked out.

"Miss Baral," the instructor began, running after her, and she snarled at him with such ferocity he fell back.

"My name is Max. Max Seventeen," she told him, and disappeared into the women's changing room.

All eyes turned to Riley.

"I think we can all agree she has natural talent," he said, getting to his feet and removing his visor. "If you'll excuse me…"

He raced through the sports complex into the main area of the club, where people sat around drinking cocktails and being elegantly witty to each other.

"Where'd she go?"

People stared at him in horror, and Riley realised he was still in his fencing gear.

"Sir, in this area of the club, sporting clothing is not —"

"Yeah, that's great, I don't care," Riley said. "Where'd she go? Max. Tall, shaved head, looks like she's going to kill someone?"

The people around him, in their cool pale suits and dresses, looked at each other in elegant bewilderment.

"She hasn't come out of—fine. All right, fine." Frowning, he went back into the changing room, stripped off his fencing gear, showered and dressed in attire the club would consider more appropriate. One of the guys from the fencing arena gave him an odd look as he reached for his shirt.

"Forgot your body protector?" he said, and Riley glanced down. Of course. That scar on his shoulder, deep and ugly.

"Word of advice?" he said, and the man, fashionably short and slender, nodded. "Anyone comes at you with a real sword, don't try fighting back with a fucking epée."

He finished dressing, ignoring the man's spluttering, and went back out into the club.

"Still nothing?" he asked the bar staff. "You'd know if you saw her."

"Sir, I am not at liberty to divulge information about our members," said the head waiter, sniffily.

"Of course not," Riley said, rolling his eyes and heading out into the sun. Maybe she'd gone back to the stables. Or maybe he should give up here and try to visit her at her home. Her father's home. Given her little outburst about her name back there, he kind of suspected all was not rosy in the Baral household.

He threw himself into a chair and ordered a beer. It came with goddamn icecubes.

How had he never realised how ridiculous this life was?

Max must be going slowly insane here. Yes, Rear Admiral Baral was a decent man, and his family were likewise good people. Yes, they had apparently been taking very good care of her. Baral had even told him how they'd cared for Max's cat, and it had repaid them with its teeth and claws. Just like Max.

"It's like putting a tiger in a fucking cage," he muttered, and received a dirty look from the gentleman at the next table. He wore a pink suit. The woman with him had some kind of snake living in her hair.

"Young man, we do not use that kind of language here," he said.

"Yeah, sorry, but I don't care what kind of language you use here. I am leaving this planet," he saluted the gentleman with his stupid icy beer, "as soon as I damn well can."

"On a Service ship, I hope!" said the older man. His moustache was the type it took hours to groom.

"Hell no."

The moustache quivered. The snake woman said, "My husband gave many years of his life to the Service, protecting people like you!"

"And I thank you for your service," Riley said, "I really do. But they've had eleven years out of me and they ain't getting any more."

"Quitter!" bellowed the gentleman.

"That's Commodore Quitter to you," said Riley, wishing he was drunker. He waved at the waiter, who scurried over. "Can I get a whiskey, please? A large one."

"What kind?" asked the waiter, beginning to list them.

"A large one," Riley said patiently.

"I don't," began the woman at the next table, but the man frowned and said, "Commodore?"

But neither of them got any further, as a chap wearing lilac tottered up on his heels, looking indignant.

"The trash they let in here these days!"

"Commodore Trash," Riley said, to no one in particular.

"That...woman. The by-blow," the lilac fellow stage-whispered. "Getting into fights now."

"Disgraceful," harrumphed the man in the pink suit.

"Wait," said Riley, getting to his feet. The waiter handed him his whiskey. "Where was this?"

"In the zen garden," the lilac-suited man said, with what was probably deserved disgust.

Riley just laughed. If anyone could get into a fight in a zen garden, it was Max.

He followed the signs to the zen garden, which was quite easy to find since there was something of a crowd gathering there. Riley shouldered his way through, draining his beer and holding onto his whiskey.

He didn't have to ask what was going on. There was Max, in some kind of dress—and there was a hat on the floor, that was how she'd got out with no one noticing! —brawling with six, seven, large, big lads.

Riley shook his head in admiration. She'd already taken out three of them, lying groaning on the floor clutching various parts of their anatomy, and she was currently in the process of knocking two more heads together. One of the remaining boys, who unfortunately didn't seem to be as sharp as his suit, looked around for an escape.

He ran off to Riley's left. Riley, not taking his eyes off Max, held out the hand with the beer glass, let the boy run into his arm, then smashed the glass over the lad's head.

Unfortunately that distracted Max, who was rightly wary of the sound of breaking glass, and as her head snapped round one of the lads landed a punch in her gut.

"No," Riley said, striding over and picking him up by the simple method of grabbing him around the neck.

"He bothering you?" he asked Max, who had stumbled but not fallen.

"Nothing I can't handle," she said, and he nodded and held the boy out for her to punch. Dammit, that right jab of hers was a thing of beauty.

The boy wailed, and Riley let him fall. That made, yes, seven of them on the ground.

"Did no one tell you," he said, "not to hit a woman?"

"You never know when they might hit back," Max said, catching her breath. She touched her nose, which was bleeding. Her knuckles were bruised and her knees scraped. Her dress, which had probably been quite pretty and feminine at one point, was stained with dust and more blood.

"Whiskey?" Riley said, holding it out to her, and she took a big gulp of it.

"I'm going to—" began one of the boys, furiously, and Riley feinted toward him. He flinched back quite satisfyingly.

"You're going to get up, shut up, and go home," Riley said. "And you're not going to pick fights with girls." The club's security people were approaching now, late and cowardly.

"She—"

"Beat the shit out of you," Riley finished for him. He turned to the security men. "Commodore Thrynn, Sigma Fleet. Nothing to see here. These boys were just leaving."

The men looked down at the seven boys, then at Max. From their expressions, they'd heard all about her.

Riley gave them all a big smile. "Miss Seventeen and I were also leaving," he said, taking her arm and towing her away.

"Let go of me," she hissed.

"When we're out of eyesight."

"Commodore fucking Thrynn," she snarled.

"Minor fib."

"What?"

Riley tugged her around a corner, under an arch, and into one of the small private arbours this type of club always had plenty of.

"I quit the Service," he said. "Properly, this time."

She let him stay, mostly because he had some ice and a handkerchief. Also, because it felt good to look at him sitting there in the sunlight, big and tanned and somehow a bit more real than all the silly men she'd been patronised by ever since she landed on this stupid planet.

It felt, in fact, far too good to see him.

"Pinch it here," Riley said, gently taking hold of the fleshy part of her nose, and she jolted away.

"I know how to deal with a bloody nose," she said witheringly, and he smiled a bit and relented. The ice felt good against her face, where one of those fecking culchies had landed a lucky swing.

"I've got soft," she said, disgusted with herself. "Taking two fucking hits like that."

"You nearly died a few months ago," Riley said gently.

"But I didn't," Max pointed out, and he blew out a laugh, shaking his head.

"No, you didn't. Tell me something, Max, are you actually made of titanium?"

"Titanium don't bleed."

He watched her doing just that, blood soaking his handkerchief and splattering onto the ground. Her dress, the one she'd brought with her in an effort to fit in slightly, was a mess. Priti and Shanti would never make a mess of their dresses like this.

"They attacked me, you know," she said.

"Bunch of idiots."

"They fucking are. I already had to hit Braiden once today."

"What for?"

"He has a punchable face," Max replied, and Riley smiled. "He was after this girl. Didn't understand 'no'."

"Ah. And then he called for reinforcements?"

"Big man, right? Seven of them against one of me."

"What were they thinking?"

That I'd beat them one on one, or one on two, or all the way up to one on six. Next time, they'll try eight or nine. Culchies were culchies wherever you went.

"What are you even doing here? Ain't you got a fleet to run? Lab-grown babies to look after?"

He watched her for a moment, then said, "I came looking for you. Because I've left the Service. And… relinquished my claim to those children. I don't want to be anyone's father any more than you want to be anyone's mother."

She stared at the spots of blood on the ground.

"Besides, I'm intending to give up this life of virtue and become a full-time pirate, and that's no environment to raise a child."

A full-time pirate. Was he serious? Was he messing with her? Was he going to betray her again?

"You can look it up if you want. I can't believe you don't still have an in with the Service files."

Of course she did. Even Romesh didn't know about it, but Max had a sneaking suspicion she was smarter than him. He wasn't the child of two tech geniuses, after all.

She chewed on her lip for a bit, then put down the bloody handkerchief and addressed her old battered micro. "Comm Romesh."

Riley's brows went up, but he said nothing as the call went through. Romesh answered promptly, as he always did. She was sure he ought to have more important things to do than talk to her, but he always found time to answer her calls.

"Max. My God, what happened?"

"Fell off a horse," she said, at the same time Riley said helpfully, "Got into a fight."

"What? Who's that?"

Sighing, she made a twirly gesture with her finger, and the micro's newly programmed sensors followed it to show Romesh Riley's face.

"Commodore Thrynn," she said glumly, "sticking his nose in where it don't belong."

"Ex-Commodore Thrynn," Romesh corrected, and hope contracted in Max's belly.

"Yeah, no," she said. "He's tried that one before."

Romesh shook his head. "This time it's real. Formal resignation. Have to say, I'm surprised, Thrynn. Thought you were doing a great job with the Big Freeze Project."

"I've laid the groundwork," he said. "There are good people working on it. People who are a better fit than me." He shrugged. "I said all this in my resignation letter."

"Which the Service will consider, but—"

"No," said Riley, quietly, firmly. "They will not consider. They will accept. When I walked out before it was with the knowledge of Admiral Orlov and no one else. I understood the risks of deserting. I didn't ever intend to come back."

"Until you'd completed your mission—" Romesh

began.

"Maybe, originally," Riley said. His gaze flicked to Max. His eyes were very blue. "But there was one reason, and one reason only, that I made that call to Orlov."

There was a beat of silence between the two men, both of whom could be bloody inscrutable when they wanted to.

Romesh sighed. "Your term of service was fifteen years—"

"I don't want to make this difficult," Riley said. "And trust me, I could. I think when the Service *considers* this, they'll decide that letting me go is mutually for the best."

At that, Romesh let out a bark of laughter. "You've thought about this, haven't you?"

"Did you doubt it?"

"No, not really." Romesh paused. "You take care of my daughter, now."

Riley gave Max a long look and a slow smile. "I wouldn't insult Max," he said, "by inferring she couldn't take care of herself."

Max couldn't break his gaze.

"I see you do know her," Romesh said. "Take care of each other," he amended, and she nodded even though she wasn't looking at him.

"I think we will," said Riley, and Romesh signed off.

For a long moment there was silence between them. The muffled sounds of genteel enjoyment wafted over the hedge.

"Okay," Max said, uncertainly.

Riley leaned back on his hands and regarded her. "Told you I'd really left this time."

"Well, if they agree—"

"Even if they don't. I'm not scared of the Service, Max. And I meant what I said. About why I called

Orlov."

Max looked down at her hands, which even here in this country club in this privileged city on this privileged world, were still bruised and bloody. She looked up at Riley, who sat there in shirtsleeves, looking like all he needed to do was sling on the right jacket and he'd fit in anywhere.

"No, 'cos that was your plan," she began. "To get the Service to shoot down Madam Savidge and then rescue us."

"Rescue the women and children in the facility," Riley corrected. "I'd kind of hoped to keep the rest of us out of it. At the least, I could take the fall and let you go free. Thought I might have to push Angharad on her own sword, but…"

"Did they ever find her?"

"No. So I suspect we'll have to watch our backs."

"We?" Max said, appalled to hear her voice shaking a bit.

Riley reached out and took her hand, his eyes meeting hers. "Can you forgive me?"

She started to tell him no, because he'd lied to her, but she couldn't make the words come. Because he hadn't actually lied, had he? He'd omitted one crucial detail, for sure, but he hadn't lied.

"Do you believe me?" he asked, softly, reading her face.

"I don't know how you do that," she said.

"I know you, Max," he said. "I love you. And I'll do anything for you, including breaking my goddamn cover and going back to the Service. The Service which, for the record, I still hate as much as I always did, and which I've left. Conclusively, definitely left."

She pulled her hand from his and stood up, taking deep breaths. Her nose throbbed. "This is too much. I can't…"

Riley sat there, big and implacable, waiting.

"I hated you," she said. "I mean…at least I tried to hate you. 'Cos you'd made me feel…"

His blue eyes were hopeful.

"…I didn't know what you'd made me feel. I still don't. I dunno if people like me get to actually be in love —"

"Whoa, whoa. Wait. People like you?"

Max shrugged, helpless. God damn him, if he'd swing a bloody punch at her she'd know how to block it, but he kept lobbing all these *feelings* at her, and she had no defence against those.

"Max, I don't think there are any people like you. I've sure as hell never met anyone so brave, and smart, and funny, and resilient, and so incredibly sexy I've thought of at least seven filthy things I want to do with you before we even leave this arbour."

She had to smile at that.

"You don't have to love me back," he said. "I mean, it'd be nice, but…"

Max put her finger on his lips. He looked up at her, not moving.

"I wanted to hate you," she said. "I tried really hard. But I came to realise that I…I mean I…I really don't… oh, fuck this," she said, and kissed him.

Riley's arms went around her and he kissed her back, and this wasn't boring or polite or gentlemanly. It was hot, desperate, longing, and it felt incredible.

"I don't hate you either," Riley said, smiling against her mouth. "Maybe we could just go on not hating each other, and—"

"Oh, shut the fuck up," she said, and kissed him some more. His hands were warm though the fabric of her dress, across the bare part of her back, her neck, her skull. Max melted into him, her legs going round his waist, skirt riding up. When Riley touched her bare thigh she bit down gently on his lip in pleasure.

"About those seven filthy things," she said, and his eyes went all hot.

"They'd definitely get us thrown out of the country club," he said, fingers sliding higher under her skirt.

"Well good, 'cos I don't want to be the sort of person country clubs accept for membership."

"Me neither."

"Riley, you are exactly the sort of person country clubs accept for membership."

"Even if I do this?" he said, slipping his fingers inside her underwear, inside her, and she moaned softly.

"Mmm, not sure. You might have to do a bit more."

He laughed softly and kissed her neck as he stroked her, making her writhe on his lap.

"I think we'd have to do something like this," she said, unfastening his trousers.

"Sure?" he said, grunting as she took him in hand. "We wouldn't have to fuck in the middle of the stableyard?"

A spasm of pleasure shot through Max and she guided him into her. "Or on the tennis courts."

"On the terrace bar," Riley said, eyes closing as she sank down onto him.

"In front of the main building—"

"—on the lawn—"

"—on Open Day—"

"—during tea—"

"—for charity—"

"—the sponsored—oh fuck, Max…"

"Sponsored fucking," she laughed, dissolving into giggles, rocking against him, kissing the laughter from his lips. "Christ, Riley, I've missed you."

Afterwards, she clung to him as the sun went down, arms and legs wrapped around him as he leaned back on the stone bench. His hands stroked her back, the fabric of her dress soaked through with sweat.

"If anyone comes in here, it'll be pretty obvious what we were doing," she murmured against his neck.

"They wouldn't have had to come in. We weren't quiet."

She lifted her head and looked down at him, this big gentle man who'd do anything for her. Around his neck were the tchotchkes he'd always worn, her old slave tab tangled in amongst them.

"Why'd you still have this?"

"It was all I had of you," Riley replied, and her heart swelled. *I love you*, she thought, and opened her mouth to tell him, then realised what he was doing behind her back.

"Are you *texting*?"

Riley looked guilty. "Um. Just arranging a ride."

"I have a HAV," she told him.

"Yeah…I thought we might want to go a bit further than a HAV's range."

"How far?" Max asked, but he was saved from having to answer by the roar of an engine above them. She stared up, astonished, to see a ship descending through the sunset.

"Is that the Eurydice?"

Riley shrugged. He was trying not to smile. Max scrambled off him and ran to the entrance of the arbour.

"It's the bloody Eurydice!"

People were shouting. Club staff, and members, and that idiot Braiden. And somewhere in the mix the Eurydice's door opened, and she heard Orpheus's distinctive rasp.

"Somebody better get this fucking cat off me."

Riley slung his arm around Max's shoulders, and she shook her head in amazement.

"Ask me again," he said, "how far we're going?"

Max leaned into him. "How far?"

"How far do you want to?" he said.

Max looked out at the ship, and the sunset, and the chaos, and she smiled.

AUTHOR'S NOTE

A year or so ago I bought a new geek t-shirt (it won't surprise you to know I have a lot of these). It had twelve little cartoon figures on it and the legend "She needed a hero. So that's what she became." The cartoon figures depicted characters like Agent Carter, Princess Merida & Hermione Granger.

It confused a lot of men.

The working title of Max Seventeen was *So That's What She Became,* to remind me that no matter how wonderful the male character of a romance novel is, sometimes a girl has to become her own hero.

Did you guess that the innocent, repressed one was the hero of this book, and the fighty angry one was the heroine? Well, maybe if you've read my books before, you did.

This book was known as the Mad Space Book for about year after writing, because it was just too insane to ever be published. I wrote it following a period in my authorial life I can only refer to as the doldrums. But sometimes a girl needs to be her own hero, which is why I published the book myself, with a little help from my friends.

You don't need to change the world to be a hero. Sometimes, you just have to rescue yourself.

ALSO AVAILABLE

The Sophie Green Mysteries: **I, Spy?**

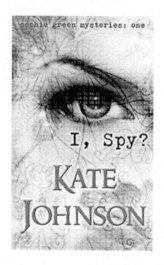

A reboot of the series you know and love...or maybe it's all brand new to you? It's certainly all new to Sophie, who's just been hired by a top-secret government agency.

All she has on her side is sarcasm, blonde hair and a small cat called Tammy, but that's not going to keep her from saving the day...once she's figured out who to save it from.

Sexy spies, plane crashes, firebombs and multicoloured cocktails: they're all in a day's work for Sophie. Roll over Bond, there's a new bombshell in town!

This is a new edition of the beloved book, containing brand new material.

Available exclusively from Amazon: August 2016.

Read on for an excerpt.

I, Spy? *was previously published by Samhain Publishing in 2007.*

But there's more...
Not only will the original books be expanded and improved, but there will be a series of companion novellas from Luke Sharpe's point of view. The first Luke Sharpe File, **Worth A Shot**, will be released in late 2016.

For more information please visit
www.KateJohnson.co.uk

EXCERPT FROM I, SPY?

Okay, I can do this. This is not a problem. This is what I'm trained for. I can stay calm in a crisis.

Only, the crisis is I switched my alarm off and now I have twenty minutes in which to get out of bed, washed, dressed, up to uniform 'neat and tidy appearance' standards, gulp down some coffee, find my keys and get to my desk.

Most days it takes me twenty minutes to find a frigging parking space.

I hit the first hurdle when I couldn't find my uniform shirt. Not by my bed. Not under my bed. Not in the laundry basket. Not in the washing machine. Christ, I only took it off yesterday, where the hell could it have gone? I found myself looking in the most insane places —under the sofa, in the shoe cupboard, the oven, everywhere—before I finally found it in the first place I'd checked. Stale and creased in the laundry basket.

I sprayed some Febreze on it, shook out the creases— I don't even know where my iron's supposed to be, let alone where it might actually have ended up—and slung it on. I nearly strangled myself with my neck scarf before I got it right. Making some heroically quick instant coffee with half cold water, I nevertheless scalded my tongue and the roof of my mouth gulping it down.

Tammy, my little tabby cat, watched with a total lack of interest as I hopped around, swearing and moaning at the pain.

"Keys," I slurred, and she blinked at me. There was no logical place for my keys; why would there be? I was nearly crying by the time I found them on the kitchen counter. A quick check of my watch told me it was ten to five—T minus 10 minutes. Even if I raced up to the airport and left my car on the front concourse, I'd still be late.

"So why am I rushing?" I asked Tammy.

Tammy didn't know.

Finally, finally finding my shoes, gulping down some mouthwash as an alternative to toothpaste (and nearly choking myself in the process), I ricocheted out of the house. T minus seven minutes. This was not going to be possible.

At least the roads would be quiet—but no, against all reasonable laws, I got stuck behind some duffer doing two miles an hour in his ancient Rover. Finally leaving him behind as I took the back road to the staff car park, I skidded up to the car park barrier—and realised I'd left my security pass at home.

Shit, fuck and bugger. With a side order of bollocks.

Slamming the car into reverse I made the world's worst J-turn and zoomed back home, startled Tammy by grabbing said pass from the back of my bedroom door—well, where would you keep yours?—and left again.

I parked up at quarter past five. T plus fifteen minutes. By the time I made it up to the terminal, breathless, red and wheezing, it had gone twenty past and the queues at check-in were hitting the desks opposite.

I slunk up to the office, ready with an excuse about my car breaking down—hoping no one would remember it's physically indestructible—and found it deserted.

Ha. I grabbed my time sheet and signed in on time. Hell, they weren't going to check.

Probably I should stop being this late every day, though.

I, Spy? is available as eBook and paperback exclusively from Amazon.

ABOUT THE AUTHOR

Kate has a second cousin who held a Guinness World Record for brewing the strongest beer, and once ran over herself with a Segway scooter. She misspent her youth watching lots of Joss Whedon and reading even more Terry Pratchett, which made it kind of inevitable that when she grew up to write romantic novels, they'd be the weird ones around the edges. A few years later, she lives with her cats who are only partially named after Whedon characters, and a dog who is only partially evil, in the south of England. She still loves Joss Whedon and Terry Pratchett.

You can follow Kate online:
www.twitter.com/K8JohnsonAuthor
www.facebook.com/K8JohnsonAuthor
http://pin.it/aNwO6Dp
or find out more on www.KateJohnson.co.uk

Want to be first to hear about new releases? Sign up to Kate's newsletter:
www.etaknosnhoj.blogspot.co.uk/p/newsletter.html

Did you enjoy Max Seventeen? Please consider leaving a review!

Max Seventeen is enrolled in Kindle's Matchbook program. For more information, see <u>Amazon.com</u>